An

Honourable Estate

by

Marie Cross

Martin Publishing
35 Exeter Close
Tonbridge
TN10 4NT

ISBN 0 9546146 0 7

Cover design by Jean Hill
Drawings by Catherine Nickford
Printed and bound in Great Britain
Typesetting by David Brown, Maynards Green, Sussex 01435 812506

Preface

'**Abbotts Lidiard**' and '**Grassenden**' are based on a hamlet and a village in Kent. They are not as close to each other as they are in the novel.

'**Abbotts Lidiard**' does have an old road, but it is not a footpath. There is a stream going under the road which flows between cottages. Unfortunately there is no Elizabethan Manor or almshouses. There was a barn shop – no longer there – and opposite is a footpath that goes to a farm

'**Grassenden**' has a public house next to a shop. There is a garage but no adjacent bungalow. Ridge House is not as grand as the one in the village. There is a school and behind it a church.

I have not met anyone who lives in either place. Any resemblance to any person in the novel is purely coincidental.

If anyone can link the two places, I shall be interested to hear from them.

Marie Cross
Tonbridge, Kent

Acknowledgments

My thanks to my goddaughter, Dr Heather Walton, for medical help, to Charlie Simmonds for assistance with farming matters, to my husband John, for cooking delicious meals while I tapped away and to Tunbridge Wells Writers' Circle for all their love, help and encouragement. Any mistakes are purely due to my incompetence.

Part I

The Manor

Chapter 1

'Sit down, Lydia,' he commanded. 'I have something I want to say to you.'

Lydia felt uneasy at his tone but she knew what was coming – her orphan background was not compatible with his lifestyle and ancestry. He had made a big mistake asking her out.

Edward stretched out his long legs, pulled them back and leaned forward.

'You remember I told you my wife and son were killed in an accident?'

What could he want to say?

'You understand the need for the Casleigh line to continue?'

'Yes,' she said, even more puzzled.

'I want you to marry me – to give me an heir.'

Lydia's eyes opened wide with incredulity and she sat stiffly trying to take in what he was saying. She stared at her hands clasped tightly in her lap, then raised her eyes to see if he had been joking. But Edward's face was perfectly serious and his eyes looked steadily and enquiringly at her.

'But I don't love you. I – I hardly know you,' she said at last.

'Love doesn't come into it.'

She went to protest but he held up his hand. 'It'll be an arrangement – a contract if you like. You'll provide an heir and run the Manor and in return you'll have a beautiful home, which I can see you love, and a certain – status. He paused, but before she could speak he said, 'I'll give you an allowance so you'll have no money worries.'

Lydia's throat contracted as she tried to swallow and her voice was uneven as she said, 'But why me?'

'Because you have a love of history, of beauty. All the things I treasure, you treasure.'

She gazed round, her eyes lingering over the fine furniture and the exquisite objects that made up this one room.

'Suppose I can't have children?'

'We'll make sure you can.'

His voice was firm as if discussing a business proposition. Lydia could not believe this was happening, it seemed like something from a gothic novel.

'But what about my job at Kingley's,' she said at last, more for something to say than needing an answer.

Edward switched on the light beside his chair then moved to turn on the others, bathing the oak-panelled room in a soft, warm light. The grandfather clock ticked slowly and loudly.

'When you have a child you wouldn't be working anyway,' he said dismissively as he returned to his chair.

'I'm sorry,' she said. 'I couldn't – I couldn't do such a thing. It's too great a step to take. In fact it's a – it's a preposterous idea.'

'What's worrying you?'

'Worrying me! You're asking me to change my life completely, to live with someone I have only just met – and you ask what's worrying me?'

'But Lydia, look what you'll have,' he said, as if this proposal were a normal, everyday event.

She looped her finger in her silver necklace and ran it from side to side, lost for words.

In a state of shock Lydia left the Manor that evening trying to convince herself Edward could not have been thinking straight. But in the brief period she had known him, she could tell he was a man completely in control of his life, someone who would not commit himself to anything so dramatic without some thought.

Lydia went to the balcony of her Clapham flat as soon as she returned home and sat amongst the hanging baskets and pots of flowers that twined and hung from the ornate, wrought ironwork. In the remaining warmth of the evening she leaned back in her chair, closed her eyes and sighed. It would be pointless going to bed. She had to sort out the turmoil in her head and bring some sanity to the situation.

∗

Lydia Abbott had been to a country house sale near Battle that hot July day when she first met Edward. She was feeling pleased with herself as she put the two vases she had bought into the boot, padded and tied them securely. She blew her curly, black hair from her damp forehead and reached for the map in the glove box. It was too hot to rush back on main roads to an even hotter

London. She would meander her way home through country villages, perhaps stop somewhere for tea.

It was as she left a small Kent village called Grassenden that she caught sight of a sign pointing to Abbotts Lidiard Lane. She swung the car left and descended between high hedges till it widened. She parked the car by a low stone wall, where a stream disappeared under the road to emerge and run between some cottages.

Abbotts Lidiard – Lydia Abbott. How extraordinary!

The lane had houses and cottages on each side, dotted inter-mittently between fields and orchards. After half a mile, the small hamlet appeared to end at a converted barn that made and restored furniture. She had been standing in the doorway taking in the smell of new wood, when the man standing in front turned suddenly and knocked into her. Caught off-balance, she hit her head against the door.

The man apologised profusely, saying he hadn't known anyone was behind him and insisted she come to his house to attend to the small cut on her forehead. Lydia protested that it was nothing and she could deal with it when she got home, but he insisted and strode away, clearly expecting her to follow.

His home turned out to be a large Elizabethan manor house close by, where the date 1578 in crooked figures over the oak door proclaimed its age. It had two upper floors, the top one with high-pointed gables. The windows, several of which were jettied, all had leaded panes. Tall, elaborate chimneys rose from the roof. Lydia was enchanted and clapped her hands in delight.

'So, you like my house?' he said when they were inside. He put a little disinfectant into warm water and fetched some cotton wool from a drawer. 'It's Elizabethan. It was built by a Nicholas Casleigh on the site of an abbey and has always been in my family, passing from father to son, though a cousin and a couple of nephews have inherited along the way.' He gave the ghost of a smile and held out his hand. 'I'm Edward Casleigh, and this is Abbey Manor.'

'Mine's Lydia Abbott.' She smiled. 'I saw the sign and just had to investigate.'

'Lydia Abbott,' he repeated, giving her a long, hard stare. 'How surprising.'

She took a mirror from her handbag and dabbed the cut. 'I'm on my way back from a house sale in Battle. I work in Chelsea at

Kingley Antiques.'

When she looked up Edward was still staring at her enigmatically. 'As you are interested in antiques, perhaps you would like to see some of the rooms before you go?'

Would she? Lydia could hardly contain herself.

Downstairs all was oak – hall, staircase, and most of the rooms. Rugs and carpets covered the polished wooden floors. In stark contrast were the uneven flagstones in the porch and passage. The doorways were low, a problem that did not bother her, but Edward had to stoop through all of them. The panelling and the small windows of the drawing room, that ran from the front to the back of the house, made it appear dark, even on that bright summer day. Only the kitchen, which had been tastefully modernised, could be described as spacious and light. Two of the rooms had doors leading on to a terrace.

The house smelled of polish so someone other than its owner was looking after it, Lydia surmised. Edward Casleigh did not seem like a man who did his own housework.

When she had seen all the downstairs rooms and assured him she was all right, Lydia took her leave and returned to her car. What a tale she would have to tell Charles on Monday.

*

'Look. What do you think of these?'

Charles Kingley inspected one of the vases closely, turning it slowly in his hand. He reached for the other one.

'What did you give for them?'

'Three hundred the pair.'

He nodded his approval. 'Very nice, Lydia, very nice. You'll soon be an expert.'

'Oh, I wouldn't say that, there's always such a lot to learn.'

'But you've done so well in two years.'

'All thanks to you,' she said, smiling at him fondly as she took the vases and placed them on a nearby shelf. 'But, listen to this, Charles.'

Lydia told him about the Manor and the furniture and all the exquisite porcelain she had seen.

'The pieces on display must have amounted to thousands, not to mention the Georgian cabinets themselves. Just two items would have made £3000 at least.

'And what did this Edward look like?'

'Now, now. What are you dreaming up?

Charles grinned. 'I just think a pretty young lady like you ought to be out and about driving men wild. When I was young I would have swept you off your feet by now.'

'I'm too boring to drive anyone wild, and I can assure you a man like Edward Casleigh isn't searching for someone like me as a soulmate. Anyway, for all I know he could have a wife. Someone was looking after him because the place looked cared for and was extraordinarily tidy.'

Charles looked disappointed. 'I'm sure he isn't married, he would have told you.'

Lydia laughed. 'He could have a wife in the attic,' she said, as she went to open the shop.

Lydia was captivated by the house and pictured herself examining the cabinets, holding the delicate porcelain and valuing it. She saw her fingers running over the shiny surfaces, admiring the wood and the workmanship.

Towards the end of the week, Edward rang the shop. Charles handed Lydia the phone, a broad grin on his face. 'For you.'

'I wonder if you would come out to dinner with me,' Edward enquired.

'Oh, er, dinner, yes. That would be lovely.'

'How about tomorrow.'

'Tomorrow? Yes, thank you, Yes.'

'Tell me where you live. I'll pick you up. You won't want to go out straight from the shop.'

Still flustered Lydia gave instructions and when she put down the phone began to panic, wondering where she would be taken and what to wear.

'There,' said Charles, 'he must be a very discerning man.'

'If he's that discerning, he'll not find much of interest in me. Still it will be rather exciting going out with a rich, handsome man, even if it will be a one-off.'

Edward took her to an expensive restaurant in Knightsbridge. The men, like Edward, seemed very self-assured and the women elegant. Lydia looked down at her black jersey dress, far inferior to anything she saw there and was convinced everyone was staring at her. Even more disconcertingly, Edward appeared to scrutinise her every movement as if she were a laboratory specimen.

'This can be a birthday celebration,' Edward said, when they had ordered.

'Oh, how old are you?' Lydia blushed, worrying that she was

being too personal.

'Thirty-eight.'

'I'm twenty-six.'

'Tell me about yourself,' he said as he returned the wine list to the waiter.

Lydia had been most impressed to hear their discussion in fluent French.

'My parents died when I was five. I was in two foster homes until I settled with Robert and Elizabeth Kentner when I was nine. My mother, I mean Elizabeth, died when I was sixteen. Robert sent me to Art College and I worked for a year after I left. Then Robert was taken ill and I left work to look after him till he died.'

'Do you know anything about your real parents?'

'Only that my father was an architect and my mother a teacher. I gathered they were quite old when I was born. That's all I know. It appears they had no relatives, or none that wanted to take on a five-year-old.'

Edward nodded. 'You inherited your father's talent it seems. What did you do after you left college?'

'I worked in a kindergarten for six months because I couldn't find anything in the art world.'

There was a long embarrassing pause while Lydia tried to think of something interesting to say. Her life was so mundane she couldn't imagine a man like Edward, public school educated from the sound of it, being interested in anything she did. What she did do amounted to little more than poring over antique books and magazines and browsing round shops looking for bargains.

'What happened after Robert died.'

'I found my present job at Kingley's.'

'Do you enjoy it?'

'I adore it. Working amongst the elegant furniture, and the china and porcelain – even the more bizarre items that come in have some story to tell. I so envy you surrounded by all that beauty. None of the families I was with had anything of great value.'

Lydia wanted to ask him questions such as was there a Mrs Casleigh and where did he work? But her lack of social contact in recent years made her self-conscious. Instead she concentrated on not making a fool of herself by breaking some rule of etiquette. Glancing up she saw Edward give her another disconcerting look and she put her napkin to her mouth in case she had a mark there.

She did learn over the dessert that there was no wife in the attic and that his wife and son had been killed in a car accident. She also discovered his father had been a diplomat and that Edward worked at the Foreign Office, but what he did there wasn't forthcoming.

After the meal he drove Lydia back to her flat in Clapham, but left so hurriedly she felt she had been at an examination and had failed whatever test had been set. Not surprising considering her unconventional background.

When she told Charles later that week she had been invited to the Manor for the day, Charles was as excited as Lydia.

'Don't forget to ask if he has anything he wants to sell?'

'Oh, I couldn't do that, Charles. He's not that sort of person.'

'Only joking, Lydia.'

*

Edward and Lydia walked down the lane and he pointed out the almshouses built by a seventeenth century ancestor, James Casleigh. Close by Stream Cottage, whose owner sold flowers and plants, he showed her the old road that was now a bridleway that went into the village of Grassenden.

Nearing the Manor on their return Edward said, 'The last of that row of four cottages belongs to me. I spent a great deal of time there as a child.'

Why on earth would he spend time in that tiny cottage when he lived at the Manor, she wondered?

They had now reached the barn shop but instead of going up the drive to the Manor, Edward took her through the hedge opposite on to a footpath.

'I'm going to take you to the farm.'

'You don't own that too, do you?'

'Yes, I do.'

'How do you find time to go to work?'

'I don't run it. Tom Cresswell does that. He's the tenant.'

The farm came into sight and they walked down a slope by a hopfield, into the yard and crossed to the kitchen door. Edward knocked and they went straight into a large kitchen.

'You there, Tom?'

A tall man with curly black hair came in from a hall drying his hands on a towel.

'To what do I owe this pleasure?' he said coolly. 'You're lucky to have caught me, I've only just come in.'

'Good. I didn't want to wander round the farm looking for you.' He turned towards Lydia. 'Tom, I'd like you to meet Lydia Abbott. I'm showing her around. She's never been on a farm.'

Lydia held out her hand which Tom shook firmly. 'Pleased to meet you,' he said.

Edward started talking to him about the good weather and the wheat harvest while Lydia let her eyes wander around the room. Books and magazines covered every surface. A large dresser faced the outside door and to the left was an old-fashioned kitchen range. A modern – if you could call it modern – cooker and a fridge were beside the range. A wooden table, with two unmatched chairs, stood in the middle of the room and a very old settee was by a wall. Lydia bet he was a bachelor.

'Will you see to that then, Tom?' Edward was saying.

'Of course, don't I always?'

On the way back Lydia said, 'Tom doesn't look like a farmer somehow, not that I've met any farmers.'

'Did you expect a yokel with straw sticking out of his mouth.'

'Not quite as bad as that, but you know what I mean.'

'Tom is – he's quite clever, you know. Could have gone to University, but farming was all he ever wanted to do so he went to Agricultural College.'

Edward sounded reluctant to admit Tom's intelligence but, at the same time, gave the impression he admired him.

It was that evening Edward made his proposal.

∗

Lydia gave a shiver as she locked the balcony door and prepared for bed. She forced herself to think of his marriage proposal, or contract as he preferred to call it. In spite of her emphatic refusal, Edward had asked her to think it over. She had to admire his persistence. 'Ring me at the end of the week with your decision' were his parting words, as if she had not already given it.

She switched off the bedside light and pulled the covers up over her ears.

A child – the reason for Edward's offer of marriage. She did like children and was good with them. Her first two families had children and she had looked after and enjoyed playing with them. But if *she* had children they would be hers, her very own.

Lydia pummelled her hot pillow and turned it over. What was

she thinking? She couldn't possibly marry a virtual stranger just because she liked children.

Eventually she fell asleep, and dreamt she was gliding down the staircase of a grand stately home, a stream of children behind her, and Edward lovingly smiling at her.

*

Charles greeted her warmly. 'Well?' he said, 'Did you have a good day?'

'Yes, yes. It was – very nice.'

He scrutinised her face. 'You seem upset. Did something go wrong?'

'No. I'm not upset. It's just…'

'Just what?'

'Nothing.'

Over the following days Lydia noticed the worried look on Charles' face and knew she ought to confide in him. She wished Elizabeth were alive, but she knew what she would have said. It *was* crazy, wasn't it? Quite out of the question.

'You love the house – all the things I treasure, you treasure.'

She did – oh, she did. The panelled rooms, the inglenook, the clocks, the antique ornaments all enchanted her – not to mention the Manor itself.

'Love doesn't come into it.'

As they did not love each other, at least she would know where she stood. It would not be like a real marriage. It would be more straightforward. You couldn't fall out of love if you were never in love, could you? There would be children to love and the garden to tend. She would belong – really belong in her own right.

Through the distracted days, the sleepless nights and all the soul-searching, the thought of living at Abbey Manor threw a spell over Lydia.

Eventually she opened her heart to Charles who was horrified.

'You've been blinded by the Manor like you used to be over the pretty antiques in the early days,' he almost shouted at her. 'You know nothing about this man. He could be a – a wife-beater. You're being naïve. The whole idea is absurd.' Charles paced the floor. 'He can't care about you to suggest this – this liaison.'

'But we know we don't love each other,' she said, defensively. 'It's not as if it were unrequited love on the part of one of us.'

'How can you say that? You've taken leave of your senses. I never thought I'd see you contemplate anything so irresponsible.

To think of you marrying, without love, in – in cold blood, is beyond me.'

Lydia felt tears pricking her eyes at the way he was speaking to her.

'I could grow to love him,' she murmured.

But Charles strode away too upset to listen.

*

Edward's voice, when she rang, conveyed a calm acceptance of her decision.

'Come down tomorrow and stay the weekend. I have important matters to discuss with you.'

'Such as?'

'The date of the wedding for one thing. I want it to be as soon as possible.'

'Why the haste?'

'Why not?'

'I suppose there's no reason.' But Lydia could not help feeling her life was rushing past without her having lived it. 'I can't come tomorrow. I work on Saturdays and we're usually very busy and close late. I shan't feel like travelling when I've finished.'

'Can't you get the day off?'

'Not on a Saturday, and certainly not in the tourist season.'

'Well, it'll have to be Sunday. Come down early.'

'Early?'

'Come to breakfast.'

*

Edward was standing at the top of the three uneven steps that fronted the studded oak door. As she stepped from the car she could not resist standing for a moment gazing at the Elizabethan façade, the early morning sun glinting on the angled panes of the leaded windows.

He gave Lydia a kiss such as he might give a visiting aunt and ushered her into the kitchen. A cuddly woman with grey hair and pale blue eyes came from the pantry in the corner and placed a pot of marmalade on the neatly laid table. She greeted Lydia with a welcoming smile.

'So you're Edward's young lady.'

'Fiancée,' he corrected.

'Of course.'

The older woman showed no surprise. Lydia, on the other hand, experienced a feeling of finality in that word. The woman went on to comment on the coincidence of her name.

'I could hardly believe it when Edward told me. Fate must have brought you here.'

Fate, yes, fate. It was meant to be.

Edward went to stand beside the woman. 'Let me introduce you. This is Margaret Cresswell, but I've always called her Cressy. Cressy has worked for the Casleighs for years. She is quite indispensable.'

Lydia saw a smile brighten his eyes and his arm tightened round the woman.

'Don't be silly,' she said, patting his hand affectionately. 'Now, let me get you some breakfast.'

'You must be Tom's mother,' Lydia said as Edward went from the kitchen into the passage.

'That's right.' She arranged bacon in a pan. 'Tom's been farming there since he left agricultural college. Edward's father paid for him.'

When Edward returned she noticed how formally he was dressed – fawn lightweight suit, pale green shirt and brown patterned tie.

'Are we going somewhere special?' Lydia asked, wondering if she were dressed appropriately.

'I'm reading the lesson at church. To tell you the truth I'd forgotten David had asked me. Come with me.'

'Yes, you go along, Miss Abbott. It'll be nice for him to have company.'

*

From the Casleigh family pew at the front of St Luke's Lydia listened as he read the lesson. At the end of the service she could not help noticing she was the cause of some interest. As they stepped from the porch into the sunlight, a tall, good-looking woman detached herself from one of the groups and came gliding up to them.

'Edward, darling.' The woman kissed his cheek and held his arm with both hands. 'How well you read, as usual.'

She was dressed in a cream suit with gold buttons. Her straight, fair-reddish hair was thick and expertly cut. Jewellery was plentiful, tasteful and expensive. The whole shrieked money and style.

'I'm glad I've seen you, Serena. I'd like you to meet Lydia Abbott.' He turned to Lydia. 'May I introduce Serena Detrale.

She is an old friend.'

Her green eyes regarded Lydia with scarce-disguised hostility but when Edward added, 'We are to be married,' her face paled, and she appeared about to faint.

Quickly she regained her composure. 'What a sho – surprise. You've kept Miss – er ...'

'Abbott,' Lydia prompted.

' ... very quiet. What a secretive man you are.' She gave a hollow laugh.

'I've been meaning to get in touch about the almshouse vacancy,' Edward said. 'I'll give you a ring, but we must go now, Cressy is getting lunch. Give my regards to Jeremy.'

As they drove back to the Manor Lydia could not help wondering about the expression on Serena Detrale's face on being introduced. Just how friendly was his 'old friend'?

A delicious smell of roast lamb greeted them on their return, plunging Lydia back to Sundays at home when Elizabeth was alive. Mrs Cresswell, her cheeks redder than before, bustled about the kitchen.

'Hello, my dears. Good service?'

'Edward read so well,' Lydia said, recalling his deep voice reverberating round the ancient walls. She had stared at those walls and the monuments that all seemed to be dedicated to members of the Casleigh family. Would she be amongst them one day – the dearly beloved wife of Edward Casleigh?

'Let's go out on to the terrace,' Edward said.

They moved into the dining room and he opened the french doors.

'An Elizabethan garden. I noticed it when I was here last time.'

'My mother supervised the building of the parterre during the time she stayed home – when I was born – before she went off again with my father. There's a wooded area over there.' He waved his hand to the left. 'We've more land at the front than the back. Both gardens follow the line of the lane and in the front at the very top are the ruins of the abbey.

'So, you own the Manor, the farm, the barn shop and Cressy's cottage. What about the pub, the church and the village hall?'

'No, I don't own those, but I do own a garage in Grassenden. Tom's brother, Jamie runs that.'

Lydia shook her head and smiled.

'So it was with Mrs Cresswell you stayed when you were

younger.'

'Yes.'

Lydia waited for him to give an explanation, but none was forthcoming.

'Mr Laurence approached me about two years ago with a view to converting the barn and renting it. I didn't think it would be a success, being so out-of-the-way, but he seems to have built up a reputation and made a go of it.'

'I'll be off now,' Mrs Cresswell called from the kitchen. 'Everything's ready to serve.'

Later, in the drawing room, Lydia studied a portrait of a man she took to be Edward's father. He was wearing a dark grey suit with a silver and blue sash with some sort of decoration pinned to it. He had dark, greying hair, and twinkling eyes and she felt sure she would have liked him.

'Is this your father? You don't look much like him.'

'So I've always been told.'

'You must take after your mother then.'

'Yes, she was Danish. My father met her when he was in Copenhagen.'

'Ah, so that accounts for your distinctive fair hair.'

Lydia examined the room to see if there were any photographs of Edward's mother but she could see none.

'Let me show you the rooms you haven't already seen.'

They went back into the passage. He opened a door opposite the dining room that looked over the front drive.

'This is my study,' he said.

Lydia put her head round the door noting one wall covered with books and a desk on which stood a computer, a keyboard and an onyx inkstand.

'It's very tidy,' she said.

They went along the passage to the narrow wooden staircase. On the first bend there was a tiny window and a ledge large enough to sit on. The bedroom above the drawing room was Edward's. As it had a large, jettied window, it let in more light then the drawing room below.

'That door in the corner of my room leads to a bathroom and connects with this room.' Edward opened the next door on the landing. 'which will be your bedroom.'

Lydia felt her face flush. So she was not expected to share his bed. She was not sure whether she was put out or relieved.

The phone rang.

'There are two more bedrooms and a bathroom on this floor. Have a look while I answer that, then go up to the top floor.'

Lydia took a cursory look at the rooms and then went upstairs. Here she found four musty, unused rooms containing oddments of furniture. Trunks and cases were stacked against the walls. She returned to the one over Edward's bedroom which, she deduced from the faded nursery rhyme friezes, was once a playroom.

She sat on a small white wooden chair and rested her arms on the child-sized table oblivious of the dusty surface. Was this room awaiting her children? How long since it had resounded to the laughter of Casleigh children? Though Edward was an only child, he must have had children in to play. Tom and his brother, perhaps?

Lydia got up and walked slowly to the window that overlooked the lawn at the front of the house. She gazed across the tops of the trees where the garden seemed to go on forever. Won't it be lovely, she thought, living in the peace of the countryside, where the only sounds would be the twittering of birds, the striking of Grassenden's church clock and the drone of an overhead plane. She looked down on to the drive and the lawn with the semi-circular beech hedge enclosing it. Lydia could hardly wait to get some order to the garden's sadly neglected lawns and flowerbeds.

She heard Edward's footsteps on the stairs. 'In here,' she called.

His eyes flicked round the rooms as he came in. 'This was once the playroom. I expect you gathered.' He gave a shiver.

'What's the matter? Do you feel all right? You look as if you'd see a ghost.'

'It's nothing. Let's go back downstairs.'

Chapter 2

The wedding, set for the last day in September, was to be at St Luke's, the square-towered Norman church in Grassenden.

Lydia asked Charles to give her away. He was so overcome that tears filled his eyes, though whether from pleasure or dismay she was far from sure. When he had seen she was determined to go ahead, he no longer prevailed upon her to change her mind, but she knew how upset he was. Lydia, on the other hand, felt easier now she had made her decision.

Edward suggested an engagement dinner so he could meet Charles and her friend Jill's family. To Lydia's great disappointment, Jill said they would be on holiday, but nothing would keep them away from the wedding and she could not wait to see Edward and the fabulous Abbey Manor that had been described in such detail.

Charles told Lydia he was going to close early next day so he could get ready without rushing.

'Why don't you come down with me?' Lydia offered, as she tidied the office prior to leaving.

'Thank you, but no. You will want time to prepare for your guests. You enjoy your day off, don't worry about me.'

'I'll meet you at the station then.'

'No, my dear, I'll get a taxi.'

The darkening clouds threatened rain as Lydia manoeuvred her car out of the service road on to the south side of Clapham Common. She reached Abbotts Lidiard about four, passing the old road that petered out into a bridleway that skirted one of Tom Cresswell's fields, then Stream Cottage that sold plants. She would be calling there soon. Next the almshouses and Mrs Cresswell's cottage. This would soon be her neighbourhood and she would make friends as she had never done in Clapham. Her spirits rose.

'While you're freshening up, I'll get Cressy to make tea,' Edward said when he had taken her case to her room. 'I'll see you in the drawing room.'

The intricately patterned box hedges she could see from her bedroom still looked trim, but the rest of the parterre was losing its form and colour. She would miss her flowers, she thought, as she opened her case and hung up her dress. The wrought iron balconies at home were a feature of the Victorian terrace where she lived. Hers had been a riot of colour all summer. To have charge of a garden this size was a challenge she was feverish to begin.

In the drawing room a display of bronze, white and yellow chrysanthemums in a large copper vase, filled the inglenook, adding to the beauty of the room.

'Mr Kingley phoned,' Mrs Cresswell said, as she put down the tray. 'He said to tell you he isn't feeling well and is sorry, but he won't be able to join you tonight.'

'Oh, how awful,' Lydia exclaimed putting both hands on her cheeks. She was concerned about Charles but felt totally deserted by those who would have made the evening more enjoyable.

Mrs Cresswell put a hand on Lydia's arm. 'There, there, dear. It's a shame, I know. Never mind.'

'I shan't have anyone here I know,' she murmured.

Oblivious of Lydia's distress, Edward said, 'Are you going now, Cressy?'

'Yes. I've put everything out for the caterers and left a note about the one less guest. I'll rearrange the dining table before I go.' She turned to leave. 'Enjoy yourselves.'

Lydia gave her a watery smile. Edward held out her tea and as their fingers touched her hand shook. The cup rattled as it settled in the saucer and he glanced at her then looked away.

'What's the name of the vicar's wife?' she asked, trying to push to the back of her mind the forthcoming ordeal, as ordeal she now considered it to be.

'Faith. Faith Tressant.'

'That's an appropriate name.'

'Appropriate?'

'Faith – for a vicar's wife, I mean.'

'Yes.' There was a long pause. 'It looks pretty grim out there,' he said, standing up to put on the lights.

Another silence.

'Our guests will be arriving about a quarter past seven and I'll serve drinks in here. I'll expect you down at seven.'

Edward spoke as if they were on manoeuvres and any moment they would synchronise watches. Lydia viewed the coming evening with even greater foreboding.

'In that case, I think I'd better start getting ready as soon as I've finished my tea.'

'Before you go I have something for you.'

He reached into his pocket and brought out a small, pale blue velvet box. He took out a ring, that flashed even in the subdued light.

Lydia gasped. She had never seen such a sapphire. Even the surrounding diamonds were large. He reached for her left hand, so tiny in his, and stared as if admiring it. She spread out her fingers and he slid the ring on.

'I have never seen anything so beautiful,' she exclaimed, stretching on tiptoe and flinging her arms round his neck. She kissed him, but felt him stiffen. Lydia let her hands drop to her sides and stood confused.

'I'll go and change,' she said.

*

As Lydia stepped from the shower and wrapped herself in the large pink bathsheet, she contemplated her future. Wiping the steam from the mirror, she stared at her blurred face. She was not beautiful like Serena Detrale. She had a nice smile Elizabeth used to say. She produced one for the mirror. All she had to do was run the Manor – she thought she could do that, and give Edward the heir he so desired – she had been told she could do that.

A sudden clap of thunder shook the house, startling her out of her reverie.

Lydia dressed, rearranged the few stray hairs that had escaped from her elegant hair do, applied her makeup and stepped into the royal blue velvet dress that Edward had paid for. It had a round neckline and bishop sleeves. It fitted closely into her waist and over the hips where it flared slightly, finishing at mid calf. She put her hand behind her to push up the zip. It glided smoothly and she reached down to pull it the rest of the way but it had stuck. Frustrated to the point of tears she struggled for fifteen minutes, but the zip would not budge up or down.

She heard a car come up the drive and crunch to a halt. She could not call Edward now. Her first undertaking and she had failed already. In one desperate attempt she wriggled the material on either side. Miraculously the zip eased and slid to the top.

Hastily she slipped on her shoes, grabbed her bag and left the room thoroughly flustered. As she descended the stairs she could hear voices, Edward's, and a well modulated one – definitely Serena's.

Three faces turned as Lydia's footsteps loudly announced her appearance along the stone flagged passage. Edward looked stern, but his face softened. Jeremy, Serena's husband, stared in open admiration.

'You didn't tell me how pretty Lydia was, Serena.' He turned to Edward. 'You certainly know how to pick 'em.'

Edward and Serena ignored him.

'How charming you look' Serena said. She leaned forward and touched Lydia's cheek with hers, which made Lydia feel more like Serena's guest.

'I am sorry I wasn't here to welcome you,' Lydia said, trying to appear relaxed, 'but the zip of my dress caught and I couldn't free it.'

'I'll have to give you the name of a dear little boutique I know,' Serena offered, 'frightfully expensive, but the quality is good.'

'Come,' said Edward, 'let me get you drinks.' He was interrupted by a knock on the door. 'That'll be Faith and David.'

Lydia led them along the passage and was just about to ask what they wanted when Edward came into the drawing room.

'I don't think you've met Faith, have you, Lydia?'

The vicar's wife rushed towards her holding out both hands.

'Congratulations. I was so pleased for Edward when David told me. I do hope you'll be very happy – both of you. And how lovely you look in that dress.' Her words tumbled out as she looked Lydia up and down. 'It matches your eyes.'

The vicar extended his hand. 'It's good to see you again after our brief meeting outside the church.'

Lydia beamed thinking that perhaps the evening would not be so bad after all.

The sight of the dining room took Lydia's breath away. It was like something from the antique magazines she read. The mahogany table had been extended and, under Mrs Cresswell's tender care, it gleamed and shone with the reflected light from the two twisted silver candelabra. There were three low displays of chrysanthemums on the table and an antique wine cooler stood beside Edward's chair.

'Doesn't the table look beautiful?' Faith said.

'It's wonderful. I think Mrs Cresswell has done a marvellous job'

Serena, seated on Edward's right, looked along the table to Lydia. 'I don't suppose you're used to dining in such style?'

'No, I'm not, which makes me appreciate it all the more.' Might as well admit my shortcomings, she thought.

'Oh, Jeremy and I have dinner parties quite regularly – business friends mostly.'

'It must be a bit of a trial always having to entertain because of business rather than the pleasure of friends,' David said, coming to Lydia's rescue. She smiled at him gratefully.

The waitress brought in the first course and Jeremy turned to Lydia.

'You know, Lydia, you look very pretty.'

'Thank you.'

Lydia appreciated the compliment but had a strong suspicion that Jeremy had been drinking well before he had arrived at the Manor.

'Doesn't she, David?'

'She does indeed.'

'I bet you had lots of boyfriends before you met Edward.'

'No.'

'I'm sure you must.'

'No, I didn't.'

Lydia looked down the table to where Edward and Serena were deep in conversation. Why doesn't he support me she thought?

'Come on – do tell.'

David protested. 'If she says she didn't, she didn't.'

'There wasn't much time for gadding about while I was nursing my father.'

Jeremy continued to ask impertinent questions which she tried to treat light-heartedly and David endeavoured to make sensible conversation, as did Faith. But Jeremy consumed glass after glass of wine and Lydia found herself increasingly miserable. Serena spoke intimately to Edward, leaning close and touching him at every opportunity, all designed, she was sure, to make Lydia feel out-of-place, which it did, or jealous, which it did not.

'Remember the May Ball you took me to, Edward. Wasn't it wonderful, dancing the night away, and walking beside the river before having breakfast. Those were the days.'

Serena smiled and peeped beneath her long lashes to see the

reaction.

'That was a long time ago,' Edward whispered, leaning his head towards her.

'This pretty young thing had probably only just started school,' Jeremy said. He caught his wife's eye. 'Oops, said the wrong thing.' He sniggered and put a serviette to his mouth.

Lydia recoiled from the constant jibes thrown at her and became quieter and more unhappy as the evening wore on. She had so wanted to appear a gracious hostess, to do her best for Edward's sake, even though she had no experience of occasions like this. But Serena managed to put her down, oh so subtly, every time Lydia attempted a new topic of conversation. It was a relief when the meal was over and they all retired to the drawing room for coffee. Faith came and sat beside Lydia.

'Did I hear you say you had to nurse your father?'

'Yes. He had cancer. I had to leave my job and look after him full time.' Lydia desperately needed someone to talk to who she felt was on her side. 'He wasn't my real father,' she confided. 'My parents were killed when I was five.

'Oh, you poor love.' Faith put her hand on Lydia's. 'Were you looked after by relatives?'

'No, I was fostered. It wasn't until I was nine that I was put with the Kentners. I call them my parents 'cause it saves complicated explanations, and I did look on them as a mother and father.'

Faith said she understood and put a finger to her lips. 'Nevertheless, it must have been hard on you.'

'Oh, I didn't mind. He appreciated everything I did for him. He was – both of them were very kind to me.'

'Did Elizabeth share this burden with you?'

'No, Elizabeth died when I was sixteen.'

'You've had a sad life, haven't you, but I'm sure you'll be happy now. You certainly deserve it. Now,' said Faith, reaching out a plump arm, 'let me see your ring.' Lydia proudly held out her hand. 'How exquisite.'

'I know. I've never seen stones so large,' she lowered her voice, 'or had anything so valuable.'

They laughed and Lydia felt she had found a kindred spirit. She glanced up and saw Serena's tormented scrutiny. Just what was the relationship between her and Edward?

Thunder had rumbled around the Manor all evening which seemed to cause Serena some distress. When it was time for the guests to leave, large drops of rain were thudding against the leaded windows. When Faith and David had gone, Lydia leaned against the wall in the porch and put her hand to her head. She was disappointed that Edward had not sat near her when the meal had finished though, she had to admit, Serena had hardly left him room to move.

'You must dine with us soon,' Serena said, as they left. 'I'll fix it with Edward.'

What's wrong with fixing it with me, Lydia thought.

Jeremy, too drunk to drive, pushed himself off the wall and followed his wife to the car. Edward bolted the doors and they returned to the kitchen. Lydia thought how handsome he looked in evening dress.

'Want a drink?'

'Just water please, the wine's made me thirsty.'

'Did you enjoy the evening?'

Tears pricked the backs of her eyes and she did not know what to reply.

'Do I gather from your silence you did not enjoy it?' It sounded like an accusation.

'I found it – it was a strain.' Didn't he realise it would be so? He knew her background – knew she had not lived his sort of life. Lydia finished the water and put the glass on the table.

'How long have you known Serena?'

'A long, long time, since we were children. Our parents, or rather our fathers, were friends. They were at school together. With my father abroad so much and her father in the army, they didn't meet often, but they kept in touch. Serena's father still lives in Berkshire. I used to stay with her parents occasionally during the school holidays – that is if I wasn't here or being off-loaded on my grandmother or left in some embassy to fend for myself.'

There was that same bitter tone she had noted before. She tried to read what lay behind the remark but his face gave no clue and she did not like to ask.

'Edward,' she cried, jumping up from her chair. 'I haven't given you my present.'

She rushed upstairs and returned, breathless, with a package wrapped in black and gold paper.

'My engagement present for you. I was so overwhelmed by my ring I forgot.' She lifted her hand to gaze at the ring now as she had done surreptitiously several times during the evening.

Edward looked genuinely pleased as he pulled the decorative string and took off the shiny paper. It was a first edition of a book on Elizabethan architecture, which had cost Lydia nearly a week's salary.

'This is lovely,' he said, somewhat stiffly. He put the book down on the kitchen table and moved towards her. Expectantly she looked up as he bent to kiss her and she rose to meet him, but his kiss was as swift and formal as before.

Still, Lydia told herself as she climbed into bed, he did like the present. Everything would be fine, she told herself – meaning it, feeling it.

*

After the reception at a country club near Maidstone, they had flown to Paris. She was excited about being in Paris, but overwhelmed and apprehensive about the situation she found herself in.

The ceremony was simple and beautifully taken by David. Edward looked his usual handsome self in a dark grey suit, and she was complimented on her pale pink, ankle length suit and a straw hat trimmed with pink roses. The ladies of the village, primed by Shirley Reece, the owner of the local store, filled some of the pews out of curiosity.

It had been lovely seeing Jill and her family, and to see how much her two goddaughters had grown and their excitement at being bridesmaids. Lydia smiled. And dear Charles, proud to be giving her away but uneasy, she sensed. He had presented her a string of pearls that had belonged to his mother. Edward's share, he had said, would be seeing her wearing it.

When they arrived at the hotel Edward ordered champagne and sandwiches, which Lydia was much too nervous to eat. She did succumb to some champagne before she went to bathe.

The bathroom held every toiletry that could be imagined – shampoo, handcream, lotions, perfume, soaps, all of the finest quality. The bath had gold taps and the shower cubicle was twice the size of a telephone box. Lydia was fascinated. How the rich live, she thought, as she sampled or sniffed every container. There was even a phone by the loo, she noticed, as she sank into the hot scented bubbles.

She slipped on her cream satin nightgown and went into the bedroom. Edward was studying the sightseeing literature spread out on the leather-topped desk. She smiled self-consciously and was rewarded with one from him. Lydia pulled down the top cover and climbed on to the Queen-sized bed.

Feeling like a child she said, 'Where shall I sleep – which side?'

'Left – is that all right?'

When he had gone to shower she jumped off the bed and explored. The room was huge. There were two armchairs and a desk with a brass table lamp and green shade. A large sideboard revealed a TV and, to her surprise, a fridge full of drinks. A consul of switches was beside the bed and she experimented, turning the lights off and on. She giggled nervously as she plunged the bathroom into darkness and Edward called out.

Picking up her glass she moved to the window and gazed at the Arc de Triomphe to the right bathed in a soft yellow light, and was that the top of the Eiffel Tower in the distance? Lydia sipped her champagne thinking she must be in a dream.

Lydia tossed back the rest of her glass, leapt on the bed and threw herself back on the soft pillows. Had Elizabeth felt like this on her wedding night? Had her mother? Though she was not a virgin, her only experience had been with a fellow art student, and that had lasted barely a month before he found someone else. Her husband was not even her lover. Would living at the Manor make up for that?

Edward came into the bedroom carrying his clothes and neatly placed them in one of the armchairs. He shut the cabinet door she had left open, slipped off his robe and got into bed.

Lydia had seen many naked men at college and recalled those weeks of figure drawing. Both sexes tried to look unconcerned whilst feeling acutely embarrassed, but soon they were concentrating so hard on deltoid muscles and dorsal aspects, that nakedness was just a part of the course.

Feeling less self-conscious now the lights were off, Lydia said, 'I wish I had my art materials with me. I'd love to draw you.'

He put his arm round her shoulders and moved his finger tips caressingly over her skin.

'Would you?' He sounded pleased. 'That could probably be....'

Why had he stopped? What was the problem?

Lydia was not sure how to respond when Edward kissed her, recalling how offhand he had been on previous occasions. Tentatively she returned his kiss. Slowly he stroked her skin as his hand eased her night-gown up her body. She lifted her hips and he slipped the gown over her head. He pushed the covers away and Lydia shivered as the cooler air hit her skin.

Edward's fingers moved lightly over her and he cupped her breast and kissed it. Lydia liked the sensations he was inducing but, at the same time, wondered what he was expecting from her. She touched his chest and spread her fingers amongst the hairs. They were soft, not wiry as she had imagined. He ran the tips of his fingers up and down her spine, which she loved. Lydia arched her back which seemed to arouse him. He parted her legs with his and his hands moved smoothly up and down her thighs, touching her expertly, making her senses tingle. She let herself be made love to, moving her body under his guidance. All was conducted in silence till he said, 'Are you all right?'

Their wedding night had not been one of unbridled passion. The thought of Edward doing anything unbridled made Lydia smile. But he had been gentle and considerate. She was not unhappy.

*

Lydia was rudely awoken. 'Wake up, Lydia. We have sightseeing to do. I have a great deal to show you.'

Viewing Paris through Edward's eyes was a revelation. She remembered it as a fifteen-year-old schoolgirl, rushing from one tourist attraction to another. Edward took her to out of the way places and restaurants he had frequented as a student. She loved listening to him ordering meals or confirming directions in French.

On their last day, when they were walking back to their hotel on the Champs Elysées, he said, 'Why won't you let me buy you something? I would like you to have some memento of our honeymoon.'

They were walking side by side returning to their hotel. Lydia had, earlier in the week, grasped his hand as they wove between the manic traffic at the Place de la Concorde, but Edward released it when they reached the safety of the gardens. She had noticed, but was enjoying herself so much, she had pushed any disquiet to the back of her mind.

'A memento?' She clutched her chin pensively. 'How about this?'

From a street vendor's stall she reached for a miniature Eiffel Tower and turned a serious face to his as she raised the tacky article to his eye level. His look of horror made her throw back her head and laugh. As he gazed at her a small smile played round his lips, but as quickly as it came it was gone. He took the offending article from her and replaced it on the stall, much to the chagrin of the stallholder.

She did allow him to buy her a mauve and green multi-patterned scarf, the price of which made her blanch. She thanked him, but did not make the mistake of an added kiss.

∗

Lydia loved seeing France from the air and had been glued to the window. Now, leaving the coast, there was only sparkling sea and dots of boats with white ribbons in their wakes. Was it really her, the five-year-old orphan, passed like a parcel from home to home, being hurtled to a life so different from anything she could ever have imagined? She raised her shoulders in a joyful hunch at the thought of spending her days as mistress of Abbey Manor. She glanced at Edward, who turned and said, 'Had a good time?'

'It's been so wonderful. I can't think when I've enjoyed myself so much.'

'Good,' he said, benevolently.

∗

At the Manor next morning Lydia woke to the familiar sound of her husband showering in the adjoining bathroom. She jumped out of bed and went to a box resting on cases brought from her flat. She found jeans and a sweater and dressed quickly so she could be down before him.

When Edward came into the kitchen the smell of coffee brewing already filled the air.

'I thought you might want to sleep in,' he said.

'But I want to get your breakfast and see you off. Isn't that what new brides are supposed to do?'

He smiled uncertainly as Lydia poured out coffee 'Do you want me to cook you something?'

'No, cereal and toast is sufficient. I only eat cooked breakfast at weekends.'

'Is there something you particularly like that I can get at the shops?' Lydia asked.

'I can't think of anything at the moment. I'll leave it to you. That's what you're here for after all.'

'Of course.' She blinked her eyes. 'What time will you be in tonight?'

'Around six thirty, depending on trains and traffic.'

When Edward had left she turned to sorting out the boxes she had brought from Clapham. Every wardrobe, shelf and drawer in her bedroom was empty. She wondered what had happened to his wife's belongings. Not a vestige of Frances could she find, apart from the jewellery case. Everything in it was hers, Edward told her, but the most expensive items were at the bank. She opened out the maroon velvet-lined box and gazed at the earrings, brooches, bracelets and necklaces lying in glittering splendour in their appropriate compartments. Laughing, she searched for her silver necklace and bracelet, a twenty-first birthday present from Robert, and Charles' pearls and put them with the rest.

Most of the rooms had only been given a quick glance. She could not wait to go into each one again. She started with the little bedroom opposite hers that overlooked the front garden and caught the sun nearly all day. She stood wondering if the women who had once lived here had been happy? Had they loved their home as she loved it? Hers was not the first arranged marriage down the Casleigh generations she was sure. Where wealth was concerned, women were just pawns in the game, though she was not wanted for her money.

At eleven Lydia came down for a drink. As she reached the passage the phone rang. She dithered at the foot of the stairs, stupidly trying to remember where the phones and extensions were before going to the one in the drawing room.

'Hello, Abbey Manor. Miss Ab – Mrs Casleigh speaking.'

'Very efficient,' drawled the voice at the other end, 'You even remembered your new name. Serena Detrale here.' Before Lydia could reply she went on, 'Did you have a lovely time in Paris? Isn't it a delightful city? We've often gone there for the weekend. Was the weather good?'

'We had a wonderful time. The weather was mixed, not bad for October.' She hoped this gave her the information she professed to want.

'On Wednesdays, a few of us get together for coffee. It's my turn this week. Would you care to join us? It'll be a chance for me to introduce you to them.'

Lydia's heart sank, but as Serena was Edward's friend she felt she must try to get on with her.

'OK, but I am expecting a few things from my flat that morning.'

'When are these few things arriving?' Serena made it sound as if they were coming on a horse-drawn cart with a carpet thrown over the top.

'That's the point. All they said was Wednesday morning.'

'I'll leave it to you. The others will be here about ten thirty.'

'I'll do my best. Thanks for....' but Serena had rung off.

*

Lydia was standing on a stool exploring the kitchen cupboards when Mrs Cresswell came into the kitchen.

'What *are* you doing up there?' she said, as she took off her coat.

'I thought I'd better see what's what, and the kitchen seemed to be a good place to start.'

The older woman went to the walk-in pantry and lifted an apron from the hook and replaced it with her coat.

'I think we need to have a chat about what you want me to do. You must have things how you want them.'

'Yes,' Lydia said, feeling important. 'but I'll certainly need your help, my whole flat would have fitted into the drawing room.' She stepped down from the stool. 'Let's have a cup of coffee and talk it over.'

'I'll get it, you carry on with what you're doing.'

When it was made, they sat companionably at the large kitchen table. Controls and timer for the central heating were explained, Edward's likes and dislikes considered and local shops discussed.

'There's a butcher and bakery, we're lucky there, though for how long I don't know. Grassenden Stores sells most other things but is a bit expensive. If you want to get to know the neighbourhood, Mrs Casleigh, there is no better place. What Shirley Reece doesn't know isn't worth knowing, so be careful what you say in front of her. I sometimes think she knows what's going to happen to you before you do. They will deliver.'

'I think I could get my own shopping. I'll have plenty of time. I must do something to keep me occupied.'

Lydia took the mugs to the sink, washed and dried them and put them on a shelf.

'Edward and Tom seemed, well, a little cool towards each other when I visited the farm, or did I imagine it?'

Mrs Cresswell did not answer immediately and Lydia looked to see if she had heard.

Eventually she said, 'They were very friendly as children – Jamie as well, but...'

Her voice tailed away and the sentence remained unfinished.

Lydia did not like to pursue it.

'Now, what days do you normally do? I don't want to upset your routine.'

'To tell you the truth, my dear, I have found it quite a strain looking after Edward. I'm well into my sixties now, but he thinks I'm the same age I was when he was at school.' She smiled. 'But I didn't care to see him struggling on his own after Mrs Casleigh died – and the baby.'

'How did it happen? Edward just told me it was in a car crash.'

'She had driven up to London to show off little Teddy to a friend. It was February and she was on her way home. The police thought she must've hit some ice and skidded, then hit a tree. She was killed outright and the tree fell and crushed the baby in his seat.'

Lydia winced. 'How dreadful.'

Mrs Cresswell began peeling potatoes she had fetched from the pantry. 'That was nearly five years ago. Edward sort of shut himself off from everyone for a while. The Detrales helped a bit and he did go to them for the odd meal, but he ate out in London most of the time. Anyway, I think David finally got through to him – had a bit of a heart to heart, like – and that was when he asked me if I'd look after him. Before that I'd only come in now and again to tidy up a bit, you know.'

There were so many things she wanted to know about, but was not quite sure if Mrs Cresswell were the person to ask. Would she not think it strange she did not know already?

'Oh, look at me peeling potatoes without asking you – force of habit. What are you having tonight?'

'You know more than I do, Mrs Cresswell. What's in the freezer?'

In the next ten minutes they decided there would be pork chops for dinner, that two mornings a week would suit them both and that they would call each other Lydia and Cressy.

*

On Wednesday, Lydia made up her mind to walk to Serena's. The carriers had been early and she had phoned Serena to say she was on her way. She pondered what to wear, but decided it did not much matter as Serena and her friends would no doubt put her in the shade.

As she turned into the Lane from the drive she saw Tom emerging from the footpath.

'Hello, again,' she called.

He looked up and lengthened his step to reach her.

'Good morning, Mrs Casleigh.'

'Lydia, please.'

'I don't think Edward would approve of that.'

'Really, why's that?'

'I always called his first wife Mrs Casleigh. I was never expected to call her anything else.'

'Well, it's my name, so I think it's up to me who I allow to call me Lydia – and you're top of the list. Well, second, actually, your Mum's top.'

'Where're you off to?'

'To have coffee with Serena Detrale. Do you know her?'

'I know her,' he said, grinning, 'but we don't move in the same circles.'

'I know what you mean, I'm not sure I do either.'

They each gave a conspiratorial laugh.

'What about you?' Lydia asked.

'Just paying Mum a quick visit to see if she wants to go into Maidstone this week.'

'We had a good chat on Monday. Your mother's one of the nicest.'

'I bet your mother's one of the best, too.'

'My mother died when I was sixteen.'

'Oh, I am sorry,' Tom said.

'My father is also dead,' she added, in case he should ask and be further embarrassed.

They had reached his mother's cottage and he unlatched the gate. 'Goodbye, Mrs Casleigh.' She glared. 'Lydia,' he corrected.

*

Tom opened the door that led straight into the living room of the cottage. He eased off each muddy wellington boot and left them on the mat in the porch. He padded over to the table and sat down.

'Hello, dear.' His mother gave him a kiss.

'I've just walked down the road with Edward's wife. She asked me to call her Lydia.'

'Attractive little thing, isn't she? So good-natured. What did you think of her?'

'Not Edward's type at all, much too pleasant.'

'Tom! That's not a nice thing to say.'

'Oh, come on Mum, you know what I mean. She's about as far removed from Frances as it's possible to get.'

'That's true,' she admitted. 'Perhaps this time he's found someone who'll make him happy, even if she isn't his type, as you put it.'

She handed him his mug. 'She also asked me to call her Lydia.'

'I wouldn't do it in Edward's hearing if I were you. He'd like to keep the master/servant relationship at all costs.'

'Don't be so horrid,' his mother protested. 'He deserves something for the miserable …'

'Yeah, yeah, I know, Jamie and I have been told enough times. Still he's always got his money to comfort him.' As his mother moved away he muttered, 'She's still too good for him.

Chapter 3

When Lydia left Tom she walked jauntily down the Lane. Everything she saw she viewed with new eyes. It was her name over the almshouses; she was part of history and when she had a son, part of the Casleigh future. The Manor was living up to expectations, Cressy was a darling and Edward – well, he was just Edward – distant, aloof, a considerate, if restrained, lover. When they had settled down and got used to one another they would find mutual interests. Life was going to be just fine.

Coming to Stream Cottage, she decided on the bridleway into Grassenden. But where the houses ended, the old road gave way to gravel and the gravel to Kentish clay, so by the time Lydia came out opposite the village inn, her shoes were caked in mud. How could she have been so stupid? Typical townie. She had not even learned from seeing Tom in his muddy boots.

The bell tinkled as she went into the shop, which was a mixture of minimarket and old-fashioned grocery store. At the back was a delicatessen and an appetising smell of cooked ham wafted on the air.

A woman came into the shop from a back room. She was a tall, well-built woman with mousy brown hair tied back with a red ribbon.

'Can I help you?'

'I'd like a box of paper handkerchiefs please. I came along the path from Abbotts Lidiard instead of the road and now I've got to get the mud off my shoes.

'It's Mrs Casleigh, isn't it? I came to see your wedding.' She warmed to her subject. 'I went with me friend, Pam, and several of the villagers was there 'cos I told them about it. You did look nice.'

'I hope you won't think I'm rude, but I have an appointment and I want to get these cleaned up.' She pointed to her shoes.

'The handkerchiefs are over there,' she said, indicating the relevant shelf, 'but tell you what, you give 'em to me and I'll clean 'em out the back.'

'No, really, I don't want to bother you.'

'It ain't no bother.' She held out her hand. 'They'll be better for a proper clean.'

Mrs Reece returned a few minutes later and handed over the shoes.

'That is kind of you,' Lydia said, slipping them on.

As she left the shop, she heard Mrs Reece say to a customer, 'That's the new lady up the Manor.'

The double gates of Serena's drive were open and on the left brick pillar was the name Ridge House. The Edwardian house, like Abbey Manor, stood at right angles to the road. It was a solid building of two storeys and across the front of the house, above the ground floor, was a glass canopy supported by iron pillars.

Serena came to the door dressed in cream tailored trousers and a long-sleeved silk blouse in pale green. Her arm, heavy with bracelets, went round Lydia's shoulders as she propelled her into the drawing room.

Lydia's practised eye took in the furniture. In keeping with the house, the pieces were in period; but Ridge House had mostly good quality reproductions. A drinks cabinet was in the window, a three-piece suite with cream coverings was in front of the marble fireplace. An unlit gas fire was in the grate. The carpet, in pale blue, had a deep pile. No expense had been spared.

Serena introduced her friends, Miriam Court and Joscelyn Maltby, who lived in the village and Anna Bartley who lived in neighbouring Grimley Heath.

'Sit down there by Anna. I'll pour you a coffee.'

'I'm sorry I'm late. I had a slight mishap.'

'You seem to make a habit of that,' Serena said.

'We hear you enjoyed your honeymoon in Paris,' Miriam said.

'It was fabulous.'

'Edward has spent a great deal of time in France. He speaks French and German fluently. He is a very good linguist,' Serena said. 'He did languages at Cambridge, you know.'

'Yes, he told me,' she lied. She had not known what he had read. How little she knew about him.

'You have a place in France, haven't you, Miriam?' Serena said.

'Yes, but we're thinking of buying another in Florida.'

'What about you, Joss? Has Stephen made an offer for that villa in Portugal? You were saying the one you had was too small now that the children were older.'

Joss uncrossed her legs and leaned back. 'I think he's decided it's too far from the golf course.'

'Has your family any property abroad, Lydia?'

'I have no family.'

'Oh.'

'That's sad,' Anna said.

Serena tried a new tack. 'I gather you come from London. Whereabouts?'

'Clapham.'

'Oh, Clapham,' she said, sounding unsure if Clapham were an 'in' place. 'Did you live on your own?'

'Yes, what makes you ask?'

'Where did you meet Edward? I am intrigued,' she quizzed, ignoring Lydia's question.

What you mean is what would Edward be doing in a place like Clapham. However, it did reveal that Edward had not been discussing her with Serena.

'I met Edward in Abbotts Lidiard ten – no, eleven weeks ago.' She beamed a radiant smile at them all and added, 'It was love at first sight.'

'How romantic.' Anna said.

Joss and Miriam exchanged glances and Serena pursed her lips. She must have thought the questioning was not going quite the way she had intended for she ceased the interrogation and started up a conversation, leaving Anna and Lydia to talk.

Anna had three young children all at school, but had once had a job at the Stock Exchange before marrying Terrence Bartley. She and Lydia warmed to each other as they discussed the work they had done and at the end of the morning Anna offered to give Lydia a lift home.

When they drew up at the bottom of the Manor drive, Anna said, 'I hope we'll meet again soon.'

'Perhaps, when I've settled, you could come here for a coffee.'

'I'll look forward to that. I've heard so much about the Manor from Serena.'

'I'll be in touch then. Thank you for the lift.'

Lydia waved as she drove off, then crossed the Lane to walk up the drive. She put the large, old-fashioned key into the oak door and let herself in to her treasured home.

That evening when Edward came home from work she told him about the day's events. He was glad about her furniture arriving, made no comment on her seeing Tom and was happy that she had had coffee with Serena and her friends. Lydia wondered what he would say if she told him theirs was love at first sight.

Later, in the drawing room, when Edward had come in from his study, he said, 'I thought we could go out to dinner tomorrow to celebrate your birthday.'

'That would be lovely,' she said, excited. 'We could go to that place you took me to in Frittingwell. We might not get a table at such short notice though. I'll ring up and see.' Lydia jumped up eagerly.

'Sit down, Lydia. If there's any booking to be done, I'll do it.'

'I'm sorry. I didn't mean…' She sat down as if pushed. The blood rushed to her cheeks.

'I like to make arrangements for any outings we undertake together. Please remember that.'

'Very well' she said tears not far below the surface.

*

Lydia sat at her dressing table after their evening out. She took off the pendant Edward had given her and held it up by the chain. As it twisted in her hand, it caught the light and changed colour. Opal – her birthstone.

She put it down carefully beside her ring and stared at the stone surrounded by its gold frame. Lydia had kissed him lightly on the cheek when he had given it to her. Would this show enough appreciation?

Lydia slipped into bed and reached for her book. She had been reading for ten minutes when Edward came into her room. He took the book from her hand put it on the table and sat on the bed.

'Did you like my present?'

'Yes, did you get the impression I hadn't?'

'No, no. I was just asking.'

Edward stared at her for some moments and she tried to read his mind. On the one hand he rejected any show of affection, on the other seemed to crave it. Suddenly he gave a smile, disarming in its rarity, switched off the light and got in beside her.

'I'm glad you like it,' he said, taking her in his arms.

*

Lydia did not know what time it was when she was jerked from sleep. She thought she must have been hit because her cheek was smarting. Edward was speaking, his voice muffled.

'What is it?'

'Don't, don't. Please ...' Edward said, threshing his arms violently.

She could not catch the next few words. She put her hand on his arm.

'Edward, what's the matter?'

She reached for a tissue and stroked his wet forehead. Slowly he calmed but did not wake. He put his arms tight around her and she heard him mutter, 'Cressy, is that you?' and felt him relax.

Waking early next morning Lydia lay staring up at the beamed ceiling. She turned to look at the clock. Half past six. She stared at Edward who was peacefully asleep. As she went downstairs, she thought of the worrying events of the night. What sort of nightmare could have tormented him so and yet had not woken him? If he thought Cressy was there, it must have been a dream he had been having since childhood. He was certainly distressed; she could still picture the sweat and the anguished look on his face. He had been restless for some time, though the nightmare had not returned.

Lydia took him tea, which she put on her bedside table. She sat on the bed and gently shook him. As he came to, she thought how dishy he looked with his blond hair falling forward. Dishy did not seem an Edward-type word to describe him, but it was how she saw him at that moment. He opened his eyes and looked sleepily at her and Lydia felt a great desire to kiss him.

'What time is it?'

'Ten to seven.'

He pushed himself up on one arm and took the cup from her. 'Did I wake you last night?'

'You were rather restless.'

'I'm sorry.'

Lydia wondered whether to mention what had happened, but all she said was, 'I'll get some breakfast. When will you be down?'

'Give me twenty minutes.'

When Edward came into the kitchen, she said, 'My car's due for a service. Shall I take it to Jamie Cresswell's garage?'

'Yes, give him a ring, I'll expect he'll fit you in quickly, depends what he's got on his books.' He poured cereal from a box on the kitchen table. 'He's very good with cars. We had hundreds of Dinky and Matchbox toys between us. I used to leave some of mine at his house and vice versa. There was more room to play here, of course. We were always keen on cars as boys – still are.'

Lydia grinned at the impeccably dressed man in his grey suit, white shirt and discreetly patterned blue tie. He glanced up.

'What's so funny?'

'Just trying to imagine you playing cars, that's all.'

Edward grunted.

'You bought the garage, didn't you say?'

'Yes. I inherited some money on my eighteenth birthday and bought it three or four years after that. I asked Jamie if he wanted to run it, but he turned it down.'

'Had he got a job somewhere else?'

'Yes, but he thought there would be strings attached. It wasn't until he decided to get married he asked if the offer was still open. I think the bungalow that went with it was the decider. I've never interfered with the running of it,' he said, defensively.

'So what to you get out of it?'

'Just the rent and I like to see him doing well. He's a good mechanic.'

Edward finished his toast and marmalade, collected his black brief case, drained the coffee cup and made for the hall.

'Won't you be cold without a coat?' Lydia said as she followed him.

'Don't fuss, it's in here.'

Edward came out of the cloakroom with one arm in his overcoat. She stepped forward to help him on with it.

'I forgot about the cloakroom.'

Edward buttoned the coat, kissed – or rather touched his cheek against hers and let himself out.

'Goodbye,' she said lamely to his back.

❋

Lydia drove the Renault on to the small forecourt of Cresswell Motors. She could hear Radio One as she went into the workshop. A head could just be seen in the pit under a Ford Mondeo.

'Hello. Mr Cresswell?' she called.

The head poked out, then he hoisted himself from the pit.

'Yes, can I help you madam?'

If Lydia thought Tom resembled his mother, Jamie was almost

a replica. Same stocky build, same ruddy cheeks and pale blue eyes.

'My car needs servicing. Edward told me to ring you, but I had to come in to shop – so here I am.'

'You must be the new Mrs Casleigh. My mother and Tom have been telling me all about you.' Quite unselfconsciously he went on, 'You aint a bit like his first wife she wouldn't be seen dead talking to me.'

His hand held hers in a grip Lydia could well imagine tightening wheelnuts without the aid of a power tool.

Jamie turned off the radio. 'What's your car?'

'A Renault 5, one careful owner but no garage – till now.'

He walked over to his office just big enough for a desk, chair and filing cabinet. He stuck his head out and said, 'How about next Friday, nine o'clock?'

'Brilliant.'

Jamie studied Lydia with ill-concealed interest. She noticed his appraisal and smiled. 'I'll see you Friday.' As she turned to leave she said, 'You know, I can imagine you playing with toy cars, but I cannot imagine Edward crawling over the floor making broom, broom noises.'

'I can assure you he did, but that was when we were…' He stopped. 'I'll see you on Friday.'

Lydia bought a loaf and cream cakes at Collins, the bakers. She made Mr Anders' acquaintance and enquired about meat for the freezer, all the while being regaled with details of his grandsons as if she already knew of their existence.

Mrs Reece greeted her like a long lost relative, which even Lydia, with her natural friendliness, found embarrassing and knew that Edward would be appalled at the woman's familiarity.

'These things in the basket, please,' she said crisply, hoping to put things on a more formal footing, 'and a four slices of your delicious ham, not too thin.'

'Certainly, Mrs Casleigh.' She began totting up. 'That'll be £10.89 please.'

Lydia put her shopping in the car, which Jamie had said she could leave on the forecourt as long as she did not make a habit of it. As she shut the boot, a woman came down the path from the bungalow.

'Hello, I'm Jamie's wife, Pat.'

'Hi, your mother-in-law has told me all about you. I'd like to meet your children one day. In fact, you must come to a meal sometime.'

Pat looked startled. 'Oh, yes – that would be…' Hurriedly she said, 'Jamie's Mum is very fond of Kim and Tony.'

'How old are they?'

'Kim's twelve in February. She's just started at secondary school. Tony's still at the village school.'

'If you'll excuse me, Pat, I must get going.' She jumped in the car and wound down the window. Nice to have met you.'

Well, thought Lydia as she turned into the lane, I seem to be making my mark. I was certainly given the once-over.

*

'We're going to a reception in London just before Christmas,' Lydia told Cressy as they were changing sheets one bitterly cold morning towards the end of November.

'That's nice dear. Are you looking forward to it?'

'Yes – no – well, actually I'm afraid I'll let Edward down. I'm not used to that sort of thing. I might do something wrong.'

'You just be your usual charming self,' she said, reassuringly. 'After all, if Edward thought you'd show him up, he wouldn't have told you about it, would he?'

'Oh, Cressy, you're so good for me. Of course you're right.'

'You're just what he needs. I think he's been very lonely.'

Lydia gave a wry smile before saying, 'Do you know about Mr Anders' latest grandchild? It's a girl at last. He's so proud.'

'No.'

'And that Mrs Reece's sister is here from Australia on a visit?'

'Nor that either. If you're getting the gossip, you must be settling in nicely.'

'I hope so, it's a bit of a contrast to my life in London – well, more than a bit.'

Cressy put the dirty linen in the basket. 'Edward certainly took us all by surprise.'

Lydia wondered if she were expected to comment further on the suddenness of their marriage, but there was no sign that Cressy awaited an explanation. She supposed that enquiring into your employer's private life was not done, however highly thought of you were.

'How many weeks have you been married?'

'Eight.'

Lydia thought back over those weeks. The Manor was all she

expected. The garden, though bare and dull now, held such promise. She was already planning what she was going to do to improve it.

Edward remained an enigma. He appeared satisfied with the running of the Manor but did not spend much time with her, nearly always retiring to his study to work after their evening meal. Still, when a child comes along he will be happier and more relaxed, she was sure. All marriages had to settle down – even a marriage as strange as theirs

That evening when Edward had finally come into the drawing room, he announced, 'I have to go to Sevenoaks tomorrow, to see my solicitor.'

'May I come with you?'

Surprised he said, 'I suppose so.'

Lydia almost declared that if he were that thrilled, she would not bother, but she did not wish to have another confrontation. She had already been censured the previous evening when she had been telling him what she and Cressy had been doing. Without warning he had shouted at her, 'Don't call her Cressy!' Then realising he had raised his voice, he said in a quieter tone, 'I'd rather you didn't call her that.'

Momentarily she was lost for words, but recovering she said, 'If that's what you wish.'

'What time are you going, morning or afternoon?'

'Morning.'

'Perhaps when you've finished at the solicitors you could help me look for a dress for the reception.'

'Why can't you choose something yourself, you have good taste. I've told you that before. Or you could get Serena to go with you?'

Serena was the last person Lydia would ask. 'I thought it would be pleasant to do something together.'

'Frances never asked me to choose clothes with her.'

'I am *not* Frances.'

'Well, if you want to come with me, I shall be leaving about nine-thirty.' He picked up the evening paper and began reading.

Lydia was ready before breakfast next morning. At nine fifteen she was sitting on the settle in the hall wearing her black coat with a small fur collar, a cossack hat, boots and gloves. The only colour relief was the scarf Edward had bought her on their honeymoon. He made no comment when he saw her and they drove to Sevenoaks in virtual silence.

While Edward went to Smith & Clint, Lydia studied the shops. He met her for coffee and then she led him round those she had found.

'I thought that smart for day wear,' Lydia said, commenting on a three-piece outfit of white blouse, dark blue trousers and waistcoat in a window. She bent down to peer at the price tags.

'Why don't you buy it?'

She wrinkled her nose. 'It's too expensive.'

'Don't I give you enough money?'

'It's not that,' she started, then angrily turned to him, tears filling her eyes. 'You do not own me, Edward, whatever else I may have agreed to. I just thought that ensemble was not good value for money. That was all.'

Lydia strode away wiping her eyes, with no idea in which direction she was heading. Edward caught up with her and grabbed her arm.

In a conciliatory manner, which she thought was about as close as he would get to easing his guilt without saying sorry, he said, 'Let's look for your dress.'

On the way home, he said, 'My mother had a mink coat, which is in store. Would you like to wear it?'

'Do you want me to?'

'You would look nice in it.'

'If you would like me to wear it, I will.'

Edward did not look happy with her reply, but Lydia was still smarting over his insulting remark and putting on a mink was not going to placate her.

*

The Christmas lights of the towns as they drove to London were reflected in the rain-covered roads. The headache she had when she woke she put down to being nervous about the evening. The ensemble finally chosen, approved by Edward with a curt nod, was of ivory lace with a beaded jacket.

Lydia's hands shook as she went into the cloakroom of the Dorchester. In spite of the mink, she felt ill-at-ease beside the other women, all of whom appeared to know each other and were used to these events.

Edward was waiting for her and she hoped he would not leave her alone as he had at their engagement dinner. Lydia had never been good at small talk and in this sort of company, she knew she would have nothing to say. He took her arm and led her into the room where the reception was being held. It was brightly lit with huge chandeliers and mirrored walls hung with heavy drapes.

They stood for a few moments just inside the room when a voice close by said, 'Edward, how lovely to see you. How are you?'

A grey haired, distinguished looking man stood in front of them holding out his hand.

'Gerald!' Edward's face lit up. 'I am well, thank you. Lydia, this is Gerald Exenton, Gerald, this is my wife.'

'I didn't know you had married again, old chap.'

'We haven't been married long.'

Edward explained to Lydia that he had, at one time, worked for Gerald. While the men chatted, two other colleagues of Edward sidled up and introductions were made. It was not long before groups formed and parted like oil on water. Soon she and Edward were separated. Lydia caught sight of him nodding his fair head and smiling, surrounded mostly by women. She, too, had gathered around her several men who made sure she was supplied with food, and kept her amused with their stories. All her fears had been groundless and she had not felt at all out of place and was having a fantastic evening.

When Edward finally pushed his way through the throng engulfing his tiny wife, she could not believe the time had gone so quickly.

'I am ready to go now,' he said, briskly.

Lydia was pleased he had come as her head had begun to thump alarmingly and she felt sick. As soon as they started for home, she fell asleep and it was not until she heard the crunch of the car wheels on the drive that she stirred. While Edward put the car away, Lydia leaned against the door waiting to be let in.

The mink was laid carefully on the settle and she went into the kitchen.

'Shall I get you a coffee?' she said, wearily.

He nodded. 'You certainly enjoyed yourself this evening.'

'I had a marvellous time. I thought I wasn't going to enjoy it – you know – amongst all those grand people.'

She turned and saw Edward's eyes. 'What's the matter? What have I done now?' Lydia passed her hand across her forehead.

'You should have stayed by me.'

'How could I? Anyway, why didn't you stay by me? You were the one who knew everybody. People were talking to me.'

'Men.'

Lydia frowned. 'What about men?'

'Men were talking to you.'

'So, men were talking to me. What am I supposed to say, "I'm not allowed to speak to strange men".'

'Don't be ridiculous.'

'If anyone is being ridiculous, it's you. I thought you'd be pleased that I had not been showing you up.'

Lydia felt almost too ill to speak. Why was he going on so? With effort she poured the coffee and handed him his mug. The pain in her head was becoming unbearable and she had to sit down. She rested her head on her arms.

'I don't feel very well,' she murmured.

'You've drunk too much.'

'I don't think so.' Lydia's voice was almost lost in the folds of her jacket.

Quickly he went round to her, put his hand under her chin and raised her head.

'Please help me,' she said.

Gently Edward raised her from the chair and carried her upstairs.

*

Mike Lucas, one of Tom Cresswell's farm hands, wiped the back of his hand across his mouth and put the beer glass on the table. 'So, Mrs Casleigh's expecting, eh? How did you find that out?'

Shirley Reece, holding court in the bar of *The Mitre*, swelled with importance.

'Mrs Detrale mentioned it when she came in the shop this morning.' She failed to let on she had overheard her telling one of her friends.

'When Edward was born,' Mike went on, 'my father said Bill Patterson was given money to wet the baby's head.'

'Very generous he was, too,' piped up Grassenden's oldest inhabitant, 'but,' he added importantly, '*I* can remember when *his* father was born.'

Smiling Mike said, 'That's worth another half at least,' and took the old man's glass to the counter.

'The new Mrs Casleigh seems very nice,' Shirley mused, 'Makes a change from the previous Casleigh women. What was Edward's mother's name – something foreign?

Jamie Cresswell joined in the conversation. 'Jette.'

'You and Tom must have known her, what with your mother

working at the Manor and you boys being friends?' Mike said.

'His mother was a right weirdo, I can tell you that. That's why Mum offered to look after Edward. She wanted to go back abroad with Edward's father. She didn't like England – or Edward from what Mum said.'

'Edward's first wife wasn't much better, was she?' Shirley queried.

'Frances? Didn't know much about her,' Jamie said, 'We'd left Edward's charmed circle long before she came on the scene.'

'Stuck up, I thought. I can't remember her ever coming into my shop.' Shirley took a sip of her lager. 'I hope it's a boy again, I did feel sorry for him after that accident. To lose your wife and son must be terrible.'

*

Lydia was soon over the awful sickness that had laid her low after the reception, though she still felt a little queasy in the mornings. They spent a quiet Christmas at the Manor alone, apart from Boxing Day morning, when they went to Ridge House for drinks. Lydia was pleased to meet Anna again, and took naïve pleasure in introducing Edward to someone he did not know.

At the Manor Lydia put in a regular order for flowers, which she placed in the drawing room and on the small windowsill on the bend of the stairs. Her few pieces of furniture she put in the little room between the drawing and dining rooms always called, for no reason that Edward could fathom, the sewing room. The button-backed Victorian nursing chair, which she had bought on impulse a year ago because she liked the upholstery, she put in her bedroom. She stared at it now, and imagined herself sitting there feeding the baby as her mother had fed her. She had often thought of her real mother, but could remember nothing about her. She had once thought that she would try and trace her mother or father's family, but had never done so. Did she, perversely, blame them for dying and leaving her?

Lydia could hear the clicking of the computer as she reached the bottom of the stairs. She wondered what Edward found to do in his study for so many hours. He said he was preparing reports or checking figures to do with the farm, but she thought he was avoiding her. She sighed as she opened the door.

Books lined two walls, and library steps stood in the corner. These made her smile because Edward could easily reach the books on the top shelves. There were probably valuable books in here, but not being knowledgeable about the antique book world, she had not studied them. That was another thing she could tackle eventually. The antiques in the house had not all been investigated, let alone valued. Careful though Edward was, she was sure they were not adequately insured. As it was the premiums must be astronomical.

He was sitting at the computer, typing four-fingered.

'Why were you so upset I went to Dr Ferguson?'

He finished what he was doing, and raised his head. 'I don't know why you didn't consult me first. None of the family has ever been to the village doctor. You will go to Robin Gilberton. I was at school with him. You will be treated privately and have the baby at St Catherine's.'

'So you don't want the baby born her, as you were?'

'How do you know I was born here?'

'Cres ... Mrs Cresswell told me. She saw you when you were only a few hours old.'

'No, I don't want my child born here – and if I did, I still wouldn't want Ferguson in on the act. I don't fancy you sitting in his waiting room with all and sundry knowing our business.'

'I don't think he conducts his surgeries in the waiting room.'

'You know what I mean.'

'Yes, I know what you mean?'

Lydia turned away. Why couldn't there be some discussion, instead of orders given all the time? He must know she would fall in with whatever he suggested if they talked about it. He spoke as though the baby had nothing to do with her and she might just as well be carrying it around in a carrier bag to be handed over in nine months' time. Lydia sighed again. She should have realised he would have private health insurance. Her humble background had not caught up with her new position. But then, she had agreed to a game where he held all the cards.

'I'm going to the farm,' he said, walking past her to the cloakroom to get his boots and jacket.

Pointless asking if she could join him. Anyway, she was not sure she wanted to – she would just like to be asked.

When he had gone, Lydia went to the sewing room and got out her sketching pad, but after a few strokes, she realised she was not in the mood and fetched her coat.

Daffodil leaves were just poking through the soil, and the red stems of cornus and the heathers, provided a gentle splash of colour in an otherwise drab brown scene. She went through the gap in the beech hedge and into the woods and sat down when she came to the scattered stones of the abbey ruins. Tears pricked the back of her eyes, but she did not know why she was so upset.

All was as expected. Edward did not love her but he was getting the child he so much desired. She loved living at the Manor, which she was managing competently, or at least she had not been told otherwise. So why did she feel so depressed? What was it Edward had said? *'You'll have a certain status.'* Not in the Manor, it appeared.

Status – what an old-fashioned word, but then Edward was old-fashioned, moulded by generations of wealth, position and power. The power had gone, but wealth and position enfolded him like a shroud.

Lydia stood up and slowly made her way back to the Manor. Why was she whingeing? Most women would think she had it made. Must be her upset hormones. Yes, of course. That was it.

Edward's study phone was ringing as she opened the front door.

'Look in the top right hand drawer of the desk, would you, Lydia, and take out a blue sheet.'

Lydia searched in the drawer, found the sheet and put it on the desk.

'Right.'

'Last year's column, see it? Read out the figures as I call out the crop. OK?'

When he had finished, she asked, 'Is Tom there?'

'Yes, why? Do you want to speak to him.'

'No, I just wanted to confirm the date I gave him for dinner, that's all. I thought next Friday. You can tell him.'

Lydia put the sheet back, neatly replacing the papers she had disturbed.

*

Edward stormed into the kitchen still wearing his muddy boots as Lydia sat preparing vegetables for the evening meal.

'Why did you ask Tom to dinner?' he snapped.

'I thought as you were at the farm, it would save a telephone call. I didn't think about it till after you had gone.'

'It's not that.'

'Well, what is it?' She looked up and examined his face. 'You don't mean to tell me you've never asked Tom here for a meal?'

'We were friends as boys, it's different now. I've – we've moved on since then.'

'I thought they'd enjoy it.'

'They, who's they?'

'I've asked Pat and Jamie as well.'

Edward's face was darkening by the second.

'You've what?' He hit his forehead with the palm of his hand, then ran his fingers through his hair. 'You've no right to ask anyone to dine here without asking me first. Haven't I made myself clear about that sort of thing?'

Lydia's cheeks flamed. 'They're my friends – I'd like them here.'

'I'd still expect you to consult me first.'

'Then I suppose you'd say no.'

'Not necessarily.'

She was not convinced. 'If you don't consider the Cresswells your friends, try to think of them as mine.'

Lydia strode across the kitchen and as she passed him she remarked, 'I'm sorry I didn't mention it first, it was stupid of me, but I thought I had some status in this household when the terms of your contract were laid down. It seems we have different inter-pretations.'

In her sewing room she shut the door and leaned against it, her heart thumping. This time she did cry, the tears falling unchecked. She should have said something, but it was not that that was so upsetting. It was the fact that Edward would have forbidden it. He was not willing to compromise on anything for her sake. Why did he have to behave like this? Lydia wiped her eyes, telling herself yet again it was because she was pregnant that she was so touchy.

Perhaps she would have tea in the drawing room for a change and she would light the fire. It would be cosy in there.

Tea ready, she went to the study.

'Edward,' she began, but he was not there. The desk light was on, and everything was in place as it might be in a glossy magazine. She searched in all the downstairs rooms. She went to the bottom of the stairs and called again.

'In the playroom.'

Lydia climbed the two flights, where she found him gazing out of the window at the dusk-enveloping garden.

'What are you doing up here?'

'Thinking.'

'I've set tea in the drawing room and I've lit the fire, so it'll be warm by now.'

Edward made no comment.

'Are you pleased about the baby?' Lydia knew he must be, but he had given no word or indication that he was.

'Of course.'

'Suppose it's a girl.'

'There'll be others.'

'What were you thinking about up here?'

'Being alone.'

Lydia took his hand. It was so large, she could hardly curl her fingers round it. She raised it to her lips and kissed it. 'Come on,' she said, 'tea time.'

Chapter 4

'You won't be late tonight, will you, Edward?' Lydia said at breakfast. 'I've planned to eat at eight and I've asked them to arrive at seven thirty. That should allow you to be a little late and still have time to shower and change.'

'Any other instructions?'

Lydia ignored the sarcasm, she knew better than to get into an argument.

With Mrs Cresswell's help, the dining room sparkled as it had on the night of the engagement party. She arranged the five places and put the wine cooler beside Edward's chair. Though she knew little about wine, she had bought red and white, trusting they were of a decent quality. Lydia knew Edward had wine laid down, but she was not going to ask him for it.

He came home at his usual hour and went up to change without speaking, apart from 'I'm home.'

When Tom arrived, Edward had not made an appearance.

'Come through to the drawing room. Can I get you a drink? A sherry?'

'I'd rather have a beer, if that's not too much trouble.'

'I don't think we have any, I'm sorry.' Why had she not thought of beer?

'Don't have any what?' Edward asked as he came into the room.

'Beer.'

'There's some at the back of the pantry.' He strolled past her and sat in his usual chair.

Lydia found the beer and, as she poured it into a jug, she heard the knocker. She went to the door, resting the jug on the settle.

'Good evening,' Pat said.

'No need to be so formal,' Jamie said, 'Hello will do.'

'Quite right.' Lydia tried to smile brightly as she stood back to let them pass, and bumped into the settle. She made a grab for the jug, but some beer spilled on to the flagstones.

'Shit.'

Pat and Jamie looked startled.

'Sorry.' She clasped her hand over her mouth. 'Here, let me take your coats and you go on through to the drawing room.'

'This way, is it?' said Jamie, pointing up the passage.

Lydia drew her fingers across her forehead. She hung up the coats and rushed into the kitchen to get a cloth. When she had cleared up, she poured the rest of the beer into the jug, but there did not seem much, and there was no more in the pantry.

Lydia returned to the drawing room. 'I spilled some beer and this is all that's left, Tom. I am so sorry.' How many times had she said that in the last ten minutes? She poured the beer into a glass and handed it to him.

'Having trouble?' Edward said, brushing an imaginary fleck from his sweater.

They had all dressed formally and though he was the odd one out, he managed to make them look overdressed. His studied nonchalance made Lydia even more uneasy.

'Don't worry, this'll be fine.' Tom said.

'Lydia's been working so hard planning this evening, haven't you, darling?'

Edward had never called her darling.

'Did you get Pat and Jamie a drink?' Lydia asked.

'No, I was leaving it to you.'

Trying hard to keep control, she said, 'What would you like Pat, we have most drinks?'

'A sweet sherry, please.'

'And you, Jamie?'

'I was going to say a beer.' He laughed. 'But I'll have a Scotch and soda.'

Lydia poured the drinks, then excused herself to hurry into the kitchen to take up the vegetables. She returned to tell them that dinner was ready. She asked Edward to see them seated.

It was while she was ladling soup into the bowls that she noticed the wine cooler beside her chair.

Jamie said, 'Do you remember, Edward, when we dared you to pick up some apple boxes and throw them in the pond?'

'He didn't do it, did he?' Lydia said, incredulously.

'Yes, didn't he, Tom?'

Tom nodded.

'You've only told me about playing with cars. I didn't know you did anything naughty.'

Edward took a sip of the soup, then asked, 'May I have some wine, please?'

Lydia stood up quickly, unable to decide whether to finish ladling, or pour wine.

'I forgot, I'm sorry. I'm not used to pouring wine.'

'Or arranging dinner parties.' Edward dabbed his mouth.

'Or arranging dinner parties.'

Tom gave Edward a withering look.

Wine dispensed and soup finished, Lydia collected the bowls. She returned with the vegetable dishes and placed them on the table. She pushed her hair back from her forehead.

'Here, let me help you,' Tom offered.

Lydia glanced at Edward, who stared back unsmiling. 'There are only two more dishes to come.'

'And the plates,' said Edward.

'I'll get them,' Tom said.

Pat spoke, and Edward turned to her. 'I didn't quite catch that,' he said, bending his head close to hers. She coloured at his close scrutiny.

'This is a beautiful room,' she repeated.

'Yes.'

There was an embarrassing silence.

'It's such a long time since I was last here, I couldn't remember where the drawing room was.' Jamie grinned cheekily. 'Not that we were ever allowed in there, were we Tom?'

'In where?' Tom said, putting the plates on the table.

'In the drawing room – when we used to play here.'

'No.'

'There is a great deal of valuable furniture and other antiques in there,' Edward said pompously.

'Yes, we had noticed,' Jamie said, winking at Tom.

Lydia passed a plate to Pat. 'Please help yourselves to vegetables.'

The click of their knives and forks sounded extraordinarily loud in the tense atmosphere. Pat tried hard to make conversation, but she was awkward as she had never been to Abbey Manor and had not met Edward socially. Lydia could see she was in awe of him and knew just how she felt. Edward did nothing to make her feel at ease.

'Tom, what's happening on the farm at the moment?'

Tom gave a potted version of the past month. Farm talk exhausted, Lydia went on to ask Jamie about cars and Pat about the children, till she ran out of topics.

Dinner dragged on through dessert, cheese and biscuits and coffee, which Lydia decided to have at the table. Whenever she glanced Edward's way, he looked at her with disapproval, especially when the four of them discussed villagers he did not know.

When Jamie regaled them with more escapades that they had got up to as children, Edward refused to be drawn into the conversation.

The evening drew to its inexorable close. When their guests were about to depart, Edward made no attempt to see them off. Lydia handed Pat and Jamie their coats, thanked them for the flowers, and said how pleased she had been to see them.

Tom stood on the top step as they waved to Jamie and Pat.

'I see you've brought the Land Rover.'

'I didn't fancy putting on boots with a suit to walk here.'

'No, of course not, I didn't think. I haven't thought very well all evening, have I?' she said, apologetically. She held out her hand

He gripped it tightly. 'Not your fault, Lydia.'

'Goodnight.' She withdrew her hand.

Tom ran across to the Land Rover, and drove down the drive very fast. Dejectedly, she turned and went into the house.

Edward had disappeared, so she locked up – something he always did. He had won again, but she was too tired and dispirited to make even the slightest protest at his behaviour.

*

'I hope you don't mind me mentioning it,' Mrs Cresswell said, as she busied herself in the kitchen, 'but did you want to do any spring cleaning?'

'Spring cleaning? I haven't thought about it, though I had considered washing the porcelain. What do you normally do?'

'We – that's Susie Patterson and me – we usually do the drawing room, kitchen and Edward's bedroom every year. Give it a thorough going over, like, have the curtains cleaned or whatever. Then one other room in the house we think needs doing. We couldn't do it all, you see.'

'No, of course not.'

'Edward's wife used to have a firm in, but he wasn't very happy. The antiques, you see, but she didn't take any notice.'

Frances obviously had more clout than she had.

'We'll do as you suggest. I've got to go into Maidstone to see the consultant and have my hair cut, so I can take the curtains to the cleaners then. What about cleaning materials? Have we all we need?'

'I'll check and make a list.'

'It's a good job Edward's away,' Lydia commented. 'It'll be an ideal time to do this.'

'Where's he gone this time?'

'Hong Kong. He's away for two weeks.' Lydia opened the dishwasher and began unloading. 'I shall miss him.'

Mrs Cresswell looked up and smiled. Lydia had surprised herself when she said that. She never missed Edward when he was at work – and when he came home, they spent little time in each other's company. But even when he upset her with one of his cutting remarks, she could not ignore him. There was, from time to time, a look of helplessness in his eyes, as if he had lost something, and no matter how hard he searched, it could not be found.

'There, I think that's all we'll need.' She pushed the list across the table.

'Mrs Cresswell?'

'Yes dear.'

'Did something happen to Edward when he was a child. I mean, something that would make him have nightmares?'

The old woman looked surprised. 'Is he still having them?'

'You know about them then?'

'I don't know what they are about, but he had them regularly when he was a child. Tom and Jamie'd moan like anything about waking them up in the middle of the night, but he never remembered what he had been dreaming about in the morning.'

Lydia was silent for a few moments, then said. 'He mentions you, you know – in his dream.'

Her jolly face clouded over and she looked uneasy as she said, 'I don't know whether I ought to say this – it's not really my place.'

'Go on,' Lydia urged.

'Edward's mother didn't love him – didn't even want any children, but, a son was expected, you know.'

Lydia knew.

'Well,' she continued, 'Mrs Casleigh – Jette her name was –

didn't like England, she liked following Edward's father around. When she was expecting she left it till the last minute before coming back, and only stayed till Edward went to school here – and that was just for appearances' sake. I think Edward's father insisted.'

'He went to the village school? In Grassenden?'

'Yes, till he was seven, then he went to boarding school.'

'But what's that got to do with the nightmares?'

Mrs Cresswell shook her head sadly and swallowed, before saying, 'I think it was because he used to be – he was left alone a lot – in the playroom – for hours on end.'

'What – even as a tiny baby?'

'Yes.'

'Oh, how awful. How could she?'

'I used to come in as often as I could, and pick him up when he was in his cot. When he was older, I used to sit and hug him. He would hear me coming up the stairs and when I opened the playroom door, he would fling himself at me.

'Tom was only seven months old when Edward was born, and when I was expecting Jamie, it became quite difficult for me. In fact Jack, my husband, got a bit fed up and thought I was doing too much. So I asked if I could take Edward with me sometimes. Edward's mother seemed quite happy with this arrangement and he spent his time between here and our cottage. I think she was glad to get rid of him. When he went to the local school, I looked after him most of the time. Sometimes he would go to his grandmother's for the holidays or to wherever his father was, but mostly he'd stay with me.'

'No wonder he loves you so much.' Lydia could imagine the lonely child waiting for someone to take notice of him, and his dear Cressy fulfilling that basic need.

'What did Edward's father think about this?'

'She probably didn't tell him. He still worked away, but returned some weekends, and she'd have Edward home then. I know he wasn't happy when she said she wanted to leave Edward here and return with him when Edward was five. But she was a strong-minded woman.'

'What was he like – Edward's father?'

'Quite a nice man really – thought the best of everyone. Completely dominated by his wife – though he seemed fond of her. Rather a bumbling man, I thought.'

'So, Edward's nothing like him?'

'Nothing at all – not in looks or temperament. He looks like his mother and ...' She stopped.

Lydia got her drift. 'But Edward wouldn't leave a child alone for hours. I know he wouldn't.'

Mrs Cresswell's face looked serious and Lydia could see she thought she had said more than enough.

'Susie Patterson – I haven't met her yet. Does she live in the village?'

'No, she lives in Grimley Heath with her mother. Susie's mother and I have been friends for years. Laura and Bill Patterson ran the farm before Tom took over. Bill had a heart attack and had to give up, and Laura nursed him till he died. They had Susie when they were in their forties and Laura had a difficult time when Susie was born and I think some damage might have been done then.'

'Does she work – other than coming here?'

'No, she can't hold down a job, but she does do cleaning for other people. Don't, whatever you do, let her near the cabinets. She can be very clumsy. Taking down and putting up curtains, turning mattresses, that's the sort of job she's best at. Susie's as strong as a horse.'

'That's something. I shan't be doing too much of that.'

'She likes to gossip, too. I let it go over my head 'cause I've hear it all before. By the way, she'll moan about Edward. She blames him for them having to leave the farm. It's no good explaining about tenancies, and someone having to run it. She's quite harmless really and she needs to have some money of her own. Laura's only got her pension. Edward pays the rent and Tom keeps them supplied with fresh veg.'

'I'll look forward to seeing her.'

'Laura's coming round for a chat this afternoon.'

'Will Susie come with her?'

'I doubt it. If she's not cleaning for someone, she'll probably be round the farm. Spends a lot of time there, does Susie.'

*

'Kettle's nearly boiled, Laura. Come and sit down by the fire.'

'It's quite cold out,' said her friend, rubbing her hands together. 'I do miss a coal fire.'

Maggie Cresswell called from the scullery, 'The boys keep trying to persuade me to have a gas or electric fire. They say that

that one makes too much work – which it does, but it'll see me out.'

She came back into the room and put a tray on the kitchen table.'Help yourself to a scone. Lydia bought them for me yesterday. I don't feel much like cooking nowadays.'

'You get on well with her, don't you?'

'She's a dear girl. That reminds me, we're going to do some spring-cleaning and I wondered if you'd get Susie to call in here so I can fix up a date. Lydia won't be able to do much lifting.'

'When's the baby due?'

'End of August I think.'

'How old is she?'

'Twenty-six, no, she must be twenty-seven. Had a birthday just after they married.'

'I've only seen her at church, but she looks younger than that, don't you think?'

'They both look younger than their ages. Edward will be thirty-nine next birthday.'

Laura grinned. 'You know, Maggie, you never mention him without smiling.'

'I know – but I do love him. I can't help thinking about when he was a child. No one should have been treated like he was.'

'Just goes to show money doesn't bring happiness.'

'Lydia'll look after him, I'm sure.'

'She's certainly nothing like Frances Casleigh.'

'That's just what Tom said.'

When Laura left, Maggie sat frowning in front of the dwindling flames. Though she did not see much of them together, when she did, she was not happy with the way Edward treated Lydia. Had he spoken to Frances the way he sometimes did to Lydia, he would have been given short shrift. Neither did he act like a newly-wed. And the dinner she had helped Lydia arrange. Jamie said it was one big laugh, as Edward obviously had not wanted them there, but Tom was unusually upset. He did not say much, but she had a strong suspicion he was getting feelings for Lydia that he should not be having.

She gave the fire a good poke, and threw on another log. She did so want Edward and Lydia to be happy.

*

It was a strange, but typical early spring day. The sky was dark, bluey mauve on one side, and dazzling sun on the other.

Travelling to Maidstone, Lydia went through two heavy showers to emerge in brilliant sunshine. By the time she had parked the sky was cloudless, more like a summer's day.

In the supermarket, contemplating which cleaners to buy, she felt a tap on her shoulder.

'Faith! Fancy seeing you in Maidstone. I hardly ever see you when I'm shopping in Grassenden.'

'I'm glad I've bumped into you. David and I were talking about you last night.'

'Really,' said Lydia, who could not imagine them having anything to talk about.

'Yes, David wondered if you'd like to read a lesson.'

'Me! Oh no, I couldn't. I've never done anything in public.'

'It's for Mothering Sunday and we thought you'd be ideal as you're an expectant mother.'

Lydia was not sure whether she were pleased, terrified or flattered. All three she supposed.

'I don't know Faith. I'm not used to that sort of thing and I haven't a lovely resonant voice like Edward's.'

'Oh, go on, they're just excuses, I'm sure you'll be excellent. You can practise at the Vicarage.'

Shoppers tut-tutted as they stood in front of the very items they all wanted at that moment.

'Look, I've nearly finished. Couldn't we chat over a coffee?'

'Sorry, I have to visit my father. He's in a nursing home near here.' She began to move away. 'Must go. You think it over and give David or me a ring.'

Shopping done, Lydia returned to the car, unloaded her trolley and picked up the curtains. On the way to the cleaners she met Tom.

'What are you doing here?' she demanded.

'I am allowed out occasionally, you know, I do have farm hands.'

'I know, I am silly. I just think of you on the farm.'

'I'm here because someone's dumped a car on my land, and I've come to see the council about getting it removed – and you're not silly.'

The crowds milled past them as they stood in the precinct.

'Perhaps you'd come and have a coffee with me.' Tom said.

'What a good idea, I was just going to have one myself. I'll pop these in the cleaners first. Shall we go to the restaurant in the store, or do you know somewhere else?'

'There's a nice café down there.' Tom pointed towards the river. 'It has tablecloths and waitresses. I prefer that to self-service.' Tom smiled. 'Most of my life is self-service.'

When they were seated Lydia said, 'I've just met Faith Tressant. She asked me if I'd like to read a lesson for Mothering Sunday.'

'What did you say?'

'I haven't decided. I'm scared. She asked me to think it over.'

'What's frightening about it? Your voice is nice and you look good.'

'Flattery will get you everywhere.'

'I mean it. Go on, I'll even come to church to listen.'

'That would make me worse.'

The waitress came over and took their order. Suddenly Lydia said, 'Do you believe in God, Tom? I haven't seen you in church though we don't go every week.'

'It's difficult to work so close to nature and not think there must be some Supreme Being. It's organised religion that I find false, but don't get me wrong, the Tressants are sincere.'

The waitress put a tray with cups, saucers, coffeepot and milk in front of Lydia. Near Tom, she put the scones and butter.

'I'm to be Mum then.' She laughed.

She poured coffee into the cups, and passed one to Tom. Lydia reached for the sugar, took one spoonful, and stirred her coffee slowly.

'Faith was on her way to see her father. He's in a nursing home. I wouldn't like to be in a nursing home and have to leave all the things I love and have lived with. I know what it's like to be uprooted, to leave homes I had become used to, even if they weren't the greatest of places.' She looked at Tom across the top of her cup. 'Did you know I'd been in foster homes for most of my life?'

'Yes, my mother told me, but said I was to keep it to myself.'

'Thank you.'

'*Are* you happy, Lydia?' Tom's words were probing.

Before she could answer, a voice beside them said, 'Lydia! How nice to see you. How are you? What are you doing here? Do you come into Maidstone often? If I had known, I could have given you a lift.'

Serena, as usual, bombarded her with several questions. Tom rose to his feet and stood awkwardly.

'Serena, you've met Tom Cresswell, haven't you?'

'Oh, yes – the farm manager.' She looked him up and down and murmured, 'Mr Cresswell.'

'Mrs Detrale.' He held out his hand, which she ignored.

'I've met more people from Grassenden today than I do when I'm there. I've already met Faith.'

'So, you two have only just met?' She looked enquiringly from one to the other, but neither replied. 'I just wondered if you came together – saving petrol – being environmentally friendly.' She gave one of her clever laughs.

'I'm sure you're busy, Serena, so we won't detain you. Perhaps I'll see you in church next Sunday.' Lydia picked up a piece of scone and put it in her mouth.

Serena, taken aback by her dismissal, could only manage an uneasy 'Goodbye.'

'Well done,' Tom said, looking at Lydia admiringly.

'I do not like that woman, and she doesn't like me, though I can't quite work out why.'

'Mrs Detrale doesn't appear to like anyone but herself.'

'Not even her husband?'

'Him least of all. Which piece of gossip, I hasten to add, I gathered from my mother.'

'And not from *The Mitre*?'

'Of course not.' Tom grinned.

'I've have to go now, Tom, I've an appointment with my gyny, followed by the hairdresser's. I have enjoyed our chat, and thanks for the coffee.'

'I hope he finds you fit and healthy. You look well.'

'I feel well. Bye Tom.'

Tom stared after her as he went to the desk to pay the bill.

Chapter 5

'Your husband turned us out of our farm. Bet you didn't know that?'

Susie Patterson was rolling up the rugs in Edward's bedroom, prior to taking them out for beating.

'Is that so, Susie.'

'Yeah, I was twelve and me Dad had a heart attack and your husband said we'd to leave.'

'But wasn't it my husband's father? He was still alive then.'

'Could be, yes, I think he was.' Susie went on hurriedly, 'but it weren't 'im what said we'd gotta go. I know it wasn't, 'cos his father was hardly ever here, and your husband looked after everything.'

Susie put the large rolled carpet and two smaller rugs across the doorway and stood leaning against the wall, her muscular arms folded.

'I liked living on the farm, I could go anywhere I liked. Now me and me Mum are cooped up in a poky house in Grimley Heath.'

Lydia felt for the girl, having to leave a large farmhouse and a garden of acres to live in a cramped house.

'Right,' said Lydia, not wishing to get involved, 'when you've dealt with the rugs, could you come back and take down these curtains? That'll be the last two pairs for cleaning.'

Susie was not to be put off. 'You know, you're much nicer than the other Mrs Casleigh. She was a right 'orror, she was. She wasn't never satisfied, always finding fault with everything. She would stand over me 'cos she said I broke things – but I didn't. Well, maybe a cup sometimes.'

Lydia continued with the tidying and dusting meticulously replacing all objects.

Susie, untroubled by Lydia's lack of response, went on, 'In the end she had a firm in once a year. They weren't as good as Auntie

Maggie and me.'

Lydia agreed and reminded her about the curtains and cleaning the windows.

'Righto, Mrs Casleigh.' She picked up the carpet as if it were no heavier than a broom, and went downstairs, leaving the small rugs blocking the door. Lydia moved them to one side and followed Susie downstairs to join Mrs Cresswell in the kitchen.

'I see what you mean,' Lydia said, as she started the percolator, 'I have had the tale of their eviction and how awful Frances was. Susie will be better than Grassenden Stores to keep me posted on village affairs.'

Mrs Cresswell was at the sink carefully washing a few items from the cabinets. She began drying those she had washed.

'You'll be kept well informed all right, but take it all lightly. Susie's got a vivid imagination and likes to put her own interpretation on the facts, depending on the effect she wishes to make.'

'In time, I want to take an inventory of everything in the house,' Lydia informed her when she came in from the dining room with a few more items from the cabinet. 'I don't suppose you know when they were last valued, do you?'

'No, 'fraid not.'

Mrs Cresswell swished the delicate porcelain in the water and carefully placed each piece on the cloths laid out on the draining board. Lydia noticed how pale her cheeks were, and that she had dark patches under her eyes.

'Are you feeling all right?'

'I haven't been sleeping well lately. I get very tired, but when I go to bed, I toss and turn.'

'You're not to do so much. Edward would never forgive me if I worked you too hard.'

The older woman smiled. 'He wouldn't notice, Lydia. Much as I love him, he is quite unaware of the work involved in keeping him and the Manor in order.'

'But I do, and I insist you do less. For a start you can eat here when you come and later, when I can't move around so easily, Susie can come.'

'You are a dear. Now, I must get back to my chores, then we'll get lunch.'

'We've done well this fortnight, haven't we?' Lydia said, as she went to the fridge to get Susie's requested coke. 'I'm glad we'll get it finished before Edward comes back.'

Lydia saw Susie pull a face at the mention of Edward's name.

*

The phone rang as Lydia came in from a walk. She had been talking to Mr Laurence at the barn shop.

'Lydia?'

'Is that you, Edward? The line's a bit crackly.'

'Yes, I'm in Bangkok and there's been some delay, so I'm not sure when I'll be home. If I get a chance I'll ring from Heathrow, but if not, I'll come straight home.'

'All right.'

'How are you?'

'Never felt better.'

'Good – I'll see you soon. Bye.'

*

Something woke Lydia. She opened her eyes, but it was dark and she could not focus.

'It's only me,' came a whispered voice.

'Edward! You frightened me. Switch on the light.'

'No.'

'What time is it?'

'About three.'

Lydia pushed herself up on one elbow. 'How long have you been home?' She could see Edward's outline against the curtained window as he sat on her bed.

'I came straight up.'

'Would you like me to get you something, coffee or a sandwich?'

'Only someone like you would offer to do that in the middle of the night.'

'Is that a compliment, or do you mean I'm stupid?'

'I just wanted to see you.'

She giggled. 'But you can't.'

'I have a good memory.'

'You'll be telling me next you missed me.'

Edward bent over and kissed her. 'I'll be with you in a moment.'

He told her negotiations had not gone well in Hong Kong, and what with that and the delayed journey home, he was exhausted – but not that exhausted.

After he had made love to her, he asked if she had liked Robin Gilberton and what she had been doing while he had been away.

He had even seemed interested in the spring-cleaning, then he fell asleep in mid sentence.

Lydia was wide-awake and moved to find a cooler spot. She plumped up her pillow and turned it over. The church clock struck the half-hour, but sleep eluded her.

Edward began talking and Lydia thought he had woken, but his words were indistinct and he began threshing his arms around, as he had previously. Lydia tried to hear what he was saying.

'Don't Mona. I don't want to, I don't like it. No, no, please!'

Mona. Who was Mona? Lydia had not heard that before.

'Edward hush, hush.' She grabbed his arms, but he was struggling furiously and she could not hold him.

Lydia knelt, and waited until some of the draining emotion subsided. She wiped the sweat from his forehead, then lay down beside him, with her arm over his chest.

'Is that you, Cressy?'

'Yes, I'm here,' Lydia said, thinking to comfort him.

'You won't go away, will you?'

'I'll always come back.'

He slept, but for several minutes muttered indistinctly.

Edward had been so pleased to be home, and when he made love to her, he was less distant – very gentle, very sweet. Why was he not always like that? Why was it he never took her out, or showed any interest in what she was doing or thinking? They never discussed current affairs or music. In fact, she only knew his taste in music because she had looked through his records and CDs. Unfortunately, his taste was classical, and even that was too way out for her as it included Mahler and Bruckner which, she decided when she had listened to some, was not her scene at all. Lydia liked pop and musicals so if she had been asked what she liked, her taste would have been denigrated, as only Edward could. So Lydia kept her CDs in the sewing room and her music preferences to herself.

All Edward remembered in the morning was his restlessness, which he put down to the taxing week and the long, disrupted journey home.

'Do you dream often?' Lydia asked, as she put Edward's breakfast in front of him.

He looked up sharply. 'What makes you ask?'

'Because a couple of times you've had a dream that's obviously upsetting. Can't you remember it?'

'No. I know I've had them since I was a child.'

'I see.' Lydia did not mention her discussion with Mrs Cresswell.

'I'm going to clean the car.'

'I'll come and help you when I've finished clearing up.'

Twenty minutes later she joined him in the front garden, bright with clumps of daffodils.

Her mind half on the garden, Lydia said, 'What shall I do?'

'When I've hosed down, you can help me leather.'

'Faith was on her way to see her father when I met her in Maidstone,' she said. 'Did you know he was in a nursing home?'

He pulled out the windscreen wipers of the Mercedes and ran the damp cloth along the blades. 'No, I can't say I did.'

'She asked me if I'd like to read the lesson on Mothering Sunday?'

'I hope you refused.'

'I told her I didn't think I could do it very well, as I've not done anything like that before.'

'Quite right.' He replaced the wipers.

Edward's outright condemnation of her ability precipitated her into thinking she would accept.

'Faith said she would help me and I could practise at the Vicarage. So I'll ring and confirm.'

He stopped what he was doing and turned to her. 'I don't want you to do it.'

'Why?'

'You'll make a fool of yourself.'

'What you mean is, I might make a fool of you.'

'Well, yes, if that's the way you see it.'

'It's not the way I see it.'

Edward went to the tap behind the garage, attached the hose and turned it on.

'However you see it, you must refuse.'

Lydia threw the leather on the ground and stormed into the house. Still wearing her outdoor clothes, she went into the drawing room and knelt to light the fire. Wisps of smoke and flames caught the small sticks, which licked around the logs. She sat back on her heels.

Why did he have to make her feel so inadequate? How could he be so tender one minute, and so hateful the next? Words were used as a cruel weapon and worse, intentionally or not, Edward seemed to raise her first, only to slap her down. She held out her hands to the flames, but there was no warmth yet. She went back to the kitchen. As she hung up her anorak in the cloakroom, Edward walked in through the front door.

'I think Frances was right, we should have had a side door made when the kitchen was re-designed – assuming we could have had planning permission.'

When he had emptied the pail, washed and replaced it under the sink, he sat at the table watching Lydia prepare lunch.

'I bought you a present,' he said.

'Oh, yes.'

'From Hong Kong.'

Lydia went to the fridge and fetched out tomatoes, cucumber and lettuce.

'Don't you want to know what it is?'

She slammed the salad down on the table and went to get bread.

'Is it something I'll like, or something you think I ought to have?' He opened his mouth to answer, but Lydia went on. 'Or maybe you had a woman in your party to go out and buy something suitable for the little lady.'

Looking hurt, he reached for a tomato and slowly sliced it.

'Meat or cheese?' she said.

'Meat please.'

She put two slices on his plate. 'Enough?'

'For now, yes.'

Lydia slapped butter on her roll and took a bite. Then, with a clatter she put down her knife and fork.

'What's the matter?'

'I'm going to ring Faith.'

'What are you going to say?' Edward looked uneasy.

She did not answer, but dialled the Vicarage number.

'Faith. Hello, it's Lydia. About the reading – Edward doesn't want me to do it.'

Lydia listened to Faith, her eyes staring over her husband's head. She could still make out the look of approval on his face.

'No, I don't think that's the reason. I think he's afraid his squire's image might be tarnished if I muck it up.'

Lydia lowered her eyes to meet Edward's while she paid attention to the voice at the other end. His face was like thunder.

'That's nice of you to say so, Faith. I am honoured you should have asked me. Perhaps, one day, I might do something Edward does approve of.'

'OK, Faith, I'll do that. Bye.' She put the phone down. 'Faith sends her regards.'

Edward was beside himself with anger and did not speak to her for the rest of the day.

When Lydia went to bed, she found a beautifully wrapped, oblong box on her dressing table. She was about to stuff it in the bottom of her wardrobe unopened, but curiosity got the better of her.

Carefully, she took off the wrapping, lifted the lid and folded back the tissue paper. Inside were two sets of silk underwear, one in pale blue the other in cream, with exquisite lace inserts and edging. Lydia gasped at their delicacy and ran the tips of her fingers over the silk.

Lydia took out the blue slip and laid it on one side. She undressed and put on the bra and briefs, then slipped the petticoat over her head. It was feather-light and downy soft. It felt as if she were wearing nothing. Edward must have taken note of her size from underclothes she had already. She could not imagine him asking Mrs Cresswell. Whatever the circumstances, he had put some thought into the gift.

Lydia was consumed with remorse, and pushed to the back of her mind why she had been so upset in the first place. She went into the bathroom and saw the light under his door, so knew he was awake. Edward was sitting in a chair by his bed in his dressing gown. A book, unopened, lay on the bed, and his hands rested on the tops of his legs.

'I've come to thank you for the present.' Lydia moved further into the room. Edward was frowning and in a familiar gesture, pushed the fingers of one hand into his hair. His eyes held that 'little boy lost' look she had noticed on occasions.

'Come here.' Lydia went over to the chair and he looked up at her. 'Have you tried them on? Do they fit?'

She untied the belt of her robe and gave a twirl. 'Too tight now, but they'll be something to look forward to after the baby's born.'

His eyes softened as he looked her up and down, but his hands were closed tightly over his knees, and his lips were drawn in. Lydia bent over and kissed his forehead.

'Thank you. They are quite, quite beautiful.'

'I did choose them myself, you know.'

'I never really thought otherwise,' Lydia said, as she closed his door.

*

Lydia and Edward continued to live in uneasy union. Overall she was treated with cool detachment and, since his return from Hong Kong, there had been no scenes, nor any rare moment of tenderness.

She asked Edward if the nursery could be in the little bedroom across the landing, preparing herself for the usual dismissal of any suggestion she made but, to her delight, he said she could do whatever she wanted.

Lydia was ecstatic and, with Mrs Cresswell, threw herself into an orgy of pouring over materials, arranging for decorators, and ooing and ahing over baby equipment and clothes in countless magazines. She drew and painted pictures, which she framed. Occasionally she wished Elizabeth were alive, but Mrs Cresswell was a good substitute. She asked her innumerable questions on babies in general – and Edward, Tom and Jamie in particular.

Remembering Edward's recent restless night, and without saying why, she asked Mrs Cresswell if Edward had known anyone called Mona, but was left with another mystery when she said she could not recall such a person.

On Easter Sunday morning when they came out of church, Lydia saw Tom standing with his mother. Lydia went over to them.

'What brought you here? I thought religion wasn't your scene.'

'Mum's invited me to lunch, and she persuaded me – didn't you?' He looked down at his mother.

'Yes, dear.' She tapped Tom's arm. 'I'm just going over to talk to Laura. I'll see you at the Landrover. Bye Lydia.'

'Bye, see you on Thursday.' Lydia turned to Tom. 'Have you noticed how tired your mother has looked lately?'

'Yes, she says she's tired all the time, but then she is nearing seventy.'

'That's not old nowadays. I am worried about her.'

'Why didn't you read on Mothering Sunday? I came specially to hear you.'

'That's not a good reason for going to church.'

'Don't prevaricate, I suppose Edward told you not to.'

'That's between Edward and me.'

They stared at each other unblinking till Tom said, 'He'll

destroy you, you know.'

'He doesn't have everything his own way,' she lied. 'I can hold my own if necessary.'

'Maybe, but will you be able to stand the strain. His first wife had him taped, you're made of gentler stuff.' He glanced over her head. 'Your husband's awaiting your return. He won't approve of you mixing with the peasantry.' And without saying goodbye, he strode down the path to the lych gate to wait for his mother.

Troubled, she turned to make her way back to Edward but was waylaid en route by several villagers she had got to know in and around Grassenden.

Serena's cultured voice reached her as Lydia approached. 'Here she comes, your popular wife. How in demand she seems.'

'Hello, Serena, yes I do seem to be flavour of the month,' she agreed as she threaded her arm through Edward's and clasped it with her other hand. She leaned against him and glanced up smiling.

Determined not to be put off, Serena said, 'You and Mr Cresswell have a lot to say to each other. Tête a têtes over coffee in Maidstone, chats at the church porch.'

Lydia felt Edward's muscles tighten but she did not release his arm.

'Yes, I told Edward four of us had met in Maidstone, didn't I darling – when you came back from Hong Kong, in the middle of the night – just before we ...'

'I remember,' he said, hurriedly.

'Well,' Serena said, pulling on the kid glove she had been holding. 'I must get back to cook lunch.'

'Edward has told me what a good cook you are. Lucky Jeremy. The way to a man's heart, and all that.' Lydia smiled sweetly. 'But we must go, too. We walked this morning. I must walk every day my gynaecologist says. Do you know Mr Gilberton? No, I don't suppose you would,' Lydia said cattily, then felt contrite as she saw Serena's hurt look.

'I'm glad you're keeping well,' Serena said as she hurried away.

'You didn't tell me you'd had coffee with Tom,' Edward said.

Lydia disengaged her arm. 'It didn't seem worth mentioning. You knew I'd seen him. Serena must have been in the café already, though I hadn't noticed her.'

'What were you talking to Tom about just now? You shot over to him as if you had something important to say.'

Lydia felt her face redden and was glad he could not see it. He would be furious if he knew Tom had known about the reading.

'I wondered why he was at church, he doesn't come often.'

'And why was he?'

'Because his mother persuaded him. He's having lunch with her.'

*

Spring slipped into summer. The bluebells in the wood by the ruins were of particular delight to Lydia. She would often sit there thinking about the coming baby and the strange twist her life had taken.

She spent much of her time gardening, till it became too uncomfortable to bend down. Then she supervised the gardener who came in once a week. She even persuaded Edward to mow the lawns at the back farthest away from the house. Lydia wanted to concentrate on the lawn at the front, across the drive. In her mind's eye it would be as good as a bowling green – a place where they could sit and eat.

One Friday, Lydia and Susie spent the morning clearing out the kitchen cupboards. As usual, Susie kept up a non-stop prattle about the goings-on in the neighbourhood – who was seeing whom, who was getting married, who had died. Lydia nodded sagely, and said 'yes' and 'no' in what she hoped were the right places. Later in the morning, she sent Susie to do the cloakroom and the two upstairs bathrooms before giving her some lunch.

As they sat at the kitchen table, Susie said she was going to the farm when she left the Manor.

'Tom doesn't mind me walking round the fields, you know. Sometimes I tidy up a bit 'cause he's ever so untidy.'

Lydia's heart went out to Tom. It was kind of him to let her wander round what was once her home.

Susie's chatter, and the effort of the morning, had taken its toll. Her back ached and when Susie had gone, she went into the drawing room and sat knitting. Just after three, she made herself a cup of tea and returned there. She rubbed her eyes and leaned back in the chair.

Lydia woke with a start and gave a shiver. The grandfather clock struck six. She stood up, placed her hands behind her back, and stretched. Smiling, she moved them round to the bump. Right – dinner. It would be a bit late and she hoped Edward would not moan. Before setting to, she went upstairs to get a cardigan.

*

Edward had had an awful journey. His train was late and consequently packed. He had stood most of the way so by the time he reached home he was decidedly weary.

He hung his coat in the cloakroom before poking his head in the kitchen. He was surprised not to see Lydia there; neither did there seem to be a smell of cooking underway. Had she decided to eat out? No, she would not do that.

He walked along the hall calling, 'I'm home, Lydia,' as he went into the drawing room. He poured himself a large whisky from the crystal decanter on the cabinet, picked up the glass and slumped in his armchair, but something struck him about the silence. Lydia must be out – perhaps she had left a note?

Edward returned to the kitchen – no note. Why on earth had she gone out at this time, he did not know where to contact her. She had so many acquaintances. Did she not realise she had a position to keep. Frances would never have allowed anyone to call her by her first name as Lydia did.

Certain there was no message, Edward made his way back along the passage. As he drew level with the staircase he heard a faint moan, then a low voice call his name. He bounded up the stairs and, as he turned at the first bend, he saw her.

Chapter 6

Lydia's head was against the wall and as she turned, he could see a gash to the side of her forehead. A trickle of blood had run down her face on to her blouse. In her hand she clutched a cardigan.

'Lydia, whatever's happened?'

'I fell down the stairs. I think – I think I must have blacked out. My leg – it's so painful.'

Tears spilled to mix with the blood on her cheek. Edward felt her hands – they were cold.

'I'll get something to cover you.'

He stepped past her and went to the cupboard for a blanket. As he came back, he picked up a can on the step behind Lydia and put it on the windowsill. He arranged the blanket round her and wiped the tears and blood from her face with his handkerchief.

'I'd better call a doctor.'

Edward ran along the passage to the phone in the kitchen. Who should he call? Gilberton? No, Ferguson – he was closest. Number? He reached for the directory, flicked the pages and ran his finger down the names, Ferdinand, Ferguson. Initial? Try Grassenden numbers – B Ferguson, G – ah, Ferguson, Dr Ian. Edward dialled. The phone seemed to ring endlessly.

'Ian Ferguson,' said a Scottish voice.

'This is Edward Casleigh – of Abbey Manor. My wife's had a fall.'

'Is she a patient of mine?'

'No – yes, she did sign on with you. Could you come quickly, she may have fallen a while ago – I've only just found her.'

'Very well. Abbey Manor did you say – up the Lane?'

Edward heard the car draw up and waited on the step.

'I left her where she is because I think her leg might be broken. She says it hurts and – and, she's pregnant.'

He led the doctor along the passage. There was no room for the three of them on the staircase bend, and Edward hovered anxiously a few steps below. The doctor removed the blanket.

'Don't move, Mrs Casleigh. I just want to discover what, if anything, is broken.'

The doctor felt round her neck. 'Can you move your head?'

Lydia did so gingerly. 'My head's throbbing.' she said.

'That's where you hit the wall. Hurt anywhere else?'

'My leg and my back a bit.'

The doctor looked down at her legs. One ankle was badly swollen.

Edward said from the stair, 'what about the baby?'

Dr Ferguson, who was taking Lydia's pulse, did not answer. 'I'll phone for an ambulance.'

He stepped down the staircase and said to Edward, 'Who's dealing with your wife's pregnancy?'

'Gilberton. Robin Gilberton.'

'Right. He's the consultant at St Catherine's so he'll see her there in due course. If she has broken any bones the orthopaedic consultant will deal with that. Can you show me where the phone is, please?'

The doctor stepped up to Lydia. 'Now you stay quite still till the ambulance arrives. They'll sort you out.' He smiled encouragingly as he replaced the blanket.

Don't mention the baby,' he said, as he followed Edward into the drawing room. 'It'll only worry her and she's already had a shock to her system. What is she – about seven months?'

Edward nodded.

'Contrary to popular belief, falling downstairs rarely causes a miscarriage,' he reassured him as he dialled.

When he had finished he told Edward the ambulance should not be more than fifteen minutes and not to give his wife anything to eat or drink.

Edward followed the ambulance in the Mercedes and stayed at the hospital while they strapped up her ankle, which was badly swollen but not broken. When he had seen Lydia settled into a private room, he returned home.

*

Edward had slept badly and was woken at eight by the phone.

'Edward? Robin Gilberton here.'

'Robin! Have you seen Lydia already?' He felt cold. 'Is something wrong?'

'They called me in. Your wife unexpectedly went into labour a couple of hours ago. Don't worry,' he said, as Edward started to interrupt, 'they are doing all they can to stop the contractions, but your wife would like you to be with her. She is very distressed and in some pain.'

'But Ferguson said her accident wouldn't cause a miscarriage.'

'That's true, but there might be something wrong with the baby.'

Edward's face was white as he put down the phone. A sensation like ice cubes went down his spine. Not again, please, not again.

When he reached Lydia's room, she was having labour pains. He wiped the sweat from her forehead, and held her hand. Periodically nurses checked the situation. During the afternoon he went to the canteen for a snack. He had hardly had anything to eat since the previous day's lunch. When he came back it was to find Lydia's bed empty.

Edward hardly heard the nurse's professional voice endeavouring to reassure him. 'Look on the bright side, Mr Casleigh, your wife is very healthy. The babe will be as well as a seven-month baby can be. The technology is so good nowadays. Why don't you go for a walk and come back a little later. There's nothing you can do here till they bring her back.'

'Yes, yes, I'll do that,' Edward said, pleased to have an excuse to be out of the building.

*

On his return, a nurse caught Edward before he went to Lydia's room and took him to the Special Care Baby Unit. His son was having difficulty breathing, he was told.

His son. He stared at the tiny body that could almost have fitted on his hand.

'It's a boy' Lydia said, as he entered the room. 'Have you seen him?'

'Yes. How are you feeling?'

He took her hand in his and kissed it. To his surprise and embarrassment she burst into loud, uncontrollable sobs. He did not know what to do. Should he call the nurse?

'There's something wrong with him, isn't there? He's g-going to d-die, isn't he?' she sobbed.

'No, he's just having breathing difficulties.'

He hoped he sounded more convincing than he felt. He caressed the back of her hand. How small it was, how beautifully shaped her nails – he had always admired them.

He raised his eyes to her face; she was still crying. He had never seen her cry. How could he comfort her, what could he say?

'I'm going to see if – I'm going to find Gilberton and see what he says.'

'You'll come back, won't you?' She grasped his hand tightly.

'Yes, of course.'

She was still grasping his hand as he stood up, and it slipped from his as she reluctantly released it.

The lift arrived with a clank and the doors rumbled open. Head down Edward went into the cavernous lift, but a hand gently rested on his shoulder.

'Come into my office, Edward.'

'He's dead, isn't he?'

'Yes, I'm so sorry. His lungs, you see, they were probably malformed – there was nothing we could do. The post mortem will tell us more.'

Gilberton guided him to a chair and sat him down. Edward put his head in his hands.

After a few moments the consultant said, 'You'll tell your wife?'

'What?'

'Edward!' he said sharply, 'Your wife – she must be told.'

'Yes, Lydia, I'll tell her.'

'Shall I come with you?'

'No, no. You needn't do that.'

He shook himself and pulled his shoulders back. He wished he were at home. He did not want to face Lydia, did not know what to say, or do. Utter devastation was all he was experiencing.

'Very well, I'll keep a close eye on her. She needs to rest. We'll keep her in for a few days.' He gave Edward's shoulder a light tap as he walked from his office.

Edward retraced his steps. Lydia looked up as the door opened. She seemed not to have moved since he left her.

'You were quick. You couldn't have…'

'It's the baby. He's – he has died.'

Edward bowed his head so she would not see the tears in his eyes. Lydia leaned her head back against the high hospital pillows and let the tears flow down her face. He took her hand, which lay unclasped in his.

'Don't cry.' He knew it was an absurd remark but could think of nothing else.

'I've failed you, haven't I? The one thing – the only thing I could have done for you, and I've let you down.'

Lydia turned her head away and wept silently. Edward could think of no words to console her, or find consolation himself. If only he had taken her in his arms and cried with her they could both have found the comfort they so desperately needed and longed for. With each of them wrapped in their own manifestation of grief, they did not notice David Tressant come into the room. Lydia saw him first.

'David.' She held out her hand.

He walked round the bed to sit opposite Edward.

'Do you know about – about the baby?' Lydia said, wiping the tears still wet on her cheeks.

'Yes. I was coming to see you, but a nurse recognised me and explained the situation. In view of the concern, I baptised him.'

'How kind of you, David. Did you give him a name?'

David glanced at Edward, not sure of his reaction. 'I chose Edward's father's name – William.'

Edward nodded. 'Thank you.' He stood up. 'I just want to – I'm going to – I want to find Gilberton. Would you stay with her please, till I come back.'

He squeezed Lydia's hand in a gesture quite inadequate to convey what he was feeling and quickly left the room.

*

It was Edward's birthday the day he brought Lydia home. He helped her into the front seat and placed a small basket of dried flowers on her lap. He shut the door and put her case in the boot. Lydia looked at the display on her knee, the only one she could bring of the numerous bouquets she had received during her time in hospital.

Edward had visited her every day straight from work. In some ways they spoke more to each other in the hour or so they were thrown together than they would have done at home – but they said nothing.

Edward told her what he had done at work, Lydia told him how she was feeling, what visitors she had had, who had written and who she had written to. Only once did they refer to the baby when she asked about the funeral, which the consultant advised her not to attend.

Serena had visited, bringing flowers of gargantuan proportions. She had made a point of telling her she was going to cook Edward a meal that evening.

Lydia looked at the birthday cards Edward had left on the table that morning. She held the one she had sent in her hand.

TO MY DEAR HUSBAND it proclaimed on the front, and inside, All my love, my darling, for a very Happy Birthday. She had just signed 'Lydia'.

'Cressy has left lunch for us,' Edward said when he returned from taking her case to her room. 'Thank you for your card.'

'I asked Mrs Cresswell to get it for me. The ones in the hospital shop were a bit tacky. I'll buy you a present as soon as I can get to the shops. Is there anything you particularly want?'

'No, I can't think of anything.'

He moved the dried flower display to one side to set the table. 'Where are you going to put this?'

'I thought it would look nice in my sewing room.'

'Who sent it?'

She hesitated a moment before saying 'Tom.'

As he filled a jug with water she glanced at his face. She knew by the tightness of his jaw that he was not pleased. She desperately hoped he would not say anything, she still felt too weak to cope with even a minor confrontation.

Edward went to the fridge, removed the film covering and put the two plates on the table. Relief flooded over her as he sat down without comment. She picked up her knife and fork and began eating.

'I expect you feel a bit strange.'

'Yes, I do rather.' She poured a glass of water. 'But I'll soon be back in the swing. I'm longing to get out to do some gardening – when I've stopped hobbling, and when Susie comes tomorrow…'

'I've dismissed her – told her never to come anywhere near the Manor again – ever.'

Lydia was shocked. 'But why?'

'Because it was her fault you fell downstairs.'

'But she wasn't here. I just went to get a cardigan.'

'She left a can on the stairs and you fell over it.'

'How do you know that?'

'Because the can was on the stairs when I found you and I went to see her and questioned her about what she'd done that day. It was obvious she had left it there.'

'She always was careless. Poor Susie.'

Lydia could imagine her confronted by Edward and browbeaten into confessing what she had done. Large as she was, she had not the mental equipment to deal with Edward.

'Poor Susie! How can you say that,' he shouted. 'My son – lost because of that half-witted girl's carelessness.'

'Our son,' she corrected. 'The fall had nothing to do with losing the baby, he would have died anyway.'

Her words and the softness of her tone brought Edward up short.

'That's what they say,' he said, bitterly. 'Don't you care?'

'How can you say that?' Lydia felt the tears forming in her eyes. 'I do know how you feel, it's just that Susie needs the money to give her a bit of independence. She would not have done such a thing deliberately. Won't you reconsider?'

'No, get Cressy to come back.'

'I'll managed,' Lydia said, too weary to argue. 'She's not well enough to cope now.'

'You're not to do too much. Get someone else, there must be somebody around who'd be pleased to do the work.'

'Leave it with me,' Lydia said. 'I can't worry about it at the moment.'

She finished the meal and put her plate to one side. She chose an apple from the bowl and began to peel it.

'Do you remember,' she said, 'we first met a year ago next week?'

'Yes, I do.'

Lydia waited for him to say something that showed he thought the past year had some significance in his life.

'When I've eaten this,' he said, taking a banana, 'I'm going to my study.'

'Oh, Edward, I thought we might walk round the garden. It's such a nice day and…'

'I must ring the office. I shouldn't have had today off as I am very busy.'

Lydia was not sure whether she should be pleased he had made such a sacrifice, or guilty that he had had to make it.

'I'm sorry I've inconvenienced you,' she said, gathering up the plates.

'I didn't mean it like that.' Edward looked shamefaced and added quickly, 'Tomorrow, let's go out for the day, to the coast perhaps. The weather seems set and the air will do you good.'

'That'll be nice,' she said, without enthusiasm.

When she had cleared away, Lydia went out into the warm

sunshine. She took each of the steps carefully. Stairs made her feel uneasy and her ankle was still painful. She bent down to run her hand over the grass, wondering whether she should start from scratch and have the whole area taken up and turfed, or use what was there and gradually improve it. She limped over the grass pondering where to put the garden furniture then turned to stare at the house.

Lydia's eyes roamed over the façade. How she loved that house. She looked to the left at the windows of the drawing room and the large jettied bay of Edward's room above. Her eyes moved to the tiny windows that marked the bend in the staircase and Edward's study window and the new nursery above it. Her mind's eye saw round that room, at the cradle and the materials she had chosen, the pictures she had drawn. Her eyes filled.

Edward turned round, phone in hand, and waved. She waved back at his blurred outline. She had done too much weeping in his present. He could not cope with tears.

Poor Edward. How terrible he must be feeling to have lost two sons. She would try to comfort him but it was difficult when he was so unapproachable.

Lydia swept a last look at the house before turning to go through the beech hedge and the trees up to the ruins.

And there she wept for the baby she had only glimpsed, for Edward's loss and the devastation he must be feeling – and her failure. Lastly, she wept for herself and the loveless marriage she acknowledged and the friendless one she had not foreseen.

Yet Edward was capable of tenderness – and then she loved him? Did she? All to often these rare moments were followed by a seeming desire to cancel out any affection he had shown.

In spite of his wealth, his looks, his intelligence, he was not a man at peace. There was often in his dark eyes, a longing, a quest for something, but she could never get close enough to find out what it was.

Lydia heard twigs crackling underfoot and quickly composed herself and hid her handkerchief.

'Are you all right?' Edward asked.

'Yes.'

He held out both hands and she placed hers in his. He pulled her up.

'Come. I'll get dinner tonight. Where would you like to go tomorrow?'

On the first Sunday Lydia attended church, parishioners surrounded her as if she were a film star. Well-wishers stopped them every few feet. Edward was grasped by the hand and sympathetic words expressed. He looked alternately uncomfortable and touched.

'I'm quite overwhelmed, aren't you?' Lydia said on the drive back. 'I never realised how concerned people were for us.'

He said uncertainly, 'I've spoken to people today I've never spoken to before.'

They swung into the drive, past the rhododendron bushes that lined it, and drew up outside the garage.

'Damn, I meant to mention the almshouse vacancy to David.'

'Why, who's died?'

'Mrs Kitchen.'

'When did that happen?'

'Last week sometime, I think.'

'You didn't tell me.'

'I forgot.'

'She was a dear old lady. I used to like visiting her – always cheery. Used to tell such tales about when she was a young girl in Grassenden. Do you remember her?'

'Vaguely.'

'So, there's a vacancy and you've to call a meeting. Just after we met you were having to do that, do you remember?'

'If I make it for Thursday or Friday week, could you set it up? Say eight o'clock?'

'Yes, of course. Who'll be coming?'

'There's David, Serena, Dr Gifford, Prue Viger, the social worker and myself.'

'What shall I do – coffee and sandwiches?'

'No, just coffee and biscuits will do. I'll hold it in the dining room.'

*

David was the first to arrive. Lydia took his coat.

'I haven't had a chance to thank you properly for what you did at the hospital – and the funeral. I know Edward was touched, and so was I.'

'My dear Lydia, we were all devastated by your loss and so concerned for you both. I know what a lot a son meant to Edward. You must get great comfort from each other.'

If only, she thought as she hung up his coat.

'Go through, Edward's in the dining room.'

The knocker went and a woman came into the hall through the open door.

'Hello, you must be Mrs Viger. I'm Lydia Casleigh.' She held out her hand to the tall women in a smart navy suit. 'We've not met before.'

'No, I don't live in Grassenden but his is part of my area.'

As she turned away, Dr Gifford came in. He was the senior partner in the practice with Dr Ferguson.

'Dr Gifford, do come in.'

'How are you Mrs Casleigh? I was sorry to hear of your accident and the loss of your baby.'

'Thank you. Dr Ferguson was very kind.'

Lydia was in the kitchen when Serena arrived. She poked her head round the door said, 'Evening, Lydia' and went into the dining room.

Lydia put biscuits on a plate and glanced around to see that all was ready for the break. She thought she might as well go in and listen as sit in the kitchen alone.

Looking back on her decision, it proved to be a dreadful misjudgement.

Chapter 7

Lydia tiptoed into the dining room from the kitchen and sat on a chair just inside the door. Edward was at the head of the table, Serena and David were facing Lydia and, with their backs to her, sat Dr Gifford and Prue Viger. Edward was speaking.

'…. will have to go up to £48 a week. Now let's turn to the vacancy.'

Edward lifted his head, saw Lydia and raised an eyebrow. She smiled.

Dr Gifford said, 'How many applicants have we to consider?'

'There are two, one from David, and one from Mrs Viger.' Edward nodded to her. 'Let's hear you first.'

Mrs Viger consulted her notes. 'Mrs Elizabeth Jenkins is 69, in reasonable health, apart from some arthritis. She is capable of looking after herself but the house she rents is too large for her. She has a daughter in Maidstone and a son in Eastbourne – both are supportive. She only has her pension plus around six thousand pounds in savings. However, she does not live in Grassenden or Abbotts Lidiard, she comes from Grimley Heath.'

'David?'

'This is a difficult one. Mr and Mrs Ninion have lived in Abbotts Lidiard for fifteen years. Mrs Ninion's mother, Jane Kirkpatrick, is 84 and is no longer able to look after herself properly as she cannot walk without aid. The daughter will see to all her needs. Mrs Kirkpatrick lives in London and her only connection with the area is her daughter. She has no savings, only her pension.'

'Thanks, David. As I see it,' commented Edward, 'neither fulfil the domicile requirements of the Casleigh bequest. Any thoughts or comments?'

The sight of Edward, authoritative and imposing, made Lydia's heart swell with pride. He looked so handsome.

'Is Mrs Jenkins a churchgoer?' David asked.

'No,' replied Prue Viger.

'Neither is Mrs Kirkpatrick, according to her son-in-law, though I have seen him and his wife at St Luke's on high days and holidays.' David smiled wryly.

'The Ninions are a charming couple' Lydia commented, without thinking.

Edward turned to the doctor.

'From a medical point of view,' Dr Gifford said, 'Mrs Kirkpatrick's need seems greater and, in all probability, she has not so long to live, but arthritis can spread and Mrs Jenkins might, in a short space of time, be incapable of looking after herself either.'

'Well,' volunteered Serena, 'at least Grimley Heath is in the area. If we start opening up to Londoners, there's no knowing what class of people we'll be getting.'

Lydia, unthinking, rose to the bait. 'I think Jane Ninion deserves some consideration. They, at least, are Abbotts Lidiard residents.'

'Don't interfere, Lydia. This meeting has nothing to do with you. Go and get the coffee.'

Lydia stared at Edward as if he had hit her. Embarrassment swept over her and the hairs on her arms stood up. She felt crushed by the way Edward had spoken to her in front of visitors, and wanted to die.

Her eyes sought Serena's, who smiled malevolently. David's head was lowered. Of Dr Gifford and Mrs Viger's thoughts, she had no idea.

After what seemed an eternity, Lydia left the dining room and went to the kitchen desperately wanting to escape, to storm out and walk for miles to rid her mind of the humiliating incident, but she had an obligation to her guests. She splashed her face with water.

As she switched on the percolator she could hear voices as the meeting resumed.

Coffee transferred to the warmed pot, she took the tray into the dining room. Her entry caused whoever was speaking to dry up, and the air felt tense and overbearing. Lydia placed the tray on the table and with as much dignity as she could muster, turned and said to the hushed company, 'Perhaps you'd like to help yourselves when you're ready.'

*

'I've had the most embarrassing evening, Faith,' David said when he arrived back at the vicarage. 'Edward was so rude to Lydia in front of us all I could hardly believe my ears.'

When she had heard the story Faith asked, 'And what did Lydia do?'

'She stood there staring open-mouthed in horror. She glared at Serena, but I'm ashamed to say, I couldn't bear to meet Lydia's eye.

'Was that all?'

'No, we continued the discussion in a somewhat strained atmosphere and about five minutes later, Lydia came back with a tray and asked us to help ourselves. I thought she dealt with the situation with the utmost dignity. We did not see her any more.'

'You know, there's something very strange going on there. You remember my asking Lydia to read on Mothering Sunday?'

'Yes, and Edward told her to didn't want her to.'

'What I didn't tell you were the remarks she made about tarnishing Edward's image and something like – "perhaps I'll do something he will approve of one day." It was so out of character for her to say that to a stranger.'

'We're not strangers.'

'But Lydia isn't the type who would say that sort of thing to anyone – unless she'd been…'

'Been what?'

'Well, driven to it.'

David rubbed his hand over his chin. 'Edward was well out of order to speak to her like that in front of us, however justified he felt. Dr Gifford and Prue Viger didn't know what to do with themselves and they couldn't see the look on Lydia's face.'

'Perhaps you could take him on one side – have a word with him.'

'I don't know. Edward's a difficult person to 'take on one side' even though I do have a good relationship with him. It wasn't easy after his wife died.'

'No, perhaps you're right, but I still think something's amiss. I mean – she's only just left hospital after losing a baby. What was he thinking about?' A puzzled frown knitted her brows. 'Maybe I'll find a chance to talk to her.'

*

When Lydia had taken in the tray, she left the dining room by the door that went into the hall. She collected her coat and left the Manor with no idea where she was heading. Shoulders hunched she went out into the summer twilight. How could he humiliate her like that? Was she so despised in her own household?

By the time her angry thoughts had settled, she realised she was on the old road bridleway to Grassenden. It was practically dark and her ankle hurt dreadfully. She should never have walked so far, but till then her emotional distress had overcome the physical pain. Lydia was just about to turn back when she noticed, coming towards her, a shadowy figure in the distance. Alarmed, she turned quickly and hobbled painfully back towards the lane. She heard the follower's footsteps coming nearer. Abbotts Lidiard Lane was not well lit and she wondered whose door she could knock on when a voice called, 'Lydia?'

'Oh, Tom, it's you.' She gave a great sigh of relief. 'I was so frightened.'

'What on earth are you doing here at this time?'

'I – I fancied a walk.'

'With your bad ankle?'

'Yes.'

'Does Edward allow you out without a chaperone?'

'I wish you wouldn't speak about him like that.'

Two cars came along the narrow road and Tom took her arm to move her closer to the side.

'How are you feeling? Glad to be home?'

'I've been home over two weeks and seem to be back into a routine.'

Lydia was about to add how much her leg was hurting, but thought this might involve further awkward questions. She did not feel in the mood for more explanations – she still had Edward to confront.

They walked along in silence till Lydia said, 'Thank you for the flowers, I brought them home. They really brighten up my room.'

'I'm glad you liked them.' He paused. 'I thought it best I didn't visit. Mum told me how you were.'

They fell silent again.

'Susie Patterson's upset. I've had her crying all over me for the past week. I suppose you know she got the sack?'

'Yes, I'm sorry. She was a great help – if you could ignore the gossip. I'm trying to get her back.'

'Was it true what she said?'

'What about, she's not very reliable?'

'That you fell over something she'd left on the stairs?'

'So Edward said – and before you ask yes, I do believe him. I had thought I caught my foot on something, but I can't really remember. I banged my head you see.'

They had reached his mother's cottage and Tom unlatched the gate. 'I'm calling in to see Mum, are you coming in?'

'No, I'd better not.'

'I'll see you around.'

'Goodnight, Tom, and thanks for your company.'

''Night.'

The cars had all left when Lydia knocked on the door.

'Where've you been,' Edward said, 'I didn't even know you were out.'

'I was upset and went for a walk.'

Edward hovered over her as she hung up her coat. 'Where did you go?' he demanded.

Lydia went past him into the kitchen and he followed. 'I went down the lane and along the old road. By then I had calmed down.'

'Calmed down?'

'I realised where I was, so I turned to come home – and my ankle was hurting.'

Lydia went to the fridge for milk and tipped some in a saucepan. She took a deep breath and turned to Edward.

'For the past year I have put up with your hurtful remarks, your disparaging comments and your general air of indifference towards me, but they have been to me alone. This evening you went too far and humiliated me in front of others.'

'You – you shouldn't have interrupted.'

'Yes, I realise that and I apologise. I wish I'd never come in to your wretched meeting, but you had no right to speak to me like you did, as if I were your servant – worse than a servant. And why didn't you tell Serena not to make remarks that were deliberately said to upset me? She only volunteered her opinion out of spite.'

'I couldn't do that, she's my friend.'

'And I'm your wife,' she cried, and ran from the room.

Edward caught up with her at the top of the stairs and grasped her arm. She glared angrily at him, her mouth set in a grim line. In a voice that sounded strangely intimidating she said slowly, 'Take your hand away.'

His arm dropped to his side and she went into her bedroom and slammed the door.

Three o'clock. Lydia had heard every chime since she had left Edward standing on the landing. Sleep? How could she sleep?

She put on her dressing gown and went down to the kitchen. The saucepan of milk was still on the cooker. She heated it, poured it on the chocolate and stood sipping it for a few minutes before switching off the light and returning to bed.

As she reached the landing she heard Edward call. She ignored it and went to her room, but had second thoughts. He might be ill. She went through the bathroom to his room.

'Are you all right,' she whispered.

All was quiet and dark in the room but as she turned to go he shouted, 'No! No! Please don't.'

Lydia padded over to the bed and put down her mug. She switched on the bedside light to illuminate the expected scene – the bedclothes awry, his arms flaying and sweat dripping from his forehead. That wretched nightmare again. This time she was going to wake him. Lydia was not sure if it were a good or bad thing to do, but she was in a less charitable mood than usual.

'Edward, wake up.' She shook him and he opened his eyes. 'What are you dreaming about?' Lydia put her hands on his shoulders and shook him again.

'Sit up,' she commanded.

Lydia reached for another pillow and put it behind him. He shook his head as if to clear it, making his blond hair fall forward.

'Here, have a sip of this.'

He took the mug from her hand and took a sip. He pulled a face.

'What is it?'

'Hot chocolate. Now I want to get to the bottom of this. What is this dream or nightmare that you keep having? What's it about?'

'Dream? Oh, dream. I don't know?'

'Well someone's hurting you. Have you been in an accident?'

'No.'

'Were you bullied at school?'

'Yes.'

Lydia was surprised. 'Were you hit?'

'No – probably 'cause I was tall for my age.'

'So what form did this bullying take?'

'Verbal.'

'What was said? What had they against you?'

He held out the mug. 'I don't like hot chocolate,' he said, like a spoilt child.

'Tough, it wasn't meant for you.' She snatched it from him and put it on the bedside table.

'Now,' she persisted, 'why were you verbally bullied?'

'Because of my hair and my height – and …'

'Yes?'

'I was very shy.'

'Shy? You?' Lydia almost laughed.

'Well, I was.'

'That can't be it,' she said, realistically. 'You wouldn't fling your arms around like that unless it were something physical, something that is being done to you. Think Edward.'

She sat on the bed.

'I'm surprised you can bear to be so close.'

'So am I, but that's not the point at issue. Now I'm here, I'm going to sort out this mystery once and for all. Who is Mona?'

He frowned. Mona?'

'Yes, you say "Don't Mona, please don't" or some similar name. She, or he, has a part in your past.'

'But I don't know anyone called Mona, never have.'

'Something that sounds like Mona then,' she said impatiently. 'You're not distinct. Jonah perhaps: Myrna, Moira? Think!'

Lydia willed him to search his mind for an experience so traumatic that it had had to be erased from his mind.

'I honestly can't think of anyone.'

Lydia was about to give up when she saw his body stiffen. 'What is it?' She took his hand and it trembled within hers.

'Mor,' he whispered, and turned his head away.

She waited for his distress to ease and after a while she said, 'Who is Mor?'

'My mother.'

*

When Lydia woke late next morning, Edward had left for work. She felt drained so knew how he must be feeling. Although she had released some anguish from his childhood to do with his mother, he would not tell her what it was, and ordered her back to bed with about as much finesse as he had previously told her to get the coffee.

She showered and dressed. As she sat at her dressing table fixing her necklace and earrings, she told her reflection she would just have to get on with her life. She had known bad times before, like the first home she had been sent to after her parents had died. Her foster parents were not intentionally unkind, but they did not realise that five years of her life had disappeared without explanation. She had been told they had died in an accident, but she believed that it was her fault they had gone, that she must have done something bad for them to leave her like that. She sighed.

Lydia went for her usual Tuesday shop. It was the first time since her return from hospital that she had been into the village apart from church. When she reached the Stores, Mrs Reece greeted her with her usual enthusiasm and expressed sympathy over the loss of the baby.

'Your husband – well is he?'

'Yes, very well thank you?'

''It must be coming up for your first anniversary.' She put the ham on the scales and raised her head to look through the bottom of her glasses. 'That's £1.32.'

Lydia reached into her handbag. 'Our anniversary isn't for several weeks yet.'

'How've you found married life? The first year is the worst, I always think, all that adjusting. I nearly left my Dave after a few months?'

Lydia did not like the line the conversation was taking and recalled Mrs Collins voicing thoughts along much the same lines.

'Can you change a five pound note?' Lydia said coolly, but noted the self-satisfied look on the woman's face as she realised Lydia was not going to be drawn on her marriage. Damned if you answer and damned if you don't.

She was almost afraid to go into the butcher's. Mr Anders greeted her in his usual courteous manner and asked after her health, but she did think he scrutinised her face closely – or was she just getting paranoid.

Faith dashed over as she was walking back to the car. 'How are you? You're looking much, much better.'

'To tell you the truth, I'm beginning to think I have two heads or something. People keep making observations about marriage, and mine in particular.'

'Come back to the Vicarage and we can have a chat. I've been meaning to give you a ring.'

Faith showed her into the living room, removing a pile of old parish magazines and some knitting to one side.

'This isn't much like the Manor, I'm afraid. I never seem to get around to housework.'

'I don't suppose I'd have much time if I did as much as you do around the parish, housework is about all I tackle. I haven't even got the baby to prepare for, or look after.'

'Oh, my dear. I felt so sorry for you. I was saying so last week when David came home from the …' She stopped. 'I meant I was sorry about the baby.' The more Faith tried to qualify what she said the worse she made it.

'So I gather David told you about the confrontation?'

'How awful it must have been.'

'Yes, it was.'

'And now everybody knows.'

Lydia jerked upright. 'What d'you mean – everybody?'

'Oh dear,' Faith said, embarrassed. 'the incident does seem to have spread around the village. You know what villages are like.'

'No, I obviously don't. I'm a Londoner remember.'

Faith gave a little smile. 'Don't be bitter, it's not in your nature.'

'So that accounts for all the strange remarks I've been getting. Who would do such a thing?' Lydia pushed out her lips. 'Serena. Of course, I should have realised.'

'I don't suppose she did it deliberately. She probably told somebody, who told somebody else. You know, once it's out of ones hands …'

'You think too highly of her,' Lydia said coolly.

Faith changed the subject. 'You know you were saying you don't have enough to occupy you.'

'Yes, I begin to miss work. The Manor is under control now so the garden is about my only interest.' Lydia did not let on she had lost all enthusiasm for valuing the Manor's contents.

'The village school will be needing a classroom assistant next term. Why don't you apply? Didn't you tell me once you had worked with children?'

'Yes, but that was only for a few months, and they were toddlers.'

'You'd be ideal. Think about it. I'll mention it to Mrs Estridge, she's the Headmistress. She'd be delighted to have you, I'm sure.'

'I would really like to work in the school,' she said. 'But….' Lydia recalled the dressing down she had received over reading the lesson and she knew Edward would certainly knock anything she wanted to do on the head. Then would follow some indulgence that would make her forget his behaviour. But this seesaw existence was getting on her nerves.

'You're thinking about Edward?'

'Pardon? I'm sorry, I was miles away.'

'You're afraid of what Edward will say, aren't you?'

'No.' Faith looked at her shrewdly. 'Yes, I am,' she admitted.

'It's up to you, Lydia. Do whatever you think best.'

And that was as close as Faith got to preaching anarchy in the Casleigh household.

*

Edward came into the kitchen from the cloakroom rubbing his damp hair on a towel. He dropped a soggy evening newspaper on the kitchen table.

'Dinner will be about ten minutes.' Lydia looked at his tired face. 'Get yourself a drink, I'll call you when it's ready.'

'Yes, I think I will,' he said wearily.

When she had taken the casserole out of the oven she went to the drawing room. Edward's long legs were stretched out in front of him and his hand clasped a glass of whisky, which rested on the arm of the leather chair. He was asleep, his head to one side. Lydia crept across the wooden floor, took the glass from his hand and put it on the marquetry table that stood beside his chair. She stayed looking at him for some moments before going back to the kitchen where she helped herself to chicken and put the dish back to keep warm.

The telephone rang and Lydia put down the knife and fork and went to answer, but it must have woken Edward because he had already picked it up.

A few minutes later he came into the kitchen, whisky in hand.

'You should have woken me,' he said.

'You looked exhausted, so I thought I'd leave you.' She lifted the dish from the oven to the table and returned for the vegetables. 'Who was that on the phone?'

'Serena.'

'What does she want?'

'She's having a garden party Saturday week.'

'You're not expecting me to go, are you?'

'I most certainly am. There'll be a great many people there who've been associated with the Casleighs for years. Some are from families as old as mine.'

Lydia was tempted to say 'ours', but held her tongue. 'Won't they feel embarrassed having a common Londoner in their midst?'

'Don't be idiotic.'

'I don't want to go anywhere near that woman. She hates me and the feeling is mutual. I don't know what I've done to make her so spiteful. I can only think she's jealous.'

'Jealous?'

'She's in love with you and can't stand the thought of anyone else loving you.'

'I didn't know you loved me.'

'I don't – but she doesn't know that.' Lydia went on, 'I'm told she doesn't love Jeremy.'

'How do you know?'

'Tom told me.'

His face clouded. 'You two seem to spend a great deal of time in discussion.'

'We do both live here. We can't help passing the time of day if we meet.'

Edward scowled. 'Anyway, to get back to Serena's party. I expect you to be with me and when you've said hello, you needn't speak to her again if that's what you want, but I must say I am very disappointed. Serena is my oldest friend and I expect you to respect that.'

'Well, really!' Lydia was beside herself with indignation. 'I never started all this. I was quite prepared to be well disposed to all your friends, but Serena started on me at our engagement dinner and hasn't stopped since – nor is likely to, as far as I can see.'

Edward stared in amazement. 'I didn't notice anything amiss that evening.'

Lydia could not be bothered to answer him. She collected his plate and put it in the dishwasher.

'Aren't we having anything to drink?'

'I was waiting for you.'

'Coffee then.' He drained the last of his whisky.

'I saw Faith today.'

'Yes.'

'She wondered if – she thought maybe I'd like to help at the local school as a classroom assistant – in September,' she added lamely, as she saw his expression.

He fixed her with a cold stare. 'I'm surprised you've even mentioned it. You know very well it is quite out of the question.'

'Why?'

'Because I wouldn't want my wife to be seen working, especially in the village.'

'But it would help me. I need something to do. I'm so …'

'You have enough to do here.' He stood up, his height making Lydia feel even more oppressed and dispirited. 'Anyway, I'm hoping there will be another child in the not too distant future, and then you'll have enough to occupy you. I'll have my coffee in the study.'

The little fight she used to have had vanished completely and she was filled with despair and loneliness. She took the tray into the study and put it on Edward's desk. He neither raised his head from the keyboard nor made a comment.

'I'm going out,' she said, and shut the door before he could question her.

She walked down the lane to Mrs Cresswell's cottage. There was a car parked outside, and as she knocked on the door, a burst of laughter met her ears. Too late to go now.

Jamie opened the door. 'Why, Mrs Casleigh,' he said, taken aback. 'Have you come to see Mum?'

'Yes, I have, but I can see you've got a family party so I'll come another time.'

Mrs Cresswell came to the door. 'Lydia, I thought it was your voice. Come in, my dear. It's Tony's birthday and they've been to tea with their old Gran.'

'I don't want to intrude. I can come tomorrow.'

'Don't be silly.' She caught Lydia's hand and drew her into the living room.

A curly headed boy with pale blue eyes was saying, 'Uncle Tom, you don't do it like that!' Tony and his sister Kim were standing behind Tom laughing at his feeble attempt to play a game his nephew had been given.

Tom looked up, raised an eyebrow and smiled at Lydia. Pat, who was clearing the table, glanced at them both.

Such was the contrast to her forlorn existence at the Manor the whole scene made her want to cry.

'Sit down.' Mrs Cresswell indicated a chair. Turning to her daughter-in-law, she said, 'Is there a spot of tea left?'

Pat inspected the pot and went to add water.

'OK kids, tidy up,' Jamie said. 'It's time we were going, you can teach your uncle how to play next time you see him. You can't expect much from these 'ere yokels.'

Kim laughed and Tom cried, 'What a cheek. I could beat you any day.'

Tony said, 'I might be a farmer when I grow up.'

'Sensible boy.'

'I'd like to go to University,' Kim said.

'I didn't know that,' her mother said, handing Lydia her tea.

'That's their futures settled then,' said their grandmother, laughing.

Lydia sipped her tea and watched as the children cleared up. She asked Tony his age and what presents he had had and said she might find him something later in the week now she knew it was his birthday. From Kim she learned that she liked English best at school.

When they had gone Lydia, Tom and his mother sat chatting. Slowly Mrs Cresswell's eyes began to close.

'Your mother must love having her family round her. How lucky she is.'

'What's he done this time?'

'I don't want to talk about it.'

'But you *do* want to talk about it, that's why you're here.'

'Not with you – it wouldn't be right.'

'Why on earth did you marry him?'

'He asked me and I said yes.'

'And that was it!' he cried, appalled. 'No courtship – no love?'

She did not reply. *Love doesn't come into it.*

They sat in silence for some minutes.

'I love you, Lydia.'

'Don't say that Tom, please don't. I entered into this marriage quite willingly and I must manage as best I can. Edward is a complex character, I shall get used to his ways, I expect.'

'I doubt that. You are gentle and sweet-natured, you need love and companionship, not wealth and position.'

'Stop it!' she cried. He was too close to the truth.

'Why couldn't I have found you first? I'd love you as you deserve.'

Mrs Cresswell stirred and opened her eyes. 'I get so tired nowadays and visitors seem to take it out of me.'

'I'd better be going now.'

'I didn't mean to chase you away dear.'

'No, I know – but Edward will be worried.'

Tom gave her an uncomprehending look and shook his head.

'I'll walk up the lane with you,' he said.

Tom kissed his mother and said he would take her into Maidstone later in the week.

'I'll see how I feel and let you know.'

Lydia gave her a kiss and Mrs Cresswell squeezed her hand.

'Night dear.'

Tom opened the gate on to the road and waited while Lydia went through. It was dark and still drizzling.

'I didn't mean to upset you, but I can't help the way I feel.'

'You should have kept it to yourself.'

They walked along in silence till they reached the drive. They stood facing each other and Tom raised his hand and traced his finger down her cheek and along the angle of her jaw. Lydia took his arm away and he spread his hands in a despairing gesture and strode on to the footpath.

Lydia shut the oak door and bolted it. How she used to delight in its age and to wonder what scenes it must have witnessed. She used to give it a little stroke each time she came in, revelling in its history. Tonight it seemed like a jail door, locking her into deep unhappiness.

Edward came into the hall.

'I'll lock this while I'm here, shall I?' She stood on tiptoe to reach the top bolt.

'Where've you been this time?'

'Mrs Cresswell's.'

'What for?'

'I wanted someone to talk to. It was Tony's birthday and they were all there having tea. Tom as well.'

'I thought he'd be in on the act somewhere.'

'Meaning?'

'He seems to loom very large in your life.'

'Like Serena does, you mean?'

'That's not the same thing.'

'Look Edward, whenever I've seen Tom it has been quite co-incidental, but if you're going to make such a fuss, then I might as well be hung for a sheep as a lamb. So, if I choose, I shall visit the farm and Tom whenever I fancy, on any pretext. Now, I'm going to bed. Goodnight.'

Chapter 8

The day of Serena's garden party dawned bright and sunny. That was one good thing, thought Lydia, as she showered – Serena and rain would have been too much to bear.

Edward came into the bathroom as she wrapped the bath sheet around herself.

'Sorry, I didn't realise you were still here. I'll come back later.'

'I'll finish in my room,' she said coolly.

Lydia escaped and threw the towel on a chair. She spread underwear from her drawer on the bed and standing in front of the open doors of her wardrobe pondered what to wear. The afternoon will be the garden party followed by a barbecue for Serena's close friends, of whom she was one – heaven help her. She clasped her chin pensively. She did not hear Edward come into her bedroom.

His arms encircled her waist and he kissed her neck. She stiffened and turned round within his arms. He moved his hands to her shoulders and slid them down her arms. His eyes, soft with longing, peered into hers. She stared back impassively.

'Don't you want me to make love to you?'

Lydia wanted to respond lovingly, but could not. Edward tore her in half. A tender lover on the one hand, overbearing and dictatorial on the other. She said nothing.

Edward let his arms drop to his side and she caught that sad, lost look so at odds with his usual high-handedness.

'I'm going to garden this morning, dress in something pretty this afternoon, to which you can give your approval if you wish. I haven't quite decided what to put on for the barbeque. How does that sound?' She gave a quick, forced smile that did not reach her eyes.

He studied her for a long moment, then said flatly, 'That sounds fine.'

*

Lydia had to hand it the woman; the setting and arrangements for her party were perfect. The front lawn was the location for a large marquee with plastic windows draped in swags of pink silk. A top London caterer provided the food. Serena looked elegant and, Lydia had to admit, quite beautiful in a chiffon suit of eggshell blue with matching shoes and wide brimmed hat. Jewellery was more discreet than usual. A well-groomed Jeremy stood dutifully in line greeting their guests.

Edward and Lydia mingled with the others on the lawn. Lydia had not, so far, seen anyone she knew. Edward, on the other hand, seemed to know everyone. She was introduced, and those who had heard, made sympathetic comments about the loss of the baby.

Lydia kept close to Edward, so close that on more than one occasion, Edward nearly tripped over her as he turned. When a moment arose when he was not talking he said to Lydia, 'Must you stand so near?'

'But I thought that's what you wanted. Remember the party in London?'

'Don't be so childish.'

'Does that mean I can move around freely? I've just seen Anna Bartley. You remember her, don't you?'

'Do as you please.'

'When would you like me back?'

'Sarcasm doesn't suit you. I'll find you if I want you.'

She crossed the lawn to Anna who was standing alone. She had visited Lydia in hospital and had telephoned when she returned.

'Lydia, how nice to see you. You're look back to your usual self, have you settled back home now?"

They chatted for a few minutes till Anna's husband came over and said would Lydia excuse them as he would like his wife to meet a friend of his.

She watched Anne and Terrance walk away hand in hand and searched for Edward. There he was just outside the marquee talking to Serena and Joss. Joss' husband joined them, said a few words, then the two of them disappeared into the marquee. Lydia studied Edward and Serena who were standing close and relaxed, he was smiling at something she said. He rarely smiled or laughed in her presence, but there was nothing to laugh about. They shared no events from the past, had no mutual friends. Their only shared incident was the loss of the baby and that Edward considered his loss.

Lydia surveyed the scene, far beyond anything she had known or ever considered being her future. Her clothes were expensive, her credentials impeccable. She had been accepted in the village and was liked by everyone. Well almost everyone, too much by one, but she could not pretend to be someone she was not; could not play Lady Bountiful.

Lydia's eyes slid back to them. Edward's blond head was lowered and he was whispering in Serena's ear. They both threw back their heads and laughed and she reached up her well-manicured hand to touch his cheek playfully. It was a spontaneous gesture, for once not done to provoke her. Lydia screwed up her eyes to shut out the tormenting scene. Edward had never made a playful gesture towards her but then, why should he?

This morning when he had put his arms round her had not been a sign of affection. It was nothing more than a response to seeing her unclothed, and a subtle reminder of the reason for their marriage.

Lydia sensed someone near and opened her eyes.

Jeremy was beside her, nodding to where Edward and Serena were talking.

'Giving you a bad time, I hear,' Jeremy said.

'What do you mean?'

He smirked. 'Your old man – cutting up rough, eh?'

Lydia felt the blood rush to her face. 'No, of course not.'

'Don't give me that. Everyone knows he put you in your place in no uncertain manner.'

'I think you're quite out of turn speaking to me like that.'

'OK, OK, sorry I spoke.'

Jeremy was slightly shorter than Edward and not as broad, but he was a handsome man with even features beneath straight, black hair. His florid skin and the beginnings of a paunch were showing the effect of too much drink and expense account lunches. Lydia had seen his type in the shop often enough, seeking some trinket to take home to placate the wife.

'What do you think of this shindig?'

'I think Serena can be very pleased with herself. It is superb.'

'Yes, the old girl hasn't done too badly.' He paused. 'It's a sort of farewell do – only no one knows who's leaving.'

'I don't understand.'

'Serena's kicking me out. Giving me the boot.'

Lydia was shocked. Though she liked neither of them, she had always thought they were admirably suited. Tom had mentioned they did not get on, but she had not thought they would go as far as separating.

Jeremy saw the look on her face and her vivid blue eyes open wide.

'Don't look so upset, we've not been hitting it off for some time now, but we've tried to keep up appearance. Now we're both past caring. I am anyway.'

Lydia murmured how sorry she was.

Suddenly he said, 'You know Serena is in love with Edward, don't you?'

'I had suspected.'

'Yes,' he said, turning to look at her. 'I can see you'd realise that.'

He took a handkerchief from his pocket and dabbed the sweat that had broken out on his upper lip.

'That's why she's got it in for you. I think she's been in love with him for years.' After a few moments, he said, 'They'd have made a good couple, don't you think?'

'Yes', she said, disconsolately, 'I think they would. Edward values her friendship I do know that.'

'Edward must have had second sight.'

'Oh, what makes you say that?'

'They said she can't have children – wouldn't have done for Edward.'

Lydia detected a note of sadness for what might have been and for a brief moment she felt they were kindred spirits.

'Well, I'd better circulate and spread my charms. Nice talking to you, perhaps we'll get a chance for a chat this evening. You are here this evening, aren't you?'

Lydia watched Jeremy saunter across the lawn one hand in his pocket. He had an air about him that comes from always have had money and seeing no reason to apologise for it. He went into the marquee where she saw him pick up a glass and down its contents in one go, then gather another from a passing waitress.

It *was* true, Edward did value Serena's friendship. What did he value in her, apart from childbearing?

*

There were fourteen at the barbeque and for once Lydia knew everyone – Serena's coffee morning pals with husbands and Faith and David. They had not been at the garden party because David had two weddings that afternoon.

The relaxed atmosphere of the afternoon overflowed into the evening. Though it had cooled down considerably the weather was still fine. Serena had replaced her many bracelets and her long legs made the most of the slacks and blouse she wore.

'Are you thinking what I'm thinking?' Anna sidled up to her. 'Why don't we look like that in trousers? Meow.'

Jeremy, already the worse for drink, had on a chef's hat and striped apron. Meat in copious amounts was already on the barbeque along with mushrooms, sausages, tomatoes and potatoes wrapped in foil. A table held more of the same covered by a muslin tent. The aroma from the sizzling food wafted tantalisingly on the still evening air.

Just inside the french windows stood another table laden with pies, gateaux, cakes, fruit, trifles and cream – enough to feed the afternoon guests as well.

'This is wonderful,' Lydia exclaimed. 'Did you make all these yourself?'

'Of course,' Serena said sharply, but nevertheless looked pleased.

Lydia had done her duty and spoken to Serena with a genuine compliment, now she was determined to relax and enjoy herself.

During the evening David regaled them with the events at St Luke's that afternoon. Evidently the bride suddenly had cold feet and it took an hour in the porch before they could get her to the altar. 'I think Mr Morgan played *Here comes the bride* three times before giving up and waiting till she was practically at the rails. Good job it was the last wedding otherwise we would have had two lots of guest vying for seats.'

'What did the poor old bridegroom do all this time?' Terrence asked.

'After about fifteen minutes,' Faith joined in, 'The bridegroom's mother, a formidable lady, joined them. She eventually got her future daughter-in-law to the altar. The bridegroom looked bewildered to say the least.'

'I bet he could've done with a large whisky,' said Jeremy, demonstrating with his glass.

'I don't know about him,' David said, 'I wouldn't have minded one myself.'

'Just think what we were all missing,' Serena said.

When they had consumed what they all agreed was too much food, Faith came and sat next to Lydia.

'Well, what happened? You haven't got back to me.'

'No, I'm sorry, Edward won't have it and I haven't enough courage to go against him, I wish I had. From what I gather Frances would have told him what she was going to do, not ask him, though I'm sure she wouldn't have dreamed of working in a school, or anywhere else, come to that.'

'She certainly wouldn't. Frances was a real snob – even more so than…' Faith clamped her hand over her mouth. 'I'm afraid I let my tongue run away with me – not a thing a vicar's wife can afford to do.'

'Thank you for thinking about me. I would have loved to do it, but then again, I could have another baby and would have to leave, so maybe it's for the best.' Lydia reached for her handbag. 'I'm going in to freshen up, see you in a minute.'

She stepped through the french windows, past the table even now groaning beneath the weight of the left-over desserts, into the hall. Compared with the Manor, the rooms of Ridge House were spacious. She was turning to go up the wide staircase when a voice called, 'There's a cloakroom out here.'

Lydia went into the kitchen. Jeremy was leaning against the fridge, a tumbler half full of whisky in his hand. Hat and apron lay discarded on a chair.

'OK, it'll save my legs. They are quite tired after standing all afternoon.'

'Through there,' he said, pointing with his drink towards an archway.

She walked through the utility room with its washing machine, tumble dryer, freezer and assorted shoes. A door ahead led to a cloakroom.

When Lydia came back into the kitchen she flashed a quick smile at Jeremy and went to go into the hall.

'Stay and talk,' he said, in a voice thick with alcohol, 'we can carry on our conversation of this afternoon.'

'I'd rather go out and join the others.'

'Back to your tiresome husband?'

'He's not tiresome,' she said hotly, 'He's just…'

'… misunderstood?'

'Yes.'

'What a loyal little wife you are.' He swung round with his arm upraised and some drink spilled from his glass.

He put the glass down on the table with exaggerated care. 'Now I've got my hands free, I can give you a kiss. It'll be better than anything that husband of yours can do.'

He lunged at her and before she could stop him, he put one hand behind her head and was kissing her with hot, slobbering kisses. She could smell his alcoholic breath and saw his wild bloodshot eyes as she struggled free. Just then Serena came into the kitchen from the garden.

'What are you two up to?'

'*I'm* not up to anything.' Lydia hurried into the hall and back through the drawing room to the terrace. She stood by Edward's chair till he had finished his conversation.

'Can we go home soon?' she whispered in his ear.

'Why, what's the matter?'

'Please Edward, I want to go. Say I'm not well, say – say anything,' she urged.

With his usual aplomb, Edward managed to make their departure look uncontrived. Lydia said goodbye to everyone with a fixed smile on her face and even took leave of Serena. Of Jeremy there was no sign.

When they were in the car Edward asked what was wrong. She told him Jeremy was drunk and upsetting her.

When he had put the car away he joined her in the drawing room. She was sitting in the armchair with her feet curled up. Her shoes lay where she had kicked them off. He walked over and put them neatly side by side.

'Don't get too upset, he's often drunk nowadays I'm told. What did he do exactly?'

'He kissed me. It was horrible.'

'You didn't say that in the car, you said he'd upset you.'

'Isn't that upsetting enough,' she said, raising her voice, 'or are you suggesting I encouraged him.'

Lydia put her finger inside her silver necklace and ran it furiously from side to side till it broke.

'Now look what's happened.' She pulled it from around her neck and flung it on the floor.

Edward bent and picked it up. 'It's not worth mending,' he said, glancing at it resting in the palm of his land. 'It's not expensive. I'll buy you another.'

Lydia burst into tears. 'That's your solution to everything, isn't it? Buy your way out, the same as your ancestors bought their way in. That was my mother's necklace – my real mother's,' she shouted. 'These earrings and Elizabeth's jewellery are the only things I have of value. *Sentimental value.* But you wouldn't know about sentiment, would you? Sentiment hasn't any meaning in your life. it can't be quantified, or insured, or locked in a safe or – or – seen by your influential friends.'

Edward stood bewildered by Lydia's outburst and watched as she slowly pulled herself together. She jumped up and held out her hand. 'Here, give it to me, I'll have it mended.'

'I'll get it seen to,' he said, putting it in his pocket.

For a few moments he looked at her woebegone face then put his arm round her. He walked her along the passage and at the foot of the stairs he said, 'You go on up while I lock the doors.'

Ten minutes later he came to her bedroom with two brandies. 'I don't drink brandy.'

'I know, but it's only a little one, it'll help you unwind.'

She took a sip, made a face and coughed. 'How can you drink anything so strong?'

'Practice,' he said. 'Go on, take another sip.'

'Are you trying to get me drunk?'

'If it's the only way I can share your bed, yes,' he grinned.

'And why are you having a large one? So you can forget all about it in the morning?'

Edward looked aggrieved but said nothing. He undressed and got in beside her. He took Lydia's glass and put his other arm round her shoulders. He raised the glass to her lips. With each small sip she spluttered.

The brandy was distributing a relaxing warmth throughout her body heightening her senses as she felt his fingers brush lightly on her skin. She pushed the unpleasantness of the evening to the back of her mind.

Edward made her finish the drink and put her glass beside his. He reached across and switched off the bedside light. As he began to make love to her, Lydia's subconscious told her this moment would have to be paid for, but she was not listening.

✳

In early September Edward took Lydia to Denmark to meet his Aunt Christina, her husband and their son Johann, who was 21 and at university. The family made her very welcome and Lydia could see for herself the strong family resemblance. Lydia took the opportunity to find out more about Edward's mother.

'I was only five, maybe six when Jette married William,' Christina said. 'When I was born, after my father came back at the end of the war, Jette was away at a school, for dancing you understand. She appeared to me always very stern as a little girl and I was not so happy when she visited our home, but I liked William.'

No much information there, thought Lydia.

When they left Aahus they went to Copenhagen. They stayed at the Hotel Opera near the theatre, in a road with a name Lydia could not pronounce. They went shopping along The Stroget, and Edward pointed out that it changed its name four times along its length. He bought her an amber brooch in one of the specialist shops. They took a canal trip and lunched or dined along the colourful Nyhavn. Lydia had never seen so many restaurants in such a small area.

He showed her the Danish Royal treasures in the Rosenberg Palace and the famous Little Mermaid. This was a little disappointing, as it was surrounded by coachloads of tourists and was so much smaller than Lydia had imagined.

On their return, Lydia felt happier than she had for several months. Not even on their honeymoon had Edward been kinder or more attentive. She was not sure why this should be, but put it down to the fact they were away from the Manor and forced to share the same bedroom and on occasions the same bed.

When Mrs Cresswell came Lydia was able to catch up on village gossip. The big talking point had been Jeremy's disappearance from Ridge House. Everyone knew he was no longer there, but no one knew the reason. This led to wild speculation in Mrs Reece's store and ribald jokes in *The Mitre*.

'Mrs Davies at the almshouse is in hospital and she's not expected to return home,' Mrs Cresswell went on, as she stacked the breakfast things in the dishwasher.

'That'll mean another vacancy at the almshouse then.' Lydia smiled to herself. As Grimley Heath had triumphed over London in the last round, Mrs Kirkpatrick might now get her place but this time wild horses would not drag from her so much as a raised eyebrow.

'Would you make some pies this morning. Use up the apples in the pantry. I'll get some more from Tom later this week.'

'Righto.' She went to get the fruit.

'And sit down to do it!' Lydia ordered.

'Yes, ma'am.'

Recently Lydia tried to arrange tasks that did not involve Mrs Cresswell lifting or standing. It had crossed her mind to suggest she no longer came, but she had had no success in getting Edward to agree to Susie's return. Anyway, Lydia valued her company as much as her help.

'Did you enjoy your trip to Denmark?'

'It was wonderful, they made us so welcome. Doesn't Edward look like his cousin – or should it be the other way round?'

'I don't know. To my knowledge he's not been here, but as I told you before, Edward doesn't take after his father or the Casleigh grandparents. I think this likeness to his mother has been a source of distress to him all his life.

Hoping to glean some extra information, she asked. 'What did Edward used to call his mother when he was little? Mummy?'

'No, it was something that sounded like 'moor'. I believe it was Danish for mother, but I'm not sure. After he was about five or six he rarely called her anything, and when he was older he called her Mother. Relations between them were always strained.'

'Did you know Edward's aunt is only nine years older than he is? That's a huge gap between her and Edward's mother.'

'All we knew when William married Jette was that she had a little sister. But we didn't talk much; it wasn't done. It was more like in his grandfather's day. Jette Casleigh was not the most approachable of women when she was here.'

As Mrs Cresswell rolled the pastry, Lydia said, 'I'll freeze one of those when it's cold. We'll have the other tonight.'

'There's one other piece of news you missed. There's been a prowler about.'

'Really, what a lot has been going on in our absence. What's this prowler been doing?'

'He's been spotted round the orchards. Tom's seen him and Mike Lucas, but when they've approached him, he's run off.'

'Do the police know?'

'Yes.'

'I'll tell Edward so he can check on our security and watch out for anything suspicious.'

*

On their first anniversary Lydia met Edward in London. They dined at the Knightsbridge restaurant where he had first taken her. She could not help marvelling at the turn of events that brought her here again. She still might not feel as sophisticated as the women around her, but she certainly was as well dressed. She smiled.

'What's amusing you?'

'I was thinking what a nervous wreck I was when you first brought me here.'

'I thought you were rather sweet.'

Why could he not have said that at the time? It was almost the only compliment he had ever paid her.

They went on to a theatre then stayed the night at the Dorchester.

'It's been a lovely evening, thank you so much.'

'It's not over yet, I have something for you.'

Lydia had showered and was drinking a glass of champagne. She was wearing the satin gown she had worn on their honeymoon. Edward had removed his tie and jacket. He handed her a square, emerald box. She opened it to reveal a gold bracelet, a solid band resting on its moulded satin cushion.

'It's beautiful, Edward. I haven't a bracelet of my own.'

Beguiled by the better relationship Lydia thought they had reached since their holiday, she put her arms round his neck and pulled his head down to kiss him. At first he returned her kiss with the same feeling, but then reached up and took her arms from his neck and she was left, as ever, deflated and uncomprehending.

Lydia brushed away the tears that were slowly forming and climbed into the double bed. She pulled up the covers till her head was barely visible.

When Edward joined her she had almost cried herself to sleep. She felt him move close and put his arm on her shoulder, brushing her skin and reaching his fingers into her hair. Lydia lay still and breathed deeply and evenly. If Edward thought she was in the mood for lovemaking, he would have a long wait. At the moment she felt so crushed she doubted she would ever allow him near her again.

After a while Edward turned over and went to sleep, leaving her bleakly awake.

*

Lydia picked up the wicker basket from the pantry and went to her car. She was about to unlock it when she felt the early autumn sunshine on her face. Leaving the car, she strolled down the drive and across to the footpath.

As usual her thoughts turned to Edward who was rarely out of her mind. How could he be when they lived together but were so far apart? Since the night of their anniversary they had returned to their strained existence. More time than ever he spent in his study. She watched TV or listened to music, then took him a drink and went to bed.

Looking for some explanation, Lydia decided it was the Manor that had a hold over them. Both Jette and Frances had fought and been released. Edward was imprisoned and would always be. And herself? The house had seduced her and she had allowed it to, and Edward was the agent that kept her there. So, from the chaos of her mind she absolved him. But why the need to find excuses? She gave a grim smile. Was it because she loved him? Could one love a man and dislike him at the same time?

A hand came over Lydia's mouth. She dropped the basket in panic as she was drawn backwards and struggled to keep her balance. She could not breathe and shook her head from side to side fighting for air. The hand moved, and in that fraction of a second, she opened her mouth and bit with all the power she could muster. Her assailant swore and she twisted free and fled without turning round.

As she neared the farmhouse she shouted, 'Tom, help. Help me.'

Lydia hurled herself at the kitchen door, crying 'Tom, where are you?'

She turned to go out into the yard, fearful that the man might be waiting for her, but Tom was standing in the doorway. Relieved, she threw herself at him and he clasped her close and stroked her hair. He could feel her trembling in his arms.

'What's the matter? Is it Edward, has he upset you?'

'No, it's a m-man. He grabbed m-me.'

'Did he hurt you?' Tom held her away and studied her face. 'Where was this?'

'Up there,' she indicated vaguely. 'On the footpath, b-by the hopfield.'

'I bet it's the same man we've seen recently.'

'He put his hand over my mouth. It was horrible.' She drew in a deep breath. 'I – I bit him.'

Tom held her close trying to calm her with soothing words. As she relaxed, he sat her in his battered armchair and went to make tea.

'Are you sure you won't have something stronger? I have whisky or brandy.'

'No.' Lydia thought of the brandy Edward had given her. 'Thank you.'

Shall I walk you back?'

'No, no! I don't want to go back along that path.'

'Were you out for a walk?'

'I was coming to get apples. I dropped my basket when he attacked me.'

'I'll get it for you.'

'Don't!' she cried, 'he might still be there.'

Tom smiled. 'OK, I'll drive you back, but I can't leave right now. Will you be all right here till I get back?'

'Can you lock the door?'

'Look, you lock it and I'll knock when I come back.'

*

Tom helped Lydia from the Land Rover and went with her into the Manor kitchen. Lydia switched on the light and sat down at the table then stood up almost immediately. She stared at the clock but did not register what it said. Tom was uncertain what to do or say next.

'You'll be all right now, so I'll go.'

'No, don't. Don't leave me alone.'

'But you're quite safe here.'

Lydia glanced at the clock again. 'Dinner, I must get dinner. He'll be home in a minute.'

'I'd better be going.'

'Wait till he comes home, he won't be long.' She heard a car door slam. 'Ah, there he is now.'

Lydia went to the front door and rushed down the steps to Edward, who was opening the garage.

'What's up?' He saw Tom and frowned. 'What's happened, Tom?'

'She was attacked by someone on the path to the farm.'

'What!' He turned to Lydia. 'What did he do? Did he hurt you?'

'No, but I was very frightened. He put his hand over my mouth and I couldn't breathe.'

Lydia turned her face into his city suit and Edward put his arms round her.

Tom looked away. 'I'd better be going. I've rung the police, I expect they'll get in touch.'

Edward kissed the top of Lydia's head and, without looking up, said, 'Right.'

Tom moved to one side to let them into the Manor.

'Bye,' they said in unison.

'And thank you for bringing me home.'

∗

'Guess what, Pat? It's the latest rumour I've picked up this morning.'

'Well, what?' she said, putting his sandwiches in front of him.

'Told to me with great glee by Chris Barrett from the farm.'

'Oh, get on with it, Jamie.'

'My big brother and Lydia Casleigh are having an affair.'

He studied Pat's face to see her reaction. 'You don't seem surprised,' he said disappointed.

'No,' she said slowly, 'I would be surprised if it had got that far, but Tom does fancy her.'

'How do you know? Did he tell you?' Jamie said, his mouth full of his favourite cheese and pickle sandwich.

'No, but you can see it in his eyes and when he speaks about her. Didn't you notice when Lydia turned up at your Mum's that evening? Who started this anyway?'

'Susie Patterson is supposed to have seen them with their arms round each other and kissing at the farm.'

'For a start you can take anything Susie says with a pinch of salt. She'd tell you the moon had fallen from the sky if she thought it would get her some attention.'

'Trouble is,' Jamie said, 'people would rather believe it than not. It's more exciting. I enjoy a bit of gossip myself.'

'That's the drawback. I expect there's some simple explanation. Your Mum'll no doubt find out and tell us in time.'

∗

That evening Jamie was in the bar of *The Mitre* when his brother came in. Conversation practically came to a stop, and even the darts players, in the throes of a match, turned to stare at Tom.

'I'll get you a beer. Pint?'

'Thanks.' Tom leaned one elbow on the bar and rested is foot on the rail, quite unaware of the interest he had caused. When the beers were drawn, Jamie took them to a table in the corner.

'You're playing with fire, aren't you?'

'What?' Tom took a swig of his beer.

'Messing around with the squire's lady.'

An awful feeling settled in the pit of his stomach. 'I haven't been messing around. Who's been tittle-tattling?'

'Susie Patterson, I gather.'

Tom looked relieved. 'That must've been when Lydia was attacked a couple of days ago. I told you about it.'

'You never told me about you and Lydia Casleigh.'

'I mean about the prowler.'

'Well, was she in your arms?'

'No – yes, but not like you think. She ran away from this man, but I wasn't in the house, but I'd seen her from the barn. I went into the kitchen and she threw herself at me.'

'Lucky you.'

'I meant she was upset, stupid!' he almost shouted. 'What else could I do? Anyway, I took her home and waited till Edward came in, so it's all above board.'

'I wouldn't bank on that. Does he know you had your arms around his wife?'

'I hardly had time to say anything. I wasn't there above five minutes after he'd come home.' Tom took another mouthful. 'What would I say – "By the way, Edward, we stood in my kitchen with our arms round each other – hope you don't mind."'

Tom met his brother's serious scrutiny.

'Did you kiss her? That's part of Susie's tale.'

'No I did not.'

'Pat says you're in love with her.'

Tom stared into his near-empty glass.

'Want another?' Jamie asked.

'No, I think I'll go when I've finished this.'

'I fancy one.' Jamie went to the bar and returned with his replenished glass. 'Is it true?

'What?'

'That you're in love with her.'

'Yes.' Tom stared ahead gloomily.

'Does she know?'

'Yes.'

'You're a fool. What on earth possessed you to tell her? She's only got to let a word slip – well, you know what Edward's like. He won't think twice about turfing you out of the farm – or trying.'

'He doesn't love her.'

'Did she tell you that.'

'Not in so many words.'

'You're assuming too much. She's Edward's, like all his other possessions. You remember that! Think about that summer he came home from school – it was as if he had never known us.'

'How could I forget.' Tom drained his glass. 'See you, Jamie. I can rely on you to put the record straight, can't I – and to forget what I said?'

As he left, it seemed more people than usual called Goodnight.

*

For a Saturday morning it was unusually quiet in Grassenden's main street. Shirley Reece went outside the store to check on the vegetables displayed in wooden boxes.

As she turned and straightened her back, she saw Edward Casleigh drive on to the forecourt of Jamie's garage. She wondered if Jamie knew of the rumours about his brother and Mrs Casleigh, and what sort of conversation they were having at this moment.

She did not believe the stories. Susie Patterson was well known for her far-fetched tales. Though Shirley Reece loved a bit of tittle-tattle as much as the next person, she did not go on this one.

Old Tom was a confirmed bachelor. Only ever had one girlfriend as far as she knew, but Joy Baxter and her parents had emigrated to New Zealand, so nothing came of that.

Funny set-up there – the Cresswells and the Casleighs. Mrs Reece recalled the boys when they were all at the village school. She would have been about ten. What a change in positions. Those two brothers used to watch over Edward Casleigh like a hawk in the playground, and outside. Poor kid, he looked scared to death most of the time, a target for bullying if ever there was one, tall and skinny with that near-white hair. Maggie Cresswell must have primed her boys well. Even Jamie, at five, used to see off anyone who dared attack Edward in his presence, and he was inches taller than either brother. Strange how it all turned sour. Good friends even after he went away to school, then suddenly....

Now there's another mystery, Shirley thought, as she watched Edward leave the garage and walk up the drive of Ridge House. Where is Jeremy Detrale?

*

'How lovely to see you, Edward, come in. Coffee?' He followed her to the kitchen. 'What can I do for you? Or have you just called to see me?' she asked, hopefully.

'It's about the almshouse. Mrs Davies has died, I've been told, so there'll be a vacancy. Instead of having a meeting, I propose Mrs Kirkpatrick be given the place, unless someone in Abbotts Lidiard or Grassenden emerges in the next few days. I'll contact David and Prue Viger. I don't suppose there'll be any objection as we discussed it fully.'

'Yes, we did, didn't we?'

Edward frowned. He did not like Serena's tone and now he thought about that evening, she had been a bit spiteful towards Lydia.

'Do Lydia and Tom Cresswell see much of each other?' she asked.

Edward's chin came up and his eyes narrowed. 'Why are you asking?'

'Oh, just a story that's doing the rounds. I expect it's just someone's idea of a joke.'

'Tell me what you've heard.'

'That your wife and farm manager were seen embracing and kissing at the farm.'

A wave of jealousy surged inside him when he thought of Tom with Lydia, but with his practised self-restraint, he gave the appearance of disbelief.

'You surely don't believe it?'

'I'm only telling you what I've heard,' she said, sweetly. 'They do seem to have a great deal to talk about, and that's only what you see and she tells you.'

Serena lifted her cup to her lips and her bracelets shunted up her arm. She took a sip, eyeing him over the rim. His face fell into bleak lines.

Serena put down her cup and reached over to close her hand over his.

'You know, she was never your type. I mean – what sort of background has she? She's out of her depth at Abbey Manor. A farmer is more her type.'

'You don't know anything about her so you're in no position to comment,' he said, tersely.

In all the years Edward had known her, he had never spoken to Serena in such a manner.

She quickly changed the subject. 'I had a phone call from Jeremy on Monday. He's bought a flat in the Barbican.'

'Oh yes.'

'He'll be near his office.'

'Yes.'

Edward looked fixedly into the garden. Serena moved his cup and saucer away and took them to the sink.

'He had to pay quite a bit for it.'

'Did he?'

She rinsed the cups and saucers and placed them on the draining board.

'I'd better be going, I have to get my car from Jamie's. He said it wouldn't be long.'

He levered himself from the chair and walked to the front door. Suddenly realising he had heard but not taken in what she had been saying, he asked, 'Are you coping?'

'Yes, it's a bit strange rolling around in this house on my own.'

'I know how you feel,' he said, recalling the years after Frances' death.

Edward opened the front door and gave her a peck on the cheek.

'I'll ring you.'

Chapter 9

'I've brought your basket back,' he said, as Lydia opened the door.

'Come through, Tom.'

'I'm sorry I've been so long returning it,' he said, putting the basket on the table, 'but we're very busy. I've brought you some apples. I wasn't sure what you wanted, so I've put in eaters and cookers.'

'Great,' she said, eyeing the fruit, 'that's more than I could have carried.'

'How are you – no after effects?'

'No, not really. To tell you the truth, I haven't been out since Tuesday. When I do, I might feel differently, especially if I go along that footpath. I'm sorry I behaved like such a baby, but I was so scared. I thought he was going to kill me.'

'I'm glad you're OK,' he said, softly.

Edward came into the kitchen.

'Do you want a coffee?' Lydia asked.

'No, I had one at Serena's.'

'Oh, I didn't know you were going to see her. I thought you were taking the car to Jamie's.'

'I did, but as I had to wait, I thought I'd call in.'

'I'll be on my way then,' Tom said.

'Tom brought my basket back – the one I dropped. He's filled it with apples.'

'So I see.'

'I must pay you.' Lydia went to her bag.

'Don't bother,' Tom said, 'have them…'

'She'll pay you,' Edward snapped.

Lydia looked from one to the other, then took a note from her purse and thrust it into Tom's hand saying, as she pushed him into the hall, 'I'll see you out.'

At the front door, she said, 'Something's upset him. I'll sort it out.'

Tom went to speak, but she put a finger to her lips.

Edward was sitting at the table scowling and drumming his fingers.

Wearily she said, 'What's up now? What've I done this time? I presume it's me that's committed some crime?'

'What does Tom mean to you?'

'Mean to me?' she said puzzled.

'Yes, are you – fond of him?'

'Fond? It's not a word I would have chosen but yes, I suppose I am. I would be upset if anything happened to him. Why do you ask?'

'There's a rumour going around that you were kissing him at the farm.'

Lydia was stunned by the accusation, but was even angrier with Edward.

'And you believe it.' It was a statement, not a question.

He stopped tapping his fingers.

'And who told you this?'

'It's all round the village.'

Lydia spoke softly. 'That's not what I asked.'

'Serena.'

'Ah, and who told her – or did she make it up?'

'Serena wouldn't do that!' Lydia raised an eyebrow. 'I don't know who told her,' he admitted.

'And you didn't think to ask,' she said, contemptuously. Her eyes flashed as she became angrier. 'And when were Tom and I indulging in this passionate embrace? Or was there more than one occasion?'

At his silence, she said, 'So you don't know when it happened, you don't know who saw it and you don't know who is spreading the rumour – apart from Serena. What you do know is that it's true.'

'I didn't say that.'

'You didn't have to, your attitude and questioning said it all.'

Lydia stood by the table looking down at him. 'You can believe what you like, Edward. Why should I deny it? As you don't love me, it can only be your precious status that's been upset. You couldn't care less about my reputation. You don't see it as your duty to defend me, or to find out the truth do you? And Tom – you don't like him, though I can't see why. But even worse, you don't like me liking him. There are many things you can coerce me into doing, but choosing my friends is not one of them.

'I trust that in Jeremy's absence you were not seen passionately kissing Serena. I would hate such a story to get about. I might, just might, be upset. On the other hand, I don't think I'd much care.'

*

His head felt it had been in a tumble-dryer. Lydia would not deny the incident – but her very words told him it was not true. She said she was fond of Tom, she said she did not care about him. Did she really say that?

Edward went to his study and stood by the window gazing at the lawn across the drive. After Frances' death he had spent hours here. It was like a cocoon and he had returned to this refuge during the past year to stop himself thinking about his marriage. Edward sat in his chair and swivelled round to face the desk. He opened the drawer and saw the box containing Lydia's birthday present. He took it out and lifted the hinged lid. Inside was a mahogany-backed hairbrush and in silver filigree were her initials. Shutting the lid and replacing the box, he removed some papers and put them on the blotter.

The pencil pointed up and down the columns, but all Edward could think about was Tom – his closest friend until he was fifteen. Unbidden a picture of the village school rose up in his mind. Whenever he passed the playground it still made him shudder. From his first day he was teased and taunted. "Are you the boy from that old house up the lane?" "How d'yer get that hair, bit early for going grey" "My mum says your mum's a foreigner and speaks funny." He was pinched and punched and had things taken and hidden. Finding all the school lessons easy was another cause for persecution. The only time he had any peace was when Tom was around. He was a year above but, whenever he could, Tom would quietly break up groups that gathered round him. Jamie, always spoiling for a fight, would see off any boy or girl who touched him. Life was little better when he was sent away to prep and public school.

In Edward's fifteenth year he filled out and was already six feet tall. His hair darkened slightly and he began to notice that girls would look at him admiringly. He realised he was not bad as he had come to believe. Villagers would tell him how good-looking he was and like an unveiling he realised he had some worth, that perhaps there was nothing wrong with him.

Edward put down the pencil and pushed back his chair.

That July was a turning point in his life. He had been to fetch his clean clothes from Matron to pack in his trunk. Everything else was ready for going home the following day. As he put the shirts on top of his other clothes Leo Sandley-Brown, a tormentor from prep school days, came to his room and leaned against the door.

'Hello Alby,' he said, using a name he had long suffered, 'going home to Mummy.'

'My mother won't be there, she's abroad with my father.'

'Oh – can't she stand you either?'

It was not the spitefulness of the remark, but the truth of the words he had uttered. Edward took a giant step towards the boy and grabbed both lapels of his blazer in one large hand, and with the other, swung his clenched fist. He swung again, but the force of the second punch tore Leo from Edward's grasp and he fell, clattering the table and chairs. This brought others from the corridor who crowded round excitedly, as boys do when sensing a fight, amazed at the identity of the aggressor.

Edward bent to pick up the luckless Leo, now bleeding from the nose and mouth, and was about to hit the staggering boy again when a hand stayed his.

'That's enough, Edward,' his friend Nigel said. 'I'm sure you've made your point. Come away.'

Nigel took him along the corridor, telling a younger boy to fetch a master and another to see to Leo, who was being helped to a chair.

The boys could not stop talking about the strange turnaround and most agreed it had done Casleigh no harm at all. Edward's housemaster had other considerations and whilst he might have agreed with the boys' sentiments, Leo and his parents might not see the fight in quite the same light.

'Hand hurt?' he enquired when he saw Edward's bruised knuckles.

'A bit, Sir.'

'What was it all about, Casleigh?'

'A remark he made, Sir.'

Mr Carradene thought the boy must have heard every insult that could have been hurled at him in his short life. 'What remark?'

Edward stared at his shoes.

'Do I gather that perhaps you had just had enough.'

'Yes, Sir.'

'Though I don't condone what you've done, I think you might find the rest of your time here less, shall we say, disagreeable. Only you can fight your battles, you can't expect others to protect you. Bullies thrive on shy and reserved boys like you are, with a distinctive feature that makes them a target.'

Mr Carradene put the tips of his fingers together and rested them on his lips.

'I think an apology to Sandley-Brown is in order and we'll hope his injuries are superficial and his parents don't pursue the matter.'

He viewed the handsome boy through his thick-lensed spectacles. He also knew what it was like to be bullied, but Mr Carradene was never destined to be the wealthy, personable young man who stood before him now. From now on this boy's life would be all plain sailing. Edward Casleigh had everything on his side.

'There will, of course, have to be some punishment for starting this fight, but we can deal with that next term.'

'Yes, Sir.'

'You can go now. Goodnight.'

'Goodnight, Sir.'

'Enjoy your holiday – Edward.'

In the light of what his housemaster had said, it was the summer that Tom and Jamie were viewed in a different light. No longer did he see them as his childhood friends, but as boys who had fought his battles. Along with his new-found confidence he acquired a chip on his shoulder and despised the brothers for what they had done.

With a fifteen-year-old's logic, he reasoned that if they had not interfered, he would have taken things into his own hands earlier and so would not have suffered all these years.

He told Cressy about the fight and she sympathised as she always had. He loved her dearly, more than anyone else in the world – the one stable and steadfast person in his whole life. How he envied those boys: Tom and Jamie always had their mother's love. All he had was a loveless home and an oppressive school.

*

Edward tipped his head on one side. The house seemed strangely quiet. He thought he would have heard Lydia moving about preparing lunch. He wandered into the kitchen and saw the note resting against the fruit bowl in the middle of the table.

> *Edward*
>
> *I have gone to the farm.*
>
> *Lydia.*

✳

When Lydia returned he was in the kitchen. She steeled herself for the recrimination she knew would greet her.

'As you weren't here,' he said, frostily, 'I started preparing lunch.'

'Good.'

'Well?'

'Well what?'

'What were you doing at the farm?'

'Why do you want to know?'

'Because you're my wife and I expect to be told.'

'You sound like someone from a Victorian novel.'

'Tell me what you were doing there', he demanded, his voice rising as he lost his composure.

Lydia's eyes gleamed with uncharacteristic vengefulness as she said, 'I ran into the farmyard and flew into the arms of my lover and we went into one of the barns and…'

'Stop it! Stop it!' he shouted.

He took a step forward and she thought he was going to hit her. She had no intention of losing the initiative, and explained, 'I went to find out the truth about these allegations, something *you* should have done.'

She saw him slowly calm himself and they prepared the rest of the meal in silence. Edward was obviously not interested in her feelings as he made no attempt to discover the outcome of her visit.

When they were seated Lydia told him that Mrs Cresswell was going to the hospital for tests.

'I'm glad she's been to the doctor; she hasn't looked well for some time. Perhaps you'd go and see her one evening.'

'Yes, yes, of course I will.'

After a further period of silence, he said, 'I have to go to New York at the end of October. I want you to come with me.'

Lydia grunted. As usual there was no request – would she like to go, would it be convenient?

'No thank you,' she said, stonily. 'I prefer to stay here.'

He stopped eating and Lydia noted his look of disbelief. She returned the look, her eyes almost black. She took her plate to the draining board.

'I'm going out again in a moment. I shouldn't be more than an hour.'

*

Lydia drove the three miles to Grimley Heath and knocked on the door of the terraced house.

'Mrs Casleigh!' Mrs Patterson stood in the doorway surprised and confused.

She was a dressed in a blouse and skirt under a shapeless cardigan, which she now drew together as if for protection.

'I would like a word with Susie, please. Is she in?'

'She's in her room.' Mrs Patterson remained flustered till she remembered herself and invited Lydia in. She moved to the bottom of the stairs, and called, 'Susie, come down. There's someone to see you.'

A radio was silenced and there was a great deal of thumping then Susie appeared at the top of the staircase.

'I would like a word with you, Susie. Will you come down?'

Seeing how frightened she looked, Lydia gave her a brief smile.

'Go in there, Mrs Casleigh,' Mrs Patterson said, opening the door to a front room, and standing back to let her through.

'I would like you to stay and hear what I have to say.'

'Now, Susie,' Lydia began, 'I went to Abbey Farm this morning because I had heard rumours were being spread that involved Tom and me. I wanted to find out who would have done such an unkind thing. Tom told me it was you.' Lydia waited for a reply. 'Was it you?'

Susie lowered her head. 'Yes.'

'What did you see that caused you to do this?'

'I was at the farm – Tom doesn't mind – and I were passing the kitchen door and – I saw you – you were standing – and – and – Tom *did* have his arms round you,' she said defiantly.

'Do you know why I was in the kitchen with Tom?'

'No.'

'A man had just set upon me. You knew about this prowler, didn't you?'

'I didn't know you'd been attacked, honest.' Tears trickled down her face.

'I was very frightened at the time and Tom was trying to calm me down. Wouldn't you have wanted someone to do that in the

120

circumstances?'

The girl nodded.

'But that only deals with part of the story. It has also been said that we were kissing. That was not true, Susie, and you know it.' Tears were now flowing freely. 'Why did you do this? It has caused me a great deal of unhappiness and aggravation. And,' Lydia emphasised, 'my husband.'

'He sacked me!' she sobbed.

'I do not like lies spread about me, whatever you think about Mr Casleigh – and I want you to do something about it.'

Susie took a handkerchief from her skirt pocket and blew her nose loudly 'I dunno what to do.'

'You can talk about it with your mother when I've gone if you like, but I suggest that you write to my husband and tell him exactly what you saw – and say you are sorry. Then apologise to Tom and lastly, that you tell everyone you meet what exactly did happen, and that the tales you have been spreading are not true.' Lydia smiled at her. 'Will you do that for me?'

'Yes, Mrs Casleigh.'

Susie's mother, who had been sitting by the window gazing at the passing traffic, turned round and said to her daughter, 'And you can start by saying sorry to Mrs Casleigh.'

'Sorry,' she said, sniffing and wiping her eyes.

'When you've done that, I will see if you can have your job back, but I make no promises. I think you understand why.'

With many embarrassed apologies, Mrs Patterson saw her out.

*

Driving back to the Manor, Lydia felt acutely despondent that she should have had to clear her name, but relieved she had found out what had actually caused the tales to circulate.

She could not help smiling at the scene at the farm earlier that morning when she had strode into the barn where the men sat eating their midday sandwiches. They positively squirmed when she demanded to know who had spread the tale. Though they had not started it, Chris and Mike had both been guilty of fanning the flames. Even Tom looked uncomfortable, and when they were out of earshot, Lydia forcefully told him she was none too pleased that it was not mentioned to her as soon as he had known – and what was *he* going to do about the gossip?

Susie managed as good a job with her second story as she had with the first. The villagers said they had not believed a word of it, and was it not funny how these stories got about – and they always knew the sweet Mrs Casleigh would never allow such a thing to happen. To add weight to Susie's declamation, the prowler was arrested the following week on a neighbouring farm.

On Lydia's birthday, Edward gave her the hairbrush and she thanked him without giving him even a cursory kiss. Lydia liked this present better than the bracelet he had given her, but she could not find the grace to say how much. She even refused his suggestion they go out to dinner.

Now, they spoke only when necessary and Lydia carried out the functions of a housekeeper. Edward began to come home late from work; sometimes he would mention it at breakfast; at others he would ring during the afternoon.

The letter he received in Susie's misspelled, large handwriting was received with nothing more than a 'umph', as he threw it to one side at the breakfast table.

'Is that from Susie Patterson?'

'Yes.'

'I get the impression that you'd rather believe the rumour than the denial.'

'I don't want to discuss it any further.' He got up from the breakfast table and prepared to leave. 'I shan't be in at the usual time tonight. I might even stay up in town.'

'You seem to be extraordinarily busy lately. What has brought this about?'

'Er – it's the trip to New York, the one you do not wish to joint me on. It's been postponed and it's caused a lot of work.'

Lydia knew he was lying. 'Very well,' she said, 'if you're not coming home, I won't bother to prepare a cooked meal.'

*

'If you're not busy, come and see me when you've finished shopping,' Faith said, when she met Lydia in the village.

Busy! She was never busy; her life seemed totally pointless. The Manor no longer cast its spell and was just a place she lived in – miserably.

When they were settled in the Vicarage's sitting room, Faith said, 'You're not looking well, Lydia. You've dark rings under your eyes.'

'I've not been sleeping well lately.'

'Something bothering you? Want to talk about it?'

'Not really. Edward and I aren't seeing eye to eye at the

moment.'

'Has it anything to do with the story of you and Tom Cresswell that went the rounds?'

'Partly.'

'Did you know,' Faith said, eagerly, 'Susie Patterson went around telling everyone she had made a mistake and what had really happened. I was quite impressed.'

'That's nice.' Lydia wondered if it had been worth all the hassle.

'Are you sure you're al right? Shall I ask David to have a word with Edward?'

'No, things will no doubt work out given time. I'm just hoping that one day I might stop being treated as an extension of my husband.' Realising what she had said, she exclaimed, 'Pretend you didn't hear that.'

'I'm really worried about you. You won't be able to go on like this. It's not good to bottle things up. I don't want to pry, but isn't there someone you know that you can talk to? What about your friend – the one who came to your wedding? She seemed very nice.'

'Jill, you mean. Yes, I'll give her a ring.'

'You do that,' Faith said, relieved.

She had no intention of doing any such thing.

∗

Lydia was preparing a drink prior to bed that evening when she was surprised to hear Edward's car draw up. She was wondering whether he was expecting something to eat when she realised from the commotion coming from the porch that he was not alone. She went into the hall and gasped in surprise.

Chapter 10

Edward was swaying in the doorway supported by his friend Nigel, whom Lydia had not seen since their wedding.

'Whatever's wrong? Is he ill?' Her stomach turned over then she realised that Edward was drunk.

'He didn't drive home like that, I hope?' she exclaimed.

'No, thank God. I happened to see him coming out of the station. I was on the same train. I could see the state he was in, so I got him to take me to his car and I drove here.'

They struggled to get him to the drawing room and into a chair.

'I'll get a strong coffee. Would you like one?'

When she came in with the tray, Edward was slumped in the chair with more of him out than in. Ill-at-ease, Nigel sat opposite.

Edward took the mug Lydia held out and grinned stupidly. 'Have you met my wife, Nigel?' He took a gulp of his coffee. 'Course you have, you were at our wedding.' He laughed inanely. 'She prefers the local farmer, you know.'

Lydia's cheeks burned and Nigel shifted in his chair.

'Edward!' he exclaimed, 'Think what you're saying.'

'Oh, yes,' he continued unperturbed, 'They were seen kissing – in the barn, wasn't it?'

'Please don't speak like that,' she pleaded, 'please.'

'Well you said – you said – didn't you – didn't you say "'I won't deny it." You did, you know.' He laughed and waved his mug in the air.

Lydia turned to Nigel. 'I am sorry about this, I don't know what to say. I'm afraid…'

'He's just had too much to drink, take no notice, I'm not.'

But Edward had not finished. 'D'you know Nigel – she only married me for my money and she couldn't even produce a son.'

Nothing Edward had ever said before compared with this ultimate humiliation. She was mortified, her face on fire, her whole body shaking. She wanted to disappear, like a cartoon character, without having to walk from the room.

Nigel also looked as if he would rather be anywhere than where he was. Both of them stared at Edward still sprawled in his chair. The grin had left his face, but his silence made Lydia angrier than his words had previously. She wanted to shout and scream – hit him even.

Perhaps sensing her need, Nigel moved towards the door. 'I must go,' he said.

Lydia had her hands clasped pressing into her lips as if she could not trust herself to speak. She followed him into the hall.

Hoping he would refuse, Lydia said, 'It is late, you could stay the night.'

'No, I don't think in the circumstances it would be a good idea.'

She fought to keep the tears back and when Nigel turned away, she quickly wiped her hand across her eyes. 'Let me drive you home'

'Oh, no, I can't impose on you.'

'Nigel, there are no buses and you live the other side of Maidstone. Are you going to walk?'

'I can get a taxi.'

'No, I insist.' Having to concentrate on driving might take her mind off this ghastly night.

As they left Grassenden, Nigel said, 'You mustn't mind what he said, he is very drunk. I'm sure he didn't mean it.'

Lydia wanted to ask him questions, but she hardly knew him. All she did know was that he and Edward were friends at school, but they did not appear close now.

'I'm sorry about this evening. We are going through…'

'There's no need to explain, I know Edward. He's not an easy person to get on with, but he needs someone like you.'

'Does he? What as?'

From the corner of her eye she saw Nigel turn his head sharply. She should not have said that.

'Which way now?' she asked, as she turned to go down towards the river.

They stopped talking while he guided her through the town. Finally they drew up outside Nigel's large detached house where, he told her, he lived with his mother.

'There is one thing you can tell me. Do you know what it was that made Edward turn against his childhood friends?'

'The Cresswell brothers, do you mean?'

'Yes, he's jealous of Tom and, as you may have gathered, thinks I am having an affair. Ever since he first took me to see the farm, before we were married, their mutual antagonism was apparent. According to Tom's mother, all three were once friends. What went wrong?'

'I don't know for sure, but what I suspect is this.'

'When he ceased to be bullied,' Nigel said, after relating the tale of the fight, 'it was like a metamorphosis. When he came back that September he was a different person. He no longer confided in me, which was sad as previously we used to talk when he had had a particularly hard time. I was his only friend in school, though even to me, he was never forthcoming – always reserved. But with his new-found confidence, he built a wall round himself which prevented anyone getting near.'

Lydia could see that – she was battering herself against it constantly.

'I don't know what happened when he went home, but if he was behaving like he did when he came back that September, they would be feeling betrayed.'

Nigel opened the car door. 'I'm grateful for the lift. I hope it's not too long before we – before Edward's recovered.'

'Goodnight, and thank you for taking care of him. I dread to think what would have happened to him had he driven.'

*

Edward was no longer in the drawing room when she returned to the Manor. She went up to his room and found him lying on top of the bed half undressed. With difficulty she pulled the duvet from under him. He stirred, but did not wake as she covered him.

*

Tom came out of the bathroom. He picked up his watch from the bedside table, wound it and set the alarm for six. He arched his back and rubbed his eyes; weary after the paperwork he had been doing all evening.

He pushed his long legs down the bed and drew up the covers. Putting his hands behind his head he gazed at the ceiling and thought of Lydia. He had to admit he was lovesick and felt more like a seventeen-year-old.

It had begun at the dinner Lydia had given. Edward had done

everything he could to humiliate her and she remained so dignified. Anyone could see she was unhappy. Even his mother had to admit the marriage was a strange one and, in her eyes, Edward could do no wrong.

'If only you were married to me,' he said out loud.

Tom looked at the clock – twenty past midnight. He switched off the light and settled down. In that limbo between being awake and sleeping, the phone rang. He ran downstairs worried that his mother might be ill.

'Hello, Mum?'

'Tom?' A woman's voice – not Pat or his mother.

'Lydia?'

'Yes, it's me.'

'What's wrong?'

'I just want to talk.'

'You're not ill, are you?'

'No.'

Tom could hear her crying softly. 'What's the matter? Why are you crying?'

'I'll be all right in a m-minute.'

'Where's Edward?'

'He's asleep upstairs. He c-came home d-drunk. Nigel, you know his friend, saw him at the station and drove him home.

'Drunk? I've never known him drunk.'

'He – he said the m-most dreadful things Tom – about me – and the b-baby.'

Lydia began to cry distressingly. He could hear her sobs and his heart ached to think he was so far away when he wanted to hold her close.

'What did he say?'

'He said I c-couldn't even p-produce a son and – and I m-married him for his m-money.'

'People do say things they don't mean when they've had too much,' Tom said, trying to comfort her, but wanting to tell her what a bastard she had married.

'That's – that's what Nigel said,' she gulped.

There was no sound from the other hand. Tom waited.

'He was – oh, why is he so cruel to me. I'm so miserable. I don't think I can stand it any more. You were right – he is destroying me.'

'What are you going to do?'

'I have to get away – I can't stay here any longer.'

'Are you going to leave him?'

'I don't know. Yes, I think I must.'

Tom was elated, his mind skipping to what might be. 'When are you going?'

'In the morning.'

'Are you going to tell him?'

'Not unless I have to, I can't face any more humiliating scenes.'

'Where will you go? Can I come and see you?'

'I'd like to see you too, to say goodbye properly. I'll find a hotel and ring you. I'm sorry for disturbing you, I just wanted someone to talk to.'

'I'm glad you did.' He paused. 'Lydia?'

'Yes?'

'Nothing, it'll wait till I see you.'

*

Edward opened his eyes and quickly shut them. Pain throbbed at the base of his neck and above his eyes. He licked his dry lips and lifting his head he saw he was partly clothed. He fell back on the pillow and tried to clear the fog that was his mind. What day of the week was it? What time? He raised an arm to look at his watch, but the light was too dim. How had he got here? What happened last night? Was someone visiting?

Edward struggled up on one arm and peered at the clock – a quarter to ten, or was it ten to nine? Gingerly he put his feet to the floor and stood unsteadily. He stumbled through the bathroom to Lydia's room. Bed was made, all was neat, unusually so. He went back to the bathroom.

He turned on the shower and let the water hit his face. He remembered going to a bar near Charing Cross Station. He was going to stay in town but he wanted to see Lydia – but she did not love him – so he drank some more till he did not have to think of her at all. He dressed and went downstairs and into the empty kitchen where he saw the envelope.

Gradually scenes from the previous night filtered into his mind. Nigel! Lydia's face! He tried to pretend his mind was playing tricks, but from the painful knotting in his stomach he knew he had said dreadful things.

Edward picked up the envelope and, with reluctant fingers, opened it and drew out the folded sheet.

Dear Edward

I have tried to be what you wanted me to be
– what I think you wanted me to be – you see I
am not even sure of that. But I've failed. Not
least in providing you with the son you so desire.

I cannot mould myself in your likeness and if
I stay, I fear you will take from me the only things
that are truly mine – my will and my nature.

I've taken the coward's way out by writing
because I'm afraid of facing you.

I'm sorry to break our contract. I did truly try
to keep my side of it.

Lydia
PS I rang your office and told them you were ill.

Edward let the letter fall from his fingers. He felt sick and rushed to the cloakroom. He took a glass from the cupboard and filled it with water, which he drank in one go. He moved to the table, drawn like a magnet to the letter. The phrases leapt out at him. *What you wanted me to be – you will take from me things that are truly mine – I'm afraid of facing you.*

'Afraid of facing you,' he said out loud. Fifteen years he had spent in fear, now he had inflicted the same on her.

Edward leaned against the worktop and her face rose before him. Her lovely blue eyes, her sweet smile. She had not smiled much lately.

Where would she go? Jill's perhaps – he'd ring this evening. Perhaps she had gone to the farm – but he could not bring himself to ring Tom.

He felt slightly better after a coffee and toast. Last night he had drunk on an empty stomach, no wonder he felt ill. What had he been thinking about?

But it was not *what* – but *who?*

He changed from his suit into sweater and trousers. As he came down the stairs of the miserable house, the phone rang. His heart leapt as he hurried to the drawing room.

'Is that you, Lydia?'

'Oh,' the voice said, 'I was expecting Lydia. Flustered the voice continued, 'Is that Ed – Mr Casleigh.'

Disappointed, Edward said, 'Of course.'

'It's Pat. I wanted to tell her – you – that Jamie's Mum has had the results of the tests and has to go into hospital. I thought you'd like to know.'

'When – when has Cressy to go?'

'Tomorrow. I don't think – it's not good news.'

'Oh.' Edward could not believe his whole life was disintegrating with every step he took. 'Oh,' he said again, 'I'll go and see her. Is she at home?'

'She is now, but this afternoon she's staying with us so we can take her into hospital in the morning.'

'Well, thank you for telling me – us. Goodbye.'

Edward put the phone down and collapsed into an armchair.

*

Lydia booked into a hotel in Tonbridge, the first she was conscious of seeing. She had no idea where she was going when she left the Manor. Her aim was to get away as fast as she could.

She lay on the bed, too dejected and exhausted to think any longer. It was four o'clock before she woke to a darkening room. She called reception and asked for sandwiches and tea, then she rang Tom.

'Lydia! Where are you? Can I come and see you.'

'Now?'

'Yes.'

Desperately wanting to talk to someone, she gave Tom instructions and said, 'I'll tell reception you are expected.'

*

'It is good to see you, Tom. I am sorry about last night, I expect you were asleep. I wasn't thinking straight.'

'I'm pleased you did.'

He studied her closely then moved towards her. He reached up his hands to cup her face and kissed her.

'Let's go away, you know I love you,' he said.

'You couldn't and I wouldn't.'

'I suppose you are thinking about Edward?'

'Of course, I'm married to him.'

'More's the pity'.

Lydia took his arms from her shoulders and her eyes were gently reproachful.

'You're doing the unforgivable, Tom, playing on my vulnerability like a drug pusher. I'm sorry if I have misled you, but I felt so alone last night I just had to speak to someone, someone I thought would understand.'

'But you don't love me,' he said. 'But you can't love Edward.

You can't. Not after all he's done.'

Lydia gazed out of the window at the shops across the High Street.

'No, but I could.'

'I won't stop loving you, you know.'

Lydia turned from the window and smiled sadly. 'I value your friendship more than I can say and I'm sorry things could not have been different for you.'

'What'll you do now?'

'I'll look for somewhere to live. As soon as I find something, I'll write to you. You won't say anything to Edward, will you? I'll get in touch with him when I feel I can cope and think straight.'

✳

Neither Edward nor Tom told anyone that Lydia had left. It was not until three days later that the village became aware all was not well at the Manor.

Edward was to read the lesson on Sunday. He did not want to and had sat by the phone in his study on Saturday wondering how he could tell David without giving anything away.

He had found Jill's number but did not ring. He came across Charles Kingley's also, but could not bring himself to phone him either. The dreadful sense of uncertainty was coupled with the fear he might never see Lydia again.

The few villagers who attended St Luke's noted Lydia's absence. Not even when she was in hospital had Edward Casleigh come alone. David noticed, and as soon as Edward reached him in the porch he said, 'Is Lydia not well?'

Edward knew the question was coming, had even rehearsed what he would say, but now it had been asked, he was tongue-tied.

'She's – I don't know, she's not ill.'

'Go to the Vicarage,' David ordered. 'I'll join you in a moment.'

When Faith opened the door Edward said tonelessly, 'I've come to have a word with David,'

She frowned. 'Come in, he's not here…'

'No, I know. I've just left him.'

Edward went to the study window and stared across the Vicarage garden to the school and its playground. It was the scene of so much misery but not as much as he was feeling now. How often had he looked over to this house and wished he could escape through its door and seek out the kindly Reverend Dunster.

David indicated an armchair in front of the Victorian tiled fireplace. He switched on the electric fire and took the chair opposite Edward.

'What's wrong?'

'Lydia's left me.'

'Why?'

'You don't seem surprised.'

'Come on, man' David admonished. 'You can't go on pretending things are all right just to keep up appearances. Why not start at the beginning when you first met Lydia.'

'Oh, it started long before that.' Edward sat, elbows on knees, his head in his hands. 'My mother never wanted me, you know. Didn't even want to come to England for my birth, but my father insisted.'

'How did they meet?'

'My father was with the Embassy in Copenhagen. She was a dancer. I don't know the actual circumstances of their meeting, but they married in Denmark soon after they met. It probably seems strange to you, but I know little about my parents. We hardly lived with each other and didn't talk much when we were.'

Faith came in with a tray and left without speaking.

'My grandmother was furious when she was told about their marriage. She'd never even met my mother till she came home to have me and by then they must have been married three years or more.'

'From what you say, you had a very unhappy childhood'

'Childhood! I had no childhood. From the day I was born, Cressy told me, I was left alone for hours in the nursery at the top of the house. She said I used to cry, but no one heard me. Cressy used to come and pick me up and eventually she arranged that I spend time at her house. After that I practically lived there. I'm sure my mother was only too glad to get rid of me.'

'Cressy? Would that be Tom's mother?'

'When Cressy wasn't there – if I upset my mother, which I did most of the time, she would drag me upstairs and shut me in the roof. There were high windows and it was dark, full of old furniture and cobwebs and spiders. I was petrified. I've had nightmares all my life that I could never recall, till Lydia made me face up to them. If it weren't for Cressy, I'd have run away.' Edward's eyes wandered round the room, and then he gave a mocking laugh. 'No I wouldn't, I would have been too afraid. I was frightened of everything and everybody. I was conspicuous when I wanted to be insignificant. I was a coward when I wanted to be brave and fearless – like Jamie Cresswell. One day I could not stand it anymore.'

'And?'

'A boy at school said something and I flipped and I hit him, and hit him again.' Edward made a fist, which he punched into his left hand and screwed up his face as he relived the moment.

'Then what?'

'I decided that no one – no one was ever going to make me suffer like that again.' Edward raised his eyes and looked David in the eye as if defying him to disagree. 'Nobody was going to tell me what to do or fight my fights. No one was going to get close to me, that way I'd never be hurt.'

'And you were happier?'

'Yes.'

'You don't sound sure.'

'Somewhere along the way I lost Tom and Jamie. I shut them out along with everyone else.'

'Why was that, do you think?'

'I was jealous.'

'Jealous? Jealous of Tom and Jamie?'

'But don't you see, they had love all the time, not just in the holidays. I was a boy who was shunted somewhere out of the way – to school, embassies, my grandmother's – or left with Cressy knowing she wasn't my mother, but theirs.'

David never ceased to be amazed at what made people tick. 'Go on.'

'Then I met and fell in love with Frances.' Edward smiled a twisted smile. 'She was beautiful and I thought at last someone will love me. But I soon found out she didn't love me either, she had only married me for the position she gained. Frances went on her own sweet way doing exactly as she wanted as if I weren't there.'

'And Lydia?'

'Ah, Lydia, she was part of a new plan. The Manor and its contents entranced her so I persuaded her to marry me to give me an heir and in exchange she would have, what I considered they all wanted, money and position. Love had no part in it.'

David gasped in disbelief at this bald statement.

'I know, David. I stood before you making vows I had no intention of keeping. No loving – no cherishing. We hardly knew each other, it was to be an arrangement.

'So I plied her with expensive gifts and resisted her at every turn. As she became liked and admired, the more resentful I became. The more I tried to keep her at arm's length, the more I was – I was falling in love.' Edward blinked several times. 'My strategy was so successful that I've driven her away. I even made her afraid of me. Ironic, isn't it? All the things that had been done to me I was now doing to her. I couldn't see she was not like Frances. Lydia wasn't cynical or calculating, Lydia was – is…

'The other night I came home drunk and I said the most terrible things. I accused her of having an affair even though I knew it wasn't true. Not only that, I said it in front of someone else. Now she's gone.'

'Do you know where?'

'No, she has a friend Jill, and the man she worked for in London. You saw them at our wedding, but I don't think she'd go to either place.'

'So you haven't tried?'

'No.'

'Why?'

'Because it would be too humiliating to admit she's left and it's all my fault.'

'But soon you'll have to admit it – to everyone.'

'I've to go to New York tomorrow and I can't get out of it. So I won't be able to do anything till I come back.'

'Would you like me to ring her friend Jill and – who was it?'

'Charles Kingley. No, I must do it myself.'

Edward pushed himself from the chair. 'Thank you for listening.'

'That's what I'm here for and as a friend.'

When David had seen him out he went back to his study and watched Edward go through the gate and across the churchyard. He wondered if he could have helped if he had known him as a young man. Somehow he thought not. Edward was a victim of both his character and upbringing. However much he now acknowledged his shortcomings, relationships were never going to be easy for him, even less so without Lydia.

Chapter 11

'A whisky and mineral water.'

'Certainly, Sir.'

Edward stared out of the aircraft's small window. He should be sorting out his notes for his report, but matters he had tried to push to the back of his mind now fought to crowd his every waking minute – and sleeping ones, too.

Lydia and Cressy – the two people he held most dear. One gone and perhaps, by now, he had lost them both. The first cable told him Cressy had cancer and the second she was failing fast and hoped he would be home soon.

When the whisky arrived he drank it straight, followed by a few sips of water. Here he was, a man adept at masking his emotions, reduced to an indecisive wreck, vacillating and irresolute. He did not know where Lydia was so he could not go and see her.

He pressed the button for the attendant. At least the drink relaxed him, though it did not make him forget, only getting drunk did that and look where that had got him. He adjusted his seat, leaned back and closed his eyes in the hope that he could find some momentary relief.

*

There was the note on the floor of the porch as soon as he opened the door to the Manor.

> *Mum wants to see you. She keeps asking*
> *for you. Come as quick as you can when*
> *you get back.*
>
> *Jamie*

The phone rang and Jamie's voice came down the line.

'At last. I saw your car pass. Can you come right now?'

'Yes, I've just read your note.'

Edward hurried down the lane and unlatched the gate to go along the lavender-bordered path. Lavender was the smell he associated with Cressy from the time she had held him close, soothing his anguished sobs in the nursery at the top of the Manor.

He turned the handle and pushed open the front door. Pat was sitting at the table. Jamie came through the door at the foot of the staircase as Edward entered the room.

'Go on up, Mum's awake.'

Jamie, usually so chirpy, looked tired and downcast. Head bowed, Edward went through the low doorway. He mounted the narrow twisting stairs he had climbed so often as a child and turned into the first room.

Cressy lay propped up. She was gaunt – her usual fat, rosy cheeks yellow and her eyes were sunk in her head. Edward could not believe anyone could change so much in so short a time. She turned as she heard the latch lift.

'Come – sit here.'

Edward perched on the chair with the cord seat. It made a pattern of four triangles. He remembered that chair because it had to come down if Tom's father were eating with them. Jack Cresswell – he had not thought about him for years. Edward was away at school when he had died but Cressy had seemed the same as ever when he had come home for the holidays. He had never known her sad. How must she have felt losing her husband? Did she feel as he did now? He had never considered how Tom and Jamie had taken the loss of their father.

He clasped Cressy's hand in both of his. He swallowed hard and took a deep breath to get his voice under control.

'How are you?' he asked forlornly, futilely.

'Not long now, Edward.' Her voice was thin. 'Lydia.'

She tried to move nearer to him but the effort was too much. Edward drew his chair closer so he could catch her words.

'You treated her very badly, you know that, don't you?' She paused, gathering her thoughts. 'And it's you that has driven her away.'

Edward nodded.

'Have you ever loved her?'

'Not to begin with. She was attractive, not beautiful like Frances – but she had – has – she was pretty,' he finished lamely.

'And she served a purpose.'

He flinched. Cressy's pale blue eyes were watering and she moved her hand from within his to wipe them. Edward left his hands resting on the counterpane.

'And now?' she said.

'I don't know what to do, Cressy.'

'Is that really true? You do, but you can't bring yourself to do it, can you?'

The clock on the bedside table showed it was eight twenty-seven. It ticked loudly in the quiet room. No sound came from below, not even through the thin plaster and lathe ceiling. The three boys could never get away with playing about at bedtime because whatever they did the noise could be heard downstairs.

'You love her now, but you didn't want to. You used her as a whipping boy to pay back your mother and Frances for the pain they had caused you. I don't know what you did to persuade her to marry you, but she didn't deserve the way you treated her.' The effort of speaking was taking its toll. 'I've never criticised you, Edward. I think, perhaps, I should have done, but I've always tried to understand. I knew of your suffering mentally and physically, but you have a nature that does not bend.' She paused, and said half to herself. 'Had you seen more love perhaps things might have been different.' She closed her eyes.

'What shall I do, Cressy? I don't know where Lydia is.'

'Ask Tom, he might know. Ask Tom. But only if...' She started to cough, but tried to finished the sentence. '... only if you love ...'

It was too much. Edward took the cover from a jug and poured water into a glass. Pat came into the room as he raised it to Cressy's lips.

'I think Mum ought to rest now,' she said.

He put the glass down and wiped her cracked lips. He bent over, clasped Cressy in his arms and kissed her, his throat closing and hurting as he tried to hold back the tears. He knew this would be the last time he would see his beloved Cressy.

Her words went round in his head as he looked back before he went down the dark staircase. *Ask Tom, he might know.*

Jamie sat at the large table where they had had their meals together. Edward remembered the rare occasions he had Cressy to himself, and how he would pretend he lived at the cottage and that she was his real mother. He made no comparisons then with the Manor and this humble room. One was a place, the other a home.

'Do you think she'll live through the night?'

'Dr Gifford doesn't think so.'

'I'm going to the farm now, shall I tell Tom to come?'

'You can if you like.' Jamie's voice, like Pat's, was cool and impersonal. 'He said he'd be coming soon anyway.'

'Well, goodnight Jamie, Pat.'

Jamie muttered 'bye' as he shut the door.

Edward walked up the lane, past the Manor and between the hedges on to the public footpath. The night was cold but still, the stars sharp and clear in the cloudless sky – a beautiful night. In contrast his heart was heavy and tears formed which he could not stem.

Lights shone from the downstairs windows as the farmhouse came into view. He blew his nose before knocking on the kitchen door.

'Oh, it's you,' Tom said. He turned away leaving Edward to shut the door. 'Beer?'

Edward sat down at the table while Tom went to the fridge and took out two cans, and from the dresser, two glasses. He poured the beer till the froth reached the top, then pushed the glass and the near empty can towards Edward.

Tom took a long draught and licked the froth from his lips. He emptied the rest of his can into the glass and sat down.

'I assume this isn't a business or social call?'

'I've just been to see your mother. She said to ask you…' He stopped, hating to ask anything of anyone, especially Tom.

'Ask me what?'

'If you know where Lydia is,' he said quickly.

'It's taken you long enough to ask. I'd half expected you to come thundering on my door as soon as you discovered she had gone. Well, she's not here, if that's what's been worrying you. My God, if anyone was too good for you it was Lydia. You must be the male chauvinist pig of all time. How my mother loves you like she does I'll never know.' His jaw tightened as his anger rose. 'Do you know, she loves you more than she loves us? She's always made excuses for you and when we could see for ourselves what an arrogant bastard you were, she still said we should make allowances.'

Edward took the onslaught of words like punches.

'Suppose I do know where Lydia's gone, what are you going to do? Get her to soothe your fevered brow – take up where Mum has left off?'

Edward reached for his glass. He wanted to assert his authority, subdue Tom to his will. He drank the beer and Tom reached over for the can and put the rest into Edward's glass. The beer brought back some of his arrogance.

'Well, are you going to tell me?'

Tom went to the shelf above the old range and reached behind the clock. He picked up a letter and gave the top sheet to Edward.

Flat C
16 The Slip
Barnes

My dear Tom
Thank you for your letter. I
was aware Edward had to go
to New York.
Do keep me posted. As you
have realised I have grown to

Edward turned the sheet over, but there was nothing on the back. He was tormented by the unfinished sentence.

I have grown to love you, Tom – I have grown to hate Edward. but she did want to know about him. Would she want that if she hated him?

Edward wanted to snatch the rest of the letter from Tom. His hand trembled as he handed the letter back.

'Don't you want to write the address down?'

Edward had memorised it, but he said, 'She'll know you told me.'

'Well, what is important to you? Do you love her? Do you want her back? If so, on what terms?'

Edward banged his clenched fist on the table making the glasses jump. A can fell over leaving a trickle of beer as it rolled across the surface.

'Don't, don't! I can't stand it.'

'Well, what *are* you going to do,' Tom insisted, ignoring Edward's outburst.

'I'll write to her – or ring.'

'She's not on the phone.' Tom took another gulp of beer. 'You won't go and see her, will you, because you're afraid?'

'Afraid?'

'You'll have to eat humble pie, climb down from your ivory tower and admit you've been unkind. No, that's too weak a word – cruel, that would be nearer the mark.'

'All right, all right,' he shouted. 'I'll go and see her.'

Edward finished his beer. 'I've just come from Cressy's. She's – she's…'

But he was unable to hide how he felt and rushed from the kitchen so Tom would not see him cry.

When Edward had left, Tom re-read the rest of Lydia's letter.

> … *to love him in spite of how he treated me. I wouldn't have thought it possible to love and hate somebody at the same time. Your mother would understand, though I am sure you don't.*
>
> *Had I told you about my former boss, Mr Kingley? I called into the shop to learn he'd died two weeks ago (I wish his nephew had told me). He has left me some money, so I'm thinking of buying a flat and with the money Edward allows me, I should be able to manage. Which brings me to my second piece of news.*
>
> *Because I wasn't feeling well, I signed on with a local doctor. I thought he'd say I was run down, but he examined me and said I was pregnant. My feelings are very mixed, as you can imagine. Please don't tell Edward. I shall have to think carefully about the baby's future before I tell him. He desperately wants a son, but a son without a mother – I don't think I could bear that.*
>
> *Anyway, you know I shall be pleased to see you – but just as a friend please. Write again, and thank you for your shoulder to cry on.*
>
> *How did the tests go? Is your mother any better?*
>
> *Lydia*

Tom replaced the letter behind the clock, took his jacket from behind the door and left for his mother's.

*

Edward stepped from the footpath into the lane. The closed and darkened barn reminded him of the first time he had seen Lydia.

He slept fitfully and dreamed alarmingly. A young Cressy was waiting for him with arms outstretched and smiling as she had when he came home in the holidays. As he ran towards her she changed into the dying woman he had just seen. Behind her stood his mother with her cold, cruel eyes, who turned into Frances with her cynical smile. He ran into the Manor desperately searching, searching, but once inside he could not remember what he was seeking. He peered through the window to the garden and saw Tom and Jamie laughing at him, and holding something in their hands like a trophy.

Edward woke with a start. His watch said five-thirty. He put on his dressing gown and walked through to Lydia's bedroom. He switched on her bedside light spreading a soft glow, serving only to heighten her absence. He wandered over to the dressing table and picked up the hairbrush with her entwined initials, which made a pattern of loops. He reached for the perfume in the cut glass bottle, which she had told him she liked.

Edward pulled open a drawer. There lay the sets of lingerie he had brought back from Hong Kong. His fingers ran over the soft silk garments and he recalled how she had come to show him, and the overwhelming desire he had had to kiss her.

He opened the doors of the wardrobe: there were the evening dresses, the blue velvet for their engagement, the ivory lace for the Christmas function, the pink and the black. Nothing he had given her or paid for was taken. Lydia had left them all wanting no reminder of him or their marriage.

He reached for the jewellery box which had been his mother's, but he could not bring himself to open it; could not bear to touch the jewels he had given Lydia, to feel the misery flow out of his fingers as he picked them up. Would her engagement ring be there, the opal pendant, her wedding ring?

When he had dressed, he drove down the lane, stopping only to enquire about Cressy before heading for London.

Skilful driving had always been something he took pride in. Even as a teenager he had had no desire to speed around just for the sake of it. Now he had to make an effort to concentrate. An irate mother, with two small boys on the back seat, had already honked at him.

He parked in a side road near the river and began searching for Lydia's address. It turned out to be a large double-fronted house overlooking the river. He walked to and fro outside, then leaned back on the embankment wall, looking at the house wondering which were her windows.

Would she be pleased to see him? Of course she wouldn't. She hated him, she was afraid of him. There was no point in seeing her: he should not have come. He turned to go back to the car as she came out from the front door. Seeing him, she smiled fleetingly and raised her eyebrows.

'Hello, Edward, how did you know where to find me? Did you ask Tom?'

'Cressy told me to ask him.'

'Ah,' she said, 'of course.'

A boat chugged down the river, a train rattled over the railway bridge, people passed – jogging, strolling, chatting. They stood facing each other waiting for the other to speak.

Edward said at last, 'I want you back, Lydia. I miss you, I need you. Please come back.' He added feebly, 'I don't know what to say.'

Lydia's face was serious and unsmiling as her eyes searched his. She seemed to have changed, grown taller, though he still towered over her.

'What is more important – needing me, missing me or wanting my return?'

'Funny, Tom said that – what's important?'

'What else did he say?' she asked, sharply.

Over the months I've grown to... 'Nothing, just gave me your address.'

They fell silent again. Eventually she said, 'I don't think coming back is a good idea. You hurt me so much. I know I must take some blame for agreeing to our arrangement, but I did think we could find some common ground, some companionship.' She drew in her breath and let it out slowly. 'I never knew I was to be the scapegoat for the women in your life who'd wronged you. You hadn't told me that was part of the contract.'

Edward recoiled. He thought of Cressy's words. *You used her as a whipping boy.*

'Cressy died last night.'

'Oh.' Lydia put out her hand and placed it on his arm. He took comfort from her touch. 'Oh, Edward, how dreadful. Tom told me she was going to St Catherine's, but I had no idea it was that serious.' Tears filled her eyes. 'I can't believe it. I'll miss – you will miss her dreadfully.'

'It was cancer, she went downhill fast, if you could've seen her.' He shot out the words as if saying them quickly would help to erase her from his mind. 'You know, she was the only person who ever loved or cared about me.'

Lydia opened her mouth to speak, but closed it and followed him as he started to walk.

He was bruised by her reaction, but half expected it. What had he to offer? The money, the house, the position, she did not want those things. He stopped and turning to face her put his hands on her shoulders.

'You don't believe I love you, do you?'

Lydia looked deeply into the sad eyes. 'I don't know, Edward. I don't think I understand you at all, though I have tried. I recognise your vulnerability, I feel your needs, I understand your motivation – most of the time, but you live in a world where only you matter. Everything you do, even what is done for other people, seems to be for your benefit. For all I know your love is the same. You told me love did not come into our marriage. I've seen little to make me think it has developed, have I?'

'Do you remember our wedding night?' Edward's head jerked in surprise. 'That huge queen-sized bed and me saying *I hope you can find me.'* Sadly she looked up at him. 'You never did, did you? But then you never bothered to look.'

'Is there's nothing I can say to persuade you to return?'

Lydia hesitated a fraction. 'No.'

The sadness in her eyes as he bent to kiss her was almost more than he could bear. He turned away and crossed the road. A taxi hooted as he stepped in front of it.

'Stupid fool,' the driver shouted prophetically.

Chapter 12

They met again at the funeral. Edward in the front pew saw her sitting across the aisle with Tom and the rest of the family.

An even more humiliating time was spent at the farm trying to make small talk while his eyes followed Lydia as she moved around the farmhouse kitchen and best room. She seemed part of the Cresswell family as she helped Pat with the food, while the brothers saw to the drinks. Edward had to make an effort to find anything to say to people, most of whom had known him all his life. He caught snatches of conversation that dried up as he approached and sensed eyes staring at him that focussed elsewhere when he glanced in their direction. He had never felt so mortified, so out of control, in all his adult life.

They were all pleased to see Lydia, and he watched as they sought her out to tell her their family news. Jamie's children chatted to her as if she had known them all her life. He had barely acknowledged their existence though he should have been like an uncle.

When most of the guests had gone and all the Cresswells were in the kitchen, he found himself alone with Lydia as she plumped up cushions and collected glasses. He recognised the black jersey dress, which she wore under a fitted jacket with gilt buttons. Round her neck was the repaired necklace and matching earrings. She looked so pretty. His eyes sought her left hand and the sight of the gold band with its fine chasing was strangely comforting.

'Lydia.' She looked up. 'Will you come back with me to the Manor – just for a while – for old time's sake.'

Edward could see she was about to refuse by the way she raised her shoulders slightly as if to say what's the point. He forestalled her. 'Please.'

'Tom's going to drive me to the station,' she said, 'my car's out of action.'

'I can take you.'

'It would be rude to leave now, I am Tom's guest.'

'But you will come?'

'No. No, I don't think so. I'm not sure it will achieve anything. What we have to say to each other can be said through solicitors, don't you think?'

Desperately, he said, 'I want you to come.'

'Is that another ultimatum?'

'No, no, I didn't mean it like that. You've got me confused.'

'You mean you don't know how to react, don't know what words to choose or that what you say will be disparaged. It's easily done, you just need practice.'

He looked at her pleadingly.

'Oh, all right, but I can't see that there'll be anything to gain.'

*

'You're doing what?' Tom exclaimed aghast.

'Please don't shout at me.'

He glared at her across the kitchen table. 'You're mad. You're making a big mistake. I only gave Edward your address because you told me you loved him. I want you to be happy, and if it has to be Edward – OK, I'd accept that. But you turned him down! What's changed?'

Hurt and confused he paced round the kitchen table like a wounded animal.

When he had written to ask Lydia to the funeral, he could hardly believe it when she told him she had refused to return to Edward. The way was now open for him.

Dolefully, Lydia said, 'He looked so unhappy.'

'Unhappy! Unhappy!' Tom shouted. 'Edward always looks unhappy. It's his stock-in-trade.' He was beside himself with frustration. 'Divorce him and marry me.'

'You know that's not possible. Even if I wanted to marry you, Edward and I couldn't live so close. Neither could you give up farming – it's your life. And there's the baby.'

Tom grappled to find a solution. 'We could emigrate – it isn't my farm.

Calmly Lydia said, 'You're not thinking straight. You've had a harrowing time – we all have. And Edward – Cressy was like a mother to him. He is bereft.'

'You don't have to tell me that.' Tom's voice cracked out. 'It was my mother who sent Edward to me for your address, even though she knew how I felt about you.' His voice rose with anger,

'Edward, Edward, Edward. I don't know what that man's got – apart from a great deal of money and no charm – but everyone makes excuses for him.'

Lydia went to speak.

'And don't tell me he had a hard childhood,' he shouted.

'Right, I won't.' Her face was grim as she buttoned her jacket, picked up her bag and left, slamming the door behind her.

*

Lydia saw Edward watching for her through the kitchen window as she walked up the drive. He opened the oak door with a flourish, pulling her into the hall.

'I was afraid you wouldn't come – that Tom would stop you,' he said, as his fingers slid into her hair. Her hat fell to the floor as he kissed her so long and hard, she had to push him away to draw breath.

'I love you, I want you, I've missed you more than I can put into words. There – that's in order of importance.'

He took her hand and hauled her along the passage and up the stairs. Her bag dropped from her shoulder.

'Edward! What are you *doing?*' she protested, as she tried to pick it up, but he continued up the stairs taking her with him.

He looked down on her from the step above and gave a lovely smile. 'I want to prove to you how much I love you.'

He raised her to the stair he was on, and wrapping his arm about her, they went to his bedroom.

He kissed her eyes, her nose, her mouth. He took off her jacket and his hands reached round and unzipped her dress, which slid to the floor.

'Let me show you how much I love you, Lydia?' he said, as he nuzzled into her neck.

'Is this wise?' she asked, weakening. But wise or not, she was in no state to refuse.

*

Lydia woke before it was fully light. She lay wrapped in thoughts of the previous night. A delicious feeling spread through her, troubling and delighting her in equal amounts. He had told her he loved her in all the languages he knew, and she laughed as she named ones more and more obscure so he had to make them up. Lydia told him these were lovelier than the real ones.

Carefully, so as not to wake him, she moved to raise herself on one arm.

'There are still problems to face,' she said softly to his sleeping face. 'Love doesn't conquer all.'

Edward's fair hair, ruffled from sleep, fell over his forehead in attractive disorder. She pushed the strands back with the tips of her fingers and was enveloped in a bear hug.

Eventually she drew herself away. 'Edward, we've got to talk.'

'I'd rather make love.'

'Yes, well, we've done that. We have to discuss things.' He began to caress her. 'Please be serious.' Fancy asking Edward to be serious.

'Then can we make love?'

'That's blackmail,' she said, but she was not laughing.

Edward sat up, a look of alarm on his face.

'About our contract,' she began.

He gave a sign of relief. 'I don't want a contract.'

'Marriage is a contract, and anyway, the reason for our marriage is still there.'

'We can still have a son? You do want children, don't you?'

'You've always known I've wanted children, but I want to know that five daughters aren't going to walk around the Manor awaiting a brother like the coming of the Messiah.'

'You don't doubt our fruitfulness then?'

Lydia smiled then. 'People don't change overnight. You're arrogant, unfeeling and thoughtless.'

'I'm not that bad. Am I?'

'And you're a bully.'

'No I'm not!' She looked directly into his eyes. 'I'll stop being a bully.'

Lydia took a deep breath and said, softly, 'I'm pregnant.'

Edward turned away locking his hands behind his head. She felt a strange chill at his silence and the change in the light, bantering mood.

'Aren't you pleased?'

'Is it mine?' he said.

Rage, swift like an avalanche, swept over her. She shot out of bed and her eyes flashed as she stared at him in horror. She tried to speak but no sound came. She wanted to scream. Edward was calling her an adulteress. She, who had upheld the sanctity of their loveless marriage. *Marriage!* The very word mocked her.

Lydia scooped her clothes from the floor and went into the bathroom. She needed to shower, to cleanse from her body all traces of Edward, but she could not bear to stay in the house. She went through to her bedroom to dress. It was as she did up the buttons of her jacket that her body began to react. Her knees buckled and she trembled so violently she had to sit on the bed. Then she flung herself across it and wept.

That is where Edward found her – face down, arms outstretched, a sodden handkerchief clutched in one hand, sobs jerking her shoulders. She felt his hand touch her tentatively as if she were a coiled spring, and he was afraid of the reaction. He lifted her so she was sitting beside him and pulled her close so her head rested on his chest. Her shoulders still rose and fell with residue sobs.

They sat like that for some while, till Lydia, her voice trembling, spoke.

'How could you make such a despicable, hurtful remark? Do you know so little of me that you think I'd come to you knowing I was carrying another man's child, or even seen anyone else.' Edward hung his head. 'Doesn't this prove what I've just been saying?'

Lydia released herself and walked over to her dressing table where she searched for a handkerchief. She sat down in her button-backed chair, calmer now, but her heart still thumped and her head ached from crying.

'I suppose you think it's Tom's – or maybe you think I've been playing the field. What cause have I ever given you to think I've been unfaithful?'

'Tom loves you.'

'So that makes *me* unfaithful?' She left her chair and went to the window. She gazed out on to the parterre. 'I wanted someone to confide in. Tom was kind and I needed kindness, but I don't fancy him and he knows that. He has always known that.'

Lydia half turned to look at Edward. His shoulders were slumped, his eyes cast down.

'I have no family – not even a Cressy, but it's never occurred to you that I might feel as you do – unloved? But I wasn't unwanted, was I?'

'I don't know why I say the things I do. I can't believe what I said just now.'

He crossed to the window and put his arms around her and pulled her close.

'I know people don't change and that I'm all the things you say

I am.' He turned her towards him and wiped a stray tear from her red-rimmed eyes. 'I suppose I can't believe someone might love me.'

Lydia wished she did not love him, it would be easy to go. She felt tired and empty and needed time to think about herself and Edward, and the coming baby. Material things had once blinded her. Was she now letting herself be blinded by promises of love – that most intangible of emotions?

'I meant what I said about loving you,' he said.

A common thought. Lydia remembered how Robert and Elizabeth seemed to be thinking about the same things at the same time. Was this togetherness? Were they getting on the same wavelength?

'I think you do, and I love you, but we can't go on as before.'

'I know.'

'I want to share with you, not be ordered around.'

Lydia looked into his sad brown eyes and knew exactly why Cressy had loved him so much – and why Tom could not understand.

'If you don't change, I'll leave you again.'

Edward could not see the small movement at the corner of her mouth. 'I don't think I could bear it,' he said.

'Not only that,' she said, grinning, 'I'll take all five daughters with me.'

'You're staying that long, are you?' He smiled his beautiful smile and kissed her the top of her head. 'I promise to be a reformed character.'

'Not too reformed, parts of you are quite nice already. I don't think I could live with perfection.'

'Not much chance of that from what you've said.'

Part II

The Farm

Chapter 13

'Do me a favour, Tom. I'm ever so busy.'

'What d'you want?'

'Run Mrs Detrale's car up to her? She particularly wanted it this morning and I said I'd do my best.'

'Must I? Can't I do something else while you take it?' he grumbled. 'You know how much I dislike the woman.'

Jamie grinned. 'Not unless you can take out this engine.'

'Oh, very well.'

'And while you're there, see if you can get her to give you a cheque straightaway. She always pays, but weeks later. I don't suppose she realises some people have to live hand to mouth.' Jamie wiped his hands on a cloth and went into his cupboard-sized office.

'You don't live hand to mouth, do you?' his brother said alarmed.

'No, not quite, but you know what I mean – cash flow.'

Jamie printed the invoice and handed it to Tom.

'Right. What shall I say?'

'Hold out the bill and say, "Would you like me to take a cheque back to save time?"' Jamie peered at Tom's face. 'Are you all right, you seem put out? Something wrong at the farm?'

'No everything's fine.'

'Good. It's the silver BMW over there.'

Tom backed the car from the garage forecourt and drove up the main village street. He turned right into the drive and drew up alongside the canopied front of the Edwardian house, the grandest in the centre of the village.

He rang the bell and stood uneasily. Their paths had only crossed when Lydia came to Abbotts Lidiard and Serena Detrale had always managed to make him feel small – either by ignoring him or making some disparaging remark. She had also made Lydia's life miserable and had probably contributed to her leaving

Edward. Mrs Detrale and Edward were two of a kind – patronising, arrogant and rich.

'Oh,' she said, taken aback when she opened the door.

'My brother asked me to bring up your car, as I believe you need it. He's a bit busy.' He held out the bill and was about to give his rehearsed speech when she said, 'Come in and I'll write you a cheque.'

He followed her into the kitchen. She took her handbag from the worktop and sat at the table.

As she wrote, she said, 'I see Edward's wife came crawling back to him. I expect she realised what side her bread was buttered.' Her eyes met his and she smiled slyly.

'That's about as far from the truth as you can get,' Tom burst out angrily. 'It was Edward who did the begging and even then she refused. He had to trick her into coming back.'

Serena jumped up. 'I don't believe you, Edward isn't like that. He'd never go crawling to anyone, least of all that – that...'

'Well, it's true. She'd be better off on her own than with him.'

Her hand swished through the air giving Tom a stinging slap across his face. He did the same.

Horrified, he could not believe what had just happened. He was even more unnerved when her face crumpled as she sat down and burst into tears. Was she injured? He did not know his own strength. Had he broken her jaw? Visions of lawsuits and newspaper headlines flashed before his eyes.

When he finally spoke his voice came falteringly. 'Have – have I hurt you? I'm so sorry – I don't know what came over me.' Tom thought she had stopped crying, but her head remained on her arms. 'Can I get you something – some water perhaps?'

Slowly she raised her head and reached into her bag for a handkerchief. She wiped her eyes and delicately blew her nose.

'This is most embarrassing,' she said, in her cultured voice. 'I do apologise.'

Tom felt some relief at hearing her speak, and the threat of court action receded, but he was still appalled by what he had done.

'I've never hit a woman in my life. I wouldn't dream of – it's not...'

Serena jumped up and straightened her skirt. 'Let me get you a coffee.'

'No, really, there's no need. I'll be going.'

'Don't look so scared, I'm only offering a coffee. Sit down.'

'Yes, right – thank you.'

She busied herself with the percolator, only speaking when she put the mug in front of him.

'Milk, sugar?'

'Please.'

She brought out a basin from a tall cupboard on the wall. 'I don't take sugar. Jeremy used to take it – three spoons – you could stand your spoon in it.' She grimaced.

Tom tipped his mug and drank half the coffee in one go, burning himself in the process. The thought of being in Ridge House was unlikely in itself, but to think he had just slapped the face of Mrs Detrale was a nightmare scenario.

She broke into his thoughts. 'I was sorry to hear of your mother's death, she was very highly thought of in the village.'

'Yes.'

'Edward was terribly upset.'

'I know.'

'They were very close.'

'Yes.' He rose, shifting his weight from one foot to the other. 'I must go. Jamie'll wonder what's happened to me.'

'I suppose he will.'

'You are all right, aren't you?' he said, inspecting her face closely.

'Yes.'

'I'm afraid I caught you with my ring,' she said, raising her braceleted arm to touch his cheek. Tom jerked his head away and backed out of the kitchen before turning to walk to the door. He fumbled to open it, but there were too many knobs and catches.

'Here, I'll do it,' she said, brushing past him. 'Thank you for bringing the car.'

'My God, you've been a long time,' Jamie said on his return. 'What d'you do, take her for a test drive?'

'She gave me a cup of coffee.'

'My, my we are going up in the world. You'd better watch your step, she'll be after you now her husband's off the scene.' He gave a loud guffaw.

'Don't be silly. What would she want with a farmer whose hands are always dirty? I probably earn in a year what she spends on clothes.'

'Did you get the cheque?'

'Damn, I left it on the kitchen table. Shall I go back and get it?'

'Don't bother, she'll bring it down. At least it's written.' He examined his brother's face. 'You've a cut on your cheek. She didn't attack you for asking for the money, did she?' He threw back his head and gave another boisterous laugh.

'Of course not, I must have caught it on something.' Quickly he changed the subject. 'Now, about that tractor. Could you come up to the farm and look at it some time? I don't think it's terribly urgent but bringing it down here causes such congestion on the lane. Mike thinks it's something that could be fixed easily.'

'If it's that simple, why couldn't he do it?'

'I told him not to meddle in case he makes it worse.'

'You're a bit of a fusspot where machinery is concerned. OK, I'll try to get up today, that suit you, brother dear?'

*

'Hey, look who's 'ere.' Chris Barratt poked his companion. 'Never seen her here at the farm, wonder what she wants?'

'She's gotta bag, so maybe she's come for apples,' Mike said.

Chris gave Mike another nudge. 'Look, 'ere comes Tom, he'll soon get rid of her.'

Fascinated, they watched from the kitchen where they were having their midday break. Serena Detrale stood in the yard, elegant in a thick camel coat, an orange scarf just visible at her throat and wearing highly polished brown leather boots.

'She's certainly a looker,' Chris said. 'I wonder why her husband 'opped it?'

'Perhaps he found someone else. I've heard she isn't the easiest of women to get on with. How old d'yer think she is?'

'Dunno, thirty-seven, -eight,' Chris said, taking a bite from his sandwich. ''ere, look at that, she's put her hand up to his cheek. Well I never. Tom don't look all that happy. Wonder what they're talking about?'

'The cut seems to have gone.'

'Yes.' His face felt hot thinking of their last encounter. 'What can I do for you, Mrs Detrale?'

'I've come for some apples.'

'Over here.' He led the way to the barn. 'I'll see what there is. What were you looking for, eaters or cookers?'

'Cookers.'

Tom pointed to the last box. 'Derbys are all I have left. I'd say there were about four pounds there, but one or two may be bruised.'

'They'll do, I'll take them all.'

Tom frowned as he selected a paper bag from the assortment on an upturned box. Why had she come to the farm? She could get all the apples she was likely to need from the Stores. He supplied the shop and so did other farms.

'I thought I would do some cooking, some pies perhaps, then I could give them to the residents at the almshouses. What do you think?'

'I'm sure they'd appreciate it – and your company.'

'Do you think so? I hadn't thought of that.'

They walked from the barn towards her car as Mike and Chris came from the kitchen.

'Afternoon,' they chorused, and Chris winked at Tom.

'Goodbye, Mrs Detrale,' Tom said, anxious to see the back of her.

'Couldn't you call me Serena?'

Not likely, he thought, as she slid into the driving seat and wound down the window.

'I'll bring you something when I've finished cooking.' Without bothering to close the car window, she reversed and drove away.

*

'Hello Tom.'

Tom wheeled round at the sound of Lydia's voice. It was both beautiful and unwelcome. He had dreaded this moment since the evening of his mother's funeral when she had told him that Edward had begged her to go to the Manor.

'Lydia.' They eyed each other uncertainly as they stood in the High Street.

'Come to do some shopping?' she asked.

'No, I'm here to give Jamie some money I owe him. And you?'

'I usually do a shop on a Tuesday. Did you have a good Christmas?'

'Yes.'

'Were you at Pat and Jamie's?'

'Where else would I go?'

Another uncomfortable silence fell between them.

'Edward bought me a new car for Christmas,' Lydia said at last.

'Was that by way of a thank you present for coming back, or a bribe to keep you here?'

'You're still angry with me, aren't you?'

'Angry? Why should I be angry? You went back to your husband.'

'I don't like us not being friends. You were there when I needed your help.'

'But you weren't there when I wanted you.'

'Couldn't you be glad that I'm happy now?'

'Are you – for how long? Edward's not going to change overnight.'

'That's my problem, not yours. Can't you get out more – meet people. Then perhaps you'll find someone else you can love.' She laughed nervously.

'It's just a joke with you….'

'No it isn't, I care about you, you know that. I hate to see you miserable, but there's nothing I can do about it. I can't make myself love you. And anyway,' she said pointedly, 'I am married to, and in love with Edward.'

'So,' Tom said, 'we know exactly where we stand.'

'I want you to be my friend, our friend. You'll always be welcome at the Manor.'

'I find that hard to believe. But I don't want to talk about it – or him – or you.' He stared coldly at her and saw in her eyes how hurt she was. Tom wanted her to suffer as he was suffering. Deep down he despised himself for saying the things he had, but it made him feel better.

'Perhaps I will get out more. Yes, I'll have to get out my little black book and see who's left that isn't married. Not that being married need matter nowadays.'

'Don't, please, I don't like you speaking like that. You're making me feel guilty and I've nothing to feel guilty about.' She reached out a hand to him.

'I must be going, I've a lot to do.' Tom strode past her and crossed the road to the garage.

*

Pat wants a word with you before you go,' Jamie said.

'What she want?'

'Something to do with Kim's birthday.' Jamie watched as his brother tore out a cheque. 'What's the matter with you? You've been so grumpy every time I've seen you lately. Are you still upset about Mum?'

'No. Well, yes, I suppose I am. I always knew she was there

even if I didn't see her every day. You never expect them to die – mothers – do you?'

'Cheer up. I don't like to see you miserable.'

Tom handed him the cheque. 'I'd better go and see what Pat wants.'

He went up the side of the garage to the back of the bungalow.

'Pat, it's me, Tom,' he called.

'I'll be right with you.'

He stood in the unexceptional kitchen which, for some reason, he compared with Serena Detrale's. The two kitchens were not much more than two hundred yards from each other, yet were worlds apart.

Pat came in from the hall. 'The reason I wanted to see you was, I wondered if you'd care to join us on a trip to London for Kim's birthday. It'll be half term, so the Wednesday would be a good day.'

'I'll say yes, but I never know when something might turn up. I can't leave Mike and Chris if we're very busy.'

'Let's go into the front room.'

'Jamie coming with us?' he asked, as he followed her.

'Doubt it. He can't afford to turn work away, or keep people of waiting.'

'Where were you thinking of going?'

'Up to London, the zoo perhaps.'

'I don't like seeing caged animals.'

'You're an old softie. I thought farmers saw animals as money on legs.'

He grinned.

'That's better. I haven't seen you laugh for weeks. What's up?'

Tom's face clouded and he was silent while he considered whether to confide in his sister-in-law. Pat was a nice, uncomplicated person, shy with those she did not know. She kept Jamie in line, controlling some of his more exuberant ideas. Tom recalled his days at the village school when he had to keep one eye on Edward to prevent his being bullied, and the other on Jamie who was always being provoked because they knew he had a quick temper. Tom thought he ought to have been nominated for the Nobel Peace Prize.

'It's Lydia Casleigh, isn't it?'

'It's that obvious, is it?' He rubbed two fingers up and down his temple. 'I can't get her out of my mind. I don't sleep properly –

and – and she was so close, then she was snatched away.'

'Don't you mean snatched back. She was never yours in the first place.'

'You know I tried to persuade her to marry me when she said she wouldn't go back.' He leaned forward resting his elbows on his knees and clasping his hands in front of him. 'Here I am, just turned forty, feeling like a lovesick cow. Joy was the only serious girl friend but she went off to New Zealand. There were a couple of others, but none I felt strongly about. Why did it have to be Lydia? Why Edward's wife of all people? Why couldn't it have been someone in the village – another town.' He threw up his arms in the air. 'Anywhere?'

'But you never go anywhere, and when you do take a holiday it's usually walking somewhere on your own. You've always been content with your own company.'

'Not any more.' He walked over to the bay window that looked out on to the front garden and the main village street.

'Unrequited love is one of the most poignant of emotions I should imagine,' Pat said sympathetically. 'but the answer's in your hands. Get out and about more. Take a holiday right away from here – abroad perhaps. Find someone to ask out.'

'That's what Lydia said.'

'You've seen her, have you?'

'Yeah – just now.'

'I think she gave you good advice.'

'She said I was making her feel guilty.'

'And were you?'

'I wanted to hurt her.'

'That's not like you, Tom. You're easy-going like your Mum. You're acting quite out of character.'

'I know, I don't seem like me at all. It's as if I am in another body.'

'Don't forget you're still getting over your Mum's death. You were very close to her, more so than Jamie. He's had us to think about.'

Tom moved away from the window and stood by Pat's chair. 'You won't tell Jamie about this, will you? He'd only tease me and I couldn't stand it at the moment. I expect I'll get over it.'

'Of course I won't.'

'I'd love to join you for Kim's birthday and I'll go straight home and put it on my calendar. How old will my big niece be –

twelve?'

'Thirteen.'

He sighed. 'A teenager – makes me feel even older.'

'Come on, lighten up, think about what I said. Find something else to occupy your mind. And if you want to talk, you know where I am.'

Tom kissed her on the cheek. 'Yes, I know where you are.'

Chapter 14

Tom opened the fridge and inspected the contents – butter, three eggs and a brown paper bag that revealed four shrivelled mushrooms. A survey of a lower shelf produced a rasher of bacon and two large sprouting potatoes.

As he closed the fridge door he thought he heard scuffling and went into the hall to investigate. All was quiet. He came back and crossed the kitchen to the side door and opened it. A woman stood there bathed into the harsh security light.

'It's a pity this light isn't round the other corner,' she said angrily. 'I nearly fell over going up that wretched path.'

'Mrs Detrale! What on earth are you doing here?'

'Trying to find my way into your damned house,' she said. 'Don't you use a front door like a normal person.'

'That door hasn't been used since – since – to tell you the truth, I can't remember it ever being used.'

'Aren't you going to ask me in. I'm not here for the good of my health, you know.'

'I'm sorry.' He stood back and she marched past him. Hastily he cleared a chair and threw the farming magazines on to a battered settee. He could see from her face what a mess she thought the place was.

'I was just about to get myself something to eat when I thought I heard a noise coming from the hall. It must have been you at the front door.'

'I never got as far as the front door. It's a death trap out there.'

Tom grinned, but quickly wiped away his smile as she turned to him and said, 'What were you going to eat?'

'That's just it, I haven't got anything decent. Since my mother died, I don't go into Maidstone as regularly as I used to. I tended to rely on her to remind me what I'd run out of.'

'That sounds pathetic.'

Tom felt as self-conscious as he had at Ridge House, but it

annoyed him that he should feel like this in his own home.

'I wasn't asking you opinion, just telling you the facts. What are you doing here anyway? It's a bit late for buying apples.'

'I brought you the pie as I promised. Here it is.' She reached into a bag and handed him a foil dish covered with film.

'So what are you doing to do?' she asked.

'Do?'

'For a meal,' she said impatiently.

'I hadn't decided. There's not much in the fridge.'

'Here, let me look.'

Before he could protest she was across the room and peering in the fridge door. She took out everything that was there.

'Like me to cook something for you?'

'I'd thought of egg and chips.'

'I always imagined manual workers needed big hearty meals.' She smiled at him. 'No, don't tell me, your mother used to provide them.'

'Not all the time,' he mumbled.

Serena took off her coat and handed it to Tom who put it over the back of a chair.

'Can't you find a hanger?'

Obediently he took the coat into the hall.

'Right,' she said, opening cupboards and inspecting the contents, 'you certainly need stocking up.'

Within half an hour Tom was sitting at a neatly laid table, complete with a cloth which had lain, long forgotten, in a drawer. In front of him was a meal he would not have considered possible from the meagre offerings at her disposal.

'I'm overwhelmed,' he said. 'Are you sure you wouldn't like something, though I can't think what. You've used everything I have.'

'No, I've already eaten.'

Tom saw her watching him with ill-disguised pleasure as he fell upon his meal.

'Why do you live in such squalor?'

'I haven't time to do housework.'

'What you need is someone to come in.'

'Susie Patterson clears up sometimes.'

'Not often enough from what I can see.'

'Look here, what's it got to do with you how much squalor I live in. Why did you come anyway?'

'I told you, to bring your pie.'

'I don't think so, not just for that. You don't even like me. How long have you lived in Grassenden? You've never spoken to me in all that time, not till Lydia came. Even then you could hardly bring yourself to pass the time of day.'

'I don't dislike you,' she said slowly.

'You give a very good impression.'

Tom finished the meal and went to the sink to wash up while Serena cleared the table. She looked distant and appeared to have forgotten what they were talking about. He studied her as she took the clean crockery to the dresser and carefully arranged the cups to face the same way, and moved the plates to look symmetrical. She stood back and he awaited her comment on how dusty they were, but all she said was, 'I'd better go now.'

He fetched her coat and held it for her. 'Thank you for the meal. It was quite delicious – not to say miraculous.'

'I'm glad you enjoyed it.'

Tom sat at the table when she had gone still trying to fathom what had made her visit him at seven o'clock on a winter's night. Funny woman – she didn't seem quite so fearsome once you got to know her, not that he was likely to do that.

✳

It was raining torrential, stair-rod rain. Bad weather had never bothered Tom. he accepted it, as he accepted everything, as a natural component of his life, but today it had depressed him irrationally.

Taking Pat's advice, he spent more time at *The Mitre* instead of reading – his usual form of relaxation. It hadn't helped. Pictures of Lydia kept flooding his mind without warning and he would suddenly be aware of the men laughing at him and asking where had he been this time.

He crossed from the kitchen to the oast and his coat and hood were soon soaked.

'I want you, Mike, to begin pruning the apple trees on Upper Field and Chris, you can mend the stile on the footpath near the pond and then help Mike. I'll join you later when I've seen to the post. You can wait a bit to see if the rain eases.'

Tom sighed heavily as he went into the room he called his office. The administrative side of farming had never been his favourite, but now it sent him into deep gloom. He sorted through his mail then sat back in the chair staring into space.

Had he reached what was called the crossroads of life? What about life begins at forty? What life? This was his life – farming. The farm was just the same; Abbotts Lidiard was the same, apart from his mother. How could Lydia, who had only been in the neighbourhood eighteen months, have wreaked such havoc on him?

The phone rang and he picked it up impatiently. 'Yes,' he snapped.

'You do sound bad-tempered – and the day so young.'

'Who is it?' he demanded.

'Serena – Serena Detrale.'

'Yes?' He stared at the rain still battering the windows. What the hell did she want? Not another home delivery service?

'This doesn't seem a good time to talk to you,' she said in a soothing voice. 'I'll ring again later. When would be a good time?'

Realising how abrupt he had been he said, 'I'm sorry. What can I do for you?'

'It's more what I can do for you? I wonder if you'd like to come here for a meal one evening.'

Tom took the phone away from his ear and stared at it, as if doing so would give him some insight. Mrs Detrale asking him to dine with her.

'Hello, are you still there?'

'Yes, I'm here.'

'Well?'

'All right,' he heard himself say before he could reason why.

He heard a release of breath as she said, 'How about tomorrow?'

'Tomorrow?'

'Is that a problem?'

'Well, no, I don't think so. What time?'

'Seven for seven thirty?' She sounded pleased.

'I might be late if something unexpected turns up. Farmers don't work nine to five.'

'I'll just have to hope you won't.' The phone clicked.

He replaced the receiver and sat astounded at what had just taken place, not only at the invitation, but also at his ready acceptance. Could it be he was recalling Pat telling him to get out and meet people? But Serena Detrale!

*

Tom had only one suit. Clothes were not high on his list of

priorities. It was not even a good one, certainly not by the standards of the Casleighs and Detrales of this world. He had little call for wearing even one and, if the truth were known, he was cautious with his money or, as his brother would have put it, stingy.

Tom looked at himself in the long, gilt-framed mirror in his bedroom. He thought he had lost weight in the last few months. He turned away and his stomach felt as if he had swallowed half a dozen frogs that now wanted out. He wished he had not accepted the wretched invitation. What could he say? What would they talk about? They had so little in common – the way they lived, their outlook, their upbringing. Still, she would be nice to look at.

*

The car was left near the church and Tom walked down the hill peering about him furtively. Approaching Ridge House he checked the main street then shot up the drive hoping he had not been seen.

Serena, wearing a frilly apron over a two piece suit of some soft green material, greeted him brightly. Tom thought how beautiful she was. She ushered him into her drawing room, a large room to the left of the hall.

'Would you mind getting yourself a drink – and one for me. I can't leave the dinner for the moment. I'd like a gin and tonic.'

She hurried to the kitchen while he looked around for a cabinet. She shouted from the kitchen. 'The drinks are near the front window.'

Tom savoured the mouth-watering smell as he took the glasses into the kitchen.

'I hope I've got the proportions right.'

'Thank you, I'm sure it'll be fine.' Serena took a sip and nodded her approval.

Tom's eyes roamed round the kitchen recalling his first embarrassing visit and felt his face flush. He watched as she deftly decorated the starter and checked the vegetables.

'Would you take my glass into the dining room. It's opposite the drawing room.'

She followed him into the room and put their starters in place.

'Please sit down.' She indicated the chair at the end of the table.

As he took his place he wondered if he ought to have pulled out her chair. Though he was not used to such high living, he had learned some of the finer points of dining from his mother.

'I hope you like this,' Serena said as she picked up a fork. 'It's salmon mousse.'

'If your improvised meal is anything to go by, it'll be great.'

They ate in silence. Several times Tom glanced in Serena's direction and on one occasion she looked as if she might speak, but then lowered her eyes.

Tom studied the room when she returned to the kitchen with the plates. It was large, but smaller than the drawing room. The furniture was solid, typical turn of the century style. The carpet was highly patterned and predominantly red. It reminded him of the one in his granny's front room. Whilst his place would never compare with a house like this, it did make him realise just how badly the farmhouse needed attention. He felt ashamed that he had let it get into such a state.

Serena returned with a large tray, which she placed on the sideboard.

'Want any help? I feel uncomfortable sitting here having you wait on me.'

'That's what going out to dinner is all about,' she said briskly, as she put a vegetable dish on the table but added appeasingly, 'But thank you for your offer.'

She served chicken in sauce on his plate. 'I hope you like chicken. This is a favourite recipe of mine because it doesn't involve too much fiddling in the kitchen. That way I didn't miss out on conversation when we had guests.'

'I'm not fussy about my food,' Tom offered.

'I had noticed.'

'My mother wouldn't let us. If we didn't like what was served we went without. No fuss, no arguing – that was just the way it was. It's surprising what you can eat if you're hungry enough.'

'Doesn't sound very complimentary.'

'Oh – I didn't mean….' Tom coloured.

'I know what you mean.' She smiled disarmingly. 'But I hope you are hungry.'

'To tell you the truth I didn't realise just how much till I smelled the food cooking. I've hardly eaten since breakfast.'

'Help yourself to vegetables,' she said, as she put the last dish on the table.

This burst of conversation seemed to break the ice and they exchanged snippets of village gossip during the following courses.

'Are things going well on the farm?'

'They're fine.'

'Good.'

Tom searched for something to say. She wouldn't be interested in sheep or hops. He could hardly ask her where her husband had gone and would he mind Tom being there?

'When was this house built?'

'Nineteen-o-one?'

'The year Queen Victoria died.'

'Was it? Shall we have coffee in the other room?' She gathered up the last of the dishes and put them on the tray.

'Here, let me carry that,' he offered.

'You go and sit in the drawing room while I make the coffee,' she said as he put the tray on the kitchen table. As he went into the hall, she said, 'Do get yourself a brandy if you fancy one.'

Tom did as she suggested feeling pleased, as he poured it into the correct glass, that he could show her he was not just a country oaf. As he sat down in the large cream leather armchair, he wondered why he should be bothered what she thought of him. He didn't even like her, did he? Or her sort. What on earth was he doing here? He was certain she was not on Lydia's or Pat's list of people he was urged to get out and meet.

Tom started as Serena came into the room. She began to pour coffee into delicate, highly coloured cups and handed him his.

'I'm trying to work out exactly why I'm here,' Tom said. He took a sip of brandy and watched fascinated as she straightened her skirt and arranged her shapely long legs side by side at a slight angle. He raised his eyes and flushed as they met hers and she smiled as if she could read his thoughts.

'Why did you ask me here?' Tom asked.

It was her turn to look uneasy and for several moments she didn't speak.

'I thought it would make a pleasant evening for you.'

'That's condescending,' he said sharply. 'I don't need you to make my evenings pleasant, I can do that for myself.'

Serena shifted in her chair. 'I didn't mean it like that. I thought you'd like to come.' Her voice then took on its usual sharp edge. 'You did want to come, otherwise you wouldn't have accepted. What's so wrong about that?'

'But,' he said, 'you must admit we are as different in every way as it's possible to be.'

'I miss cooking for someone. You see it's the only thing I'm any good at. Most often the dinners I planned were connected with business – not wholly relaxed affairs, but I enjoyed them because I like entertaining. I miss it now Jeremy's gone.'

Tom was not convinced by this explanation. Surely there were friends of her own class she could have invited.

Serena rose from her chair and moved to the cabinet, her hips making the soft folds of her skirt sway from side to side. As she poured herself a drink he studied her.

Her gold hair, on its way to red, was thick and straight and cut just to cover the bottom of her ears. Her skin was light and translucent. The features that lifted her from good-looking to beautiful were the high cheekbones and her green eyes fringed by long, thick lashes.

Her figure, Tom noted, was well proportioned, but she was too thin for his taste. It was particularly noticeable because she was tall. He though of Lydia and the only time he had kissed her. She had been warm and soft against his body, and even though she had reproached him for taking advantage of her situation, he carried with him, like a photograph, the feel of her body against his.

'You're not very communicative, you're in a little world of your own most of the time, aren't you?'

'The result of living alone I expect. But you didn't ask me here for my scintillating wit. You hardly know me. You must have friends…'

'They're all married. I never get asked out now – only to coffee mornings. Couples are wary of dining with a single woman. They think I might have designs on their husbands now I've got rid of my own.'

'So, what are your designs?'

'You intrigue me.'

'That's it then, you want to delve into my soul.'

'No, but I'd like to know why you slapped me the day you brought the car back.'

'Doesn't that amount to much the same thing? Anyway, what's more to the point is why you hit me. I hadn't been in your house five minutes and I only mentioned how Edward had got Lydia to return…' He stopped. 'Are you in love with Edward?'

The thick hair fell forward as she bowed her head. Tom had rarely seen Edward and Mrs Detrale together though he knew they were friends since childhood. Edward used to stay with her parents some summer holidays.

'Yes.'

'How long?'

'Forever. Since we were children.'

'Was it because Edward lived here that you moved to Grassenden?'

Serena nodded. 'We lived in Epsom and I just told him it would be quieter further from London. We'd visited the Manor often so I suggested we look in this area.' She took a sip of her coffee. 'I suppose you think I'm feeble.'

'No, I understand perfectly.'

'You do?' she said, opening her green eyes wider.

'Yes, I do.' He drained his coffee cup and stood up. 'At least you've had one less lonely evening,' he said. 'I'd better go now.'

'Must you?' she said. 'Couldn't I get you more coffee?'

'No, thank you. Us earthy types have to get up early.'

'Yes, of course,' she said, rising gracefully to her feet. She walked with him into the hall and fetched his coat

'Thank you for the dinner. You really are a very good cook.'

'I'm so pleased you decided to come, whatever the reason.'

He left her drive as he had arrived – like a spy. He peered up and down the street, then hurried past the school towards the church car park.

In bed, hands behind his head in his usual pre-sleep pose, he thought of Serena Detrale. Deftly he had managed not to call her by name all evening. Calling her Serena would have given her a familiarity with him he was not willing to give. On the other hand, Mrs Detrale sounded deferential. Now their relationship had reached a different phase – somewhere between the two.

Lydia was second in his mind. He still loved her, wished it had been her he had dined with. He took his hands from behind his head, extinguished the bedside light and prepared for another restless night.

Chapter 15

'Tom? It's Edward here. Come up tomorrow evening, I've something I want to talk over with you.'

'Not tomorrow, sorry, some other time?'

'Day after then. Come to dinner.'

'Dinner! Good Lord, Edward, I bet that wasn't your idea. No, I won't come for a meal. I'll be up about eight. There's something I'd like to discuss as well.'

Edward went into the kitchen. 'Tom can't make tomorrow, said he'd come the day after. He was very abrupt.'

'Neither of you has ever been chatty, have you? He's probably taken my advice and is going out more.' Lydia put pastry on top of a pie and crimped the edges.

'When did you see Tom?'

'I told you! I saw him on Tuesday, in the High Street.'

'Yes, yes, so you did. He's not coming to a meal, by the way.'

'He's obviously still angry with me, but he'll have to get on with it.' She touched his cheek. 'Don't look so miserable, you've got nothing to worry about, I still love you.'

Edward gave a wan smile. In spite of her return and her assurance that she loved him, he couldn't believe that Tom would not one day whisk her away.

'I wish I didn't have to deal with him.'

'Don't be silly, Edward, he is extremely efficient and you'd have to go a long way to find someone of his calibre. And think how unhappy you must have made Cressy over the years with your attitude to him. There's no need to carry on this antagonism.'

'No, I know,' Edward said, without conviction.

*

Tom walked to the Manor. It was a cold, late January evening and the frost which had lain all day in sheltered spots, was now re-freezing the areas that had melted. He moved briskly and emerged from the footpath to cross the lane and go up the drive to Abbey

Manor. After taking his coat and cap, Edward followed Tom along the passage to the living room.

Tom's heart gave a lurch as Lydia raised her face to welcome him. She was sitting to the right of the inglenook where a large fire, piled high with logs, was blazing. The flames licked round the wood, which hissed with remnant sap and the smell of burning apple wood filled the room. A white, cobwebby material lay piled in Lydia's lap like a cocoon.

'Hello, Tom,' she said, laying down the knitting needles. 'Did you have a good time yesterday?'

'Yesterday?'

'Edward said you had another engagement.'

'I don't think I said I was going out, did I Edward?' He smiled to himself because he had decided on the spur of the moment not to be at Edward's beck and call.

'What would you like to drink? Beer?'

'No, I think I'll have a gin and tonic.'

'That's unusual for you,' Edward said.

Lydia resumed her knitting. 'You seem pleased with yourself. Things going well at the farm?'

'Much the same as usual. Ground's very hard with the frosts we've been having.'

'Edward said you'll be busy with the pruning now.'

'That's right and repairing wirework and posts for the hops. We're also grubbing out some of the windbreak trees and hedges and replacing them.'

'Right,' Edward said, 'to business. I've been thinking about converting the oast house on the farm into a dwelling and selling it.'

Horrified, Tom said, 'But we use that for storage, and garaging for the tractors and other machinery.'

'We can get a purpose built structure for that.'

'What about access? There's already a quarter mile track from the road to the farm, and then the residents would have to drive through the yard, which might be cluttered with machinery. No, it's quite impracticable. Anyway, you'd never get planning permission.'

Disconcerted, Edward ran his hand through his blond hair. 'I said I'd been thinking about it – not that it was going to happen tomorrow.'

'Well I don't go much on the idea. Let me know when you've

'delved into it a bit more, but I think it's a non-starter.'

'I was hoping you'd do that.'

'Oh no, I've quite enough on my plate. I haven't got time to look into schemes I know are doomed from the start. If you want it, you do the work, they're your buildings.' Tom took a gulp of his drink.

Edward stared at him with a mixture of surprise and aggravation. He went to speak but Tom saw Lydia glance at him and imperceptibly shake her head. Good, he thought, that's one good thing, she is getting him under some sort of control.

The grandfather clock chimed the half-hour, fire crackled, knitting needles tapped rhythmically.

'The other thing I wanted to bring up was Cressy's cottage. I'm not sure…'

'You want it cleared? I think Pat and Jamie have almost finished.'

'It's not that,' Edward said, 'you can take as long as you like. It's what to do with it.'

'Oh.' The thought of someone else living in his childhood home suddenly made him immensely depressed.

'It's sad for you, isn't it – and Edward? Had your parents always lived there?'

'They went there in fifty-one.'

'My grandfather owned all four cottages at one time,' Edward explained to Lydia, 'but when he died three of them were sold to help with death duties. Jack and Cressy had the one that was left and she continued to live there after Tom's father died.'

Edward gazed into the distance and Tom knew from his expression that he must have been feeling just as emotional about the little cottage as he did. He almost felt sorry for him.

With a slight shake of his shoulders, Edward pulled himself back to the present. 'I was thinking of selling it.' Tom said nothing. 'Well, what do you think?'

'It's up to you, it's your cottage.'

'Oh, do stop saying that, I know it's mine.' He went to get another drink. 'Shall I sell it or keep it to rent out? You can give an opinion, can't you? I don't know what's the matter with you, you're not like your usual self.'

'Acquiescent?'

'What's that supposed to mean?'

'Rubber stamping any scheme you think up – like I usually do.'

'I've always asked your opinion,' Edward said stiffly.

'And then badgered me till I've agreed with you.'

Tom looked at Lydia who was trying not to laugh. 'Now stop this,' she said, standing up and putting the mound of shawl on the chair, 'or it'll get out of hand and you'll start saying things you'll regret.'

Tom smiled sheepishly and Edward scowled.

'You can manage to stay for a coffee, I hope?' Lydia asked.

'Yes, thank you.'

'Well, what do you think about the cottage?' Edward repeated as Lydia left the room.

'I think it would be best to keep it. Chris Barratt and his wife aren't living in a very good flat at the moment. It's the other side of Grimley Heath and he has to bike in. You could rent it to him. If, in the future, they find somewhere else, you never know when a new farm hand might be needed. Accommodation is always a draw. People aren't exactly queuing up to work on the land.'

'I see what you mean. OK, you find out if he's interested and let me know.'

'I'll tell him you want to see him.'

Before Edward could remonstrate against this further act of insubordination, Lydia came in with the coffee.

'Now, what was it you wanted to say?'

'I'm intending to do some decorating. The inside hasn't been done for years. I'd be grateful if a few structural repairs could be put in hand, windows mainly; most of the frames are rotting. The farmhouse is listed so that'll have to be considered. I'll find out about that.'

'Are you going to do all the rooms!' Edward exclaimed.

'Eventually, but I'll start on the kitchen and the best room, so I'd like the downstairs windows done first. I'll let you know as soon as I find out how they've to be replaced and the cost. Can it be done soon after that, do you think?'

'I, er, suppose so.'

Tom sat back in his chair, extended his legs and flexed his feet before saying, 'I'm thinking of buying a car.'

'What's wrong with the Landrover suddenly?' Edward asked.

'It's used about the farm and is perpetually dirty. I thought I'd have something a little more sophisticated.'

Edward and Lydia exchanged glances.

'What kind of car had you in mind?' Lydia asked.

'Dunno – thought I'd have a word with Jamie and get his advice.'

When Edward came back after seeing Tom out, he said, 'Well, what do you think of that?' I've never known him behave in that way. He appeared – I don't know – he seemed like a different person.'

'He behaved more like you do.'

'What d'you mean?'

'Well, he did, didn't he? He wasn't uneasy like he usually is when you're around.'

Edward grunted. 'I preferred him the way he was.'

'I'm sure you did, but I have a feeling we'll not see him like that again.'

*

Tom picked up the phone to arrange a return meal with Serena. It was a month since he had dined at Ridge House and apart from sending her some flowers, they had not come across each other since. He had wondered about contacting her at all. Though it was a more pleasant and enjoyable evening than he had anticipated, he was not completely at ease in her company. In the end he decided an evening out would make a change. There would be no need for any follow-up after that and she would drift out of his life as she had drifted in.

'I would ask you here,' Tom said, when she told him she would be delighted to go out to eat, 'but I'm afraid you'd find it too basic compared with what you're used to, and anyway, I can't cook – not anything you'd care to eat.'

Tom chose a pub in a village the other side of Maidstone in the hope that they wouldn't been seen by anyone he knew. He was too uncertain of himself to face the villagers. Their remarks would be bad enough had he acquired any female companion, but to be seen with Serena Detrale would give them apoplexy.

'Is this where you usually bring your girlfriends,' she said, looking round the pub restaurant.

'No, I've never been here before – and I've never had a girlfriend.'

'Never!' she cried.

'Nothing permanent. There was Joy Baxter, but she and her family emigrated.'

'Ah, at last I've got you to tell me something about yourself.'

'Not something, more like everything. I lead a very uninteresting life. I'm just a farmer.'

'You must do something in your spare time. You can't farm twenty-four hours a day.'

'I go down to *The Mitre* a couple of times a week, have a meal with Jamie occasionally. I used to take my mother shopping and have meals with her.'

'What do you do in the evenings when you're not at the pub?'

'After the paper work you mean.' Tom grinned.

'All right, I get the picture, you work all the hours God gives you.'

'I read a lot,' he volunteered.

'I rarely read. I don't even glance at the newspapers now because Jeremy doesn't bring them in. I have a couple of magazines. I used to cook a great deal, but as I told you before, I have no-one to cook for now.'

Serena reached for her roll and broke it between her fingers. Her engagement ring, an oblong emerald, flashed as it caught the light.

'What do you read?'

'I particularly like Dostoevsky.'

'A bit highbrow for me.' She popped a piece of roll in her mouth. 'Where did you go to school?'

'The grammar school in Maidstone.'

'Couldn't you have done something else – gone to university or something?'

'Just because people choose to work on the land, it doesn't mean they can only read comics.'

'So-rree,' she said, 'you are touchy.'

Feeling he ought to explain himself, Tom said, 'My Dad and my teachers wanted me to go to university, but I've always wanted to farm, ever since Edward, Jamie and I used to play there. I've never regretted it.'

'Well, I'm not ashamed to say I couldn't read such books – way above my head.'

'But you can get away with it. You only have to open your mouth for people to know that you've had an expensive education. You have money – that says everything. People without money behind them have to prove themselves all the time.'

'You've done all right though. Edward sings your praises and everyone knows what a good farmer you are.'

'But it's never going to be my farm, is it?'

'One thing you've certainly got is a big chip on your shoulder.'

Tom went to deny this, but she went on, 'I get terribly bored. I haven't enough to occupy me.'

'Can't you use your talents.'

'What talents?'

'Cooking, of course.'

'Cooking?'

'Yes, cooking. Why don't you turn it into a business?'

'A business?'

'Serena – stop repeating everything I say.' Tom realised he had called her by her first name. 'You could get Edward to help you,' he added.

'Why can't you?'

'Me?'

'Now who's repeating?'

Tom laughed and felt himself relax. On neutral ground the conversation flowed more easily. The evening, which he had planned solely to reciprocate his visit to Ridge House, was turning out to be a satisfying break in his otherwise uneventful life. He was surprised how much he was enjoying himself.

'You're older than Edward, aren't you?'

'Yes, forty last month, so life's just beginning.'

'Mine's in March,' Serena informed him, 'I'm older than you.'

'Really,' he said, surprised.

'Do you think I look younger?'

'Stop fishing for compliments.'

Receiving flattery must be like food and drink to her, he thought, as a flush of embarrassment suffused her cheeks. He was caught between contrition and getting even for past humiliation at her hands.

The waitress brought their coffee but as she went to leave she caught the cream jug and the contents spilled on to the table and trickled into Serena's lap. She leapt up brushing her skirt with her paper serviette, which added a pink stain. She turned on the girl.

'You stupid ninny look what you've done, you've ruined my skirt. How could you be so careless?'

The girl, who could not have been much more than seventeen, blushed and stammered her apologies. The commotion gave rise to unwelcome attention, which brought the restaurant manager to the table.

'What's the problem, Madam?'

'This chit of a girl has knocked over the cream and ruined my skirt.'

'It was an accident, Mr Ponting, I caught it with my hand. I'm sorry.'

'Sorry, sorry! What's the good of that?'

Serena held out her skirt and the young waitress began to cry as all eyes turned their way.

Tom said, 'Calm down, can't you see the girl's upset.'

'Upset!' she shrieked. 'What about me?'

Mr Ponting assured her that he would pay for madam's garment to be cleaned.

'I should hope so. Meanwhile I have to go home smelling like a dairymaid.'

Roughly Tom grabbed her arm. 'Go out to the car, I'll deal with this.'

'What about…'

'Do as I say.'

Serena glared angrily at Tom and looked prepared to argue, but she picked up her bag and flounced out of the restaurant, all eyes following her progress. Five minutes later Tom joined her in the car park where she was furiously pacing up and down.

'That was a disgusting display of ill temper. You ought to be ashamed of yourself.'

'Me ashamed.' She was beside herself with rage. 'Just look at this.' She pointed to the pink stain and the congealing cream. 'And it stinks.'

'Just like your behaviour.'

Two couples came out of the pub laughing and stopped when they saw them.

'Get in the car,' Tom ordered. Serena went to get in the driver's seat. 'Other side.'

'I'm not insured for you.'

'Do as I say – you're in no state to drive.'

Heedless of the contradiction, Tom drove too fast for the narrow, twisting Kent lanes. Neither spoke, apart from his throwing a ten pound note into her lap. 'The manager gave me this.'

They bumped down the farm track and drew up in the yard. Ignoring Serena, Tom jumped out of the car, slamming the door and strode to the farmhouse. Inside he turned on her.

'That may be how you behave in your type of restaurant, but

in a quiet country pub we have more control over ourselves. That was just a young girl, still at school most likely, trying to earn a bit of pocket money. She was not a fully trained professional. You are just what I've always thought you were, a stuck-up ungracious, bit... snob.'

Serena's slim body shook with rage, her fists clenched and unclenched at her sides and her mouth was set in a grim line. Tom thought he had never seen anyone look so ravishing – her hair, the flawless skin flushed with anger, and her green eyes, darker now with dilated pupils. She took a step towards him and from the corner of his eye he saw her hand rise. Calmly he caught her swinging arm by the wrist.

They eyed each other for several moments then he pulled her towards him and kissed her. He felt her stiffen and waited for her to pull away. When he finally released her he whispered, 'You are lovely.'

'That's not what you said just now.'

'You know what I mean.'

'Do you really hate me so much?'

'You have a filthy temper.'

'You're very uncompromising in your criticisms.'

'If you'd like me to pretend your nature is as lovely as your face, you've got the wrong man.' Tom was still holding her in his arms. 'May I kiss you again.'

'You didn't ask last time.'

'I'll take that as a 'yes'.'

*

'I didn't tell you, did I, Serena?' Tom said, when he rang next day. 'Jamie has found me a car.'

'What did you decide on?'

'A Volvo. Jamie thought I needed something robust, as it'll have to travel over that rough track from the road.'

'Is it a new one?'

'No, it's a year old. You'll also be pleased to know I'm having my place decorated – two rooms anyway. I thought you'd like to help me – choose colours and things. You'll know a lot more about that than I do.'

'I'd love to.' There was a pause. 'When will I see you again? You won't leave it another month, will you?'

'No, but I must go now, I can see Mike waiting for me.'

'See you soon then.'

'I'll ring you later. Bye.'

＊

'Hi Mike, d'you know if Chris has seen Mr Casleigh yet?'

'I don't know. I haven't seen him this morning.'

'Well, if you do, mention I want to see him. I'll be up by the gate to the road. I noticed last night when I came in that the gate was off its hinges. Someone's idea of a joke, no doubt. While I'm up there I'll look at the hedges and fencing and see if anything needs attention.'

'OK boss, I'll give him your message.'

In the light of day, as he trudged up the track to the road, Tom wondered if what had happened last night had actually taken place. If anyone had asked him a few weeks ago what he thought of Serena Detrale he would have said she was a bitch. In fact, he had nearly called her so. Now he had kissed her – and taken pleasure in it and so it appeared, had she.

He heard a car draw up in the gateway and turned to see Lydia winding down her car window.

'Hi, Tom.'

He walked over to her car and he realised that she had not invaded his mind for at least twenty-four hours. He still remembered her heartrending telephone call in the middle of the night and kissing her in the hotel room, but the intensity had diminished.

'Hello, Lydia, pleasant morning, isn't it?'

'You seem happier than when I saw you in Grassenden. Have you taken my advice?'

'Don't preach. It isn't as if I thought you were going to be any happier with Edward.'

'I am happy, believe me, but you did seem different the other night, you can't deny it. I could see you were goading Edward.' She giggled. 'He was quite thrown.'

'Good, I meant him to be. I'm turning over to a new page in my life. My mother's dead, you are lost to me so, instead of living my life wholly for farming – on a farm that isn't mine – I'm going to do what I want when I want to do it.'

'I'm pleased you're taking this view. Your happiness is what I want, really it is. Don't spoil our friendship, I wouldn't like that. And if you're worried about Edward – I can handle him. We have come to an understanding and I realise what makes him tick.'

'I wish you'd tell me.'

'Your mother knew, that's why she made excuses for him.'

'You're looking well.'

'Yes, I'm feeling great. Edward keeps fussing in case I have another fall. But I'd better leave you to get on, I'm sure you're busy.'

Tom watched as her car disappeared round the bend and felt more at ease than he had for months. To hell with accounts tonight, I'll ask Serena to come round.

*

It was nearing lunchtime when he eventually made his way back to the farm. In the distance he saw Chris moving up the track towards him.

'Sorry I didn't catch you yesterday,' Tom said.

'I went home early 'cos Wendy wasn't feeling well. The doctor says she's to rest if we don't wanna lose this baby.'

'Yes, I understand. I just wanted to know if you've seen Mr Casleigh.'

'Yeah,' Chris said excitedly, 'last night. 'e said we could rent the cottage in the lane. 'e said we could go and see it any time. We're ever so pleased. We'll be able to grow our own vegetables and there'll be somewhere for the washing instead of hanging it around the flat, and somewhere for the baby to play – when he's old enough, of course.'

Tom smiled at his farmhand's face alight with anticipation at what the future held. 'I'm glad it'll be in the hands of someone I know. I hope you'll be happy there.'

'We will, I'm sure we will.'

'Give my regards to Wendy. When's the baby due?'

'Three weeks. I might stay on a bit tonight Tom, to make up for yesterday.'

'What about Wendy?'

''er mother's come for the day.'

'You don't have to Chris, we can manage.'

'I don't like to take off too much time. I've already got a week off when the baby comes. Thought I could do those odd jobs you wanted done that I 'aven't got around to yet.'

'OK, if you're sure. You will make certain everything's locked up when you go? I'm going into Maidstone when I've had a bite to eat. I won't need to check when I get back if I know you've done it. Tell Mike you're staying.'

'Will do.'

'Look,' Tom said that evening, flinging open the fridge door. Serena peered in. 'My, my, I am impressed.'

'But wait.' He went to the wall cupboard. 'Voila!'

He moved to the middle of the room arms akimbo, looking smug and self-satisfied. Serena gave him a playful push and he fell laughing into the dilapidated settee. He settled himself comfortably and patted a place for her.

'Come and sit here.'

'I'm going to put the kettle on for a cup of tea.' She went to fill it.

'Oh dear,' he tut-tutted, 'I've forgotten to buy any tea.'

She turned sharply, 'You haven't…' then she saw him laughing at her.

He patted the settee again. Serena glided over and he caught her hand.

'Kiss me,' he said.

'I kissed you yesterday.'

'You didn't – I kissed you.' Tom pulled her down. 'Didn't you like it?'

She smiled and nodded.

'Kettle's boiling,' she managed to say eventually.

'It'll turn itself off,' he murmured into her hair.

It was sometime before they got around to discussing colour schemes.

Chapter 16

Tom and Serena came in from shopping late one Wednesday evening. He had met her and they had bought paint and brushes and rollers and paper and all the things she considered he needed. She also chose new curtains. Tom was alarmed at the amount of money that was being spent, but because he had little idea how much decorating materials and furnishings cost, he let Serena have her head.

'I think you ought to keep the range,' she had said when Tom suggested asking Edward to have it taken out. 'You kitchen is enormous. It isn't as if you need the extra space. they're all the rage now, so even if you never intend to use it, you can make it a feature.'

Tom wasn't sure what making it a feature meant and did not like to ask. She went on to tell him that as most of the kitchen windows faced north, and the farmhouse was in a dip, it needed to be light with bright curtains – and couldn't something be done about the ghastly furniture.

'That furniture has been here as long as I can remember. I don't know if it's mine as the tenant or Edward's.'

Serena found this extremely amusing. 'Tell you what,' she said, 'I'll ask Edward to buy you something decent.'

'You'll do no such thing,' Tom cried outraged, 'I can buy my own furniture – that is if I've any money left after you've spent it all.'

'You're an old skinflint,' she said as she sorted out the bags. 'I was only joking.'

'It's all very well for you, money's no object if you've got plenty.'

Serena stopped unpacking and tapped her foot on the flagstoned kitchen floor. 'I'm beginning to get a bit tired of you whingeing about money all the time. You're not searching around for the next penny, but I don't see you giving your money away.' She looked at his face. 'Stop sulking and set the table while I put these things in the office.'

When she came back she said, 'Have you decided if you're going to do it yourself, or get someone in to do it.'

Tom was about to say that it would cost too much, instead he said quickly, 'I'll do it myself.'

She went over to where Tom stood searching for the resurrected tablecloth in the drawer. She slid her hands round his waist and he turned round.

'I am grateful for your help Serena.' He kissed her.

'I'm enjoying it.'

'Kissing or decorating?'

'Both.'

'You do realise,' he said, 'that we are taking advantage of each other?'

'Yes, I suppose we are, but is that a crime? I was lonely – you intrigued me. And you – well I'm not sure about your motive, but I seem to be fulfilling something missing from you life.'

'You do, Serena. I haven't felt so contented for a long time.' After a moment he said, 'Are you divorcing?'

'Yes, it's in the hands of my solicitor.'

'On what grounds? I don't know anything about divorce.'

'Neither do I, except it is not very pleasant. It's called irretrievable breakdown of the marriage. My petition is unreasonable behaviour.'

'How long have you been married?' he said as he spread the tablecloth.

'Eighteen years.'

'You must have been happy some of that time. What went wrong?'

Serena continued her preparations and was silent for such a long time he thought she had not heard his question.

'I think it partly stems from not having children,' she said eventually. 'We both wanted them and – and…'

Tom raised his head. She had stopped what she was doing and stood leaning against the cooker, her back to him.

'Serena?'

She did not move and he went over and stood beside her. 'Serena, what's the matter?'

She turned towards him and he saw the tears running down her face. He drew her close and let her cry while he stroked her hair.

At last he said, 'Come and sit down – supper can wait.' He

settled her on the settee and went to a cupboard. 'Here, drink this.' He handed her a brandy.

Tom pulled out a handkerchief from his pocket and wiped Serena's damp cheeks.

'I don't like to see you crying. Do you want to talk?'

'I met Jeremy in the city. I was employed to do directors' lunches at the firm where he worked. I wasn't immediately attracted to him; in fact he pursued me. I'd never had any difficulty finding boy friends. I usually had more than one on the go and was always out. At the time I shared a flat in London with a couple of other girls. Jeremy was very persistent and eventually we got together. I did love him when we married.

'Jeremy was already comfortably off. We were able to buy a lovely house in Epsom and I shopped and cooked and held dinner parties. Jeremy was rising fast in the firm so entertaining people who might be influential was vital.

'While I was enjoying all this we awaited a baby. I went to doctors who said not to worry, it was early days. Then I went to specialists and they all said they could find nothing wrong. Jeremy had tests and he was all right. So we waited and waited.

'Meanwhile Jeremy was becoming more successful and began to drink as the pressure grew. Then he started coming home late and sometimes stayed away all night, ostensibly on business, but I suspected there were other women. We acquired more and more money and spent more and more, but life began to seem pointless to me. It was at this time that I asked Jeremy if we could move but being near Edward made things even worse and then he married Frances and when she was expecting a baby I thought I would die.' She turned to him. 'I suppose you think I'm being over-dramatic.'

Tom thought of his feelings for Lydia. 'No, Serena, I told you, I understand.'

'But you can't understand about wanting a baby,' she said fiercely, 'nobody can unless they've been in the same position.'

'No, no, but a longing for anything is a longing, it tears you apart if it's deep enough.

'Then Frances and the baby were killed. I felt guilty because – because – I thought it was my fault. Well, not my fault exactly – guilty because I didn't want him married and was pleased she was dead.'

More tears of anguish and guilt squeezed from her eyes and

clung to her thick lashes.

'And – and…' she sobbed, gasping for enough breath, 'I was T-Teddy's g-godmother.'

Tom pulled her close and rocked her as she wept. He let her cry hoping the tears would release some of her remorse.

After a while he said, 'Feeling better?'

'I haven't told you everything yet.'

He began to wonder if he might be getting out of his depth. It upset him to see her so distressed, as it had with Lydia.

'Then Lydia came along,' she said.

The simultaneous mention of her name and his thought made him start.

'What's the matter?'

'Nothing.'

Serena raised her eyes to his and he saw her examining them, darting from one pupil to the other.

'Our marriage was all but over,' she continued. 'We'd more or less decided to go our own ways. We had a big row and I told him he could go whenever he liked. I thought, given time, I'd get a divorce then I'd set about capturing Edward. I didn't think it would be hard. We were close friends, I knew he liked me, even held me in some esteem. We'd been good to him after Frances died and he'd seemed so depressed. You'd remember, of course. Then, just as I thought I would be free to pursue him, along comes that woman. I couldn't believe it – she wasn't his type, wasn't even good-looking though she was attractive in a sort of way. She certainly wasn't in his class.'

'That's very arrogant.'

'You know what I am, you've told me in no uncertain terms. Anyway, you're a fine one to talk about class, you're always on about it. There's such a thing as inverted snobbery you know.' She got up from the settee. 'It all happened so suddenly, one minute she arrived, next they were married. I didn't have time to adjust.'

'Don't you think it wouldn't have mattered who it was, you'd never have been reconciled.'

'How do you know?'

To confess or not to confess. 'Because I've experienced something similar.'

Serena stared at him for some moments. 'You're in love with her, aren't you? That rumour was true then.'

'No, it wasn't, but I once wished it had been.'

'So, you've taken advantage of me to get over her.'

'It was you who pursued me, not the other way round. But I won't deny you've helped, and haven't I done the same for you to some extent?'

'True.'

'And you said it wasn't a crime.'

'True.'

'Well, then, I've helped your loneliness and you've brightened my life. Surely we can accept it for what it is, and I am fond of you, in spite of your foul temper.'

'I've always had a bad temper.'

'Nice making up though,' Tom said.

*

'It's beautifully wrapped,' Pat said glancing at Tom as her daughter excitedly opened her birthday present.

Kim folded back the tissue paper to reveal a soft pink jumper. She picked it up her eyes shining and as she held it against her she said, 'Oh, Uncle Tom, it's lovely.' She waltzed round the armchair in the small room. 'It's the loveliest present I've ever had.'

Tom gave an embarrassed smile. Tony glared with disapproval at something he could not play with and left in disgust.

'Can I wear it now, Mummy?' Kim said, but before Pat could answer, she was undoing the buttons of her blouse.

'Kim! Go and do that in your bedroom,' she admonished. To Tom she said, 'She hasn't quite realised she is growing up – though you seem to have cottoned on. How did you decide what to get – and the size?'

'The assistant helped me,' he lied.

Kim came back and gave a twirl. 'Do I look nice, Uncle Tom?'

'You look lovely.'

Kim rushed over, flung her arms around his neck and kissed him.

'Go and get Tony, then we'll be off,' Pat said.

When the train came in it was fuller than expected. Kim proprietarily took hold of Tom's hand and rushed for the only two seats that were together. Pat and Tony were forced to sit apart in another part of the carriage.

'Uncle Tom?' Kim said as the train moved off.

'Yes?'

'I do love this jumper.'

'Do you. I am pleased.'

'How did you know what I'd like? Did your girlfriend help you?'

Tom turned sharply. 'What makes you say that?'

'I heard Mum and Dad talking.'

'And what did they say?' he said alarmed.

'That they hadn't seen much of you recently and that you must have a girlfriend.'

Tom relaxed. 'They were just joking. I've been decorating. Why don't you come and have a look before you go back to school?'

'Mummy won't let me walk along the footpaths by myself, not since that man attacked Mrs Casleigh last year and it's a long way round by road.'

'I'll come and fetch you. You'll hardly recognise the kitchen and I'm starting the best room now. You've not been in my new car either, have you?'

'You still haven't told me how you chose my present,' Kim persisted.

'I asked the lady in the shop to help me. She said I could take it back if it wasn't right.'

'You are clever, Uncle Tom.' She squeezed his hand and smiled up at him coquettishly. Tom could see that his niece was already practising her womanly wiles, albeit unconsciously. He was surprised how he was succumbing to her charm, like he had to Serena's. What a lot he had to learn about women.

'What other presents did you have?'

Kim held up her hand. 'Mum and Dad gave me this watch. Trudi gave me some handkerchiefs, Tony gave me a cassette for my radio, Grandma and Grandpa Hudson bought me some gloves and Mrs Casleigh brought me a brooch.' She pulled her coat to one side to show him. 'Oh, I've left it on my blouse. Never mind, I'll show you when we get back.'

Kim turned to look out of the window and Tom recalled his discussion with Serena about what to get his niece.

He had asked her what toy she thought Kim would like.

Serena frowned. 'How old is she?'

'Thirteen.'

'She doesn't want toys! She's a young woman, she wants pretty things, something personal, something to wear.'

'If you say so, but what? I don't know sizes or anything.'

'Tell you what, when the school bus comes in, I'll be at the

Stores and take a good look at her.'

'Do you know what she looks like?'

'Look Tom, you may think I'm a bimbo, but I have lived in the village a good few years and your brother practically lives next door. I do have eyes you know.'

'OK, OK,' he said, raising his arms in mock fear.

On their way to Tunbridge Wells to look for materials and curtains for the best room Serena suggested that a blouse or sweater might be a good present. Tom said if that is what she thought, go ahead.

If he had known what it was going to entail he would have sent her to shop alone. They had gone into two shops and Serena had queried all the stock causing assistants, and Tom, to raise their eyes to heaven. As they came to a large store Tom said he had had enough and he would see her in the café.

When she finally met him and showed him what she considered was appropriate, he asked. 'Are you always like this when you shop?'

'There's no point in buying something with which one is not satisfied,' she had said imperiously.

Kim broke into these thoughts.

'Mrs Casleigh's nice, isn't she? She came in yesterday on her way to the shops to give me the brooch. Do you like her, Uncle Tom?

'Very much, she is charming.'

'She doesn't seem to go with Mr Casleigh, does she? He always looks so serious – and unhappy.'

'You're very perceptive.'

'What does that mean?'

'That you can see things about people without them, or anyone else, telling you.'

'Dad said you all used to be good friends as children. I can't imagine you playing together – well not Dad and Mr Casleigh, anyway.'

'They both liked cars though, that's the reason Mr Casleigh asked your Dad if he'd like to run the garage he owned.'

Tom reflected upon their very early days, before Edward went to boarding school. They were almost inseparable and in the holidays they'd all three had such fun wandering round the farm, getting in Bill Patterson's way and generally being naughty boys. It was in those early days that Tom decided he wanted to farm.

Tom was not aware what a miserable life Edward was leading. His mother only hinted at it, but he and Jamie did not take it in – or understand. All they knew was that Edward's mother was a very peculiar woman. In contrast, he thought how happy his and Jamie's childhood had been. He couldn't imagine how being unloved and sent away from home at seven, might colour the rest of a person's life. Even so, there was no call for Edward to have dropped them when he was in his teens. Jamie said it was because Edward suddenly realised that they were labourer's sons, while he was lord of the manor.

'Mr Casleigh practically lived with us at Granny's in the school holidays, because his mother was hardly ever at the Manor.' Tom told Kim.

'Granny loved him very much, didn't she? Perhaps he's happier now he's married to Mrs Casleigh, she'll make him happy.'

It was a neat solution of Kim's, but Tom had his doubts.

'Why aren't you married, Uncle Tom?'

'Never had time for girlfriends. I was happy just farming.'

'Aren't you any more?'

'Of course, what makes you ask?'

'You said, "I was happy"'.

'Just a way of speaking.' Tom did not care for the line the conversation was taking.

'I'd like to marry someone like you.'

Tom smiled at her as they stood waiting for the train to come to a halt. 'You'd find me very boring.'

'But you'd buy me nice presents.' She grinned.

'You're a scheming little monkey and I pity the poor man who does marry you.'

She laughed and took his arm as they waited on the platform for Tony and Pat to join them.

*

When Tom came home that evening he saw Serena's car parked at the end of the track near the farmhouse. He drew up beside it.

'Serena?' he said as he tapped on the window. She jumped and flung open the door almost hitting him.

'Why the hell are you so late?' she said, getting out of the car.

'Pat and Jamie asked me to stay for dinner,' Tom said. 'I was going to treat them to a meal, but Pat said she'd prepared something for the evening, so I had to stay. Anyway, I wasn't expecting to see you.'

He unlocked the door, took off his coat and hung it behind the door as usual.

'I wish you wouldn't do that.'

'Do what?'

'Hang your coat on the door.'

Tom stared at her and went to speak, but he was feeling in a good mood and wanted to stay that way. He filled the kettle.

'Fancy a tea or coffee?'

'Coffee.'

'We had a great day. Serena. The jumper was a huge success and Kim couldn't thank me enough. It was rather embarrassing because she said it was the best present she'd ever had, and her Mum and Dad had given her a watch. She changed into the jumper straightaway and wore it up to town.'

Tom made the coffee and pushed a mug across the table to Serena. She closed her hands round it and took a sip.

'Why don't you get filter coffee, I hate this stuff.'

'Why didn't you ask for tea. I don't have the time to make proper coffee. I haven't a machine either which makes it doubly difficult,' he said jokingly, before continuing. 'We went to Madame Tussauds and the Planetarium and on to McDonald's.'

Serena pulled a face.

'The kids loved it. Then we took the tube to Trafalgar Square and fed the pigeons before catching the train home. I haven't enjoyed myself so much for a long time.'

She gave a grunt.

'For heaven's sake, what's the matter with you? You're like a bear with a sore head.'

'It was cold out there waiting for you.'

'I didn't know you were there, did I?'

'I wanted to see you.'

Tom scrutinised her face but could not read her expression. 'That's very gratifying, but you knew I was going out.'

'I'd forgotten.'

'Don't lie.'

'Well, I thought you'd be home earlier. I've been waiting ages and ages and it was cold.'

'The reason you're cold is that you don't eat enough. You're as thin as a rake. Get some flesh on you.'

'I suppose you'd like me to look like that wife of Edward's, all cosy and fat.'

Tom ignored her exaggerated criticism. 'You should have gone back when you saw I wasn't home.'

'You've no sympathy, have you?'

'No, not when you're being stupid.'

'I thought you loved me.'

Tom burst out angrily, his face reddening. 'I've never said that! You know I've never said that!'

'Don't you care about me at all?'

'Of course I do, don't I show it?'

'You kiss me occasionally.'

'Well?'

'I thought you loved me,' she repeated.

'I didn't say that. I've never said that,' Tom said angrily.

She stood up abruptly and the chair clattered across the stone floor.

'I'm going,' she said, marching to the door.

'Serena,' he called, but she was gone and the door slammed behind her.

Tom rushed to follow her into the yard, but she was already manoeuvring round his car and he watched her drive furiously up the track.

As he went back into the kitchen and locked the door, Tom realised exactly what Jamie had meant when he used to complain that he couldn't understand women.

Chapter 17

Tom rang Serena twice next day but there was no reply. When he still hadn't heard over the weekend he thought he would go into the village for shopping and, at the same time, call on her. As he pushed open the tinkling door of the Stores and grabbed a basket, he could hear Shirley Reece talking to a customer at the back of the shop. He wandered vaguely round the shelves not knowing what he needed, his mind on Serena's strange behaviour and sudden departure from the farm. Why had she said what she did? She knew the score. He did not love her, had never professed to; and she could not be in love with him either. Why had she come last Wednesday and why in such a bad mood? He suddenly wished he were like his brother. He could have teenage children now – older than Kim perhaps.

'Can I help you, Tom?'

Just as he thought his life was cheering up a bit, it now seemed to be getting complicated and intense. What was he looking for on this shelf?

'Tom Cresswell!'

He raised his head above the shelves. 'Yes?'

'I said, do you want any help.'

'No, I'm all right.' He reached for a tin of beans, searched for a few other items he may or may not have needed and walked to the back of the shop to get something for lunch.

'Mrs Detrale's father is ill, I hear,' Faith Tressant, the vicar's wife, was saying. 'She's gone to Berkshire to see him.'

'I thought I hadn't seen her lately. Not that she comes in here all that often.' Shirley Reece sniffed.

'Hello, Tom. I haven't seen you for ages.'

'I've been busy, Mrs Tressant.'

'I thought this was a quiet time of year.'

'Quiet?' he said, grinning. 'No time is quiet for a farmer. Actually I've been decorating.'

'It does need doing, doesn't it? When I was at your place for your mother's funeral I thought the rooms could do with a…' She stopped. 'I'm sorry, that was rude of me.'

'You're quite right, the rooms are in a state. The window frames were in a dreadful condition, so Edward's had the downstairs ones done. They've had to be replaced in wood to the same design 'cause it's a listed building. It's costing him a tidy sum, though no doubt I'll end up paying for it in raised rent.'

'My Dave says you haven't been in the pub much lately. Got yourself a young lady?' Shirley smiled artfully and gave a wink.

Why was everyone so obsessed with his social life? It dawned on him – his mother had kept them up to date and there was no one around now to inform the village of his movements and they had to speculate what he was up to. There were advantages to living in an isolated spot.

'You're niece is growing up into a lovely girl, isn't she?' Faith said. 'I noticed last Saturday when she came with Pat to do the flowers.'

Tom was grateful for the change of subject. 'She certainly is. We went up to London a few days ago and she was good company.' He smiled, recalling their tête a tête on the train.

Pleasantries exchanged, Mrs Tressant left and Tom paid for his purchases assuring Shirley that yes, he was missing his mother and no, he was not neglecting himself.

He walked home in pensive mood, annoyed that Serena had not seen fit to let him know about her father. At least this bit of village gossip had been informative, but he wondered how long before their friendship became public knowledge.

Enlightenment, when it came, did not hit the village. It seeped, like food through a sieve. Mr Anders, whose butcher's shop was almost opposite Serena's drive, noticed Tom's car there, but thought he had been delivering fruit and vegetables. The barman at the pub believed he had seen Tom and Serena in Maidstone, but they were lost in the crowd and the idea that they would be together was so unlikely he had dismissed it as an illusion. Chris Barratt saw Mrs Detrale's car at the farm at what he thought was a strange hour to call, but he assumed she had come for more apples.

It was only when villagers began to compare notes that they realised what had been going on. To say they were stunned was an understatement. They also resented the fact that it seemed to have been going on for some weeks without their being aware. Shirley Reece felt particularly incensed.

It went without saying that by the time each account had been told and re-told in homes, shops and pub, it was considerably embellished to suit the mood of the storyteller.

It was when he and Mike were working on Toilers Field a few days after he had been to the store that Tom knew their secret had been discovered.

'Tom?'

'Yes, Mike.'

'Er, I don't know how to put this.'

Tom thought he sounded guilty. 'Something wrong? What's up? Forgotten something I've asked you to do? It can't be that serious – out with it.'

'No, it's nothing like that.'

Mike stopped what he was doing and Tom stood up straightening his back.

'It's nothing to do with the farm,' he said 'it's, er, it's sort of personal.'

'You in some sort of trouble? If I can help, you only have to ask. Is it Sheila?'

'No, no, she's OK,' he said flustered.

'Well, what is it?'

'It's about you and, er…'

'Let me guess. It concerns me and Mrs Detrale, doesn't it?'

Mike stood awkwardly. He pushed back his cap and scratched his thinning hair. 'I thought you ought to know, that's all. I know it's nothing to do with me but I just thought you ought to know what's being said.'

'And what's that?'

'That you and Mrs Detrale are…'

'Yes?'

'Having an affair,' he said quickly, shuffling his feet.

Tom was not surprised they had been discovered, but he was surprised it had developed into an affair.

'And what do you think?'

'Think?'

'Has been happening between me and Mrs Detrale?'

'It's nothing to do with me. I just thought that if the gossip wasn't true, you ought to do something about it.'

Mike, at least, Tom was gratified to note, had some doubts.

'We're not having an affair, but we have been out to meals together and she's helping me with the decorating.'

'Well, Tom, you want to hear what's being said in *The Mitre*, and coupled with last year's story…'

'Last year's story? Oh you mean Susie's daft tale – well that wasn't true either as Mrs Casleigh informed you in no uncertain terms, if you remember.'

'Well – if there's nothing in it.' Mike shrugged and went back to work.

Tom supposed he had been naïve. As he had lived in a village all his life and heard the gossip, he should have realised how people made mountains out of molehills. It was more interesting to pep it up a bit. Unfortunately, fiction soon turned into fact, and as he and Serena were the least likely of souls to get together, Tom thought they must be having a field day. Had he been on the outside looking in on a similar situation, he would have enjoyed the tittle-tattle, though he liked to think he would not have believed all the tales.

Later that afternoon, Tom was sitting in the office tapping figures on to the computer with four fingers, when one of the men came in from the yard. Tom crossed the hall to the kitchen to see what he wanted, but it was not Chris or Mike.

'What do you think?' Serena cried as soon as he appeared. Her lovely eyes flashed as they had on the night he kissed her.

'Hello Serena, nice to…'

'What do you think people are saying?'

'What are they saying?'

'That we're having an affair.'

''So I've heard,' he said grinning. 'Mike told me this morning. The news broke, as the papers say, while you were away. When did you come back? You might have told me where you'd gone, I was worried.'

'We are not having an affair, and it's not funny. It was my turn to have the girls round for coffee this morning,' she said, placing herself in one of the new chairs, which had arrived in her absence.

To his disappointment she did not arrange her skirt and legs in the manner that always fascinated him.

'But Joss rang and said she wasn't coming and rang off. When I told Anna and Miriam about Joss, they sat studiously trying to avoid my eye. I asked what was wrong and had I said anything to upset her, but Anna said she didn't think it was anything I said.

When Miriam said, "don't blow your top", I knew something must be up.'

Tom smiled at Miriam's preventative measures, but quickly wiped it from his face when Serena raised her head to pin him with a steely eye.

'They said didn't I think I was stupid carrying on an affair with you what with the divorce and all that, and the reason Joss was upset was because Stephen did business with Jeremy.'

'Who's Stephen?'

'Joss' husband – does it matter?' she stormed.

'Can I get you something, Serena?'

'I kept assuring them there was nothing to the gossip and we'd just been out together, but I could see they didn't believe me – though Anna assured me she did.'

Serena stood up and paced around the kitchen. 'How dare Joss snub me like that. Who's spreading these lies?' She glared at Tom accusingly.

'I don't know exactly, but this is a small village and we could hardly keep our meetings secret for long. What are you so worried about, it isn't true?'

'It's all very well for you, you're not married.'

'You won't be soon.'

'I do not want to lose the few friends I have, and it might jeopardise my divorce.'

'You should've thought about that before.'

'Thank you for your sympathy, nothing's changed in my absence I see.'

'What exactly do you want me to do?'

'You could tell everyone it isn't true.'

'But who's going to believe me?' Tom said. 'You know this place. Once the village has got something into its head, it's the devil's own job to get the true story believed. Perhaps I could find out how it started.'

'How are you going to do that?'

'Dunno, Lydia managed to find out last time.'

'Yes,' she said scathingly, 'you do seem to make a habit of this sort of thing.'

'Prerogative of a bachelor.'

'Don't be so insufferable.'

'Sorry, I was only joking. But it was inevitable that someone would see us, either in the village or out and about.'

Serena sat down again and tapped her fingernails on the wooden arm of the chair. 'It was you who didn't want anyone to know we were seeing each other. You don't seem to care now.'

'I wasn't in the mood to be tormented by my brother or anyone else a few weeks ago. I was…'

'Trying to get over that stupid woman of Edward's,' she finished.

His tolerance exhausted, he said angrily, 'Stop running her down. Just because some stuck-up friend of yours doesn't approve of you consorting with a farmer, there's no need to take it out on me. You find out who's making a mountain of a molehill. You're the one who's upset, I couldn't care less. We've hardly done anything earth shattering, it's all in people's minds. What they don't know they make up.'

'Whether it's made up or not I've got to live with it,' she shouted.

'Pity you didn't think of that before you chased after me,' he countered.

'Of course, you haven't got anything out of seeing me, have you? "You looked so beautiful, I was bewitched",' she mimicked. Her voice trembled.

'That's about it,' he said callously.

Small tears formed on her lashes and trickled slowly down her cheeks. Tom hated to see her cry, but did not want to comfort her either. He considered she had got herself into this and wanted him to get her out of it.

'I don't suppose Jeremy really cared for me either,' she said, looking down at her hands. 'He might have done to begin with, but I suspect it was my looks that bewitched him. I probably came as a package, expensive house, good job, matching wife who looked the part.

'Everyone thinks that being attractive must be marvellous. It has its advantages, but it's like being wealthy, you never know if you're loved for yourself or your money.'

Serena rose from her chair and Tom stepped towards her intending to take her in his arms and apologise for being so insensitive, but she moved from his reach and went to the door. As she opened it she said, so quietly he hardly caught her words, 'It was pleasant while it lasted.'

'Serena,' he called, but made no move to go after her.

Tom sat for a long time after she had gone, his eyes roaming round his transformed kitchen – at the yellow walls, the bright check curtains, the 'featured' range, which he had learned meant blackening, and covering with ornaments and pictures. They had ordered two chairs in a cottage style which, she assured him, were just right. Serena appeared not to have noticed.

His life would not be the same. In spite of what she thought he did care – was fond of her even, but that did not stretch as far as loving her, did it? His life would go back to what it was before Lydia arrived. At least Serena had got him over his intense feeling for her. Perhaps he was meant to be what he had always been, a bachelor farmer in a small, quiet Kent hamlet he had never left. His attempts to rationalise his life left him feeling hollow and deeply despondent.

*

Tom walked from the farm to the lane on his way to see Wendy's new baby. An excited Chris had issued the invitation that morning. They had now moved into the cottage though, as Chris said, they could not say they were settled.

As he passed Mr Laurence's barn shop and drew parallel with the entrance to Abbey Manor, he saw Edward's Mercedes coming down the drive. Tom raised his hand. The car screeched to a stop beside him and Tom turned sharply, thinking Edward had had an accident. The door of the car flew open and he strode across to Tom.

'I suppose you did this to spite me,' Edward spat out.

Tom said nothing.

'Well, what have you to say?' he demanded.

'I haven't anything to say, I'm not answerable to you for what I do.'

'You've done this on purpose, haven't you? You couldn't have Lydia so you thought you'd have my best friend instead.'

'What's worrying you? Has Serena asked you to speak to me? Perhaps you consider you're her guardian in her estranged husband's absence.'

He saw Edward trying to curb his rising anger. 'I haven't seen Serena, but I think it's despicable the way you're behaving.'

'You haven't yet told me exactly what I've done that's upset you.'

'You know very well, it's the talk of the village. Lydia told me there's only one topic of conversation. Do you want me to spell it out?'

'Yes.'

'Your affair, man,' he shouted, 'your affair with Serena! Are you denying it?'

'I don't see what it's got to do with you whether Serena and I are having an affair or not, so I'll thank you to mind your own business. And if you're as worried about Serena's morals as you seem to be about mine, why don't you go and question her – that is if you dare. I don't know whether you've ever been at the end of her tongue, but it's quite an experience. However, I can't stop to chat any longer, I have a new baby to see. Goodbye.'

Edward's car passed him at great speed as he unlatched the gate and walked up the brick path.

'Come in and sit down, I'll get you a beer.' Chris danced round the room with such joy Tom thought he looked more like a ballet dancer than a farm hand.

'I'd rather have a tea or coffee, Chris, if you don't mind, but I'll wet the baby's head later.'

Wendy came down from upstairs followed, to Tom's surprise, by Lydia.

'Here he is, Daniel Peter Barratt,' said proud father.

Tom dutifully went to look at the little bundle and Wendy pulled the shawl away from the baby's face. He studied the tiny features and immediately thought of the last time he had looked at a new born baby – Kim, no doubt, probably in this very room.

'He's lovely, Wendy. How are you?'

'A little tired, but it's so wonderful being in our own place. You don't know how happy we are to be here. It's almost as wonderful as having Daniel.'

'Mrs Casleigh has come in to help.' Chris said. 'She has some furniture she thought we might like. We're so excited.'

Tom looked at the pair of them standing close together, Chris' arm round his wife and the baby moving its little arms in the air. Would I be like that if I had children, Tom wondered? His eyes moved to Lydia who stared at him, but not with the smile she usually bestowed.

When Tom had drunk his tea and considered he had spent a suitable length of time with the Barratts, he made his excuses and prepared to leave.

'I'll go, too,' Lydia said. She turned to Wendy. 'I'll come again in the week, but if you want any help meantime, you only have to ring.'

'Oh, thank you, you've been ever so kind. Bye Tom, bye Mrs Casleigh.'

When they were out in the lane Lydia said, 'How could you Tom? How could you consort with that ghastly woman? I feel betrayed.'

'Why is everyone so worried about what I do with my life?'

'But Serena Detrale – why her? Couldn't you have found someone else, there must be plenty of girls more your type.'

'That's rich, coming from you. How do you know what my type is? You urged me to find someone to vent my pent-up passion on you may recall? Well, I did. I'm sorry she doesn't meet with your approval, but it has nothing to do with you – either of you, as I told Edward just now.'

'But how could you carry on with her? She was so rude to you – and malicious. It was Serena who passed on the rumours to Edward last year, stirring up trouble.' They had now reached the Manor drive. 'I thought you were concerned about me you've told me enough times.'

'Ah, it's different now, I see. You can marry someone out of your class for the status it gives you, but I'm not allowed to dip my toe in these exalted waters.'

'But at least I'm married!' she cried.

'What exactly is being said about us and where has it come from this time?'

'That you're having a love affair and it has been going on since Christmas. You've been see together in Maidstone and – well, various stories are circulating.'

'And, of course, you've believed them, as has Edward and half the village it seems. A bit like the Susie Paterson incident last year.'

'Say they aren't true, Tom?'

'No, why should I? It's nothing to do with you.'

*

He had intended going to the pub in an attempt to scotch the rumours, but because Chris had taken a week off, he was too busy. He had also been trying to finish the best room, but his enthusiasm had waned now that Serena was no longer there to support him. Several times he had picked up the phone then put it down again.

He enjoyed Serena's company. How they'd laughed, especially at what she saw as his lack of sophistication and what he considered her incomprehension of farming and what went on in the real world.

He supposed she was in a difficult position still being married, but it was not he who started this fling, or whatever it was to be called. He wandered from the kitchen where he had just finished his evening meal and went into the best room. All he had to do now was clear up and hang the curtains Serena had chosen. She had dealt with the ones in the kitchen, spending ages pulling strings, tying knots and putting in hooks. He had not a clue what to do. She told him his suite was quite good and he should get new cushions and perhaps a couple of throws. Needless to say, he did not know what a throw was, but was now brave enough to ask. Tom longed to see her and yearned to hold her close and kiss her.

Tom shut the door of the best room. It was like closing a book one was enjoying but had no time to finish. He heard a car come down the track and pull up in the yard.

Serena! His heart leapt.

The kitchen door burst open. 'What the bloody hell d'you think you're playing at? What you trying to do – make up for lost time or something?'

Jamie slammed the door angrily behind him.

'Hello to you too. What are you doing here?'

But Jamie could not wait for polite greetings. 'Do you know what's being said about you this time?' Before his brother could reply, he went on, 'That you've been having it off with that Detrale woman?'

'Don't be so crude, and I…'

'Pat told me but I didn't believe her. Now everybody's talking about it and they're telling me as if it's my fault.'

'From the way you're acting it might as well be. I've not asked you to defend me.'

'So you're not denying it?'

'What are you accusing me of exactly?'

'Carrying on a – a love affair with that woman.'

'What's your definition of an affair?'

'Stop pussyfooting about. You know very well what an affair is.'

'In that case, no, we're not. We've had a couple of meals out together and she's helped me with the curtains and things – as you can see.' Tom spread one arm in an arc to take in the kitchen.

'But why her? You've told me enough times how much you hate her – and she's married.'

Tom shrugged. 'It just happened.'

'Happened my foot, something triggered it off.'

'It was your fault actually – when you asked me to take back her car, remember? She slapped my face and I slapped her back.'

'Oh what a good basis for a romantic affair,' Jamie said, incredulity written all over his face.

'I keep telling you it is – was not an affair.'

'Was? It's finished then?'

'This gossip has upset Serena. I won't be seeing her again.' When Tom said these words it felt like a stab.

'You want to see her husband.'

'Is he back?' Tom said alarmed.

'Not 'arf. He evidently went up to his house and she wasn't in so he came to the pub, presumably looking for you – or maybe just to have another drink. He was already pretty tanked up. He found me instead.'

'What did you say to him?'

'Not a lot at first, I hadn't been there for a few nights, so I hadn't heard all the stories, but he went on and on accusing you of seducing his wife and how you were going to regret it, etc, etc, till in the end I hit him.'

'You did what! My God, Jamie, I seem to be in enough trouble without you putting in your two pen'th. Who started this story anyway?'

'As far as I can make out everyone and his wife has seen you and Mrs Detrale everywhere, doing everything. From the tales circulating I think you two have had the whole of Grassenden travelling in the back of your cars, not to mention staying at both your homes.'

'But Serena only comes here when the men have gone home.'

Jamie studied his brother closely. 'So that bit's true.'

Tom coloured. 'Yes, but we've not done anything wrong.'

'I don't know what to say Tom, I just don't know what to say.' He shook his head slowly. 'I can't believe it – you and Mrs Detrale. As you said yourself, she's about as far removed from you as it's possible to get. What on earth do you talk about?'

'She was lonely – and she's good company. We just like to be together and I find her attractive.'

'That I can understand. But what on earth made her pick on you?'

Tom bristled. 'I'm not that repulsive. You'd better ask her.'

'I wouldn't go near her and I'd advise you not to either. There's a lot of trouble brewing and whatever you say did or didn't happen, people are going to suspect the worst. I bet this wouldn't have happened had Mum still been alive.'

'I don't see how you can say that,' he said indignantly. 'I wasn't tied to her apron strings.'

In his heart of hearts he thought Jamie was probably right. He would have talked to his mother about Lydia, got if off his chest and he would not have re-bounded into Serena's arms – at least he did not think so, though she had been persistent and he had become fonder of her than he liked to admit.

'I seem to have managed without women for over twenty years why, suddenly, do I have to get involved with two married women – albeit ones who appear about to shed their husbands.'

'I hope all works out well,' Jamie said, 'but I must admit, I wouldn't like to be in your shoes.'

'So, I cannot count on your support?'

'I hit a man on your behalf – what more do you want?'

'I don't somehow think that was very helpful.'

'What you going to do now?'

'Nothing. Go to be – alone.'

'Right then, I'll be going,' Jamie said, moving towards the door. 'I must say I wouldn't have recognised this room. Kim told us about it. It's a great improvement on what it was before. The woman's certainly got taste as well as good looks.'

Jamie opened the door but as he went to shut it he poked his head round and said, 'She didn't pay for all this, did she?' and quickly retreated.

'It's a good job I haven't a temper like yours,' Tom shouted after him, 'or you'd be found buried in the shit pile on Toilers Field.'

Chapter 18

Serena drove the car into the garage, turned off the engine and lay back in the seat. She was near to tears. In fact she could not remember when she had last felt so wretched – Edward's wedding most likely. Even the break-up of her marriage, whilst distressing, had been a protracted business with no very violent troughs, just endless rows. They had grown tired of each other and she had grown tired of the pretence that all was well. Now something that had put some zest into her days had ended.

Tom had brought a new dimension to her life. He was strong, though he gave the impression he was unsure of himself. He would let her push him so far, but no further. All the men she had ever known she could manipulate, even Jeremy most of the time.

She seemed assertive and tough, but nobody saw her sensitive side. Her bad temper and sharp tongue kept people at bay. She knew it, but seemed powerless to keep it under control. Though she enjoyed, and was used to being the centre of things, she always felt she was on the outside looking in. She could not call any of her friends close, except Edward, who had always accepted her as she was.

Serena shut the garage door and as she turned towards the house her eye caught sight of a figure turning into the drive. Her heart gave a lift – could it be Tom? Then she recognised the unsteady, sadly familiar gait of her husband.

'What are you doing here at this time of night?'

'Come to check up on you, sweetie. You weren't in earlier, so I went down to the pub. Thought I might see your lover there, but as he wasn't, I presumed you were with him.' Serena opened the front door. 'Were you?'

'Was I what?'

'With your lover.'

'I haven't got a lover.'

'That's not what I've heard.'

'Who from?'

'Stephen Maltby. Joss told him you were seeing that farmer chappy, Tom – Tom…' The effort to remember his name was too much. 'Mind if I get a drink?'

'Help yourself.'

She went through the kitchen to the utility room and hung up her jacket before returning to the drawing room. There she found Jeremy about to sprawl in a chair, a very large whisky in his hand. Serena sank into a chair opposite.

'I have been seeing Tom, seeing being the operative word. He's been here to dinner and I've had a meal out with him. I've also helped him decorate. End of story.'

'What about being seen kissing?'

'By whom?' she said disdainfully.

'Nearly everybody from the tales I've heard.'

'So, I've kissed him, what about it?' Serena tried to sound nonchalant.

'You're telling me that you've been kissing him in that isolated farmhouse and it stopped at that? C'mon, pull the other one. He'd be a fool not to take advantage.'

'Not everyone's like you.'

'You're a very beautiful woman.'

'So I've constantly been told. Sometimes I wish I'd been born ugly.'

'Oh, darling, you wouldn't have like that.'

'At least I would have found out…' She studied his face. 'What have you done to your lip? It's all swollen.'

'That brother of Tom's punched me.'

'Jamie, you mean, from the garage?'

'Yes.'

'Why did he do that?'

'Defending him I suppose.'

'He wouldn't just hit you for nothing. What were you saying?'

'Just telling him what was going to happen to his brother and he didn't like it.'

Alarmed, she said, 'What are you going to do?'

'I shall cross-petition for adultery – and I shall cite Tom what's-his-name.'

'But we haven't done anything!' she cried. 'Why are you being so spiteful?'

'I shall also bring charges against that garage man.' Jeremy took another swig from his glass.

Blearily, he looked across at his wife as she returned to her chair after pouring herself a large gin and tonic.

'There's something different about you, sweetie.' He peered at her through slitted eyes. 'I can't put my finger on it. You're not excitable, not so…'

'Exhausted is how I feel, so it's probably how I look. When are you going?'

'Expecting a visitor?'

'No, I want to go to bed, I'm very tired.'

Jeremy stood up unsteadily, drained his glass and waved it in the air. 'One more before I go?' He raised a questioning eyebrow.

'No, you've had more than enough already.' She eyed him. 'You're not driving I hope?'

'Still concerned about me then?'

'I wouldn't want you injured – or your Porsche damaged.'

'I haven't got the car, I came by train straight from work.'

'Shall I call you a taxi?'

'You wouldn't drive me to the station, would you?'

'No.'

'Oh well, a taxi then.'

Serena went to phone. When she returned Jeremy was leaning against the banister his face flushed. Beads of sweat stood out on his upper lip.

'Are you all right?'

'A bit breathless.'

'Why don't you stop drinking so much. It's not doing you any good. Have you seen a doctor?'

'Don't nag, at least I don't have to listen to you going on at me anymore. What's the point of seeing a doctor? He'd only nag as well and I'd have exchanged a nagging woman for a nagging man.'

In the past Serena would have been blazing with anger by now and they would have been well into on of their slanging matches. She heard a car draw up.

'Here's your taxi,' she said, handing him his coat.

'Well, sweetie, watch this space. You'd better warn that farmer to expect a letter from my solicitor.'

'You're going ahead with this then?'

'Of course, why should I be the guilty party.'

'You are the guilty party. You want to be thankful I didn't use your adultery as grounds for divorce.' Jeremy lifted his head in surprise. 'You didn't think I knew about your women, did you? The odd overnight stays, the weekends abroad. I chose to ignore them. I didn't want to be humiliated.'

Seeing no movement from the house, the taxi driver rang the bell.

'Goodbye, Jeremy.'

'Bye, sweetie.' He bent to kiss her, but she moved her head. She had shut the door before Jeremy reached the cab.

She ran a bath, needing to unwind and think. The warm, soapy water swirled about her and she let her thoughts roam.

Her father, Jeremy, Edward, Tom. Four men in her life and not one able to comfort or support her. Never had she felt so alone, so in need of sympathy and love.

Her father had had a stroke and as her brother lived in Connecticut, it was left to her to make arrangements for him to be looked after. He needed to be moved to a nursing home but where – here in Kent or in Berkshire? Could she perhaps look after him at Ridge House with the help of a nurse?

Jeremy. How could he be so vindictive? She hoped, for Tom's sake as well as her own, he would think better of it when he was sober.

And Edward. She had been so embarrassed and upset when he had tackled her after church last Sunday – in front of Lydia, too, though she had had the grace to move away. Everyone had been staring at her which, normally, would not have bothered her in the least. This time she felt like a museum exhibit.

*

'Serena,' he had said, staring sadly at her from his dark brown eyes, 'I've, er, there have been, er, stories circulating. I expect you've heard.'

'Yes, Edward, but do we have to discuss them here.' She looked around and faces turned away or eyes stared at some object that had amazingly appeared in the sky at that moment.

'Is it true? I tackled Tom and he – well, he didn't deny it. He told Lydia the same, told us to mind our own business.'

Serena was surprised, but smiled. That sounded like her Tom.

'I'm inclined to agree with him. I think we're old enough to look after ourselves.'

'But why him?' Edward said, clearly puzzled.

'Why not? He's nice looking, kind, decent.' She paused. 'Doesn't always let me have my own way. I like him, that's all there is to it.'

'But an affair. What did he do to – to…'

'Seduce me?' she said, the smallest of movements at the corner of her mouth.

Edward appeared shocked and Serena could well understand how Tom chose not to deny or explain. Edward was being so pompous, anybody would think she was his daughter.

'The truth is Edward, I was lonely and I asked him to dinner at my place. He asked me out for a meal, as a duty no doubt, and things developed from there. I've also helped him decorate – and that's it.'

His mouth dropped, whether from disbelief or disappointment she was not sure.

'But.' Serena went on, 'you're not the only sceptic, Jeremy is going to cite him.'

'Really?'

'You're pleased, aren't you? You're upset that Tom and I are friendly and are taking great delight in Jeremy's part in all this.' Serena began to see a new side to her friend. 'Why don't you like Tom?'

'He's in love with Lydia.'

'I know – he told me, but he isn't any more.' Serena said this with more conviction than she felt. 'You know, Edward, none of this would have happened had you married me.' He stared at her. 'You've never realised I've loved you, have you? All my life, ever since I was a child, I hoped you'd notice me in that way, but you never did.'

'You never said, Serena. Lydia guessed, but I didn't believe her.'

'Did she now? She's more astute than I've given her credit for. Women's intuition I suppose.'

'What are you and Tom going to do now?'

'Nothing. I can't speak for Tom, of course, but Jeremy's got to prove adultery, which he can't, as there hasn't been any. I can't do anything about the gossip, people believe what they want to believe and I'm inclined to agree with Tom, that it's none of their business. In my case, I am still married. Tom's in a different position, so let's say it's been a nice interlude in my otherwise lonely life.'

'We were going to ask you to dinner, weren't we – last year, before Lydia left?' he said guiltily. 'I'll have to have a word with her.'

'I don't think I'd be very welcome. Let's leave things for now, I've too much on my plate at the moment. My father's had a stroke, you know.'

They discussed her father, old times and childhood holidays, then, from the corner of her eye, she saw Lydia approach. Serena said goodbye and raised her hand to Lydia. Curious, hostile, but she hoped some sympathetic eyes followed her disconsolate steps as she walked home.

*

The water cooled and she gave a shiver as she stepped from the bath and reached for her towelling robe.

In the large four-poster with its pale green drapes, surrounded by the tasteful furnishings of her bedroom, Serena thought of the fourth man in her life.

Serena had never been upstairs at the farm, let alone in Tom's bedroom – but she could imagine it: spartan in the extreme, cold, untidy and in need of decorating. Decorating! What fun that had been – explaining to Tom about colours and design and his look of incomprehension. He had been wary of her at first and hardly dare speak, but after he had kissed her… Now she would never see the best room finished (what a funny name for a room) or the furniture they had ordered. She frowned. Or had it been there when Tom told her it was only her beauty that attracted him. He had been so unkind. Did he really only admire her looks, was there nothing about her he loved – no, liked, he had told he did not love her?

All the men she had ever known professed to love her – even after she was married. She could have had plenty of affairs like Jeremy had. How ironic she should now be accused of adultery with someone who had made clear his lack of feeling for her.

Serena plumped up her pillows, settled down in her lonely bed and wept tears of misery and self-pity.

*

'Serena! I'm so pleased you've rung.'

'Jeremy's going to cite you in our divorce.'

'What!'

'I know, I told him he would need proof but I'm hoping he was drunk and didn't mean it. He also said he was going to have your brother charged with assault. Whatever possessed Jamie to punch him?'

'He's like that, he loses his rag easily. Does that mean I can't –

you don't want to see me any more?'

'I didn't think you wanted to.'

'I didn't mean what I said, I was just annoyed.'

'No, I don't think it's a good idea for us to see each other.'

'I've missed you so much, Serena.'

'No one to hold your hand while you're decorating?'

'Don't speak like that, please.'

'Well, if there's nothing else I'll ring off.'

'No, don't go Serena. I want to talk to you.'

'What about?'

'I don't know – just talk. Has Edward spoken to you?'

'Yes, I was called to account.'

'What did you tell him?'

'More or less, I gather, what you did, that it was nothing to do with him.'

'Good for you.'

'But I did give him the facts, I felt I owed him that much. He is my friend, probably the only one I have left.'

Tom waited for her to go on, but all she said was, 'Is that all, Tom?'

'I – yes,' he said sadly, 'I won't keep you.'

'Bye Tom.'

Tom replaced the phone like an old man with aching bones, but it was not his bones that were aching.

Chapter 19

Tom took the post from the box outside the kitchen door. He rifled through the pile and picked out a thick envelope with an unfamiliar feel. Ponsonby, Jackson and Tope, it proclaimed on the back. This was what he had been dreading – the letter from Jeremy Detrale's solicitor.

Before he could open it, Chris bounded into the room still euphoric over the birth of his son. Tom listened respectfully to the latest report before telling him what was to be done that day.

'I thought I'd stay this evening like I did before, to catch up for the time I've had off.'

'There's no need. What about Wendy? Won't she want you at home?'

'No, her Mum's 'ere. I told her what I was going to do. They'll be happy together nattering.'

'OK Chris. Mike and I didn't get round to checking and cleaning all the machinery. He'll tell you what still needs to be done. I'm going round to Jamie's tonight, so make sure everything's locked up.'

When Chris had gone and he had dealt with the post, he went into Maidstone to see his solicitor and explained the situation.

Mr Dredgar said he would write a disclaimer and thought, in all probability, it would be dropped because to cross petition in a divorce would cost a great deal of money. In view of what Tom had said, Mr Detrale would have to prove adultery, also costly, and it seemed to him an expensive way of annoying his wife.

When he left the solicitor he went to the café near the river. He felt considerably cheered by what he had said, but it still hung over him. He had done his best to tell those he had come across that there was no truth in the rumours, but he was sure most were sceptical if not downright unconvinced.

He sipped his coffee and glanced across the tables where he saw Serena, beautiful and elegant as usual, sitting alone. His heart went out to her and he longed to go over and touch her, to take her home and kiss away the sadness he could see on her face. She was desultorily moving a spoon backwards and forwards in her sugarless coffee as she gazed at the tablecloth. He wrestled with the desire to go over, but instead drained his cup and hurriedly paid at the desk before driving back.

*

'Have you brought me anything nice, Uncle Tom?' Tony said, as he came in the back door of the bungalow that evening.

'Tony! Don't say things like that!'

'I was only asking.'

'Well, don't, it's rude. I keep telling you about asking for things.'

Tom laughed. 'I've brought your mother some apples and a bottle of wine for your dad. Is that all right?'

'S'pose so,' he said grudgingly as he left.

'Sorry about that, he's been driving me mad all day – well ever since he came in from school, just seems like all day.'

'I have got some chocolate for them both, but I thought I'd better hang on to it. Where's Kim?'

'In her room, doing her homework. She's very tetchy.'

'Oh, what's wrong.'

'I don't know for sure. She's at a funny age, all moody and morose. I think it has something to do with you.'

'What have I done? I haven't seen her since she came to see the kitchen.' Pat did not answer, but began to strain the vegetables. 'Do you know?' he persisted.

'Hello brother dear,' Jamie said coming into the kitchen. 'Want a beer? Come on through.'

He followed Jamie into the living room where the dining table was set at one end. Pat came in with two vegetable dishes. As she went back to the kitchen she called, 'Come on kids, dinner's ready.'

Tony rushed from the far end of the room where he had been watching television. Kim did not appear.

'Look, Pat, if you think I've upset her, shall I go and see if I can find out what's wrong then I can sort it out. You start.'

Pat looked sceptical, Jamie puzzled and Tony looked hungry and impatient.

'If you like.'

Tom left the room and knocked on Kim's bedroom door. There

was no answer.

'Kim, it's Uncle Tom, may I come in?' Still no answer. He turned the handle and poked his head round the door.

'What's wrong? Your Mum thinks I've done something to upset you?' There was no acknowledgement that he had even entered the room. 'Have I?'

He walked over to where she was sitting on the bed reading a book. He sat down and reached for her hand, which she pulled away.

'Is it to do with me and Mrs Detrale?'

'You told me lies,' she hissed. 'You told me the lady in the shop helped you. She didn't, did she? I thought you'd chosen that jumper yourself – just for me, but it was Mrs Detrale. She bought it, didn't she? And,' she said, shaking with outrage and resentment, 'you told me you'd never had a girlfriend but you were seeing her all the time.'

'Don't you want me to have some company? It gets a bit lonely at times.'

'You said you didn't have time for girlfriends.'

'I know, Kim. I'm sorry, I did lie to you.'

Kim was not going to let him salve his conscience with an apology.

'The children on the bus tease me because they know you're my uncle. They all think you're disgusting,' she spat out.

'But Kim, what's being said isn't true.'

'No one believes you and neither do I. If you can lie to me about my present, you can lie about that.'

Tom thought the comparisons hardly in the same league, but to Kim his deception was tantamount to treason.

'What can I do to make amends?' Tom said at last.

'Nothing.' Kim stood up. 'I'm going to have my dinner and I hope I'm not sitting next to you.'

'I was going to buy you a toy till Mrs Detrale pointed out you were now a young lady,' he said, hoping to placate her. It did not.

'Don't pat – paten – talk to me as if I'm a little girl. You can take the jumper back as far as I'm concerned. I shall never, ever wear it again.' She went to a drawer and wrenched it open. 'Here.' Kim flung the pink jumper on the ground at his feet. 'Get her to return it, she might get your money back.'

She flounced out of the room with all the dignity she could muster.

During the course of one of the most wretched mealtimes he had ever experienced, Tom learned that Jamie was to go to court in a couple of weeks on a charge of assault. Kim muttered that she could not imagine how her father could stick up for such a horrible man.

Tom went as soon as the meal was over, too uncomfortable to stay. He put the two chocolate bars on the worktop in the kitchen, certain both would end up in the same mouth.

On his return he went into the best room which he had finished. He had even put up the curtains after studying the ones in the kitchen. He reached for a book from the case and settled down to read *Crime and Punishment* which, in the circumstances, he thought most appropriate.

He opened the book, but the episode with Kim kept circling in his head causing him to read the same sentences over again. He did not know how to put things right. Should he try to talk to her again – or phone perhaps? Or would it be better to see her? Perhaps he should he speak to Pat first?

Deep in thought, the sound of the phone ringing made him start. He put the book down and went to his office.

'Hello, Tom?'

'Yes.'

'It's Wendy.'

'Hello Wendy, how are you? Bet your mother's having a great time? What does she think of her latest grandson?'

'She thinks he's lovely.' She sounded agitated. 'Tom, do you know where Chris is? I was expecting him home by now.'

'He was going to do some overtime. Didn't he tell you?'

'Yes, I know, but he said he'd be home around eight at the latest and it's now half past nine.'

'I expect he's forgotten the time. I'll go and have a look and ring you back.'

'OK, thanks.'

Tom took his coat from the door and walked out into the yard heading for the oast. As he rounded the barn he could see in the distance the glow of light from the oast doorway shining on the ground and as he drew closer, the sound of a radio. He called as he went into the oast.

'Chris, where are you? Wendy's rung.'

He went back outside and saw one of the tractors over by the wall, which he thought a funny place to leave it. He presumed

Chris must have wanted it out of the way. Tom strode over and saw Chris lying on the ground looking underneath.

'What on earth are you doing down there? Wendy wants to know why you aren't home yet?'

*

'I must see you Serena,' Tom said desperately.

'What is it? What's wrong?'

'There's been an accident here.'

'What sort of accident – something on the farm? I thought I heard an ambulance last night. Are you all right?'

'I'm all right, but I don't want to talk about it on the phone. Please let me see you Serena – now.'

'Now? Well, you can't come here and I'm certainly not…'

'I know, I know. Can't we meet somewhere else?'

'How far away?'

'Oh, I don't know, at one of your friends' perhaps.'

'What friends?'

'What about Anna?'

'Meeting at her house isn't much better than meeting here. That Susie Patterson lives there with her eagle eyes.'

'She's away at the moment. Anyway, ring Anna, please Serena.'

'What about our cars being seen outside?'

'I'll walk.'

'But it's miles away!'

'I walk that daily on the farm.'

'Oh, very well, I'll get back to you.'

*

Tom went up the short path of the double fronted Victorian house which lay on the outskirts of Grimley Heath. It stood alone with a field between it and the beginning of the village. Serena had passed him a couple of hundred yards back and her car was parked outside in the road. The front door was ajar and he pushed it open and stepped into the hall.

'In here, Tom.'

Because Serena had sounded less than pleased at his summons, he had determined to keep as detached as possible, but when he saw her his resolve melted and he went to her, anxious to find some consolation as he clasped her to him.

'Chris Barratt died last night,' he informed her dully.

'Let's sit down,' she said leading him to a chair and going to sit opposite.

'What happened?'

He told her about Wendy's call and finding Chris.

'It was terrible,' Tom said rubbing his fingers up and down his temple. 'His legs were crushed and his head was – was resting beside the front wheel.'

Serena reached out both hands and rested them on his.

'I checked his pulse, which was weak and called his name. He murmured something and I put my head down to catch his words. I just caught – caught – one word.' Tom found it difficult to go on and Serena waited till he gained control. 'One word – Daniel.'

She went round the table and stood behind his chair. He reached up for her hand as she put her arms round his shoulders.

'Daniel is his three week old son.'

A few moments passed while Tom struggled to continue. 'I called an ambulance, but in the confusion I forgot about Wendy. She'd seen the ambulance come up the lane and had a feeling something was wrong. She walked to the farm and arrived just as they were putting him into the ambulance.'

Tom turned his head into the sleeve of Serena's coat and his muffled voice said. 'He died on the way to the hospital.'

There was a light tap on the door and it was pushed open. Anna stood hesitantly in the doorway carrying a tray.

'I thought you might like a drink.'

Serena beckoned her in and returned to her seat.

'Shall I go?' she whispered to Serena.

'No,' Tom said, 'Don't go. I appreciate your letting us meet here. You understand our position.'

'Tom has just told me that one of his farm hands was killed last night on the farm. His wife has only just had a baby.'

Anna turned to Tom. 'How awful for you, I am so sorry. Did you – was it you who found him?'

'Yes.'

'What a shock.'

Anna heard her phone ring and excused herself. Serena sipped her coffee, Tom stared unseeing into his.

He had not slept all night. A near hysterical Wendy went with the ambulance. He went to explain and console Wendy's mother and offered to take her to the hospital then he rang Abbey Manor. It was nearing eleven when Edward answered and he arranged for Lydia to baby-sit Daniel. Tom eventually arrived back at the farm around three, but was by then past sleep and too distressed to attempt it.

They sat silently for several minutes each waiting for the other to voice feelings and answer questions neither could put into words.

'Why did you ask to see me? Why not your sister-in-law or Jamie?'

'I'm not very welcome there at the moment. Kim found out I hadn't bought the jumper and she's going through a bad time on the school bus because of us.'

'Oh,' she said, in a small voice.

'And – I desperately wanted to see you.'

She smiled. 'Have you heard from Jeremy's solicitors?'

'Yes. My solicitor seems to think it won't come to anything because of the expense.'

'Yes, that's what my man said. Jeremy wouldn't worry about the cost, but I wouldn't have thought him that vindictive either. His pride was hurt.' She paused. 'The damage is already done as far as we are concerned, hardly anyone believes our denials.'

'I know.' Tom took her hand. 'I saw you in Maidstone yesterday.'

'Where? I didn't see you.'

'In Delaney's. You looked so unhappy I wanted to come over and hug you.'

After another silence she said, 'Have you finished the best room?'

'Yes, you must come and see…' He stopped. 'When's this going to end?' he said despairingly. 'I can hardly bear to go back home. Everything is looking better than it's ever looked but I'm…'

'… unhappier than you've ever been. Me too.'

Tom wearily pushed himself up from the chair and put his untouched drink back on the tray. She came round and stood in front of him. He put his hands on her shoulders and went to speak.

'No need to ask, Tom.'

He pulled her close and his eyes roamed over her face as if memorising every feature. He put one hand behind her head and bent to kiss her – gently at first, then passionately, almost roughly, putting into it all the frustration he felt life was unjustly handing out to him. He let her go and, without speaking, left the room.

*

Tom and Mike sat in the impersonal room of the Coroner's Court. Tom had not known what to expect, something large, the word Court bringing to mind cavernous rooms that he had seen on the television. They had heard the reports from the police and consultant pathologist and the Coroner was now speaking to Tom.

'Mr Cresswell – could you tell us your version of events on the day in question.'

'I saw Chris – Mr Barratt – in the morning and he told me he was going to stay late that evening and look over the machinery in the oast – that's where we keep most of the farm tackle.'

'And the tractor?'

'Usually two of the tractors are in there. There isn't room for all of them. Sometimes there's one in the barn or even left in a field. It depends what we have been doing that day – or what we are doing the next.'

'Continue.'

'I told him to tell Mr Lucas, my other farm hand, that he was staying late and he would tell him what machinery still needed checking and cleaning. I also asked him to lock up to save me having to do it as I was going to my brother's for a meal.'

'Did you usually supervise security on the farm?'

'Yes, because I'm on the spot, though I might not physically do the padlocking, or whatever.'

'Go on.'

'I came home earlier than expected and sat reading. Then Chris' wife rang saying she had expected him home and was worried. I said I'd go and investigate and ring her back. I thought he'd probably lost track of the time.'

'What time was this?'

'About nine-thirty.' Tom licked his dry lips. 'The oast is about three or four minutes from the farmhouse, but it's out of sight. I came round the barn and I could see lights on in the oast and I could hear a radio. I went into the oast and called, but there was no reply. I came out again and saw Chris on the ground close to the tractor. I hadn't noticed him as I approached because the tractor hid him. My first thought was that he was looking underneath, but when I came up to him…'

Tom had tried to blot out the picture from his mind.

'There's no need to hurry, Mr Cresswell.'

'The tractor appeared – appeared to have run over his legs and the front wheel was resting – it looked as if it were resting by his head, but I think it had hit him. I knelt down and called his name. His eyes were shut but he murmured – murmured something. I felt for a pulse but it was very weak. I took off my coat and covered him then rushed back to the farmhouse to phone for an ambulance.'

'Did you inform the police?'

'Not straight away, the ambulance men told me to do it. I hadn't thought about phoning them.'

'That'll be all. Thank you Mr Cresswell.'

Tom was relieved when the coroner dismissed him. How many times had he re-lived that scene in his head and Wendy arriving in the farmyard from the footpath in time to see her unconscious husband put in the ambulance. He did not think he would ever forget the scream that rent the air that night. He still woke up in a sweat hearing her.

It was Mike's turn as the inquest resumed.

'Mr Lucas, we've heard from the police that the handbrake might have been faulty. Would you say that the machinery at Abbey Farm was well maintained?'

'Yes, Mr Cresswell was very fussy. He hardly let us do even small things to the tractors or any of the machinery, even though we could. He always had it seen to by his brother, what runs the local garage.'

'And the faulty handbrake?'

'The handbrake wasn't faulty, but it did need pulling on to the last notch.'

'Did Mr Barratt know this?'

'Yes.'

'And Mr Cresswell?'

'I don't know, prob'ly not. He didn't drive the tractors quite as much as we did, and he might not have driven this partic'lar one lately anyway.'

'If he had known the handbrake was getting slack, what would he have done about it?'

'Oh, he'd have told us not to use that one till Jamie had seen to it. Very partic'lar, he was.'

'In the absence of any witnesses,' the Coroner summed up, 'the police deduce from their inspection that the handbrake was not engaged and the tractor had begun to run backwards. It could be that Mr Barratt saw the tractor moving, ran to try and pull the handbrake up another notch but it had gained too much momentum. He fell and a wheel ran over his legs and then hit his head. The consultant pathologist has told us that the crushing of Mr Barratt's legs would not have killed him, but that the fall, plus the wheel hitting the side of his head, fractured his skull and caused the fatality.'

The verdict was accidental death.

Chapter 20

Most days tended to pass in a haze and Tom functioned around the farm rather than worked. Though twenty years Chris' senior, Mike too, had had a good working relationship and they often drank together.

Everything undertaken reminded them of Chris, but as they worked in an almost trance-like state, neither could bring himself to talk to the other about the accident.

Tom went to see Wendy one or twice a week, but there was little he could do to help. He thought he received more from the visits than Wendy did. He only knew he needed to do it, though it broke his heart to see her red-rimmed eyes and the way she sat gazing at Daniel's little face. That she drew some comfort from the bittersweet reminder of her husband was all Tom could hope.

Once or twice he saw Lydia there, but he could now look at her quite dispassionately. He began to compare her with his fiery Serena who, since their enforced absence, seemed to haunt him as Lydia had once done. But the feelings were different. Lydia had never been a part of his life; he had loved her in his imagination.

Serena had enhanced his days, made his house a home and stirred in him desires he had not known were missing. Was that love? And if it were, where could it lead?

Edward came to broach the subject of the cottage and what was to be done if a new farmhand needed accommodation.

'I don't know,' Tom said listlessly. 'I could try a bit of poaching – see if I can find someone working on a farm round here who already has somewhere to live. I haven't been out and about lately to hear any farming news.'

'I'll leave that to you then. Perhaps you'll get back to me.'

'I'll see what I can do.'

'You've got someone from the agency to replace Chris, haven't you? What's he like?'

'Competent enough, but a bit surly. Doesn't do much to lift the gloom.'

'No, I'm sure.'

*

Tom had not seen Serena since their meeting at Anna's, and though he had been invited to Jamie's for meals, he had declined when he knew Kim would be there.

Pat told him to ignore her. 'She's at a difficult age and your affair will be a nine-day wonder. She'll soon forget and come round in the end, then you'll be her favourite uncle once more.'

Pat's attempt at reassurance had not been reassuring at all, and her remark about his affair only served to annoy. What was the point of denying anything if his own family did not believe him?

He looked at another room in the farmhouse wondering if he could face decorating it, but he had shut the door decisively, not having the energy or heart to tackle something that reminded him of happier times. There was no point anyway he convinced himself. The upstairs windows would have to be replaced and Edward was not likely to have those done in a hurry.

So he did his work, kept the farmhouse reasonably tidy – in deference to Serena – and tended his garden, another neglected area.

There were only two things that had lightened the past weeks. One was the dropping of Jeremy's petition; the other was the result of the assault charge. When Jamie went to write the cheque for the fine, he was told that it had already been paid. On his return from court Jamie rang to thank him, but in spite of Tom's denial, he was convinced it had been him. Tom suspected it had been Serena. Heaven forbid that Jamie should find that out.

A cold, wet spring had done little to raise the spirits of the little hamlet still traumatised by the accident. It seemed there had been no sun for weeks, just dull leaden skies. May, however, arrived bringing cloudless skies and hot, summer-like sunshine.

Tom was in the garden, which extended to two sides of the farmhouse. The front, if the front door indicated the front of the house, and the side farthest away from the farmyard.

The L-shaped garden was prettily designed thanks to Laura Patterson. She had, over the years, created it from scratch. There was a small vegetable plot that Tom endeavoured to keep up mainly so he could supply Pat and Laura with fresh produce. It was this area he was tending now.

He put his hand in the small of his back as he stood and held his face towards the sun. Some lines from a poem he had learned came into his head.

> *And sweet the hops upon the Kentish leas*
> *And sweet the wind that lifts the new-mown hay,*

Not quite new-mown hay time, he thought. He could not remember who had written it or where he had learned it. It sounded like something Miss Quentin, or Miss Cretin as Jamie called her, would give them. He laughed. If that were the case, it would have been the village school.

He heard a car coming down the track. He stuck his spade in the ground and carefully picked his way along the path that had so annoyed Serena on her first nocturnal visit.

Jamie leapt out of the car. 'I've come to look at that trailer.'

'I'll just go and wash my hands.'

While he stood watching his brother at the sink Jamie said, 'I saw an ambulance turn into the Manor drive as I came up the lane. D'you think it's something to do with the baby? When's it due?'

'About mid July I think Lydia said when she was still speaking to me.'

'In that case it's very early.'

'It's Sunday so Edward's home.'

'Right, where's this trailer then, in the oast?'

They walked across the yard.

'It's the one over there,' Tom said. 'There's something wrong with the wheel.'

Jamie bent down to inspect it. 'You know, I think you're getting a bit too worked up about the equipment on this farm. You could easily have done this up yourself. That's all it needs. Look.'

Tom stooped to see what Jamie had done. 'Yes, I see. I expect Mike would have done if I hadn't noticed it first. I can't forget – that's the trouble. I keep thinking if I'd known Chris wouldn't have been allowed to use that tractor.'

'Tom, you can't go on saying what might have been. Chris did know – it was not your fault. I know you won't forget, but it's gotta be put behind you.'

Jamie dusted his hands one against the other. 'Trust Mike. He's been working with farm machinery for years, and so have you. Mike knows what he can and can't do.'

Tom locked the doors and they walked back to the farm.

'You're right, I'll try and do as you say. How's everyone?'

'OK, 'cept Kim. She wasn't very well this morning, said she felt sick so she's stayed in bed.'

'No good me coming to see her, I suppose.'

'Dunno, she never speaks to me 'bout you – she may do to Pat.' He sat down in one of the new chairs. 'How's your new chap shaping up?'

'He's OK.'

'You don't sound thrilled.'

'He works well enough but I don't care for him. He's sullen and rude, especially to Mike. I have an awful feeling he's going to ask to be taken on permanently.'

'You know Kim's doing ever so well at school,' Jamie said. 'Me and Pat went there last week to a Parents' Evening and they had nothing but praise for her in all subjects.

'Even yet,' Tom said dryly, 'the Cresswell labourers might compete with the Casleigh elite on equal terms.

'Twenty-five odd years and you still can't forget.'

'And you!'

'Yes, but you were closer to Edward than me.'

'Well, it's a long time ago now. I don't even lust after his wife any more.'

'You know, you're a dark horse. I'm your brother and I just dunno what makes you tick. Take this Mrs Detrale business....'

'I don't want to talk about it,' Tom said sharply. 'Fancy a beer, or is it too early?'

※

Later that evening Tom was sitting in the best room with his feet up in the armchair opposite. He was deep in his book when the phone rang.

'Tom, can you come down quickly? Kim's been taken to hospital and Pat's gone with her, but I want to go too. I'd like you to be here with Tony in case – in case we're back late.'

Tom heard the panic in Jamie's voice. 'What's wrong?'

'You know I told you she wasn't well. When I got back Dr Gifford was here. Pat'd called him 'cause Kim seemed a lot worse. She was complaining about the lights being bright and her neck hurting and he called an ambulance straightaway.'

'What does he think it is?'

'He thinks – oh Tom – he thinks it's meningitis.'

Tom felt as if someone had hit him hard in the chest. What

have I done to deserve this he asked an unnamed deity?

*

'Kim's gone to hospital Uncle Tom,' Tony said as soon as he saw him.

'I know, your Dad told me. I'm going to stay while he goes to the hospital.'

'That's good, you can play with me. Dad says I needn't go to bed yet.'

Tom looked at Jamie to see if this were a figment of his imagination, but Jamie had already put on his jacket and was going out of the room.

'See you later. Behave yourself Tony' he said automatically.

'Yes Dad,' he replied equally automatically as he went to a box in the corner and pulled out several games.

'You're not very good at board games, are you?' Tony said with some glee. 'Nowadays Kim always beats me and I get fed up playing with her. She isn't like she used to be, she treats me like a baby.'

Tom grinned as he remembered having the same feeling of superiority over Jamie.

As his nephew had so shrewdly assessed, Tom was not good at games, but even if he had been, he would not have been able to concentrate. By the time Tom considered Tony should be in bed, he had lost all they had played.

Pat and Jamie came back about midnight and said Kim was very ill and it was just a matter of waiting. The hospital said Pat could stay, and she had only returned for some suitable clothes and washing bag.

For the next few days Kim hovered between life and death. The first time Tom went to see her she appeared to recognise him and squeezed his hand. He could hardly stop himself crying.

Tonight he was at the hospital with Pat and Jamie and Kim was unaware of his presence or anyone's. Pat sat on the opposite side of the bed crying.

Jamie came in from the corridor and said, 'Look, darling, why not go back home. A sleep in your own bed will give you a break. I'll stay here and call you if anything changes.'

Pat drove her car on to the garage forecourt and turned to Tom as she switched off the engine.

'You quite sure you wouldn't like me to take you right home?'

'Quite sure, I'd like to walk, it'll clear my head a bit.'

Pat put her hand on his knee. 'I understand.'

'Are you all right? Would you like me to stay for a while?'

'No, I want time to think, like you do – and rest if I can.'

Pat locked the door and came round the car. Tom gave her a hug and kissed the top of her head. 'Let's look on the bright side.'

She smiled weakly and he watched her slow steps as she made her way up the path to the front door.

Instead of crossing the road and going home via the footpath into Abbotts Lidiard Lane as he originally intended, he turned and went up the High Street towards the church. He felt drained, bloodless and empty, like a slowly deflating balloon.

Almost without realising he turned into Serena's drive. It was deathly quiet in the village apart from the church clock striking the half-hour. He rang the bell and stood shivering though the night was not cold. After a few minutes he saw a light come on in the hall and Serena's outline showed through the stained glass.

'Who's there?'

'It's me – Tom.'

The bolts clattered, the locks clicked and the door opened a crack revealing her lovely face. She pushed the door to and took off the chain.

'Serena, oh Serena. I just want to see you.'

She reached for his hand and pulled him into the hall. His face was haggard and the eyes dull from lack of sleep.

'Is it Kim?' she said, 'I heard she'd been taken to hospital. She's not died, has she.'

Tom shook his head slowly, unable to speak

'I don't think I can take much more,' he said eventually.

Still grasping his hand Serena drew him into the drawing room and led him to the settee. She put on the fire and returned to sit beside him, putting her arm round his drooping shoulders. He managed to tell her it was touch and go with Kim, and then he rested his head on her shoulder and fell into a deep sleep.

He was at home in the cottage. His mother was comforting him. Why was he upset? Was it something at school? But he liked school – was good at his lessons. No, he was desperately, deeply sad, not just upset. His father was dead. That was it! His father had died, quite suddenly of a heart attack. Here he was sitting on the little settee in front of the living room fire with his mother's arm around him. He could feel the tears that made his cheeks itch and his throat hurt trying not to cry because he was too old for that. Now he would have to take care of his mother and Jamie. He forced his eyes open and saw the fire burning brightly in the hearth.

But it was not his hearth, and where was his mother? He rubbed his eyes and lifted his head. Serena was curled up in an armchair, eyes closed, the flames from the fire playing over her face accentuating her bone structure.

All the misery came flooding back. His mother dead. Chris. Kim.

He raised himself on one elbow and saw he was covered with a travelling rug. The movement woke Serena.

'What's the time?' he asked. 'How long have I been sleeping?'

Serena glanced at the clock on the marble mantelpiece. 'It's twenty to two and you've been asleep over an hour.

Tom sat up and pushed the cover from his legs. 'I shouldn't have come, I just didn't want to be alone. I'm sorry. I'll go home now.'

She rose from the chair, tightened the ties of her pale green dressing gown and bent to turn off the fire. She came over and smoothed her fingers across his brow and he turned his head to kiss her wrist.

'Don't go,' she said softly, 'Stay with me.'

For several moments they held each other in the silent, darkened room, a beating heart all each could hear. They climbed the stairs hand in hand.

* * *

Tom slowly roused and without opening his eyes he stretched his legs down the bed and felt the warmth of Serena's body along the length of his. He put his hand across her and moved it over her stomach and up to caress her breast. He opened his eyes and in the faint light he gazed at her beautiful face, serene in sleep, just like her name. Her hair was attractively tousled and he could study her thick, curling lashes now her eyes were shut. He traced his finger over her cheek and down to her chin. Sleepily her eyes opened and her lips moved in a Mona-Lisa-like smile. He twined his fingers in her hair and kissed her,

'I have missed you so much.' He kissed two fingers and put them to her lips and she put out her hand to touch his face. 'But I didn't mean this to happen.'

'Don't be sorry, I'm glad you came. Must you go now?'

'Yes.'

Tom sensed her eyes watching him as he dressed. The pale, dawn light filtered through the slightly parted curtains. He reached across to kiss her again fighting the desire to stay and tell her he loved her.

'May I borrow this comb?' He pointed to the dressing table.

'Don't you want to wash or anything?'

'No, I'll do that at home. Goodbye.'

'Tom, couldn't we....' But he did not hear her as he left the room.

*

Tom bathed, shaved and made himself breakfast. As he sat with his elbows on the wooden kitchen table, mug in hand, he turned over the events of the last few hours. Making love to Serena had been the most wonderful experience of his life arousing in him deep emotions and sensitivities he had not realised he possessed.

The softness of her skin to his touch and the feel of her fingers on his. Her scent – not perfume – but a sweet, womanly smell, and the warmth and silence when they had lain side by side before falling asleep in each others arms.

He glanced at his watch, drained his coffee and went to his office to ring the hospital.

'Christian Ward.'

'I'm enquiring about Kim Cresswell.'

'Who are you?'

'I'm her uncle.'

'Just a minute.'

Tom looked around the table that served as his desk and desultorily moved papers around dreading what he might be told.

'Your sister-in-law said she will ring you in a minute,' the nurse said, 'but your niece is over the worst.'

Could the nurse really have said that?

'Oh, Tom, you'll never believe it, Kim's over the crisis.' Pat sounded breathless.

'Is she awake?'

'Awake and has even had a little to eat.'

'Really?' Tom gave a sigh of relief. 'That's marvellous. Is Jamie still with you?'

'Yes, but he's going home in a minute. I came early this morning. I couldn't sleep last night, could you?'

'Er, yes, I did sleep well. Can I come and see her?'

'Of course.'

'Hadn't you better ask Kim first, I don't want her to have a relapse.' He was only half joking.

'Don't be silly, I'll see you later.'

St Catherine's was a compact 1920s building, not large, but then not small enough to have been closed in the cause of efficiency. Tom walked into the front hall, his nostrils invaded by that smell peculiar to medical institutions – something other than disinfectant – that he could never define. He was about to head for Kim's ward when he chanced upon Edward coming down the stairs.

'Hello, is Lydia here? Jamie thought he'd see an ambulance going into your drive a few days ago. How is she?'

'She had severe pains and we thought the baby was on the way, but Mr Gilberton had her in to get things under control. She'll be here a little longer, but I'm not sure how long.' His voice took on a serious tone. 'What's this I hear about Jamie's daughter?'

'I'm thankful to say she's over the worst. It was meningitis you know. I'm off to see her now. Want to come?'

So certain was he that Edward would refuse, he started to mount the first step, but to his surprise he followed him and the look on Pat's face when Edward appeared was a picture.

'Pat.' Edward gave a slight nod of his head.

'Hello – Mr Casleigh.'

Edward turned to Kim who, in Tom's eyes, seemed to be a living miracle, sitting up as if she had nothing worse than a bout of flu.

'I heard you had been unwell, how are you feeling now?'

'I'm much better – I think – I can't remember much.'

'She's a bit tired, weak really,' Pat said.

'Obviously.'

'Mum said Mrs Casleigh's in here.'

'Yes, they're keeping her in for at least another day, maybe two.'

'I might be able to go and see her if I'm allowed,' Kim said.

With motherly concern Pat said, 'You're not to overdo it. You don't realise how ill you've been.'

'Oh, Mum, don't fuss.'

Edward said goodbye and took Tom by the arm as he moved away.

'I want to apologise for what I said about you and Serena. I should not have jumped to conclusions.'

'No, you shouldn't, but Serena tells me she explained the situation, and I'm sure you will believe what she says.' If only he know what had happened last night.

'It wasn't that....'

'Wasn't it?' Tom raised an eyebrow. 'But I'll tell you one thing that will relieve your mind. Any feelings I once thought I had for Lydia have gone. I don't know what Lydia has told you, but I can assure you that she has never, ever given any sign she felt the same way.'

'Yes, yes, she told me. Will you go up and see Lydia?'

'No, I don't think so.'

*

Driving home, much relieved at Kim's recovery, the one thing that now dominated his thoughts was last night. Their relationship had moved into yet another, deeper phase. He could have left last night, but he wanted to be with her and make love and it was Serena who had asked him to stay.

Did he only want comfort? Were they using each other as they had once agreed? But then they had not gone as far as this. Their enforced separation had not made their feelings for each other any less intense – rather more so if anything.

Serena was still in a difficult position. When would her divorce come through, it must be soon? Then he could – then he could what?

*

As he parked the car he could see Mike talking to Joe Lotter, the hand from the agency. Tom could see Joe poking his finger towards Mike and Mike leaning forward angrily.

'What's wrong?' Tom enquired, going up to them.

'I particularly asked Joe to leave a space and not put the tractor away in the oast, but when I went to put the trailer away, he'd blocked it.'

'He never said no such thing. Trouble is he's getting too old for the job.'

Mike looked as if he would explode.

'Come over to the house a minute, will you Joe?'

Tom walked away but he could not hear Joe following. He looked back.

'Now,' he shouted as Joe made a further comment to Mike's retreating back.

'Sit down.' Tom was going to offer him tea, but thought better of it. 'What's this all about?'

'He don't know what he's talking about half the time. Keeps giving me orders.'

'That seems perfectly OK to me. Mike has worked here for twenty-five years and I've known him all my life. What he doesn't know about this farm is not worth knowing and I still ask for his opinion and advice. If he says he asked you to do something then I believe he did. This isn't the first time, is it? On several occasions I've heard you being rude to him. '

Joe moved shiftily. 'I didn't hear him say nothing 'bout leaving room for a tractor.'

'So, if you didn't hear, then in your mind it wasn't said. Even if you had not heard his request, was there any need to make a big issue of it? You could have apologised and offered to move it.'

'Me, apologise, just 'cause I didn't hear him.'

'He is considerably older and more experienced than you are. Have you no respect?'

'Not for that old man.'

Tom leaned forward resting his knuckles on the table. 'In that case, I shall ask the agency to send someone else next week.'

Joe stared at Tom with incredulity. 'Don't I work well enough for you?'

'I have few complaints about your work.'

'Well then.'

'But working on a farm, to me, is more than just the jobs that have to be done. I feel I am part of a team. Chris Barratt's death was a terrible blow and we lost a friend as well as a work mate. You do not fit in with this, so I think it best I ask for someone else who does.'

'But – but I was going to ask if you'd take me on permanently,' Joe said, a more conciliatory note creeping into his voice. Tom did not reply.

'I'd better go then,' he said, standing up suddenly and glaring at Tom. 'Fat lot of good me working hard when you prefer someone like that old chap.'

'Give me any overtime you've done and I'll inform the agency.'

Joe left the kitchen and the door crashed behind him. Tom gave a sigh of relief. It was the first time he had ever dismissed anyone. It brought to the fore that he had to get a permanent hand – and soon. It was not long till harvest.

For fifteen years he had run the farm with nothing other than minor irritations. Now his whole life was in turmoil and he could see no end.

Chapter 21

Blue plastic sacks, which had been neatly stacked just inside the barn, swirled about the yard that early July morning. Tom had just started rounding them up when he heard the telephone.

'What can I do for you?' he asked, surprised at Anna Bartley's call. He had not seen her since the morning after Chris had died.

'It's Serena.'

'What is it? Is she ill?'

'I don't know exactly, I can't put my finger on it. At coffee yesterday she looked awful. I thought she hadn't been herself for the last couple of weeks – but we all have our off days.' Anna gave a nervous laugh. 'I asked if she were feeling all right and she said, yes, but in such a way that it was obvious she wasn't. Do you know what I mean?' She paused. 'I'm not putting this very well, but she seemed distant, as if she were in another world.'

'Has she seen a doctor?'

'She said she hadn't.'

'Sounds very strange, what do you think's wrong?'

'Maybe – and this is only a theory mind, maybe she thinks she has something incurable and she won't see a doctor because she doesn't want to know. Some people are like that.'

'That doesn't sound like Serena to me – and anyway she's so healthy. She's told me she never visits her doctor as she never has anything worse than a cold.'

'But I know something isn't quite right,' Anna insisted. 'I said she looked distant, but then I'd see her give a sort of secret smile when doing something automatic, like pouring coffee or washing cups. It's the same when she comes to me. I am worried.'

'OK Anna, thanks for telling me. I'll go there tonight.'

'Did you know Lydia had a baby girl last night?'

'No.'

'They're both well, I gather.'

'Not the longed for boy then?'

When Serena opened the door, Tom was not prepared for what he saw. Her cheek bones now served to make her look gaunt instead of beautiful, the hollows deeper, her skin sallow, the green eyes lifeless.

'Hello Tom,' she said, moving to one side to let him in, 'I presume Anna called you. She said she would.'

He kissed her then held her away from him. 'Why didn't you tell me you weren't well?'

'What would you have done?'

Taken aback he said, 'What I'm doing now – come to see what's up. What is wrong? Anna thinks you might have some incurable disease and won't do anything about it.'

'Anna has a vivid imagination.'

'I must say I didn't think that – you're much too strong a character.' He followed her into the kitchen.

'You mean an incurable illness wouldn't dare attack me.'

'What I meant was you're not the type not to want to know if you are suffering from something serious.'

'Sit down. Shall I get you something to drink? Tea – or something stronger?'

'No, nothing thank you – I can't stop long.' He noticed a plate with two biscuits on it – one half eaten. 'Are you eating properly?'

'I don't feel much like food.'

'Come on – tell me what's up?'

Serena started preparing a coffee for herself then stopped and turned to fix him with a strange, enigmatic stare before saying, 'I've had a miscarriage.'

In the space of a few seconds emotions sped through his mind like scrolling on the computer – how awful for Serena, how amazing that their only night together could start a life and that he could have become a father. In a state of shock he stared at her.

'Close your mouth, Tom.'

'I can't believe it,' he said.

'These things happen.'

'But you said you couldn't have children.'

'Well, not exactly, they could find no reason why I couldn't. I assumed there was something wrong with me they couldn't discover – but it seems not.'

Now Tom noticed the secret smile that Anna had mentioned. 'When did this happen?'

'Two weeks ago – yesterday.'

'And you coped by yourself? Why didn't you call me? Anna says you haven't seen a doctor – why?'

Serena poured out her coffee and added the milk.

'Why on earth not?' Tom repeated.

'I'm too embarrassed. I have a private doctor in Maidstone. He's a friend – not close, but he and his wife have dined here.'

'But he's a professional man, he wouldn't say anything.'

'That's not the point, I know him, and anyway, I'm not convinced he wouldn't let slip something to his wife, or say something by implication. I didn't want to take the risk.'

'You should see a doctor. There could be complications, especially at your age.'

'Thank you Tom, that's made me feel much better.'

'I am worried – truly I am.'

Serena sat down and stirred her coffee as she had done when he saw her in the café. 'You haven't said what you think.'

'About your miscarriage? I'm very upset for you and I want to know how you feel and what I can do. I'm very uneasy about all this.'

'Are you?'

'Of course I am.'

'And supposing I hadn't lost the baby. What would you have said if you were about to become a father?'

There was the slightest hesitation before he said, 'I don't know, you've taken me by surprise. We would have had to talk it through.'

'Would you have married me?'

'I said we would have discussed it.'

'And then you would have married me?'

Tom raised his eyes to hers. 'What do you want me to say? What have I got to offer you? I'm a farmer, I have no desire to be anything else. I couldn't give that up and live your sort of life.'

'Do you love me?'

He looked down at his hands resting in his lap. 'I – I don't know. I'm not experienced with women.'

'You were a wonderful lover.'

Tom felt his face redden. 'You were easy to love.'

'There you are then.' She looked at him over the rim of her cup.

'But – but supposing it were just comfort we were seeking,' he said, 'I was upset – I needed you.'

They sat silently for several minutes. When he looked up Serena was staring at him gravely. He reached out his hand and she put hers into his and he gave it a squeeze.

'Please see a doctor. If you don't want to go to one in the village, you can find another private one. I'd worry if you didn't get your health checked. Would you like me to come with you? I will, you know.'

'You do care about me then?'

'Do you doubt it? I've missed you more than I can say. Every time I stand in the kitchen I see you. You changed my life and made a dingy, purely functional house into a home. Not only that, I think of the fun we had together. ' He smiled. 'I even miss your temper, but where can this lead? Do you see yourself as a farmer's wife? Bill Patterson would almost have been tugging his forelock to you. He would have done to Edward's father, and called him Sir, as my father and I called him Sir. Do you think you could transplant yourself to that sort of position after the life you've been brought up to and led?'

'But things are different now, you don't call Edward Sir.'

'I bet he'd like me to, but that's more by accident than design.' Her eyes filled with tears. 'Don't cry, Serena, please, I can't bear it.'

'I'm so unhappy, you've no idea. It never occurred to me when I was being sick I might be pregnant. I'd given up all thoughts of children long ago. It wasn't until I had these terrible griping pains I began to wonder. I was scared and worried about what you'd think. Then – then it was all over.' She wept.

Tom knelt beside her chair. 'I know I don't know how you feel, but I do want to help you. I'll do whatever you want me to.'

'But you won't marry me?'

'It's not that – but we live such very different lives. Let's leave it until you've got over this. Mammoth decisions have to be made by both of us, but mostly by you.'

Serena wiped her eyes and stood up purposefully. 'Yes, you're right, I'm not in a fit state to make decisions. You go home and tomorrow I'll find a doctor.'

'Come home with me and I'll look after you.'

'And suffer all the rumours and finger pointing.'

'And you don't want me to stay here with you?'

'That would be even worse.'

'OK, I'll ring in the morning and come again tomorrow.'

Tom picked up his coat and she went with him to the door. He took her face in his hands and wiped the stray tears with his thumbs. He kissed her.

'Promise me you'll see a doctor. If you don't,' he admonished, 'I'll ask Doctor Ferguson to call whether you like it or not.'

She gave him a weak smile as she kissed him goodbye.

Tom should have felt relieved but he did not like the way she was behaving; she was too bright, too practical. She had gone through a dreadful experience on her own and she was not fit to be left alone – he could see that. Who could he turn to? Anna? But she had young children and her husband was away. Pat? No, that wasn't on. As he signalled in the driveway to turn right he hit on an idea. He turned into Church Lane and drove through the car park to the Vicarage.

Giving Faith only as much information as he thought she needed, and avoiding having to tell her how he was involved, he explained that Serena was not well and seemed depressed. When Faith assured him she would go and stay with her, he went home.

✳

Faith followed Serena into the drawing room of Ridge House and, like Tom, was appalled by her appearance.

'I was just going to bed,' Serena said, requesting Faith to sit down.

'I've been meaning to come and see you,' Faith began. 'I didn't see you at church two weeks ago but thought you might have gone away – to your father, perhaps. But when you weren't there last Sunday I thought I'd better call.'

'I haven't been well.'

'I can see that. What's wrong?'

'I've had gastro-enteritis.'

Though Tom had not given her much information, Faith had gathered enough to know this was unlikely.

'How awful for you – what did the doctor say?'

'I haven't seen one.'

Faith gave her a searching look, before saying, 'Don't you think you ought to get some advice. The gastro-enteritis might have taken more out of you than you think.'

'Yes,' she replied vaguely, then without warning Serena said, 'Tom didn't send you here, did he?'

Disconcerted by the suddenness of her question, Faith said, 'Oh dear, I'm not very good at lying. It's just that he didn't think you should be here on your own – and now I've see you I'm 'inclined to agree.'

'It's kind of you, but you needn't have bothered.'

'Well, now I'm here I'm going to stay.'

'What did he tell you?'

'That you weren't well, you seemed low and he was worried. He said your friend Anna had called him. He's very thoughtful, isn't he?'

Serena stared at her then burst into tears.

'Bed,' Faith said, taking Serena by the arm and marching her upstairs. 'Have a bath and I'll go and get you a hot drink.'

While Faith went to heat the milk, she brooded over the events of the past hour. If Anna Bartley was worried, why ring Tom? Was there more to the rumours of a few weeks ago? She had not thought them true, and she was surprised that Tom and Serena should – well, even be friendly.

And the gastro-enteritis – it could be debilitating, but was it likely to cause her to be so depressed? Something did not quite add up. Then again, there was the divorce. Faith knew Serena was anxious to be divorced, but it had been a long drawn out affair. Could it be delayed reaction?

The milk began to bubble. She took the pan from the stove, poured the milk and went into the drawing room to search for some whisky. She measured out a little and added some sugar.

'Here you are, my dear,' she said, as she went into Serena's bedroom, 'I don't know whether you like this, but I want you to drink it up as if it were medicine.'

Serena did just that without comment.

'Settle down now, I'll be here all night, so don't worry.' Faith pulled up the covers, tucked them in and ran her hand across Serena's brow. 'Have a good sleep. Goodnight.'

Faith rang Tom and David then went back. Serena looked peaceful enough, but Faith thought she had been crying. She found herself a blanket and settled in an armchair close by the bed.

Faith woke with a start. Serena was sitting up in bed, her eyes wide and scared. 'I can't find it! I've lost it! Where have I put it?'

Faith gently eased her shaking body back against the pillows and she turned unseeing eyes to Faith.

'It was there – in the supermarket. I was shopping. It's gone. Where's it gone?'

'There, Serena. You're having a bad dream.'

She wiped the perspiration from her face, then held her hand till she had settled again and was sleeping.

Faith went over to the window and pulled back the curtain. She could see the vicarage and church through the trees that edged Serena's garden – dark outlines in the night.

Her mind went back twenty years. David's first parish in Nottingham; newly married and a child on the way. I know what's wrong – I'm sure I know what's wrong. Poor Serena.

*

To the emotions that Tom had on hearing Serena's news were now added others. It was his fault; he was guilty and selfish. Look what he had put her through. She was suffering just because he wanted someone to console and comfort him. Serena wanted reassurance and he had not given it to her. She wanted to marry him and he would not even tell her he loved her. Tom had known it all along but would not admit it.

Should he ask her to marry him now? Would she not think he was only asking out of duty – or pity? She must not think that. He must talk to her, but was she fit enough to make decisions of such a far-reaching nature when she was so depressed?

Faith let him in.

'How is she?' he asked anxiously.

'Not good, we must send for a doctor. She keeps weeping and has had a nightmare. We'll talk it over when you've seen her.'

'Hello darling, still feeling bad?' He stooped over and gave her a kiss. She smiled but tears filled her eyes as he sat on the bed and put his arm round her shoulders. 'Mrs Tressant tells me you've had a poor night.'

'I can't remember, I feel so tired and listless.'

'We want to send for a doctor. We think it's important you get some treatment.'

'What does she know? What have you told her?'

'Only that you weren't well and seemed depressed.'

'I think she knows.'

'How?'

'I don't know, I just think she does. The way she looked at me this morning, sort of sympathetic.'

'She would be sympathetic seeing you like you are.'

'No, it's more than that.'

Tom tightened his arm round her shoulders and said, 'What shall we do? Call your own doctor or ask Dr Gifford or Ferguson.'

'What do you think of Dr Ferguson?'

'He's not my doctor, but from what I've heard he seems well liked. He was the Barratt's doctor and was very kind to Wendy – after Daniel was born and Chris' accident. He's quite down to earth, so if you want someone to fawn over you, he's not your man. Lydia said he was good when she fell downstairs.'

For some reason this made her cry. What had he said now?

'I want a baby – everyone's having b-babies,' she sobbed. 'I want one so much. I thought I had g-got over it, now I've had one and it's g-gone.' Her shoulders heaved with sobs as she buried her head in his chest.

Of course, Tom should have realised. Edward would have rung her, which partly accounted for her behaviour last night. He rocked her gently, making soothing noises like a mother to a child and his heart went out to her.

'Will you marry me, Serena? I do love you and I can't think of anything I'd like more than to have you by my side, but it's you who'll have to make the sacrifices. Can you do that?'

She raised her tear-wet face to his. 'Do you really want to marry me?'

'Yes, I do. Absence has made the heart grow fonder. It's taken me a long time to realise it because I don't know much about these things.'

'An innocent abroad, eh?' She gave a sniff and Tom handed her a paper tissue from a cream, satin-covered box beside her bed.

'I certainly was and if I'd known you were going to lead me astray, I'd never have left the farm.'

'But look what you'd have missed?'

Faith tapped on the door. 'I've brought you something to eat. It's quite light,' she added hurriedly, seeing the look on Serena's face.

'I've decided to see Dr Ferguson,' she said, taking a sip of the orange juice on the beautifully arranged tray complete with a red rose from the garden.

'I'm so relieved.' Faith looked at Tom. 'Shall I phone him now?'

'I'll do it, you go home. I can look after her.'

'You sure?'

'Yes, we'll be fine.'

'Right, now take care of yourself Serena.' She turned to Tom, 'I'll come back this evening if that's OK.'

'Yes, I'd be grateful, Mrs Tressant, I don't want Serena to be on her own.'

'I must say you look much better. It's marvellous what a visit from a handsome man can do.'

'You see,' Serena said when Faith had left the room, 'She knows.'

'But she doesn't know for certain, does she? What does it matter anyway?'

'My divorce came through,' she announced.

'When?'

'Day before yesterday.'

'Why didn't you tell me? What a lot you've had to cope with on your own. I'll take care of you now. I don't want you to worry or make decisions till you're better. There's a lot to talk about – but not yet.' He paused then added gravely, 'There's just one important matter.'

Alarmed she cried, 'What is it?'

'You've never told me you love *me.*'

'Oh, Tom, how can you doubt it? I've chased you so hard I thought you'd never catch me. Shall I let you into a secret?'

'Yes,' he muttered suspiciously.

'I've always rather fancied you when I saw you about the village.'

'Then why on earth were you so rude when we met?'

'Because you were with Lydia and I didn't like her – didn't want to like her I suppose.'

'I can see you need a firm hand and I shall have to do something about it when we're married.'

*

Dr Ferguson came during that afternoon. Tom only left Ridge House to tell Mike he would not be back that day. When the doctor had left he rushed up to Serena's bedroom.

'Well, what did he say'?

'He wants me to go to hospital for a check, in case – in case…' Tom waited for her to continue. 'It's hard to talk about. He was so sympathetic and kind. He said a miscarriage was just like losing a child no matter how tiny or malformed it was, and I wasn't to hesitate about getting some counselling. He appeared really sad for me.'

'What about you having more children?'

'No reason why not, he said, but the risks were higher as for any older woman. A miscarriage didn't necessarily mean I couldn't carry full term. And I was to tell my partner that I would not get over this for some time.'

'Partner? Sounds nice, like working together.'

'We'll do that Tom. I will try hard to be a farmer's wife.'

*

'Can I go and see Mike, Uncle Tom?' Tony said.

Pat has just dropped the two of them to spend the day with him. It was nearly the end of the summer holidays. Tony had been at the farm a few times in the last five weeks, but for Kim, the farm did not hold the attraction it once had. She had also been away on a school trip.

'Yes, you go off, but you are to do as you're told. Don't ask to ride on the tractors or other machinery, it's dangerous and illegal. Do you understand?'

Tony's face dropped. 'Yes.'

'Remember Chris Barratt? He was used to dealing with machinery and look what happened to him.'

'Can I go now?'

'OK you rascal, but remember what I said.' His words were lost on the disappearing boy.

'Right Kim.' He turned round to find her at the sink stacking the breakfast dishes.

'There's no need to do those, I can wash up later. I want to talk to you. Get yourself a coke from the fridge.'

When they had settled themselves at the table Tom said, 'I want to tell you something important, something I haven't even told your Mum and Dad.' He wondered if what he were about to say would upset Kim even more than before.

'You're going to marry Mrs Detrale, aren't you?'

His niece never ceased to amaze him. 'How do you know?' he said.

'I guessed.' She giggled. 'You said I was perceptive.'

'Was it something your Mum said?'

'Not exactly, but I've seen your car go into her drive several times recently. I know her divorce has come through 'cause I heard some ladies in the church talking about it when Mum was doing the flowers – and I remember what you said about being lonely.'

'Kim, you've no idea how relieved I am. I was dreading telling you because I thought you would stop speaking to me like you did last time. It was true you know when I told you I was not having an affair, but I have fallen in love with her.' Tom put his hand on hers. 'I've got a favour to ask you. Mrs Detrale isn't going to find it easy to adapt to life on a farm. She's like Mr Casleigh – they've always had lots of money, lived in big houses, had the best of everything – holidays, clothes – so she's going to find it difficult to adapt to my kind of life. I want you to be friendly to her. You don't have to like her but try to make her welcome, like one of the family. Her only brother lives in America and her father is in a nursing home, so she hasn't any relatives she can talk to. Will you do that for me?'

'I'll try.' Tom gave her hand a pat and they sipped their drinks in silence. 'What happened to my jumper?' Kim demanded suddenly.

'I returned it and got my money back,' he said, 'like you said.'

Her face dropped and Tom laughed. 'You mother's got it, you ghastly child. She said you'd ask for it one day. You've no idea what you put me through when I came to dinner that night. You wait till you get a boy friend, I'm going to tell him a few home truths about you before he gets his heart broken.'

'No you won't.' She laughed and shook her curly head at him.

Tom picked up Kim's glass. 'Come on, let's find out what mischief that brother of yours is getting up to. Do you know I've taken on a new farm hand? He lives at Hemlow, not far from Granny Hudson. His name's Ian, you'll like him.

Chapter 22

Serena and Tom were married in mid October the only witnesses being Pat, Jamie and the children. Serena was not happy at just being married in a Register Office and asked Tom if he minded if they had a blessing in the church. He would have granted her the moon so pleased was he to see her almost fully recovered. He was certain that when she started cooking for him she would feel more like eating and put back the weight she had lost.

Bouts of crying occasionally overwhelmed her, brought on by seeing prams outside shops or something relevant to babies on television. One of the hardest things she had had to do was visit Lydia when she returned with the baby from hospital. Serena begged Tom to go with her. The baby, they were told, was to be called Philippa, after Lydia's father and it was the first daughter the Casleighs had produced for four generations.

They wanted a small reception after the blessing but could not decide where to have it. Tom said he didn't like the idea of Ridge House and the farmhouse was not considered quite the right setting. In the end David offered the Vicarage and Faith and Serena set about catering. Tom was worried Serena would take on too much, but Faith assured him it was just what she needed to occupy her mind, and because she was competent, she would not find it irksome.

The village was aware of the forthcoming marriage – still amazed, but more prepared. Those who thought they had had a relationship knew they had been right all along – no matter what Tom and Serena said – and gave the marriage six months. Those of a more charitable nature hoped it would last.

Tom and Serena no longer cared what anyone thought and behaved more like teenage lovers than mature adults.

'You look so beautiful.' Tom said when they arrived in the Vicarage drawing room after the brief ceremony. Serena was wearing a peach wild silk dress with small pin tucks on the bodice and wide puffed sleeves. Her straw hat was trimmed with matching peach chiffon and on her feet were beige shoes. She wore pearl earrings and necklace and the gold bracelet Tom had bought her as a wedding present. 'Have I told you that before?'

'Not since yesterday.' She kissed Tom's cheek.

Pat, who was wedged between a stack of parish magazines and a gate-legged table, studied her new sister-in-law. She had been nowhere near as surprised as Jamie had when she heard they were going to marry. He kept walking round the bungalow shaking his head from side to side and saying, 'Who'd have thought it' over and over again. She had to agree they seemed so unsuited. Was love enough to overcome the inevitable problems that were going to arise when Serena had to pig it – what an appropriate phrase – on a farm?

'Don't worry, Pat,' a voice said beside her, 'I believe it'll work out better than we think.'

'Faith! How did you know what I was thinking?'

'Because we're all thinking the same. There seems no accord, I know, but I'm sure Serena has respect for him – something she ceased to have for Jeremy.'

'And Tom?'

'He won't let her laud it over him, even though he is besotted at the moment. He's a late developer where love is concerned, but he has discovered companionship. He realises what he's been missing and doesn't want to spend the rest of his days completely devoted to farming, large though it looms in his life'.

'But will she adapt? She has the most to lose.'

'She will if she loves him enough – and I think she does.'

'I've been told she can fly into rages.'

'He must have come across that by now and decided he can live with it,' she replied. 'He may be in love, but he's not lost his wits.' Faith patted Pat's shoulder. 'Don't worry.'

'I don't want to see him hurt.'

'I'm sure we're worrying unnecessarily. But I must circulate, I'm supposed to be the hostess but I saw Serena handing round food when she should be standing around looking decorative. She looks very pretty, doesn't she?'

Pat nodded. She took another bite from her quiche and surveyed the guests. Mike and Sheila Lucas standing stiffly in their best clothes, thrilled at being asked, but looking ill at ease in surroundings and company they were not used to and Anna and

Terrence Bartley, seemingly the only friends of Serena's who had stuck by her, with their three beautifully behaved children.

Pat could not make up her mind what Edward and Lydia were thinking. She had never seen him look happier or more relaxed. He was constantly going over to look at his sleeping daughter, but his thoughts about Tom and Serena she could not divine. In an unguarded moment Pat saw Lydia give Tom a look of resentment, almost hostility. Might she be feeling a mite jealous now she no longer had his adoration? Or was it Serena she disliked?

Pat sought out Kim looking, she thought with a pang, very grown-up. She had been amazed at the way her daughter had made a point of speaking to Serena and the look of pleasure on Serena's face. She grinned as she saw Jamie sidle up to his brother. What outspoken words of wisdom was he about to impart she wondered?

'Now look here, Tom are you happy, really happy? You haven't rushed into this without thinking?'

'No, Jamie, I've given it a lot of thought and I'm sure – we're sure we are doing the right thing but, as Mum would have said, we can't be sure of anything in this life. We just have to do our best – so I'm going to do just that.'

'There's no need for me to tell you I wish you everything you wish yourself.' He clasped Tom in an emotional embrace.

'Thanks Jamie.'

'Unhand that man,' Serena said, pushing a plate of vol-au-vents between them.

'You look after him, d'yer hear.'

'Don't forget,' she said, wagging a finger at Jamie, 'it was you who started all this.'

'So Tom said. You'd better not send him on any errands, there's no knowing what might happen.'

Only one small thing marred the day for Serena, and that was when Edward came to say goodbye, holding the baby in his arms. Tom felt her hand grip his tightly.

'My, hasn't she grown since we last saw her, Serena? What a difference in only three months.'

'Yes,' she said in a strangled voice. She cleared her throat and said more boldly, 'Is she good?'

'Wonderful,' Edward said proudly, and Tom was pleased for him and Lydia. He had been afraid he would take it out on her for not producing the much-wanted son.

'You're flying to Boston tomorrow Faith tells me. Are you going to see Gerald while you're there?'

'Yes, we're touring, but we'll stay with him for three or four days. I haven't seen my niece and nephews for five years.'

'It must be over twenty years since I last saw him.'

Lydia crossed the room and joined them. 'Here, I'll take her.'

'We're off now,' Edward said, 'Philippa's due for a feed. Good luck and have a safe journey.'

'Every happiness to you both,' Lydia said.

Edward kissed Serena and shook hands with Tom. Lydia gave Serena a quick kiss on the cheek and a longer one to Tom, whispering in his ear 'Be happy'.

∗

In the impersonal bedroom of the plastic hotel near Heathrow, Tom and Serena lay in bed, their arms round each other and their legs entwined.

'Tom?'

'Yes.'

'Do you think – wouldn't it be funny – if, well, if I'd conceived again, just now – like I did before.'

Tom was disconcerted. Conceiving a child had not been on his mind when he had made love to Serena and hoped it would not have been on hers.

'No reason why not, darling. Relax, let's enjoy each other. We're on holiday. You've not been well and I'm tired after a hard year. Don't think about it.'

As soon as he had uttered the last sentence he wished he could have taken it back.

'It's all very well for you, you can go on fathering children forever.'

Tom thought he might get into deeper water if this conversation developed further, so he kissed her, hoping to divert her baby introspection back to him.

∗

Serena ran upstairs to fetch another jumper. It had snowed in the night and a soft covering swirled in the yard outside.

In all her deliberations over the adjustments she would have to make on marrying Tom, the lack of heat at her future home had never entered her mind. She had known it was cold at the farmhouse but she had not stayed long enough to realise it was never warm. Serena was convinced that the only time she was at a comfortable temperature was half an hour after they had gone to bed when Tom had warmed her up. Trouble was he found her discomfort a great source of amusement.

'Just put on more clothes – buy warmer underwear. Those frilly things wouldn't keep a fly warm.'

'You didn't mind looking at them when we were on our honeymoon.'

He grinned. 'I still would, but you're out of them and in bed before I've even had a chance to get excited.'

'Well I don't think it's funny.'

Tom came in for his mid morning coffee and an icy wind blew across the room bringing with it a few flurries of snow which lay melting on the flagstones beside the coconut mat.

'Wonder if we're in for a white Christmas?'

'There's still two weeks to go,' Tom said. 'This doesn't look as if it's setting in.'

He took off his anorak and cap and hung them on the back of the door.

'I bow to your superior weather knowledge. Want a bit of pie with your coffee?'

'I'm fast getting used to this life. I rarely used to stop for coffee in the past – except perhaps in cold weather like this. Now I look forward to it.'

'You do think it's cold then?'

'Are you still suffering?'

'Couldn't we have central heating put in. These electric fires don't do anything, especially in this enormous kitchen with that door constantly being opened.'

Tom's expression changed immediately. 'That's Edward's department,' he said coldly, 'and he's already had the top windows replaced this year by way of a wedding present because he knew you were going to live her. And anyway, I can't afford it.'

'But I can!' One look at Tom's face and she knew she had said the wrong thing.

Serena had been left a wealthy woman after her divorce. Tom had been happy for her to have a room upstairs she could call her own, decorated as she wanted and filled with furniture and possessions from her house. She had paid for all that. Other furniture she had taken from Ridge House was stored in the remaining rooms. Anything else to do with the farmhouse, Tom told her, was for him to decide and, if it concerned her, they would discuss it. Serena had nodded submissively – much to her amazement.

'I'm sorry,' she muttered.

She went to the walk-in larder, nearly as cold as the fridge which it had preceded, and cut him a slice of apricot pie which she slid on a plate and put before him.

'Thank you.'

'Ask Mike and Ian if they'd care to have their lunch break in here as it's so chilly,' Serena said as Tom finished and put on his anorak. His dark curly hair stuck out round his cap as he put it on. With his arm in one sleeve he returned to the table, picked up the mug and drained his coffee. Serena frowned. Tom slipped his other arm into his coat, gave her a peck on the cheek and said, 'I'll ask them.' Another rush of cold air came into the room.

Serena shivered. By the time it gets back to the temperature it was before that damned door was opened, she thought, they will all have blown in for their lunch. She sat down resignedly, putting both hands round her mug.

They had been married just over eight weeks, almost the same length of time after Tom had stayed the night when she had had the miscarriage – but there was no sign she was pregnant. Tom was always so gentle, so loving, yet he didn't seem to understand how deeply she felt now she knew she could have a child. She desperately, desperately wanted another.

'The more you worry, the less likely you are to conceive,' he said realistically. Knowing he was right was no consolation when she was tossing restlessly in bed while he slept the sleep of the dead.

She took the mugs and plate to the sink. She was settling down to being a farmer's wife. Tom had taken her round the farm explaining the different kinds of apple trees and method of pruning. He told her the type of hop they grew was Target, and about training the bines round the strings, the spraying, picking and pulling down of the old bines. One hundred acres were divided between apples and hops, sheep accounted for around thirty acres and the rest was cereal. Serena had been amazed at the amount of machinery on the farm and could not get over the need for six tractors. Hop picking was about the only thing she knew a little about and Tom told her there were two families who still came picking, but that most of it was done by machine. Another surprise was the New Zealander who came over every year to shear the sheep and covered several farms in the area.

'I would advise you to get some strong shoes or wellingtons. It can be very muddy in the yard and you never know when you might have to traipse around the fields.'

Serena rather hoped she wouldn't, but she bought some just the same and they were kept, along with Tom's, just inside the kitchen door. She stared at them now still looking as pristine as they had left the shop.

Tom never asked her to do anything connected with the farm, but she found herself selling apples because people would knock on the kitchen door when they could find nobody around. This necessitated her going upstairs to get a coat, so eventually her jacket hung on the back of the door with the others.

Serena tidied up, cut sandwiches for midday and prepared vegetables for the evening. She muttered to herself she really did not see why Tom should get so het up about her contributing to the farm. After all, she was his wife and it was her home too.

A flurry of activity outside the window and the unwelcome gust of cold air heralded Tom, Mike and Ian.

'Thank you for asking us in Mrs De – Mrs Cresswell,' Mike said shyly.

'There's an icy wind out there,' Ian said, rubbing his hands together.

'So I'd noticed,' Serena commented, deliberately avoiding Tom's eye. 'Can I get either of you a hot drink?'

'Yes please,' Ian said eagerly, 'I drank all my coffee during the morning.'

'Not for me, thank you,' Mike said formally.

Companionably they sat around the table and Serena studied them.

Mike, whom she had only known by sight around Grassenden, was a real countryman whose family had always been farmworkers since time immemorial. He was a short, lean man with thinning hair and sharp features. He was absurdly respectful and avoided her if he possibly could.

Ian, on the other had, was a good looking lad with thick, light brown hair, tanned face and wide apart grey eyes that gave him a look of wonderment as if the whole world were a surprise to him. He was a bit shorter than Tom, just under six foot perhaps, good-natured and got on well with Tom and Mike. He was in his early twenties and lived in Hemlow. She had noticed him on more than one occasion eyeing her up and down with scarce concealed admiration.

Tom still looked angry – no, not angry – serious. Perhaps she ought to apologise this evening. She might even be able to talk him round. If she had ever wanted anything in her life she had just asked and expected to get, or she would go ahead and do whatever it was she wanted. Perhaps that was another reason her marriage failed. She and Jeremy had lived as individuals. But was that not what Tom was doing?

'You look nice, darling,' Tom said when he came in at the end of the day. He noted the cream and grey diamond patterned jumper with a large roll collar and matching grey skirt. He couldn't remember seeing it before. Serena seemed to have an endless supply of clothes. He doubted he had seen her in the same outfit twice running since they had been married. She always made a point of changing in the evening and this had encouraged Tom to do the same.

'Dinner will be ready in fifteen minutes,' she said.

'I'll wash and change and then I'll be with you. We have been so busy today,' he called as he left the kitchen. 'I feel quite tired.'

Tom sat down in his place. 'You know, I'll never get over having a meal put in front of me like this. I keep thinking I'm dreaming and I'll soon wake up. I used to come in, wash and sink into a chair. Only much later did I think about eating. Funny part was, I never looked for anything else, never thought life would be any different – certainly not as wonderful as it is now.'

He put his arms round her as she stood beside him serving steak and mushroom pie on to his plate.

'Careful,' she said.

'I'm so pleased I married you,' he said, giving her a squeeze.

Serena bent and kissed his forehead. 'I'm sorry about this morning. I want to help you, I wasn't trying to take over.'

'What you don't seem to grasp is that it isn't my farm. Under my Tenancy Agreement Edward is responsible for the farmhouse and each time an improvement is made the rent goes up. This has to come out of any profit the farm makes. We've had some good years, but I have to have money put aside for the bad ones. Mike and Ian still have to be paid and expect a bonus in a good year. If the farm were mine, it might be different.'

'But can't I contribute anything? If I didn't have a lot of money you'd be willing for me to share it with you.'

'You've contributed more than enough. Don't go on about it any more.' He released his hand. 'Sit down and get on with your meal.'

But the sleeping tiger that had been slumbering longer than it had ever been suddenly roused at this cursory dismissal. Eight weeks of being cold, disappointment at not being pregnant and now Tom shutting her out because he was too proud to accept her money was more than she could take.

Chapter 23

Had Tom been facing her he would have seen the warning signs, the flashing eyes – the two pink spots on her cheeks. As he put a fork to his mouth a crash made him jump. Serena had hurled the hot dish on to the table where it had broken into three and the contents scattered, some of it hitting and burning him. Tom let out a yelp.

'How dare you shut me out,' she shrieked. 'How dare you! You're nothing more than an inverted snob, resentful of me and Edward just because we have money. You glory in your so-called lack of it just as you say we do with ours. Whatever you think of Edward, don't take it out on me.'

Nursing his scalded arm, he shouted, 'I'm not having heating put in whoever pays for it and that's final.'

'You don't care that I'm perpetually cold,' she went on, near to tears. 'You don't even take it seriously – it just amuses you. I – I don't want to keep piling on more clothes. I – I want to look – to look...'

Serena threw the cloth at Tom and spun round to leave. Tom caught her hand but she wrenched it free.

'Don't touch me,' she cried and flew upstairs.

Tom removed the food that had splattered over him and went upstairs; Serena had locked herself in her own room.

'Serena, let me in, I want to talk to you.'

'You've talked to me and I don't want to hear any more.'

'Let's discuss what's upset you.'

'You know that too. Go away.'

'I don't want you sleeping in there by yourself.'

'I'll please myself what I do, just like you do.'

'That's not true. I do try to please you, but some things don't concern you.' There was no reply. 'We'll talk about it later when we go to bed.'

Tom returned to finish his meal. He contemplated leaving the dish where she had thrown it, but eventually cleared up. He heard her moving around during the evening, but refrained from going to her earlier hoping she had calmed.

'Serena?' He tapped on the door and tried the handle. She was sitting up in bed reading.

'You're not sleeping here,' he said warningly.

'Oh?' She barely raised her head from the magazine.

'I told you that you were not to sleep here unless you were ill – and I meant it.'

'I don't want to discuss it, it doesn't concern you.'

'But it does – it concerns me very much and I don't intend to discuss that either. You sleep with me.'

Tom went downstairs and brought up another electric fire to add to the one already in their bedroom. When Serena joined him – and he had not decided what to do if she did not – he would try to straighten things out.

He went into the bathroom and cleaned his teeth. That Serena had to be handled he knew, but he was not going to allow her to sleep on her own.

He had not taken the fact she felt the cold seriously, but central heating was out of the question, he had to stand firm over that.

'Serena, you coming?' he called as he left the bathroom.

He picked up his book and went round to her side of the bed to warm it up. He started reading but the tiring day began to take its toll. He woke to find himself being pushed across the bed.

'It's warm enough,' Serena said as she climbed in beside him. 'You can go over to the cold side now.'

She snuggled up close to him. 'You've got to kiss me now,' she said. 'That was our agreement.'

'Why stop there?'

Things would have to be straightened out another time.

*

'I couldn't eat another thing, Serena, really I couldn't.' Jamie leaned back in his seat with the palms of his hands resting on his stomach.

'That's the best Christmas dinner I've ever had,' Pat said, 'and so much nicer when I haven't had to cook it myself. For the last few years we've had the family at our place, before that we all went to Jamie's mum and on Boxing Day to my mother's.'

'Tom as well?' Serena queried.

'Well, we couldn't very well leave him behind. He isn't good at looking after himself,' Pat said laughing.

'Why do you think I got married,' Tom said. 'I knew I was on to a good thing when she rustled up a meal from shrivelled mushrooms that would have had Egon Ronay drooling.'

'Whose Eager Ronnie?' Tony said and looked puzzled when they laughed at him.

When Serena had suggested to Tom she would like entertain on Christmas Day, she was afraid Pat might take offence. She was not sure what Tom had said to his sister-in-law, but the message came back that they would be delighted to spend the day at the farm, and from the way they were all behaving, they appeared to be enjoying themselves.

Serena thought of previous Christmases. She had frequently entertained, but these had never been family affairs. They were with friends but most of them were associates of Jeremy's.

Today had been like no other Christmas since she had been a child. The farmhouse kitchen was as far removed from the elegance of her former dining room as it was possible to get, but it seemed to her the ideal setting. She, too, reckoned it was the best Christmas she had ever spent.

On the large, oak table in the kitchen, covered with a damask tablecloth from her house, little remained of the festive meal. Serena sighed contentedly even though the sight of the dishes and pans on the draining board looked daunting.

'Right, everybody, into the best room and I'll bring you a drink when I've cleared up,' Serena said.

'You'll do no such thing. Everybody help clear up – and I do mean everybody.' Pat said glaring at Tony. 'Then, when Serena and I have washed up we'll bring you a drink. State your preference before you go.'

When all had done their bit and Pat was satisfied, she and Serena started on the dishes.

'You have done us proud. Tom said you were a good cook, but I didn't realise just how good.'

'I do enjoy it. It was my job before I got married – to Jeremy, I mean.'

'The presents you bought us – they are lovely.'

Pat sounded reticent. Had she gone over the top and made them embarrassed. It seemed to her the only way she could express herself, to thank them for accepting her.

'Pat?'

'Yes.'

'Is Tom happy? I mean – does he think he's done the right thing? I'm not always sure what he thinks. He's – he's very self-possessed.'

'You must remember he's been a bachelor a long time. He's never had to think of anyone else in all that time, apart from his Mum and she was never demanding. He's bound to appear, as you say, self-possessed. What's brought this on?'

'He seems not to take what I say seriously, as if it's unimportant and isn't worth considering. He'll discuss things with me if he wants to discuss them, but if not....'

'Well, he's not said anything to me and I doubt if he would, but we don't see as much of him as we did before he went out with you. If he were unhappy surely he'd find excuses to go out. He's not done that, has he? He's never in *The Mitre* Jamie says, and he certainly doesn't look miserable – far from it.'

Serena dried the few remaining pans, then said, 'I expect you're wondering why I'm asking you this.'

Pat poured the water away and took a towel from the rack.

'There's handcream over there if you want it.'

'What's worrying you?' Pat said, smoothing a little cream on her hands.

'Why are Tom and Edward at dagger's drawn all the time. He seems jealous of Edward's money but, from what I've gathered, the Casleighs have been very good to him. He probably wouldn't be where he is today if it weren't for them.'

'I don't think it's Edward's money that's the trouble, though he may make this an excuse. You know, don't you, that Tom's Mum practically brought Edward up, that's why he was so devoted to her – she was the mother he never had, in spirit at least. Did you ever meet Edward's mother?'

'Yes, on a couple of occasions. She certainly seemed strange, very cold and unwelcoming to me as a child.'

'Tom's Mum told me that when Edward was little she was cruel to him. She didn't go into details because it upset her. Edward more or less lived at the cottage when he wasn't away at school. It's hard for me to believe, but I'm told Edward was very shy and timid. I didn't live in Grassenden then and knew nothing about the family.'

Serena said, 'I used to find his shyness very endearing when he came to visit our family in the holidays. I liked to mother him.'

'Well.' Pat went on, 'I gather Tom used to be Edward's protector and tried to stop him being bullied. Serena?'

'Sorry, I was miles away.' Talking about age made her think about being pregnant. 'Go on.'

'All three of them went around together after school and in the holidays but, as they got older, Jamie was more the odd one out because he had a different temperament and found friends of his own.'

'Then, when Edward was about fifteen he came home from boarding school one summer holiday a changed person. Jamie said he wasn't anything like the boy who had been playing with them at Easter. He started treating them more like acquaintances – worse than that, with certain disdain. Jamie was upset but he just thought that if that was the way he wanted it, get on with it, but Tom was devastated and dreadfully hurt that someone who was like a brother should reject him like that. He has never forgotten.'

'Or forgiven it seems,' Serena added.

'The rest you know. Edward's father paid for him to go to college but Tom considered it was a gesture to his mother rather than for his benefit. I think he was wrong there personally.'

'I see,' Serena said, arranging cups and saucers on a tray.

'I'll put the kettle on, shall I?' Pat said.

'So you think Tom equates having money with being betrayed.'

'That's a very simple way of putting it, but yes, in Tom's case, I believe he does.'

'Yes, that figures.'

'You've found this, have you?'

'He won't let me contribute anything to the farmhouse. He says it's Edward's farm and his responsibility and any improvements he ultimately has to pay for in raised rent, and he can't afford it.'

'That sounds like Tom.'

'But he won't let me help,' Serena said despairingly, pouring the coffee from the percolator into the pot and placing it on the tray. 'All he has let me do is furnish a room with stuff from Ridge House, which can serve as a guest room. The rest of my furniture is crammed into the other rooms. He won't even let me have those decorated and sorted out.'

'He seems easy going at first, doesn't he, but he can be pig-headed. It's one of the few traits he has in common with Jamie. Give him time, Serena, sharing is new to him, just give him time.'

The door from the hall flew open and Tony said, 'Uncle Tom wants to know when the drinks are coming, he's gasping.'

'Tell him if he's that thirsty, why isn't he out here doing it himself – and he shouldn't have drunk so much wine.'

'OK, can I have a coke?'

They heard him crash into the best room repeating the message word for word.

*

When the evening had ended and Serena was tidying up, Tom put his arms around her.

'That was a wonderful day. Are you pleased with the way things went?'

'I can't remember when I have ever had a better Christmas. Do you think they all enjoyed themselves? Kim seemed a bit quiet.'

'I know they did, and Kim's at that in-between age. She told me she liked the scarf you bought her.'

Serena released herself from his arms to finish clearing up.

'Tomorrow will be an easy day, I won't have much to do at Anna's.

Tom turned her round and looked into her eyes. 'You're feeling OK, aren't you? You've not done too much?'

'No, I'm all right, just tired. It's been a long day and I'm not as young as I used to be.'

She wished she hadn't said that.

*

'Is this where we come for apples? We couldn't see anyone around.'

Two walkers stood outside the kitchen door looking, Serena thought, disgustingly hearty. They were in boots, corduroy trousers, brightly coloured waterproof jackets and each had a rucksack. She reached for her coat and slipped on her wellingtons.

'Yes, I'll show you what we have,' she said. 'Follow me – over here in the barn.'

With an expertise she had gathered over the last few months, she explained the types of apples and what they were like.

'There's a choice of eating apples – Coxes, Jonathans or Golden Delicious. The Spartans have nearly all gone I'm afraid. The cookers are in these three boxes.' She pointed to each one and explained how each differed when cooked. 'Perhaps you would like to taste them before you decide.'

Tom had been most impressed with this and said he had never

thought of inviting people to sample the goods, and she would make a farmer's wife yet. Serena considered she was already a farmer's wife – still, it was nice to have a compliment.

When the walkers had divided the apples between them, Serena thinking it was bad enough to be out walking let alone loading themselves with apples, she led them back to the footpath and left them pouring over their map.

Tom was in Maidstone and would not be home till lunchtime. She took her coffee into the best room where the low winter sun streaked into the room, lighting up the throws that Tom had chosen for himself when their meetings had come to an abrupt end. He had been quite cocky when he had eventually shown her what he had bought.

Serena slumped into a chair. A sudden cramp-like pain reminded her that she was not pregnant this month and a wave of hopelessness washed over her. Entreated by Tom, kindly enough, she endeavoured not to think about babies, but her body was a constant reminder. She asked him one night if he ever thought about the baby and he said 'What baby?' and wondered why she had cried. She went to ask him once they could think of a name for it, but she knew he would say she was being silly and torturing herself, which she supposed she was, but it was real to her – this sad and wondrous event she had not believed possible.

She took her cup to the kitchen and went upstairs to her own room. Two mahogany wardrobes from the house held all her clothes, at least half of which she would never have occasion to wear. She didn't miss the life she had once led, but she had hoped for a chance to stamp a little of herself on the farmhouse. Tom's attitude made her feel like a guest rather than his wife.

She wandered into another room where furniture was shoved in and stacked at all angles. She longed to make some order out of the chaos. Old cheap furniture was farthest away from the door to make room for hers.

If Susie Patterson was an only child, these other bedrooms on this floor and the attic rooms had not been occupied in over fifty years. No wonder they smelled musty.

Serena crossed to a chest of drawers that had been Jeremy's. He had taken all he wanted from Ridge House. Some of it he put in his flat and some of it was in store. They had been surprisingly amicable over the division of their possessions, mainly because she felt too weak to quibble and had let Jeremy take what he wanted.

She mentally gauged what would fit into the rooms at the farm with the intention of arranging them after they were married. She hadn't known then that Tom would be so intractable over what he would let her do.

She ran her fingers over the smooth yew surface, leaving streaks in the dust. She lifted the metal handle and a drawer slid out smoothly. All their furniture was of good quality. She pushed it back and pulled out the one next to it. It moved jerkily and stuck. She wriggled it shut and tried again – the same thing happened.

Serena put her long fingers into the half-open drawer and felt round. There was a piece of paper, or stiff card caught at the side towards the back. She tried to grasp it between two fingers, but could not get enough purchase. She removed her hand and tried moving the drawer from side to side and with a sudden jolt it came free and the paper dropped into the larger drawer below.

The letter with the shiny black embossed heading proclaimed that it had come from Harley Street. It was addressed to Jeremy at their old house in Epsom.

Her eyes flitted from side to side as she scanned the page. It finished conventionally but she turned it over nonetheless hoping to find a denial of what she had just read. Serena moved across the landing to her room and sank into a chair feeling numb as she read the letter once more.

The deceit. How could Jeremy have let her suffer all these years thinking that she was the one who could not have children? He had told her the results of his tests were positive, there was nothing wrong. She felt a rising tide of hysteria travel from the pit of her stomach to her face, which burned with an intensity as if she were sitting too close to an open fire.

Tom's car drew up in the yard and she heard him come into the kitchen.

'Serena, I'm back. You upstairs?'

His steps thumped up the stairs and he went into their bedroom, then pushed open her door.

'What's the matter, darling, you look dreadful?' She stared at him as he crouched in front of her. 'What is it? Are you feeling ill?' He took the hand that hung down by the side of the chair and he noticed the letter held lightly between her fingers. 'Is this what's upset you? Who's it from? Is it about your father?'

She shook her head and handed him the letter. 'Read it?'

When he had finished he folded the letter and handed it back.

'Well?' she said.

'It's been a shock.'

'Is that all you've got to say,' she cried. 'All those years when I could have had children – wasted.'

'But you were married to Jeremy, even if you had known, you still would not have had children, were unlikely to anyway.'

'Married! Married! I was just an appendage to his business interests. He carried on with his women and I ignored it, as I ignored his drinking till I couldn't stand it any more. If I'd have known I'd have divorced him years ago.'

'Don't you think you're being wise after the event.'

'That's right, take his side.'

'I'm not taking sides, I'm just trying to get things in perspective.'

'I'm not pregnant again.'

'I'm sorry, Serena,' he said sympathetically.

'You're not really worried, are you?'

'Yes I am, I very much want to have a son or daughter. I, too, never thought to have a child.'

'But you could have gone out and got yourself a woman if you'd wanted children.'

'I'm not like that. I wasn't married before because I had not met anyone I wanted to spend my life with. It's true that I never went out of my way to seek a woman's company but, if I had, I wouldn't have married anyone purely to have a child.' He stood up and looked down at her. 'Your obsession is beginning to worry me. I thought you loved me, now you make me feel no more than a means to an end.'

'You don't understand,' she exclaimed.

'No, I don't. I try, but I don't. I want to be supportive, caring, concerned, but I obviously fail at that too. What else can I do, Serena?'

He regarded her with such a look of utter sadness that she said, 'I don't blame you, I just feel so betrayed.'

'I'm going to get some lunch,' he said, leaving the room.

Serena followed him downstairs and went to where he was standing beside the fridge.

'I'm sorry,' she said. Tom put his arm round her and drew her close. 'I do love you, Tom, really I do, I don't think I have enough to do. Won't you consider letting me spend some of my money so I can….'

'No, no, no,' he said with sudden savagery. 'I've made my position quite clear. When I've worked out my financial position, then I'll decide what can be done.'

Her anger, never far beneath the surface, flared at his words and her eyes smouldered through half closed lids. She drew herself up and took a deep breath.

'That's not my idea of a partnership. All I hear is what you'll decide. Where do I come in all this? Pat told me to give it time and you'd get used to being married and sharing, but you have meals put in front of you, a clean house and clothes and a bit of sex added for good measure. What have I got?'

'So you've been discussing our private affairs with Pat, have you?' he said angrily.

'I want someone to talk to – you won't listen.'

'I do listen,' he shouted, 'and I explain, but you....'

'You can explain till you're blue in the face, but all you want is a housekeeper. So, if that's what you want, that's what I'll be.'

She strode to the door, unhooked her coat and picked up her bag.

'Serena, where're you going?'

'To keep house.' She slammed the door behind her.

She jumped in her car, put it into reverse and swung it round. She grated into first gear and shot dangerously up the track missing Mike by inches as she went past.

*

Serena returned home well satisfied with the start she had made for her new-planned life. Tom was not there when she let herself into the kitchen. Later she would put her mind to getting the kitchen warmer, she thought, as she sorted out her shopping.

When Tom came in at the end of the day she had nearly finished preparing the meal. She noticed him look at her face closely as he came to kiss her.

'I'll just go and change then, shall I?' he said uncertainly.

'You do that.'

'Where did you go this afternoon?' he asked when they were halfway through their silent meal.

'I went to do housekeeperly things.'

'Is there such a word?' Tom said grinning, hoping to break the frosty atmosphere.

'Whether there is or not, that's what I was doing. I've ordered a new cooker and freezer and I've bought...'

'You've what!'

'I've ordered a…'

'I heard what you said. Haven't you taken in anything I've told you?'

'The position has changed. I'm your housekeeper, living in your house – sorry, Edward's house. However, I can't cook on that antiquated stove and do my cooking justice, so I've bought a new one. I badly need a freezer, and then I can cook in advance and leave food when I go out – on my days off. As buying these things with my money is clearly against your principles, you can pay me back in instalments as and when you can afford it.' She raised her eyes to his and smiled sweetly.

She had never seen him so angry, would not have believed her Tom could look at her the way he was. His pale eyes were the colour of steel and as hard. His mouth was set in a white line as he drew in his lips. She waited for him to explode with anger as they faced each other across the table.

Finally, his voice icy cool, he said, 'Very well, if that's what you want.'

This was not the reaction she expected. Serena thought he would rant and say he would send the goods back and she would row with him and say he was being stupid. Then he would give in and she would have started her campaign to get him to see things her way.

'Oh,' she said in a small voice.

It was as Tom came out of the bathroom before bedtime that Serena discovered just how intractable he was going to be.

'I think you will agree it would be unseemly for a housekeeper to be sharing a bed with her employer, so I'll say goodnight. I'll see you in the morning.'

To her consternation he strode into their bedroom and shut the door firmly. She couldn't believe what he had done. It was Tom who had been so adamant she was not to sleep alone. Hot tears welled up in her eyes, overflowed and ran down her cheeks as she turned away.

In her room she undressed and shivered as the cold air touched her skin. Tom should be hugging her now as he had done every night since they were married.

Serena opened the door of their bedroom. Tom was naked and she noticed the white of his body against the faded tan of summer. He turned at her entry and reached for his pyjama bottoms. She rarely saw him without clothes and his modesty, which she had once found endearing on their honeymoon she now thought prudish and silly.

'I've come for the electric blanket?'

It had been one of his Christmas presents to her. She waited for him to say 'You won't need that, come here, let me cuddle you like I always do', but he threw back the covers, took the blanket off and pulled out the plug from the wall.

'Shall I come and put it on for you?'

'I am quite capable,' she said, tossing her head as she took it from him.

He will come in a minute, Serena said to herself as she arranged the blanket on her bed and crawled over the floor to push in the plug. He just wants me to suffer. She waited and waited but by the time she had cried herself to sleep, he still was not with her.

Chapter 24

The cooker was installed three days later. When Tom came in for lunch the men were just about to leave.

'There you are, Mrs Cresswell, ready to cook your husband a nice, tasty dinner.'

Tom glowered.

'You are taking this one away, aren't you?' Serena queried, indicating the old stove. 'I expressly requested in the shop that this is removed, otherwise I would not have had the new one.'

'I ain't got no instructions 'bout that, Mrs Cresswell,' said the man, whose name was George.

'In that case, you can dismantle this and take it away.'

'We can't do that!' he said aghast. 'We're only allowed so much time for these jobs.'

'Now look here,' she said, pointing an imperious finger at the luckless man, while his assistant looked on with a faint grin at the prospect of verbal fisticuffs, 'the man at the showroom assured me it would be taken away – and taken away is what it's going to be. If you had room in your van for an appliance to come, you've room to take this back, so get on with it before I lose my temper.'

From her tone and stance George realised he had more than met his match. He threw a look at Tom for masculine support, which was not forthcoming.

'They'll have to sort it out at the depot,' he muttered, gesticulating to his lad to grab the other side of the offending stove.

'Good,' she said, as they manhandled it towards the door. 'Have I got to sign anything?'

Thoroughly flustered George was not sure whether to leave the cooker and wait for her to sign the relevant paper, or continue to take it out and come back. A compromise had the paper left with Serena, which she had signed on his return.

'Now – that wasn't painful was it?' she said. 'I've kept the customer copy. Good morning.'

Conducting this dispute had made Serena feel more like her old self. The adrenaline had run but, as she turned from the door, she saw Tom's face.

'What do you think?' she said, running her finger along the shiny white edge.

'I'd used that old cooker ever since I first came here,' he said, making it sound as if she had rid him of his best friend.

'I didn't know you were that attached to it?'

'I wasn't asked.'

She felt a pang of guilt at her peremptory behaviour. Still, he was the one keeping her out of his life with his condescending, old-fashioned ideas about money. She put sandwiches and apple tart in front of him and went to the fridge for the cream.

Tom reached for the invoice on the table. 'Do you want me to write a cheque for this, or shall I wait until the freezer arrives and do one for both,' he asked, his voice impersonal as if he were talking to the man who delivered cattle feed.

'It's paid for – can't we leave it at that?'

'No, you know my views.'

They ate in uncomfortable silence till he was ready to go back to work.

'I'm on Toilers Field should anyone want me.'

'Haven't you got your mobile?' It was a present she had bought Tom for Christmas.

'It costs too much to run,' he said as he put on his coat.

Serena stared at him as if he had hit her and as soon as he was out of sight she put her head despairingly on her arms.

*

'I was wondering what to get Serena for her birthday next week. You haven't any ideas have you?'

'Can't say I have, Pat,' Faith said. 'Pass me that vase will you?'

'She's always so generous to us, but I can't think of anything she hasn't already got.'

Pat was standing by the pulpit arranging yellow and white chrysanthemums in a large display. Their two voices echoed round the ancient walls.

'I like arranging this display best of all,' Pat said, stripping the leaves from the thick stalk. 'My eye gets drawn to it as soon as I walk down the aisle.'

'Everyone else's too, I expect.'

'Perhaps it's my way of showing off.'

'You're the least showing-off person I know,' Faith said, giving her a friendly tap.

'So you can't help me?'

'What about a large bouquet? I know she always had flowers about the house. I am afraid I used to envy her. Some came from her garden and I think Jeremy used to buy some quite regularly – peace offerings no doubt.'

'That's not a bad idea. There aren't any flowers in the farm garden – not ones that can be picked anyway. Yes, I'll do that. Tony can give her some hankies, they're always useful. Kim's making something that seems to be a big secret.'

'How are they? Do you see much of them?' Faith asked, resting her well-padded frame on the front pew.

'Not a lot. They entertained us at Christmas and we had a great time.'

'I see her at church sometimes.'

'She still comes regularly then? I know Tom's not a churchgoer. I don't see her 'cause she prefers an early service I believe.'

'I don't see her every Sunday. Last week I thought she looked a bit peaky, but she disappeared so fast I didn't have a chance to talk to her.'

'Funny you should say that. I saw her coming out of the Stores on Wednesday and I swear she saw me, but she jumped in her car and was off.'

'Maybe she's not well again?'

'I'll give her a ring,' Pat said. 'I suppose I ought to see her more. I'm never quite sure what to do. This time last year she was the posh lady who lived up the road. Now she's my sister-in-law – the other Mrs Cresswell.'

'Still having misgivings?'

'Not really, not from what I saw at Christmas, but I still can't see what they – how they got together. She is used to getting her own way, but….'

'But what?'

'Tom's probably not the pushover she thinks he is.'

'Perhaps that's what she likes about him.'

As Pat walked home along the footpath between the church and school she felt guilty about not seeing Serena more often. It was not that she didn't like her, but Pat found it difficult to overcome the feeling of inferiority. Serena was so good looking and dressed so beautifully. Added to which, she didn't want to appear to be interfering, they were newly-weds after all.

*

Pat tapped on the kitchen door and waited. She usually knocked and went straight in because the door was always unlocked – something that she and Jamie had constantly warned Tom he should not do.

'She isn't in.'

She turned. 'Oh, Tom, you made me jump.'

'She's gone out – to have her hair done – or something.' Warning vibrations went through her at the way he spoke. 'Did you come for anything in particular?'

'No, just thought I'd have a chat as I haven't seen her for a while – or you come to that.'

'I'll tell her you've called and she'll give you a ring.'

Tom was speaking to her as if she were a door to door salesman, a complete stranger rather than a relative.

'Anything wrong? She's all right, isn't she? Faith was saying she thought Serena hadn't looked wall last Sunday.'

'She's fine as far.... She's fine.'

Pat studied his face. She knew he was hiding something but his expression told her he was not in the mood for explanations.

'OK Tom, I'll wait to hear from her. Busy are you?'

'It's lambing time.'

'Of course, I should have known. Bye then.'

As she drove home Pat realised that was the briefest and most unfriendly conversation she had ever had with her brother-in-law in all the years she had known – and loved him.

*

Serena walked down Grassenden High Street towards the Stores. She had just met Lydia pushing a buggy. Philippa was now eight months old and there was no doubting she was a Casleigh with her white-gold hair and large dark eyes. Lydia informed her she was expecting again, plunging Serena into deeper gloom. Would she never feel happy and settled?

In the butcher's Mr Anders greeted her with pleasure as she had always been a good customer of his, preferring local meat to that from a supermarket.

'Mrs Detrale, how lovely to see you. How are you settling into your new life?'

'I'm getting into the swing, I think.' She did not bother to correct him over her name.

'I miss seeing you come out of the drive. Funny how you get used to people and their habits when they live near.'

'There's no one to see my comings and goings now, Mr Anders.' Or care, she thought.

Meat bought, she was on her way to the baker when she noticed the tall figure of Mrs Reece outside her shop giving a man directions. As she drew closer her heart leapt.

'Fenton?' The man looked up 'Fenton McGuire!'

Serena rushed forward and threw her arms round him. Mrs Reece stood by, intrigued and thrilled by this display of affection. She was already weaving a story around this encounter to pass on to the more receptive villagers.

'Serena! How extraordinary. I was just enquiring about you.'

'What are you doing in this country?' she asked excitedly.

She took his arm, forgetting she had not finished her shopping, so delighted was she at seeing her old friend.

'Come home with me, the car's over here.' She almost dragged him across the road.

'I'm in England to see my mother. I try to get over every four or five years – sometimes with the family – but mostly on my own because of the expense.'

Serena noted the soft Irish lilt she remembered.

'I've tried to persuade her to come and live in South Africa, but she says she's too old to make a new life out there.'

'Oh, Fenton, it's so good to see you again.'

'My mother went away yesterday on one of her senior citizen outings which was arranged some time ago so as I had a day in hand before flying back, here I am. I went to your old address but they said you lived on a farm close by, but they didn't know exactly where to direct me and suggested going to the shop.'

'You've no idea how pleased I am to see you,' she repeated, as they drove out of the village.

'Tell me about yourself,' he said. 'I gathered from the chatty lady at the shop that you're divorced and have re-married. If you hadn't come along I'd have had a blow by blow account.'

'We were married last October. Tom is a local man – a farmer.'

'You must find life totally different now.'

'Yes, I do. You'll meet him this evening. You will stay for a meal, won't you?'

Serena turned down the track from the Grimley Road.

'Here we are – part of my new domain.'

When they were in the kitchen, she said, 'Here, let me take your coat. Sit down there.'

As she put his coat on a hanger she called from the hall, 'Do you like the colour scheme? I chose it and we decorated together.'

Serena hurried back into the room. 'I'll get you a cup of tea then we can go in the other room and chat. I can't get over seeing you. How long since you left England?'

'Twenty years.'

'Twenty years. Fancy that, twenty years.'

'I left as soon as I knew there was no hope of marrying you. Jeremy had appeared on the scene and seemed to sweep you off your feet – and had so much more to offer you than I had – so I packed my bags and sought sunnier climes.'

Serena stopped pouring the hot water into the pot. 'You never said. I – I never knew you had considered marrying me.' She endeavoured to keep her voice calm and resumed making the tea.

'It's of no importance now,' Fenton said airily. 'I'm happily married and we've three children, as you know from my Christmas cards.'

'Excuse me a moment, Fenton, I – I must get another jacket. This place – it isn't – it's not very warm, as I expect....'

She rushed from the room. My children. They could have been mine, she kept saying as she snatched a cardigan from her wardrobe. She blew her nose vigorously before returning.

Fenton was walking round the kitchen. 'This farmhouse is very old, isn't it?'

'Yes, definitely pre-1800, but no one knows exactly when it was built. Parts quite possibly a hundred years before that.'

'Is it your husband's farm?'

'No, but he's been the tenant for many years. Do you remember my talking about Edward Casleigh?'

Serena explained the connection and how she came to live in Grassenden. So caught up was she in Fenton's visit Serena lost all track of time and it was not until she heard Tom come into the kitchen she remembered she had a meal to prepare.

'Tom,' she called as she went into the kitchen. 'Come and meet an old friend of mine. He's here from South Africa to see his mother.'

Her face was radiant. Serena danced back into the best room.

'Tom's just washing his hands.'

No sooner had she spoken than Tom appeared. Fenton stood

up and held out his hand as she made the introductions.

'Fenton was an old boyfriend of mine, but he went to South Africa. You have a natter while I get dinner.'

'Is she still a good cook,' she heard Fenton ask as she left the room.

'That's only one of her attributes,' Tom said, but it did not sound like a compliment.

If Fenton thought things were strained, he gave no sign as they sat eating their meal.

'When have you to go back?' Serena asked.

'Tomorrow.'

'Oh, what a shame. I was going to ask if you could stay the night. It's my birthday tomorrow.'

'I know.'

'Really? You remembered after all these years. I am touched.'

'I've even brought you a present.'

Fenton reached into his inside pocket and brought out a small package, which he handed to her.

'Oh, look Tom, it's a brooch in the shape of a deer.'

'A springbok,' Fenton corrected.

'How lovely, thank you so much. Isn't it pretty Tom?'

'Yes,' he said dully.

When they had finished the meal Fenton said he would have to go.

'I'll drive you to Maidstone,' Serena said. 'You coming, Tom?'

'No, you'll still have a lot to talk about.' He turned to Fenton. 'It's been nice meeting you.'

'And you,' he replied. 'Take care of her and if you ever get as far as Cape Town, look us up.'

'That's unlikely. I don't think Tom's the travelling kind.'

*

Serena burst into the kitchen and threw her bag on the table. She sat back in the cottage chair, stretched her long shapely legs in front of her and crossed them at the ankle. Her arms hung loosely over the wooden arms. Her cheeks had the two pink spots that appeared when she was angry, but her green eyes were not flashing – they were bright and sparkling, the pupils enlarged accentuating her beauty.

Tom was sitting at the table reading a farming magazine, a small notebook and pencil beside him.

'I cannot get over seeing Fenton,' Serena said. 'We used to have such fun. I met him at a rugby match, you know.' Her brow creased as she recalled her early twenties. 'Sally – was it Sally? Yes, Sally had a boyfriend who played rugby for London Irish and she asked me to go along and watch with her. Neither of us knew anything about the game and Fenton who was standing nearby, explained some of the finer points. We made up a foursome that evening. We went out together for about a year I should think.'

She gazed dreamily into space. After a few moments she said, 'Fancy him remembering my birthday.'

'Fancy,' Tom muttered, without raising his head. He wrote something in his notebook.

Serena watched him beneath lowered lids. She saw the muscle in his jaw twitch, a sign, she had come to learn, that showed he was nettled. He rubbed two fingers up and down his temple. That he should feel jealous of someone who lived thousands of miles away she thought gratifying and laughable at the same time. The day had made her feel like a new woman and sent her mind back to old times when she was the centre of attraction – adored by men, envied by women. She felt devilish.

'I was thinking on the way back, that I might take up Fenton's invitation to visit him. I might as well spend my money on something I want to do that won't rock the boat.'

Recklessly she went on. 'You wouldn't mind, would you darling? I don't suppose you'd even notice I'd gone.'

'Don't!' he shouted, standing up.

'Don't go?'

'Don't taunt me like you do.'

'Me taunt you? Why we hardly speak.'

With feigned innocence she opened her eyes wide and slowly licked her lips. Seeing Fenton had brought back all the feminine wiles she had practised as a young woman to such satisfying effect.

'You know what I mean. I've not seen you so – so....'

'Happy? Admired? Beautiful?'

'The way you flirted and drooled over that present. I suppose you gave him a lingering kiss on the station platform?'

'But of course,' she lied. 'It made a change to feel appreciated, to know that I was still attractive and not a forty-three year old past her sell-by date.'

The smile on her face disappeared like sun behind a cloud as she stood up. She walked by him but he positioned himself between her and the door into the hall.

'I'm tired. I want to go to bed,' she said pushing past.

Tom caught her by the shoulder and moved her till she stood in front of him. He pulled her close and kissed her, digging his fingers into her shoulders. Serena neither responded nor resisted.

'What do you want me to do now?' she said. 'Slap you? Arouse your passion so that you have an excuse for making love to me against your principles, so you can say that I drove you to it?'

Serena raised angry eyes to his and saw the hurt in them, but she hardened her heart.

'I'm going to my room where I was banished.'

Chapter 25

It was inevitable, Pat supposed, that whatever the rift was between Tom and Serena, it would become public knowledge sooner or later. Some villagers were expecting it as the time limit they had put on the doomed marriage approached.

Pat had told Faith of her cool reception by Tom, but apart from her she had not even mentioned it to Jamie. Faith suggested that Pat could have a word with them, but she shook her head vigorously.

'I'm too close. Whichever one I chose to single out, the other would feel I was taking sides.'

Ian Walker was the courier who unwittingly let slip all was not quite as it should be. The news was transmitted the evening he had gone to *The Mitre* to celebrate Mike's birthday.

'That was a bit of a funny do today, wasn't it, Mike?' Ian said as he leaned on the bar counter. It was quiet as they had come straight from the farm after work and only two other men were in the pub.

'About the shelf, you mean?'

'Yeah.'

'What happened exactly? Mrs Cresswell asked you to help move the freezer, didn't you say – then what.'

'Well, she was in a bit of a mood like she gets sometimes. She told me she'd ordered a freezer some weeks ago but when it came there was a scratch and dent down one side. She then had to wait for another of the same make so by the time it arrived she wasn't half annoyed.' Ian drained his glass. 'Want another Mike? You're not eighty every day.'

'Half a pint will do, and don't be cheeky.'

'Two halves please, Ron.' Ian turned back to Mike. 'Where was I? Oh yeah. I was passing the kitchen when she called me in. She asked if I could hold up a shelf. I said I could hold it up and do the screwing as well if she liked, and she left it to me. I'd just started when in comes Tom. "What d'you think you're doing?" he shouts at me. "I've been waiting for you in the barn." "I'm sorry," I says, "Mrs Cresswell asked me to do this shelf for her."

'His face was like thunder and he said, "I don't pay you to do jobs about the house, finish that and then come outside." And he left without even looking at her. She wasn't half embarrassed, I can tell you. What d'yer think is up?'

'Dunno, but all marriages have their ups and downs. Perhaps Tom got out of the bed the wrong side.'

Ian shrugged as he took a swallow of his lager. He was not that concerned about them and was not a gossip by nature, he had just been taken by surprise by the usually easy-going Tom's reaction. Beside him, however, someone's ears were flapping and by closing time the embellished story had spread like ripples in the pond at Abbey Farm.

So those interested, or just plain nosy, began studying evidence and sought clues to fit their theories.

*

Faith was uneasy. She felt she ought to do something to ease the situation, but she was not sure which of them, Tom or Serena, she should tackle. Who was upsetting whom? And if she did know all the facts, who was she to judge who was in the right – she could make matters worse?

It was obvious Serena was miserable. The weight she had put on now seemed to have left her and she was almost as thin as she was last summer when she was ill. Faith did hate to see marriages fail, especially when those concerned were known and loved by her.

An answer to her skyward prayers was presented to her unexpectedly one evening.

*

A note told Tom what and where his food was when he came in for lunch. He and Serena seemed to communicate more by writing than speaking. How had they reached this point?

He sat down at the place set for him. Knife, fork, spoon, serviette, glass and jug were set with precision on a yellow and white check cloth. The food today, cold sausage and onion pie would be delicious but he might as well be eating sawdust he was so depressed. He had given up coming in for coffee or tea and latterly Serena would find some excuse to be out at lunchtime. Eating together in the evening was even worse than eating alone.

And sleeping alone. If only she had not said in her haughty voice that she was quite capable when he had offered to plug in the blanket, he would have taken her in his arms as he had done before.

Why did she make the most cutting remarks – saying he treated her like a housekeeper and deliberately setting out to annoy him? She had never mentioned the stove before, never said a freezer would be handy. There was a vast difference between installing central heating and buying two kitchen appliances. They could have discussed that!

Tom pushed his plate away and rested his head in his hands. He thought he could handle her but all he had done was to make things worse.

His head jerked up as Serena came in the kitchen door. She put her packages on the chair and with her customary poise she carefully eased each finger of her gloves before taking them off.

'What have you bought?'

'Nothing for the farmhouse, so you can rest easy.'

'I wasn't asking for that reason, I was trying to be interested.'

Serena reeled off in a monotone that she had bought a summer skirt, a blouse and some underclothes. Tom did not know what else to say.

'Didn't you like my pie,' she said, looking at the untouched portion.

'It was up to your usual standard, I just didn't feel like it,' he said, getting up from the table. 'I'm at a farmers' meeting tonight. Could we have dinner a little earlier?'

'As you wish,' she said.

*

As Tom left the centre of Maidstone along the Tonbridge Road, he saw Mrs Tressant standing at a bus stop. He drew in and leaned across to wind down the window.

'May I give you a lift?'

'That would be lovely. It's a bit breezy standing here.'

'Your husband has the car I presume?' Tom said, as Faith put on the seat belt and settled herself.

'No, it's in your brother's hands unfortunately. I've been to see my father. They called me late this afternoon as he had had a bad turn. How's Serena's father?'

'Not too bad. Serena's been to see him a few times since Christmas.'

'I know she was worried last year whether to move him to a nursing home here. She asked about the one my father's in. She had even thought of having her father to live with her – before you were married, of course.'

They travelled in silence for a while then Faith took a chance. 'Neither you nor Serena seem happy. Am I right?'

There was a lengthy pause while Tom was no doubt thinking whether he was willing to talk. The longer the pause, Faith had gleaned from years of experience, the more likely a person would unburden him or herself.

At last Tom said, 'I don't know precisely where I've gone wrong, Mrs Tressant.'

'Call me Faith. You sound as if you think it's all your fault.'

'No,' he said forcefully, 'It's not all my fault. Serena doesn't or won't understand my position. Everything I do on the farm is my responsibility, but the farmhouse is Edward's. She wants to spend money on it and I won't let her. My income isn't regular. I have to keep money back for the unprofitable years and I don't have unlimited money like she's used to.'

'Let's stop at the next lay-by,' Faith said practically. 'We can't talk properly if you're concentrating on driving.'

Tom turned into a gateway and switched off the engine.

'Did you explain your position to Serena?'

'Yes, more than once.'

'Did she understand?'

'I supposed so, I don't know. She's never been short of money, has she?'

'But?'

'She says I won't let her contribute anything, but I did. I said she could have a room of her own which she could have decorated and furnished with all her own possessions. She paid for all that and brought masses of other stuff – furniture, crockery, cutlery, that sort of thing. I thought that was enough for her to do. She says if she only had a little money I'd be willing to share it and that I resented the fact that she was wealthy.' Tom gave a sigh. 'And she said I had a chip on my shoulder.'

'She did put you through it.' Faith smiled to herself in the darkness. 'How much of what she said is true?'

There was another period of silence but Faith didn't press the point.

'What first attracted you to Serena? You're not the first couple that comes to mind for compatibility.'

'We aren't compatible. Everyone was right after all,' Tom said bitterly.

'I don't believe you believe that. You're much too sensible to marry someone without thinking it through.'

'I wasn't attracted to Serena, in fact I positively disliked her. I only met her through Lydia, and then she was rude and condescending. She – we didn't move in the same circles.'

'Ah, that answers one of my questions.' Faith heard him give a faint laugh. 'What do you love about her? It must have been strong to overcome the aversion you had,'

'She's beautiful.'

'Yes, that's a strong pull for any man, but you'd need more than that.'

'She's alive, energetic, full of ideas. We had such fun decorating and she's a marvellous cook, as you know.'

Tom was being superficial, she needed to probe. 'Anything else?'

'Dignity, elegance. I love watching her, she has a lovely body. I don't think I've ever seen her make an ungainly movement. Even when she flops into a chair there's a certain grace to it. I don't even mind too much when she loses her temper.' He laughed. 'It makes her even more attractive and...' There was an expectant pause. 'and she loves me. Nobody has ever loved me – not like that.'

Faith felt she had gleaned what she wanted to know.

'So, how did you get together?'

Tom gave her a potted version of their early meetings, Jeremy citing him and their enforced separation.

'I'm sticking my neck out here and I hope you won't think I'm being too impertinent but, last year when Serena was ill, had she – was it a miscarriage?'

'You guessed, Serena said you had.'

'I had two miscarriages myself when we were first married. It was what she said in her nightmare that made me suspicious.'

'That's another thing we argue about. She can't seem to forget and thinks I'm unsympathetic. I try not to be but she keeps on and on and I can't see any point in going over something that's past – that we can do nothing about.'

'I presume you want children?'

'Yes, of course, but not with the same intensity – I suppose because she is a woman.'

'And time's running out, don't forget Tom.'

'She keeps telling me that too.'

'So – let me sum up your position as I see it. You love Serena but you feel she is undermining your position as the breadwinner by wanting to use her money. You think she is over-reacting to the loss of *your* baby.' The emphasis was deliberate and Faith hoped he had noticed.

'Yes, that's about it.'

'Now – let's look at it from Serena's point of view. We'll have to assume she loves you, as she's not here to ask. As you say she made all the running when you positively disliked her, she must have found you attractive. She told you, and David and I too, that she was lonely – that figures. For over twenty years she has led a life – how do they put it nowadays – in the fast lane. If not that then at a level that meant she was spending much of her time socialising.

'I know that a great deal of entertaining and being entertained she enjoyed. One, because she was helping to further Jeremy's career and two, she was good at it and enjoyed being admired. In later years it took her mind off the fact she was not expecting the children she so desperately longed for.

'With Jeremy gone life as she had known it disappeared completely. She had devoted herself to Jeremy's needs and now she had nothing – few friends, most of them Jeremy's who felt more loyalty to him than her, no social life and the trauma of divorce and her father to worry about. Serena seeks your company for whatever reason and falls in love. She finds she is having a child and immediately loses it but, if I've read the situation correctly, she doesn't know exactly how you feel about her, let alone what you think about being a father. She is at her lowest ebb. What is she hoping from you now?'

Tom started at the sudden question. 'That I will ask her to marry me?'

'Yes, but more than anything to know you were there supporting her, loving her, realising the child was yours, not just hers.'

'Didn't I do that? Surely to ask her to marry me showed I loved her. I didn't marry her because I felt sorry for her you know. For weeks I didn't know if what I felt was love, and anyway, what had I got to offer her?'

'And the baby?'

'It was only one night. It wasn't as if we were married and I knew I was to be a father, then I would have had some of the same expectations.' Tom paused. 'I didn't think about it as a baby, only as something that had made Serena ill.'

'That's why she keeps going on about it. She thinks you don't care – that you should be more upset than you are.'

'I try to understand,' he said forlornly.

'Let's leave that for a moment. She's married – her days are now as far removed as they can be from those she knew. She has to adapt to your needs in an environment that is completely alien to her. How well is she doing that?'

Again Faith sees that he is surprised by the question.

'She's – she's very good.'

'What does she do?'

'She cleans and cooks – I've never eaten so well and makes everything homely and,' he said smiling, 'she sells apples sometimes.'

'And what do you do for her?'

Tom was quiet for a long, long time.

'Nothing, I don't do anything, I've only gained. I asked everyone to make allowances for her, but I haven't made any.'

'But she has your love, she'd settle for that, wouldn't she?'

'No.'

'No, she wouldn't settle for love, or no she doesn't have it?'

'Serena doesn't have my love. We had a row and she said I treated her like a housekeeper. She stormed out and bought things for the house and said I could pay her by instalments if I was upset. I – I didn't know what to say. She can make me feel so – so…'

'Out of her class?' If Tom caught her irony he made no comment.

'And then I said, because I wanted to hurt her, a housekeeper shouldn't sleep with her employer.'

'Oh, Tom, how could you? That was very cruel.'

'I know, I know. I regret it, but I don't know how to put things right. We've both dug our toes in and I'm afraid she'll say something humiliating if I try – if I try…' His voice faltered.

'Do you think Serena wants to spend her money to show off to you that's she's wealthier than you are?' Faith asked.

'It all started when she was cold. She suggested paying for central heating.' Suddenly Tom turned round to face Faith. 'This must sound silly to you – you must think we're a couple of spoilt children arguing over nothing?'

'You are a couple of spoilt children arguing over nothing. Having money has not spoiled you, but you've been pretty autonomous in your little world. Day to day you've rarely had to consult or account to anyone. You love farming and are successful and your decisions make you feel secure.

'Serena, on the other hand, is not sure of herself in this unfamiliar world she has entered for love of you. She knows she's not clever, but she is a homemaker and therein lies her confidence. You are denying her the things she does best. Remember the fun you said you had? What were you doing? What she enjoys most – making a home. In those early days she didn't know she was going to share it with you. Do you see what I'm trying to say? She wants to spend money to make her house into a home. Nest building you might call it.'

'But Edward….'

'Bug – blow, Edward,' Faith exclaimed, stopping herself from uttering an unladylike word. 'Do you think he is going to mind if Serena spends money on the house even if it is his responsibility. They've been friends since childhood, good, close friends. If it's not his money that's being spent, he's not going to raise the rent to pay for it, is he?' Tom did not answer. 'But you'd feel beholden?'

'Yes, Serena and Edward are alike, I'd feel they were ganging up on me.'

'I see what Serena meant about a chip on your shoulder. But Tom – she is your wife – your wife – and she loves you. I don't suppose thoughts of Edward enter her head when she wants to do something to please you both. You're not going to give up farming, so it's always going to be your home. You've everything to gain and nothing to lose as far as I can see.'

Tom was quiet for a while, as if digesting this fact. He turned on the engine.

'We'd better be going, it's getting late. Serena will be worried.'

'I hope you don't resent my talking to you like this, but I hate to see you both so unhappy.'

'If my mother had been alive, she would have told me not to be so stupid, just as you have done.'

Tom brought the car to a halt outside the Vicarage.

'Thanks for the lift.' Faith unclipped her seat belt and reached for the door handle.

'You're welcome and thank you for your advice. I'll talk to

Serena straightaway.'

'And Tom, this has been a private conversation.'

*

Tom left Grassenden and turned into Abbotts Lidiard Lane, where the tall hedges were beginning to burst into bud. The road widened and the old road into the village went left to end opposite pub. He passed Stream Cottage, where the stream that came under the road ran along the front of the garden and on to empty into the pond on his farm.

On up the gradual incline past the cottage where he, Jamie and for a good part of his childhood, Edward had lived. Wendy was still living there, a sad figure in the village, pushing little Daniel who was approaching his first birthday. Opposite was the three-sided layout of the almshouses and further on Abbey Manor. They were a part of Tom's world for as long as he could remember, and would remain so.

He parked the car beside Serena's and felt in his pocket for the keys.

The kitchen light was on.

'Serena,' he called. 'I've something to say…'

Then he saw the note, in her round child-like writing, propped up against a cup on the table neatly laid for breakfast.

> *Tom*
> *I've gone to bed. There's food in*
> *the pantry should you be hungry.*
> *Serena*

Disappointed, he dropped the note on the table and went to the fridge. He opened the door, then shut it again without taking the beer he had intended. He locked up, switched off the lights and miserably climbed the stairs. There was a light under Serena's door and he tapped lightly and turned the knob.

'Serena,' he whispered.

She was asleep, a book falling from her hand. He crept over to the bed and gazed down at her. 'You are so beautiful,' he murmured.

If he were awake first Tom used to like studying her thick, curling lashes – but he never saw her sleeping now.

Gently he took the book from her hand and glanced at the title. He had never seen Serena with a book, and *Anna Karenina* seemed a bit heavy to begin her literary education. He sat on the bed and took her hand, hoping she would wake so he could apologise for his insensitivity.

He ran his thumb over her wedding ring. Their engagement ring they had chosen together. Tom could never afford anything like the emerald Jeremy had given her, but Serena said she would like a ring totally different from anything she possessed and something he would like too. She had chosen a three-diamond band. He glanced at her bedside table, but could not see it there.

She turned without waking, freeing her hand from his. Tom pulled the bedclothes over her shoulders, switched off the light and went to bed.

∗

When Tom came into the kitchen next morning, he found Serena standing by the door. She was wearing a cream suit with a long line jacket with thin, widely spaced navy and maroon stripes. A maroon blouse showed at her throat. As always, her looks bowled him over.

'I'm going up to London,' she announced. 'I've left everything ready for your breakfast.'

'I didn't know you were going to town, you never said.'

'Well, I'm telling you now.'

'Are you meeting someone? When will you be back? I wanted to talk....'

'I don't know what time I'll be back so you can go ahead with your evening meal whenever you feel like it. There's plenty of food – you shouldn't starve.'

Tom's heart sank 'But Serena....'

'Yes?'

'Don't be late please. We must talk.'

'Well, I wouldn't wait up. I might take in a show, supper maybe, make a day of it.'

'And a night,' he said sharply feeling his temper rise at her attitude and his disappointment.

'I hadn't thought of that,' she said, with a malicious smile. 'I could book into a hotel, it would save me having to rush for the last train.'

'Serena! We can't go on like this.'

She glared at him angrily. 'I never started it, it's you and your stupid pride. I'll see you when I return.' She picked up her handbag. 'Whenever that may be.'

Tom waited up till twelve-thirty allowing plenty of time for

Serena to have caught the last train and driven home. When reluctantly he want to bed, he lay listening for her car.

'I haven't seen Mrs Cresswell this morning,' Mike said next morning. 'She gone out?'

'Yes, she went up to London.'

'Spending lots of money on clothes I expect. These women. She always, um, she always looks – well, very nice, doesn't she?'

'Yes, Mike, she is a very beautiful woman.'

Tom saw Mike give him a strange look before he headed for the oast.

Throughout the morning Tom would move to areas in the fields where he could see if Serena's car was in the yard, or he would find an excuse to go back to the farmhouse. He finished early but all he did was pace around the kitchen. Tom was torn between anger and worry that something might have happened to her and was not sure what to do.

Why had she gone to London? Was she meeting someone? When she said she might not come back that night he thought she was getting at him. Even if she had stayed – surely she would have rung him. Could she have gone to see Jeremy? Should he ring him? What would he say? "Is Serena with you?" and he would say "Don't tell me you've lost her already. I knew it would never last. Serena could never stand being cooped up in a tatty place like yours." and he would laugh cynically.

'Stop it, stop it.' he said out loud. 'She does love me, she does, and I love her.'

The phone rang and Tom dashed to answer it.

'Mr Cresswell? Tom Cresswell?'

'Yes.'

'Is your wife Serena Cresswell?"

'Yes, where is she? Who are you?'

'This is Horton General Hospital. Your wife has had an accident.'

Tom's stomach churned. 'What's wrong? Haw badly is she hurt? Can I see her?'

'Your wife was knocked down last night and we could not find anything to identify her. She was unconscious but when she came round she seemed to have lost her memory. Then the taxi driver brought in her handbag. Even then we could only find a credit card, so we had to ask the police for help.'

'Are there – is she badly hurt?' Tom felt sick.

'She has a broken leg and she's badly bruised and concussed.'

'When can I see her?'

'Whenever you like.'

Tom debated whether to get a train or drive to London. Unwisely he plumped for driving. He searched out an old A-Z.

Tom was flustered driving in an unfamiliar area and worried about Serena. When he did find the hospital it took fifteen minutes to find somewhere to park and then he had to find his way back. By the time he reached Serena's ward, he felt physically ill with frustration and anxiety. A nurse asked if she could help and directed him to a bed at the end of the room.

Serena was lying still, her head on one side away from him. A cradle was over her legs.

'Hello,' he said quietly, afraid she might wake her if she were asleep.

She turned on hearing his voice. 'For God's sake, get me out of this dump.'

'How are you feeling?' He leaned over to kiss her. 'I was so worried about you.'

'I'll feel much better when I've left here. Do you know this is a mixed ward – men and women together.'

'I hadn't noticed to be honest.'

'I asked about a private room but they said they were all occupied. See what you can do.'

'Right now? Can't it wait? I want to know how you are and what happened to you.'

'Aren't you worried about me stuck here?'

The harassing journey and the worry engulfed him in a sea of anger. 'Don't you ever let up? Don't you realise how I've felt? I've been worried sick and all you can talk about is getting a private room. You haven't even said hello. You're lucky somebody bothered to pick you up. If you've been behaving like this since you've been here, they're probably wishing they hadn't.'

Tom strode down the length of the ward till he reached the outside rooms where he almost knocked a nurse off her feet. They glared at each other till Tom realised what he had done.

'I'm so sorry,' he said. 'I wasn't looking where I was going.'

The nurse said in a calm and professional voice. 'You look upset. Is it someone you are visiting? Can I help?'

'It's my wife, she's – well she wants a private room?'

'Ah, you must be Mrs Cresswell's husband. We've explained the situation.'

'Yes, she told me, I wasn't coming to ask again. We've had a sort of argument.'

'I see,' the nurse said. 'She could be transferred to a private hospital near you. There's no reason why she can't be moved, but we're only keeping her in another night – unless there are complications. Then she'll be under her own GP.'

A voice behind him said severely, 'Are you Mr Cresswell?'

Tom swung round to be confronted by an older, frighteningly forbidding nurse.

'Yes.'

'Your wife is very distressed. She has had an accident you know and is concussed. Would you go to her please.'

Tom retraced his steps and he was full of remorse at the sight of the curtains round her bed. A nurse moved away as he came through the curtains. He sat down on the red plastic chair beside the bed and took her hand. She was crying.

'I'm sorry darling, I didn't mean to upset you. It's just that I've had a dreadful journey – and I was so anxious about you.'

Serena smiled tearfully. 'I know, I'm sorry too, I didn't mean to start on you like that.'

'I've been so stupid,' Tom said, raising her hand to kiss it. 'I really cut off my nose to spite my face, didn't I?'

'I didn't mean the things I said,' she admitted.

'Faith has told me off. She said we were behaving like spoiled children.'

'Did she? When did you see her?'

'I gave her a lift back from Maidstone and I was going to talk to you when I got home but you'd gone to bed. I was so disappointed. I saw you light on and came to see you but....'

'So it was you who turned off my light. Why didn't you wake me?'

'I was afraid to, but I kept hoping you would.' They laughed and Tom squeezed her hand. 'We'll get things sorted out, won't we Serena? We mustn't let anything like this happen again. I know I've been pig-headed. When you're better we'll set about making the farm a wonderful home just as you like it. You can talk to Edward and see what can and can't be done.'

'*We'll* talk to Edward. It's our home and we'll have it as *we* like.'

'You've no idea what a relief this all is. They're letting you out tomorrow, they said. Now, tell me what happened to you.'

Serena explained that she had been hurrying to catch the last train when she tripped at the curb and fell in front of a taxi. Luckily it was not too close and the driver slammed on his brakes, but not before hitting her. She cracked her head causing her to black out and her leg was broken. She could not remember anything when she woke up.

'The nurses kept asking me what my name was and where I lived, but by the time I remembered, they had managed to find my address through the police. I had changed my handbag and took the very minimum I needed.'

'Did you have a nice time?'

'Not really. It's not much fun going to a show by oneself.'

'If anything had happened to you, I wouldn't know what to do, I don't think I'd want to go on living.'

Tom took her in his arms and kissed her as passionately as circumstances permitted. He did not notice her wince at the eagerness of his embrace.

*

Mike and Ian had been her first visitors, Mike poking his head warily round the kitchen door and stumblingly muttering how pleased he was to see her back; and Ian, asking her about the accident and peering closely at the cuts on her face with more than medical interest.

In the afternoon an exuberant Faith breezed in. No mention was made of the lecture she had given Tom, but Serena noticed a look of self-satisfaction on her face as she regarded them both. In the evening Anna came, followed by Pat, Jamie and the children. Tony wrote his name on her plaster and drew a funny face.

Kim stared out of the window most of the time and Pat whispered that she thought her daughter was lovesick, but had not found out who for. Serena nodded knowingly.

Dr Ferguson called, examined her and said she was to take it easy because of the concussion. In two weeks the plaster would be removed and then it would be another four weeks before she would be back to normal. To her surprise he then broached the subject of her miscarriage.

'You've not been back to see me, Mrs Cresswell? How are you feeling now? Are you coping?'

'I'd expected to become pregnant straightaway after we married. Silly, wasn't it?'

'No' silly at all?'

'What do you think my chances are?' She knew, but felt she must ask.

'Same as I told you before. Can you bear it?'

Something in his voice made her look at him closely. 'It's a case of having to.' She smiled wryly. 'Have you any children Dr Ferguson?'

He shook his head and with both hands carefully adjusted his glasses. 'My wife has had four miscarriages.' He paused. 'Life's so unfair, isn't it?'

As he shut his case, he said in a more professional voice, 'Call in if you're worried about anything. You were lucky you were not more badly injured.'

'I know. I shall be more careful in future.'

Chapter 26

'I want to do that,' Tom said, as he came into the bedroom.

'Do what?'

'Unzip your skirt. I want to see how your bruises are progressing.'

'Liar.' She gave a huge smile and he laughed too. Tom started undoing the buttons of her blouse.

'All right then,' he said, running his hands over her shoulders as the blouse slipped down her arms, 'I want to kiss them better.'

'That sounds more like it – but they've gone.'

'You're playing hard to get,' he whispered in her ear.

'Would I do such a thing? You know, for an inexperienced lover, Tom Cresswell, you're a remarkably fast learner, or were you having me on when you said you'd never had a girlfriend? And stop doing that!'

'Don't you like it?' he said, kneeling and kissing her hip where the pale yellow bruise had all but faded.

'Yes – that's the trouble,' she giggled.

'I've time to catch up. Weeks since I've made love to you – and twenty odd years when my charms were lost to the world at large – the female half anyway.'

'You insufferable oaf.'

Tom got to his feet. 'But you were worth waiting for.' He eyed her up and down lasciviously. She backed away and he chased her round the bed but she managed to jump into it and pull the covers up over her head.

When they had made love she lay in the crook of his arm, her head resting on his chest. His fingers traced the small, fading scar on her forehead. He bent his head to kiss her. 'I do love you,' he said.

'I know, I love you too.'

They lay in the quietness of lovers till Tom broke the silence.

'Do you remember when I first took you out for a meal.'

'And you called me a stuck-up bitch.'

'I didn't, well nearly – you were anyway.'

'It's a good job you've already made love to me because your chances now would be nil,' she said, reaching up and tweaking his ear till he shouted out in pain.

'Do you remember,' he repeated, holding her hand tightly so she could do him no more damage, 'I mentioned setting up a business of your own?'

'Yes, vaguely. I didn't think you were serious.'

'Why don't you think about it – start making some enquiries? It's a shame not to put your flair for cooking to some purpose.'

Serena wriggled with pleasure. 'Do you think I could?'

'I don't see why not. I expect I can help you find out about the business side – or Edward can.'

'You wouldn't mind Edward helping me?'

'Not if it would make you happy. Mind you, I wouldn't want him down here helping you make pastry, or anything like that.'

Serena laughed so much she could not speak and the tears ran down her face. In the end he had to tell her his arm was going to sleep and he wanted the rest of his body to follow, so would she stop behaving like a giggly schoolgirl?

'You've made me happier than I ever thought possible,' he mumbled, as he fell asleep with Serena's arm round his waist and her body closely moulded round his.

Serena lay for some time listening to her husband's steady breathing.

Their marriage was a strange one. She knew people had not given it any chance of success but she had been confident and made up her mind she would not dwell on her past life. Tom had a calming influence on her, but the village had nearly been right. She had not known about his pride and stubborn streak. Faith had certainly been right about their childishness. Serena wondered how she had broached the subject without Tom telling her to mind her own business as he had once told Edward.

Her thoughts drifted to the day Tom came to the hospital. What a cow she had been. There he was, anxious about her, driving in a London of which he had no experience then having her bawl at him. Poor dear. That was six weeks ago and now she felt fit and well and ready to start her new life in earnest.

*

Tom sipped his coffee as Serena put a plate of bacon and eggs in front of him next morning.

'What are you having? More than that piece of toast I hope.'

'I've never eaten much breakfast, you know that.' She saw his disapproving look. 'All right, I'll get myself an egg.'

'Good, you must put on some weight. I'm sure you'll feel much better. You're tall and can take it, if looking fat is what's worrying you.'

Tom dived into his breakfast. 'About what I said last night – why don't you ask Edward and Lydia to dinner and we can kill two birds with one stone, discuss what can be done in the farmhouse and see if he has any ideas about setting up a business.'

'OK, what about Friday?'

At eleven Serena went into the best room with her coffee. She took a piece of paper from the bureau and wrote Central Heating – that was definitely number one. Next she wrote Bathroom – that certainly needed money spent on it. In fact it needed demolishing and starting again. Would Tom go along with that? Would Edward? Well, she could but ask. Third Bedroom? She crossed it out. Better not push her luck.

She tapped her pencil on her bottom teeth. Running a business – could she do that? Cooking was no problem and spending money she was good at – making it was a different matter – but it was rather exciting whatever the outcome.

On Friday evening Serena stood in her kitchen and surveyed the scene. The smell of cooking made it warm and inviting. There had been no point in preparing a table with candlesticks and the trappings that she would have for a party at Ridge House. She had studied recipes and pictures in her magazines and decided to prepare a farmhouse dinner in keeping with a farmhouse setting.

She bought a pinafore check fabric to make a cloth that adequately covered the large wooden table. She rummaged through the boxes she had brought from her old house to see if she had enough matching crockery. Delighted, she found the four settings she needed, plus dishes, plain white with a raised pattern. Little of the cutlery matched so she bought a set with wooden handles.

Food was to follow the country theme – carrot and orange soup, a chicken dish and apple pie and cream. Cheese and biscuits and fresh fruit were to complete the meal.

As she admired her handiwork Tom came down. 'It looks lovely darling. Everything is just right. What a difference from when you first came here.'

'You mean when you had to throw books on that battered settee so I could sit down.'

'It was awful, wasn't it? Even I blush to think about it. It's amazing what a good housekeeper can do.' He let go of her quickly before she could attack him. 'Do you think I'm suitably dressed to match the surroundings?' he said, standing smartly for inspection.

Serena looked him up and down examining the smart grey trousers, the muted check shirt and blue tie which she adjusted.

'Yes, you'll pass. You're not bad looking really. You smell nice too.'

'You look as gorgeous as ever.'

She went over to inspect progress. 'They should be here in a minute. Do you think I've covered everything?'

Tom looked around. 'Yep, they'll be most impressed. Ah, there they are now.'

Edward gazed around the kitchen marvelling at the change and complimenting Serena on her creativity.

'It's amazing what a woman's touch can achieve,' Lydia said, and Tom and Serena smiled at each other.

Serena asked how Philippa was and almost wished she hadn't because Edward imparted, in great detail, what a marvellous and unique child she was.

'We've got something we want to ask you. Edward,' Tom said, when they had gone to the best room for coffee.

'Oh, what's that?'

Serena said, 'We'd like to modernise the farmhouse – put in central heating for a start – update the bathroom, maybe.'

'I've already spent a great deal of money on the windows, you know. They didn't come cheap having to be specially made in wood and I had the upper windows done, which I hadn't intended.'

'Yes, we know, but we don't want you to pay for it, we'll foot the bill.'

Edward ran a hand through his hair. 'In that case, I suppose I can't have any objection.' He turned to Tom. 'You won't be biting off more than you can chew, will you?'

'We've worked it out carefully, but you know me, cautious in the extreme.'

'Right, well go ahead then, but keep me posted.'Serena jumped up, flung her arms round Edward and gave him a kiss.

'That's marvellous. Thank you so much.'

'I'm not sure that it isn't me that should thank you.' He gave a rare smile.

'The other thing we wanted was advice.'

Edward looked both surprised and pleased.

Tom went on, 'Serena's thinking about setting up in business.'

She continued excitedly, 'Catering for parties, dinners, that sort of thing. We wondered if you had any helpful advice.'

Lydia, who had been particularly quiet all evening, suddenly remarked, 'You have to be very diplomatic when you're in business dealing with the public.'

Two pairs of eyes jerked her way. Edward cleared his throat and Tom shot a glance at Serena who stood rigid pot in hand, eyes cast down. He saw the telltale signs appear on her cheeks and waited for the storm.

'I'm sorry,' Lydia said, embarrassed, 'I shouldn't have said that.'

There was a silence that seemed to stretch interminably till Serena said at last, 'Yes, I will have to get my temper under control. It wouldn't do for my clients to end up throwing food at me – or me at them.'

She filled Edward's cup and handed it to him and an audible sigh went round the room as Edward quickly took up the conversation. 'The best thing to do is go to a business seminar. I believe they run them in Maidstone.'

'I've seen them advertised in the local paper,' Lydia said looking relieved. 'They're usually held on Saturday mornings.'

'You should try and meet people already running such a business. Do you know anyone?'

'No, and would they be willing to tell me anything if I were a potential competitor?'

'Perhaps not. You must have been to enough of these things. What about the caterers at the garden party you held a couple of years ago?'

'They would do larger events than I'm intending. I want to do something that I can cope with more or less by myself.'

'You need to have a basic plan,' Edward said. 'There's capital – are you going to borrow? If so, what's the interest and for how long? Transport, tax, VAT, equipment, pitching the price, and how much you are going to take as salary. Will you want to expand or keep it small?'

Serena's face fell as his list discouragingly lengthened.

'And,' he added, 'Will you be allowed to run a business from here? I've no objection but there are so many regulations nowadays.'

'I'll help if you tell me what you want finding out,' Lydia offered, 'then it won't seem so demoralising.'

'Oh,' she said surprised at her offer.

When they were getting ready for bed Tom said, 'How do you feel about it now?'

'It's rather daunting.'

'It is a big step, but look at all the support you'll have – there's Edward and Lydia, and Jamie runs a small business, he can point out pitfalls.'

'I didn't realise there was so much to it, I don't think I'll be able to cope. I'm not clever like you and Edward.'

'Of course you can. Take it slowly, find out what you have to do by going on this course.'

Serena climbed into bed her face solemn and thoughtful.

'Cheer up. Think of it as an exciting adventure.'

She did not speak for some moments. 'What did you think of Lydia's comment?'

Tom grinned. 'I was waiting for coffee and cups to land all over the room.'

'They nearly did but, for one thing I didn't want to give her the benefit of being proved right and for another, what she said was true.'

They cuddled up together and, for once, Serena was asleep first.

*

When she had been assured she was capable, Serena started making plans. Tom would watch amused as she sat, a frown creasing her brow, a pencil tapping her teeth, surrounded by paper, notes and books, concentrating on the task in hand.

In September she went to the first of four morning courses for new business ventures. When she returned at lunchtime she told Tom that her fellow students were all beginners just as he had thought and none of them was going into catering. She told him smugly that many of them had not done as much background work as she had.

Tom studied her face, eyes bright with child-like anticipation. How could this person, the woman who had changed his whole life and whom he held most dear, be the same one he had all but despised two years ago. Unhappiness, he supposed, coupled with frustration and disappointment at being childless.

Serena no longer mentioned babies and he, being a coward and not knowing what to say, never brought up the subject. She no longer had nightmares or mentioned to him that she was not pregnant that month.

Tom tried not to admit it, but he too was disappointed. It was the birth of Nicholas to Edward and Lydia, and the village celebrations at the pub, and more intimate ones at the Manor, that had suddenly intensified his desire. He supposed in part that it was the underlying conflict between him and Edward. Tom wanted to prove he was just a capable of producing a child as Edward – a son and heir. Not that his child would have an estate to inherit.

*

Since Edward had given the go-ahead, they had arranged for central heating to be put in. Tom kept well out of the way as Serena made sure the men did the work exactly as she intended it to be done. The fact that she knew nothing about it did not seem to inhibit her and only when she was assured several times that it was impossible to put a radiator where she wanted it did she retract – reluctantly.

When the installation had been completed, she turned her thoughts to renovating the bathroom, but Tom called a halt and said it should wait until next year. She was about to argue but he said, 'Don't Serena, please don't rush me. We've spent a great deal of money – most of it yours – and if you are going to cater, you'll need money behind you. We can think about the bathroom for next year.' He paused and said laughing, 'then you can do bed and breakfast in your spare time.'

'That's a good idea, do you think I could?'

He cast her a look of amiable hopelessness. 'Serena, I was joking!'

Her innate energy flowed through her like an electric current as she threw herself into her business venture. She was granted planning permission, found an accountant and had the place inspected for hygiene. Stacked in the kitchen was all the equipment needed for cooking on a large scale. Tom said he would have to have the front door opened so he could get into his own home, but she retorted that such a grave step would have the whole farmhouse fall down.

At coffee mornings, she, Anna and Lydia discussed menus, costs and prices. Lydia had the audacity to arrange a buffet lunch and a few weeks later a small dinner party, each time unashamedly quizzing the organisers.

'I don't know how you had the nerve,' Anna said laughing.

'And I thought I was the brazen one,' Serena added, 'but I was cringing at the questions you were asking.'

'But I'm not the one going into business, am I?' Lydia said innocently.

*

'I don't know what I'd do without you,' Serena said to Faith on the way back from visiting her father in Maidstone. 'Tom knows what it's like having looked after his own mother, but he doesn't understand about my father being so awkward and pathetic. He didn't know him when he was a tall, handsome figure in his army uniform. I was always so proud of him even though we were never that close because he was abroad much of the time. When he was at home he was rather strict, a bit forbidding to Gerald and me, though I'm sure he loved us both. To see him now makes me want to cry.'

'Cry, my dear, cry. You should always cry if you feel like it. By all means in private, but never hold back your tears. They are a release, a necessary part of living.'

'It is hard to see him like he is.'

'It must be. Now, how are your business plans going?'

'Everything is fine so far. Jamie keeps frightening me with tales about customers who don't pay up or, in his case, accuse him of damaging their car while in his garage when the marks have been there all the time. He said that I'll turn up with a buffet for fifty only to find they had ordered a four course dinner for ten.'

'He's an awful tease, isn't he?'

'Trouble is, I can never tell when he's telling the truth or spinning me a tale until I see that cheeky grin.'

'You are happy now, aren't you, Serena?' Faith said as they drove through the car park to the Vicarage door.

She turned her head slightly and gave a quick smile. 'More contented than I would have believed possible. I thought Jeremy and I were happy in the early days, but I see now it was a sham. All surface glitter and glitz – no depth, no strong feelings. Tom is so affectionate; nothing is done for effect like Jeremy used to do. He won't flatter me, or indulge me. If only I'd met him when I

297

was younger.'

Faith forbade telling her Tom wouldn't have been given a second glance. It was maturity and experience that made her appreciate someone like him.

*

'Happy birthday, darling.' Serena held up her glass in salute.

'Thank you, here's to the New Year and the launch of your business.' They chinked glasses and sipped their wine.

'I feel hot,' she said, brushing the back of her hand across her forehead.

'Aren't you ever satisfied, woman,' Tom said. 'This time last year you were moaning about the cold.'

'Well, I have been cooking. But isn't it lovely to be warm all over the house – and I'm sure you appreciate seeing the frilly underwear more often.'

Tom watched as his wife cut herself a second portion of cake. Now there's something, Serena taking a second helping of anything.

Preparing for her business had, in a strange way, relaxed rather than stressed her. She had certainly gained weight, giving him more to cuddle as he told her one night, ably demonstrating to their satisfaction.

'What's it like being an old man of forty-two,' she said, taking a bite of her fruitcake. 'I've noticed one or two grey hairs appearing lately.'

'You ought to know, you've been there. Anyway, a few grey hairs at the temple make a man more attractive and distinguished.'

'I can never understand why that is, and I don't think it very gallant to comment on my age.' Serena raised one of her long fingers to the corner of her mouth to remove a crumb and her bracelet slid up her arm.

'Ah, but not many women are as beautiful as you at any age.'

'Nice man,' she said.

*

Serena scanned the advertisements in the local paper with excitement. There it was under CATERING.

SERENE CUISINE
Buffets, lunches and
dinner parties
Grassenden 269713

She and Tom had sat for ages trying to think of a name. Abbey Farm Caterers sounded as if they sold meat. Abbotts Lidiard Caterers and Abbey Cuisine were also discarded. They had decided on Serena's Cuisine when one evening she hit on the present name, which combined rhyme with mood.

Now all I have to do is wait for the rush she said to herself as she folded the newspaper. No sooner had she said this than their phone rang.

'I've seen the advertisement,' Anna said.

'Yes, it looks good, doesn't it? But will anyone ask me to do anything?'

'I'm sure they will,' Anna said, 'but I'd better get off the phone in case someone is eager to contact you.'

'No problem, I've a number of my own and an answerphone.'

'What a good idea. I never noticed the different number, shows you how observant I am.'

She had just put the phone down when Lydia rang, then Faith, all offering their best wishes.

Two weeks into the year and no business had come her way. Tom tried his best to keep her spirits up. It was not long after Christmas, he told her, and people were short of money and the party season was over so there was not much call for that sort of thing.

Serena said in that case she should have begun earlier and she was stupid not to have realised this and she was never going to be a businesswoman.

What Tom thought was consoling now seemed like criticism. In fact, since the beginning of the year life in the farmhouse had been fraught and he had to be extremely careful what he said.

When she went into Grassenden everyone she met enquired how things were going. Did she have much work? Was she keeping busy and did she enjoy it? She found it humiliating to have to confess that nothing had got under way. She had thought of lying but decided too many people knew the truth.

Mrs Reece had a particularly smug look on her face and took great delight in telling her she had not noticed anyone looking at the card in the window. The fact that Mrs Reece would not be able to tell who was reading what, even if she had been standing watching all day, did not detract from the feeling that she was a failure. By the time Serena had returned to the farmhouse she was deeply despondent.

Tom came in as usual and Serena shouted at him to shut the door or all the heat would go. He gave a resigned sigh as he hung his coat on the door. She put a plate of cold meat before him and pushed the salad bowl in his direction.

'No calls yet, darling?'

'No.'

Tom reached out his hand. 'It's very early days. Don't give up hope.'

She smiled weakly then they both jumped as Serena's phone rang. Her chair scraped across the floor as she hurled herself across the room to the little table beside the pantry that was her 'office'.

'Serene Cuisine, may I help you?'

A faint voice began, 'I – my husband has died. I can't face getting food after – after the funeral. Can you help me?'

Serena was sure the woman was crying.

'What food would you require – a buffet or a sit down meal – for how many?'

These questions were too much for the woman and definite sobs could be heard.

At last Serena said, 'Will it help if I come to see you. We can discuss it better than.'

'Oh, will you really, that is kind. I'm sorry to embarrass you like this.'

'I understand. Give me your name and address and tell me when I may call.'

As she replaced the phone she wondered how she could feel elated and sad at the same time.

'Your first customer.'

'Yes, a Mrs Darbyshire. Sadly it's for a funeral – her husband's. I'm going to see her. She only lives in Grimley Heath so I said I'd go there this afternoon.'

'I knew things would soon get going. Good luck.'

＊

Serena passed Anna's house and drove into the village. The directions were vague, but eventually she found the 1930s semi and drove on to the drive. As she locked the car she heard the front door open.

'Come in – I am sorry, I don't know your name.'

'Mrs Cresswell.'

Mrs Darbyshire led her into the front room furnished with a good, but old three piece suite in uncut moquette, covered with lacy chair backs, the square arms protected with the same material. The tiled fireplace had a small electric fire and on the mantelshelf above were various ornaments of little value.

'I'll get us some tea, I won't be a minute.'

While she was gone Serena looked at the photographs. A wedding, the man in an army uniform, the bride obviously Mrs Darbyshire. Another of two young children, a boy and a girl, dressed in similar clothes to the ones she and Gerald wore as children. A smaller frame held a picture of two boys standing in a garden with a vivid blue sky behind them.

'They're my grandsons, Gary and Charlie. They live in Australia.' Mrs Darbyshire put the tray on the table and asked Serena if she would move the plant standing on a lace mat.

'I've never seen them. They can't afford to come here or for us – me to visit them.'

This slip of the tongue made tears well up in her eyes. She reached for a handkerchief from a pocket and blew her nose. Serena was not sure what to say, she had never been called upon to give consolation to anyone.

'Shall I pour the tea?' she said.

When they were seated, tea in hand, Serena said, 'Now, could you tell me what day the funeral is and how many people you are expecting?'

'It's on Friday, but I'm not sure how many people. There's my sister in Maidstone, and I have another sister and brother-in-law who live in Northampton, but they're in their eighties. Then there's my husband's brother and his wife. They're coming down from North London with my niece and nephew.'

'That's a possible eight. Anyone else?'

'My neighbours next door. They've been so good to me since Paul was taken ill. Do you know we've been neighbours for over forty years?' This recollection brought fresh tears.

'Think what wonderful memories you must have.' Serena said, thinking some comment was called for.

'I know, I shouldn't be crying like this – in front of a stranger, but I can't bear to think of living alone without him.' She wiped her eyes and replaced her handkerchief.

Serena contemplated living without Tom and she couldn't bear to think of it either.

'Are you married, Mrs Cresswell?'

'Yes I've been married about fifteen months.'

'Only that long – a pretty woman like you!'

'I was married before.'

'Do you live locally?'

'At Abbey Farm – in Abbotts Lidiard.'

She frowned. 'Cresswell? Any relation to Margaret Cresswell?'

'She would have been my mother-in-law, she died two years ago. Did you know her?'

'Not very well, but we met on and off – at WI functions and such like.'

Serena got her client back to the matter in hand. 'So, that's ten people.'

'There's no one else. My daughter's in Australia and my son was killed in a motor bike accident when he was nineteen.'

'How tragic.'

Mrs Darbyshire sighed deeply, then said, 'So, what do you suggest?'

'If you're not sure who's coming I think a buffet would be best. Everything not eaten can then be put into the freezer. If you have a hot meal, what isn't eaten will have to be thrown away. On the other hand, if you can tell me for sure the exact number, then a sit down meal might be better. You won't have to think about preparing a meal in the evening. None of you will feel like doing that I'm sure.'

'You are very thoughtful. How late can I leave it?'

'Wednesday preferably, early Thursday at the very latest if it's a cooked meal you're wanting. I must be able to get to the shops for fresh meat.'

'I'll confirm on Wednesday then. You've taken such a weight off my mind.'

This job is not going to make much money, Serena thought as she drove back. She passed the end of Abbotts Lidiard Lane then turned left down the track to home – but it is a start.

She saw Tom in the yard and waved as she manoeuvred the car beside his. She jumped out eager to tell him how she had got on. What a dear to come and meet her – but then she saw his face.

'What is it, Tom? What's wrong?'

He put his arm round her shoulders and led her to the farmhouse.

'It's your father.'

Chapter 27

Holding a replete and contented baby in her arms, Lydia looked from the window of the nursery across the drive to the lawn. Edward was bent over his daughter holding her hands above her head as she attempted to walk. He let go and she sat on the grass. He picked her up in his arms clasping her close to his chest as he swung round. Lydia could see her smiles of delight.

'Daddy's having a lovely time, isn't he darling?' Nicholas smiled at his mother's soothing voice and gave a burp.

'That's better, now let's put you out for a breath of air and if they don't make too much noise, you might go to sleep.'

The phone rang and she went to answer it.

Lydia bounced the buggy down the front steps and pushed it over to the grass. She gave Nicholas a kiss and tucked him up.

'Tom's just been on the phone.'

'Pardon?' Edward said, pretending to chase his daughter till she fell back on her bottom.

'Tom's just told me that Serena's father has taken a turn for the worse and is not expected to live. He wondered if you wanted to go over there.'

Not looking thrilled at the idea, he said, 'I suppose I ought, it is a link with my father. Poor General Bowlett. Did Tom say when?'

'You can go any time you like he said.'

'Perhaps I could take Philippa with me.' He tickled her under the chin and made her chuckle.

'I don't think going to see a dying man is quite suitable for a baby. In the normal course of events I expect they would love to see a young child.'

'I suppose you're right. I'd better go now.' He bent down and kissed the top of Philippa's gold hair. Lydia took her hand and she toddled back to the house between them.

Edward drew into a parking place at the front of the purpose-built home. He pushed the button and a disembodied voice asked him his business. The door clicked open and someone came to meet him as he turned into a corridor.

'General Bowlett is down this corridor, turn left and his is the second room on the right.'

The room opened into a narrow passage with a bathroom to the right. It widened revealing a bed and a window straight ahead. Serena was sitting with her back to the window holding her father's hand. She gave Edward a wan smile as he moved to kiss her. Tom was perched on another chair gazing out of the window. He turned as Edward came in.

'How is he?' Edward said in a low voice.

'Failing fast,' she said. 'But I can't say I'm sorry. I can't bear to see him like this, not when I remember what he used to be like – so capable, such a proud, handsome man.'

He turned to Tom. 'Have you been here long?'

'I came about ten. Serena has been here since yesterday afternoon.'

She stood up suddenly. 'He's gone – I think he's gone.'

Tom put his arm around her. Edward took her father's wrist and felt for a pulse.

'I think you're right. Shall I fetch the Matron?'

'Please,' Tom said, 'and the doctor might still be around.'

Serena turned her head into Tom's sweater and cried.

'I'm so sorry, darling. It's sad to lose a parent; I've not forgotten how it feels. It's the link with childhood that makes it so poignant.' He kissed her hair.

'Yes, I'm sure you're right.' She looked down at her father, peaceful now, the lopsided features less pronounced.

'I want to go home, Tom.'

'Haven't we to do something before we leave?'

'No, I don't think so. I've a terrible headache.'

The room was suddenly crowded as the Matron and doctor came in with Edward.

Tom said, 'My wife wants to go home, as she isn't feeling well. Is there anything she must do right now?'

'No, I have to write a death certificate and inform the authorities.'

Edward said he would stay a little longer and report back.

'I don't feel like driving, Tom,' she said wearily when they were outside. 'We'll go back in your car and we can come for mine later.'

When they were back at the farmhouse she sat at the table while Tom prepared a drink and made sandwiches.

'I'd better think about a meal for tonight.'

'Don't worry about that, I can get something or we'll go out.' Her shoulders drooped with relief. 'How's your head?'

'Thumping. Funny my first catering assignment should be for a funeral. The funeral! What shall we do about the funeral?' she said agitated. 'There'll be army friends who'll want to come – there won't be enough room here.'

'Hush Serena, relax. You needn't think about it this very moment. Sit down and have something to eat. I don't suppose you've had much.'

'I haven't had anything at all since I left here yesterday apart from countless cups of tea and biscuits.'

'No wonder you've got a headache.'

When she had almost finished her sandwich Serena said, 'I really must go and lie down, I feel awful.'

Accompanied by Philippa, Edward came later in the afternoon just as Serena came into the kitchen.

'Your father's body will be taken to whatever funeral director's you name. I didn't do anything about it as I thought you might have an undertaker in mind.'

'Thank you. There is one thing, would you be willing to have the reception after the funeral at the Manor. I wouldn't ask if it were just family, but there'll be army colleagues who'll want to be there and I don't know how many. There won't be enough room here.'

'Of course, I'm sure that'll be OK. Lydia won't mind.'

'I'll do the catering so Lydia won't have anything like that to do.'

'Are you sure you'll be up to that,' Tom said.

'I'd rather be doing something.'

Philippa began to grizzle and Edward said they had better be going. 'Would you like me to ring Gerald when I get home?'

'Would you? I know I ought to do it, but if you'll explain that I'm not feeling too good.' She went over to the dresser. 'I'll give you his number. I hope they can come – all of them'.

'I could have rung Gerald,' Tom said.

'I'm sorry, I didn't think, but it'll be one less thing to think about immediately. I shall have to ring Gerald later this evening, but the sooner he knows the better. What you could do for me is put a notice in *The Times.*

'OK. Don't forget Mrs Darbyshire.'

'Who's she?' Edward said, trying to distract his daughter from grabbing everything within reach.

'My first customer,' she said, pulling her shoulders back and lifting her head. 'Rather prophetic it should be for a funeral.'

Returning to the kitchen after seeing Edward to his car, Tom saw Serena put her hand to her head and sway. He rushed towards her and caught her as she fell.

✳

Tom showed Dr Ferguson upstairs and hovered anxiously at the foot of the bed. Serena lay propped up by pillows, her normally pale face grey and strained and for the first time Tom thought she looked her age.

'My wife's been under a lot of strain. Her father has just died after being moved to a nursing home and she's set up a business. I think it's taken its toll.'

'You're probably right.' He turned to Serena. 'But let's give you an examination.'

'She hasn't had much to eat in the last twenty-four hours.'

'In that case, it's not surprising she fainted.'

Dr Ferguson pushed his glasses further up his nose with one finger and went to his case.

'I'll go, shall I?' The doctor didn't reply which Tom took to mean he would rather be left alone with Serena. 'Let's take your blood pressure,' he heard him say as he left the room.

When the doctor came downstairs he said, 'I'd like to do a few tests. If she's feeling well enough on Monday I want her to come to the surgery. As you say, the strain and lack of food is probably the reason she fainted, but I'd like to make sure there's nothing else.'

Tom rushed upstairs and sat on the bed.

'Go easy – my head.'

'Sorry.'

'Did he tell you he wants to do some tests?'

'Yes. I expect he wants to make sure you haven't diabetes – or something like that? He gave her face a closer scrutiny. 'What are you smiling like that?'

'He said I could be pregnant.'

'Oh, Serena, how marvellous.' He went to fling his arms round her but saw her screw up her eyes and gave her a very gentle kiss instead.

'You'd think that'd be one of the first things we would have thought of,' Tom said.

'I've been so wrapped up in what I was doing – my father and everything, that I never gave it a thought.'

'I can't get over it – me a Dad, fawning over my little girl just like Edward does.'

'It could be a boy.'

'I'd still fawn.'

'Nothing's been confirmed and anyway I could still lose it.'

'No you won't, I can feel it in my bones. You're definitely pregnant and the baby'll be absolutely fine. You are clever and I love you to bits.'

*

Serena met many of her father's friends at the funeral who all said they remembered her as a little girl. She had to admit she couldn't remember any of them – they had changed so much. Gallantly they told her a pretty girl had grown up to be a beautiful woman.

Tom's prediction about her pregnancy proved right. He was teased relentlessly. At one time Tom would have been embarrassed at some of the coarser remarks, but he was so cock-a-hoop he took it all in good part and agreed with everything they said.

'Hope it doesn't look like you,' Dave Reece said, 'when it could look like your missus.'

One small thing clouded the news and that was when Dr Ferguson confirmed she was expecting.

'It was awful, Tom. I swear there was a tear in his eye. Just think how many times he has to tell a woman she's pregnant when he and his wife are so desperate.'

*

Apart from the odd occasions when she felt a bit queasy, Serena remained disgustingly well. She had limitless energy and carried on with catering as if everything were as usual.

Serena found she was becoming more sympathetic towards others as she encountered people in the course of her business. This was an aspect of life that she had barely considered in her Ridge House days. People were happy at christenings, had mixed emotions at weddings and brave and sad ones at funerals. Anxiety and tension at business lunches was one with which she had particular empathy.

She had Tom to thank for this change in her outlook. It started with that waitress who spilled the cream. What had Tom called her – a stuck-up, arrogant bitch? If had not kissed her, she would probably have killed him.

She gazed around the farmhouse kitchen, warm, bright, lived-in – worked in – full of love. What a marvellous place in which to bring up a child. Why stop at one? She probably had time to fit in another.

Tom came up behind her as she stood stirring soup. He kissed her neck.

'How's my mother hen?' he said, resting his hands on her stomach and giving it a pat.

'Mother hens cluck around their chicks, I haven't any.'

'Stop being pedantic. Since you've been expecting this baby you've got far too big for your boots. I shall have to take you down a peg or two.'

'What had you in mind?'

'Don't know yet,' he called as he went up the creaking stairs, 'but I'll think of something.'

'I can hardly wait.'

Chapter 28

Kim came into the kitchen and dropped her school bag on the floor.

'Nice long rest now, eh, Kim?' her mother said.

'I never want to see a school book again,' she said, going over to the tin and taking a biscuit.

'You look tired, want me to make you a cup of tea?'

'Thanks, Mum, I'll just go and change.'

Kim picked up her bag and munching the biscuit went to her room. She threw the bag under her desk and gave it a kick for good measure. She changed out of her uniform and as she turned, caught sight of herself in the long mirror on the back of the door.

Average height. Nice figure? She turned sideways to study her outline and stuck out her chest. Not bad – she was a bit stocky like her father, but she was as tall as him already and much taller than her Mum. Perhaps she would grow some more. She wished she had long legs like Serena. Now she was beautiful.

Kim faced the mirror. Am I good looking? Mrs Tressant always said she was a lovely girl, but that could mean anything. She put the fingers of both hands through her curly hair, which was like Uncle Tom's, not like her parents. Dad said she looked like his father who had died long before she was born.

'Tea's ready.'

'What are you planning on doing now?' Pat said.

'Now this minute, or in the next few days.'

'Both I suppose. You've got to get ready for our holiday and I want you to sort out what clothes you want to take. I don't want to be washing and ironing the night before we go away. Oh, and I'd be grateful if you could go into Tony's room and sort through some of his things.' She saw Kim's face. 'Don't worry, I don't want you to mend them, but it would help if you cast an eye round his bedroom. I expect half his clothes are under the bed.'

'OK. Do you mind if I ring and see if I can go to the farm.'

'No, of course not. I expect Serena's feeling the heat during this hot spell. You like going to the farm, don't you? I've never known you spend so much time there as you have recently.'

'Up until this year you wouldn't let me go by myself because of that man who attacked Mrs Casleigh.'

'Yes, I know, that was Dad's idea.'

'I can't see what's different now.'

'Well, you are over fifteen, we've got to let you go sometime. Just be aware of the strange people there are around and don't take risks.'

*

There was no doubt her daughter was growing up fast. She had been restless for some time, but nothing that Pat had not expected. But somehow she had been distant – her mind far away. Could be next year's exams – she knew Kim wanted to do well. Perhaps it was because Trudi had a boyfriend and Kim was feeling out of it. She was not sure whether to broach the subject but thought it best to wait till Kim brought it up. It might not be long before she was taken into her confidence now that Trudi was no longer such a bosom pal.

*

As Kim knocked and put her head round the farmhouse door, the warm smell of baking greeted her. That was something new since Uncle Tom had married. She did not know what he had eaten when he lived alone, but she rarely recalled any cooking smells.

Serena was at the table rolling out pastry. She looked flushed and there was a smudge of flour on her cheek.

'Hello, Kim, not out with Trudi this afternoon?'

'No,' Kim quickly changed the subject. 'Mum says you're probably feeling the heat.'

'She's right and my ankles have swollen.'

'Do you resent looking like you do now. I mean, you always look so lovely.

Serena smiled. 'I don't like looking so ungainly but I'm thrilled about the baby. I've always wanted to be a mother.'

'Why didn't you have any before?'

'Just one of those things – it's a long story.'

Kim thought that a typical remark always dished out when grown-ups thought the explanation would not be understood. Nothing would be understood unless someone explained it. She was a bit annoyed because one of the things she especially liked about Serena was the fact that she did not treat her like a child.

'Tell me.' Kim could see she had put her on the spot.

'Just let me finish what I'm doing and when I've cleared up, I'll tell you all about it.'

Twenty minutes later, when the kitchen hardly showed that a buffet for twenty had just been completed, Kim said, 'Would you show me your jewellery?' She went on hurriedly, 'You showed me some once, but you said you had lots more.'

'Of course. We'll go upstairs to my room and we can talk at the same time. Bring your coke with you, but don't spill it on the carpet.'

Kim quickly drank half before following her. Serena went over to a large mahogany wardrobe. She knelt down awkwardly and pulled out a drawer by its brass handles. She took out two large jewellery boxes.

'Here, take these.'

Kim put them on the bed.

'Can I open them?'

'There's some more yet.'

'How many have you got?' she exclaimed.

'Five.'

Kim thought of the tiny red velvet lined box she had been given for her birthday last year. it had a little section that would take about four rings or earrings and the rest would hardly hold the few items she had.

'My husband often gave me jewellery and there were presents from relatives and friends. Some were gifts from my husband's business colleagues – and a few pieces belonged to my mother.' She stood up clumsily.

While Kim studied the items carefully, Serena imparted to her facts, thoughts and feelings about her first marriage which, she told Kim, she had not confided to anyone except Tom.

'That was awful what your husband did, wasn't it?'

'I think so.'

Serena took one of the boxes and tipped it up. A gold and silver cascade spread out over the cream lace bedcover.

'These are all bracelets.'

'I like bracelets and bangles.'

'Yes, everyone knows you like them.' She did not add that she was known as Rattling Annie by some, including her Dad. Kim picked up one studded with rubies. 'I like this.'

Serena sat at the end of the bed. 'That was my mother's. I had all her jewellery. I am going to give it to my niece.'

'What about your children?'

'I've have plenty to pass on, as you can see.'

Kim reached for the next case shaped like a miniature wardrobe. The tiny doors opened to reveal four drawers, which held rings, brooches and earrings. Kim inspected each piece in silence, quite overcome by their beauty. The others held mainly necklaces. Kim had no idea of the value but with a discerning female eye she was sure that thousands and thousands of pounds were lying on that bed. She gazed at the glittering array and her mind wandered to when she would be an adult, working and able to buy anything she wanted.

'You seem rather sad,' she heard Serena say. Kim had been aware of her close scrutiny while she had been looking in the cases, she also knew she would ask what was wrong – had wanted her to – but at the same time did not know what she would say. She was confused and unhappy but she knew she had nothing to be unhappy about. She was expected to get all her exams with good grades and this had once seemed important. Now she wished all her books would disappear and she did not feel so pressurised all the time.

'Kim?'

'Yes.'

'Is it because Trudi has a boyfriend that you feel so unsettled?'

'I feel sort of all mixed up like. Mum says it's how teenagers are, but it doesn't help.'

'I can remember being like that. I was at an all girls' boarding school so we tried to go for walks in the direction of the boys' school because we finished our lessons before they came out. This was frowned on as you can imagine. At least you can see the boys every day and check what's on offer.' Serena laughed.

Kim remained silent.

'Have you seen someone you fancy or would you just like to have a boyfriend?'

Still she made no comment.

'It's a bind being a woman and having to wait to be asked, but there are things you can do to speed up the process you know.'

'Really,' Kim said brightening.

'You can make sure you are often near. Watch him playing football or whatever he does at your school. Keep yourself in his eye, subtly of course.'

'He doesn't go to my school.'

'Oh. What school does he go to then?'

'He doesn't go to school, he's at work.'

After another long pause Serena said, 'Can I be told who this boy is? I assume from what you say he doesn't know you like him?'

Slowly Kim put Serena's jewellery back in the last case.

'Would you like to choose something?'

'Oh, no, I couldn't possibly.'

'Shall I pick something for you. Here, what about this?' She picked up a gold chain from which hung a pearl drop. 'That's the sort of thing that will go with almost anything and you can take off the pearl and put on something else. Here, take it.' She thrust it into her reluctant hands and Kim stared at the necklace lying in her palm.

'Is this boy someone in the village?' Serena persisted.

'Yes, well, in Hemlow actually. I can't stop thinking about him.' Serena waited. 'It's Ian.'

'Ian who?'

'You know, Ian, Uncle Tom's Ian.'

'Was that Kim I saw just now cycling up the track?'

'Yes. We've had a long chat. She's in love.'

Tom went to get himself some water. 'A boy at school I suppose. Did she give you a name?'

'It's Ian.'

'Ian who?

'That's what I said. Ian Walker,' Serena revealed.

Tom almost choked. 'But he's years older than her. Jamie would have kittens if he knew.'

'Well, I wouldn't get too hot under the collar, Ian remains in ignorance of his admirer. I personally hope it stays that way. Ian has a great deal of charm and I like him, but I believe he likes safety in numbers. He'd break Kim's heart. She hasn't the temperament or experience to deal with a relationship and keep it casual. She strikes me as a girl who would want to give her all.'

'Like me.'

'Just like you, my darling. No wonder she says she was in love with you. What good taste she has.'

Chapter 29

Tom walked through the open door of *The Mitre*.

'Well, look who's here,' Dave Reece's voice boomed as he caught sight of him.

'Hello, long time no see,' said Len Stott, a neighbouring farmer.

'He's not let out often,' Dave chortled, 'got a pass for this evening, or are you in the dog house?'

'Remission for good behaviour,' Tom said.

'I haven't seen Jamie either recently. Your missus and Pat haven't been getting together thinking up ways of keeping you at home?' Dave said, poking him in the ribs.

'Jamie's on holiday.'

'Course, should have known, garage's been shut.'

'They came back yesterday so I expect he'll be in later. Can I get either of you a drink?'

Tom leaned on the bar talking to Len while Dave drifted off to a table in the corner. It was stifling hot even though the windows and doors were open and not a breath of air stirred the curtains looped over their brass rails. He thought of Serena as he mopped his brow. Though he was quite happy to stay in, it was her suggestion he should go out for a drink. He had not missed the pub since they had been married, but now he had made the effort, he felt himself relax in the near all-male bar.

A sudden slap on the back made him spill his drink.

'Hello, what you doing here? Serena given you permission?'

'Don't you start Jamie, I've already had all that from Dave. Had a good holiday?'

'Yep, sun, sun and more sun.'

'I can see you're brown. Did you have a good time?'

'We three did, don't know about Kim. She put a right damper on things. Pat said to ignore her, so we let her go off round the shops or whatever. I think Pat was a bit narked she wasn't asked to go with her – but you know what women are like, you can never understand what makes them tick. Even you must have found that out by now.'

'Yes, they are a bit of a puzzle. Serena hasn't long to go now and she's feeling the heat. She's a bit – well you know, a bit…'

'Go on, say it – bloody minded.' Tom grinned. 'When Pat's caught up with the washing, I expect she'll ask you round for a meal.'

'Serena will appreciate that. At least she's relieved she doesn't have to cook many hot meals though I must confess I feel I never want to see another lettuce leaf.' He glared at his brother. 'And don't you dare tell her I said that – not even as a joke.'

'You're realising marriage isn't all kissing and cuddling.'

'True, but it certainly beats living on your own.'

Jamie drank his beer and wiped his mouth with the back of his hand. 'Kim spent a lot of time at the farm before our holiday. What's so special at your place?'

Tom wondered what was coming next. Did he know about Kim's infatuation?

'She usually comes down in the holidays, and Tony. What's worrying you?'

'It's just she never seems at home.'

'She's back at school next week, isn't she?' Tom said, hoping he had put his brother's mind at rest. 'Then we won't see so much of her.'

*

Eventually the weather broke and there were violent thunderstorms. Due to the hardness of the earth, the sudden excess of water caused flash floods and the stream that ran under Abbotts Lidiard Lane flooded for the first time, causing the pond on the farm to overflow.

Serena was relieved at the drop in temperature but Tom discovered something he had not previously known – she was terrified of storms. It distressed him to have her clinging to him shaking with fear when lightning flashed and the rigid way she held her body awaiting the crack of thunder. What she had done when Jeremy was at work he could not imagine and was glad storms were comparatively rare and short-lived.

Kim and Tony came to inspect the overflowing pond and Tony threw sticks and stood too close to the edge while Kim talked animatedly to Ian.

'She's managed to make contact I see,' Tom said when they had gone home. 'They were talking while Tony was doing his best to ruin his shoes.'

'I suppose that's my fault. I told her if she fancied someone she should endeavour to be wherever he is – keep in his eye.'

'But I thought you didn't approve.'

'I don't, but I gave her that advice when I thought she liked a boy at her school.'

'Jamie won't be too happy if he hears about it. He's already put out about the amount of time she spends here and how moody she is.'

'I gathered that when we went there. Kim looked a bit sheepish when she came in late for dinner. I bet she had been somewhere in the hope of seeing Ian.'

'You know, I never knew women could be so cunning and devious. Us poor men don't stand a chance.'

She patted his arm. 'I know, the trouble is some men manage to escape far too long. It isn't any wonder our wiles have to be brought into force if they hide away deep in the Kent countryside.'

'You were a scheming hussy.'

'Were? What makes you think I've finished.' Her green eyes twinkled.

'Heaven help me,' Tom said.

✳

'Kim, where've you been? I waited dinner for a quarter of an hour, but couldn't leave it any longer.'

'Sorry, Mum. I got talking and forgot the time.'

'Well, sit down now,' Jamie said, pointing his knife at her place, 'and try to be a bit more considerate. If you're going to be late, ring up and say so.'

'I forgot the time, I told you,' she said.

'Who were you talking to anyway?' Pat said putting the hot plate in front of her and placing the oven glove on a shelf.

'Out with some boy I 'spect,' Tony offered.

Interested, Pat said, 'Were you?'

'I wasn't out with him – just talking.'

'Well, who is it?' Jamie said, 'Don't keep us in suspense.'

'It's Ian, who works at Uncle Tom's farm.'

'What's he got to say for himself?' Jamie asked.

'We were talking about the floods and the pond on the farm

and – and....'

'Yes.'

'He asked if I'd like to go to a disco with him.' She saw her father's face. 'In Maidstone,' she finished lamely.

'No way, he's much too old for you. Why he must be twenty-four or five at least.'

'Twenty-three.'

'That's still eight years older than you. No, Kim, it's not on.'

'Why not? He's only asked me to a disco, we're not eloping.'

'What's eloping mean?' Tony asked.

'The answer's still no,' Jamie said. 'Get on with your dinner, it's getting cold.'

Kim pushed her plate away. 'I don't want it.'

'I'll have it,' Tony said, reaching for her plate.

'You must eat something,' Pat said. 'What about pudding?'

'I shan't want that either.' She stood up. 'I'm going out.'

'Where?' Jamie demanded.

'Just out – to Granny's. Perhaps she'll treat me like an adult.'

Kim's chair toppled over as she moved but she did not pick it up.

'Kim, come back here.'

'Leave her, Jamie. I'll talk to her later.'

'What's wrong with her and why's she so aggressive?' he grumbled.

'It's her age, not to mention some of your genes coming out in her.'

'What d'yer mean?'

'Think about it. I'll go and see to the pudding. It's Kim's favourite, she'll be sorry she missed it.'

*

Kim's grandparents did not have the pleasure of her company when she left the bungalow; instead she went to Ian's house.

'Hi, Kim, come on in.' He showed her into the kitchen of the terraced house.

'Mum, this is Kim Cresswell, she's Tom's niece and her Dad runs that garage in Grassenden.'

Ian's mother held out her hand. 'Hello Kim. Ian tells me he's asked you to join him and his friends at the disco on Saturday. You been to a disco before?'

'Only the ones at school.'

'Let's go in the other room,' Ian said taking her hand. The

effect was electrifying. 'Are you coming on Saturday.'

'Er, yes.'

'I'll pick you up.'

'No – no, don't do that. I'll meet you at the end of Hemlow Road then you won't have to turn round.'

'OK, see you at seven.'

*

'I had a chat with Kim today,' Pat said as they prepared for bed.

'And?'

'She's still upset with us.'

'And well she might. I won't have it – I mean, she's only fifteen.'

'You will have to tread carefully. The more you say can't, the more defiant she'll get. She's not your little girl any more – or mine,' she added sadly. 'Serena seems the one who has her confidence.'

'Serena? What's she got to do with it?'

'Kim said they had chatted about boyfriends and what to do about them – or lack of them.'

'What a bloody nerve! What's it got to do with her? I suppose she's encouraged Kim.'

'I believe she told Kim to keep herself in his eye,' Pat said.

'I don't want her giving Kim ideas it's nothing to do with her. I bet she's led men a merry dance in the past.'

'Just try not to be too heavy handed for once, Jamie.'

She turned off her light, wriggled herself comfortable and closed her eyes. It was not Ian and Kim going out that upset her. It was the fact that Kim had sought out Serena as her confidante.

*

Where's Kim?' Jamie said as he skimmed through *Motoring World*, while Pat and Tony watched television.

'In her bedroom.'

'No, she isn't,' Tony said. 'She's gone out.'

Jamie looked up sharply. 'When?'

'About fifteen minutes ago. I saw her go out the back door. She had on her best jacket.'

Pat observed Jamie's darkening face. 'Don't jump to conclusions, she could be at Trudi's.'

The rest of the evening was spent in a state of high tension with Jamie working himself up and Pat trying to think how she could calm the situation she foresaw looming.

It was eleven when they heard a car draw up outside and a noise at the back door.

'There she is now.'

'I've locked that door, she'll have to ring.'

'Now don't go mad, Jamie, please.'

'What do you expect me to do?' He strode into the hall and opened the door just as Kim was about to ring the bell.

'Go in there,' he shouted, holding the front door wide and pointing to the living room. 'Where've you been?'

'Out.'

'I can see that. Where?'

'To Maidstone, to a disco.'

'I thought I told you you weren't to go there.'

'No, you said I wasn't to go out with Ian.'

'Stop splitting hairs. Are you telling me you went on your own?' Kim coloured. 'So you did go with that Ian deliberately against my wish.'

'I couldn't see any reason why I shouldn't go. What's wrong with going out with a boy. Serena says….'

'Leave her out of this. *I* told you not to go out with him, and you disobeyed me. You can stay in for the rest of next week.'

'Anyone would think I'd been to an orgy the way you're carrying on. I've only been to a disco. Lots of girls at my school go….'

'I don't care about other girls. You're my daughter and you should do as you're told. How do you know what an orgy is anyway?'

'You just don't want me to enjoy myself, do you? I am on holiday you know, or perhaps you haven't noticed.'

'Don't speak to me like that.'

'And don't you speak to me like that either,' Kim shouted. 'I'm not a baby. I do everything you ask, work hard at school and at home. Don't you want me to have any fun?'

Pat stared at her daughter. Her first reaction when she came in was to ask if she had had a good time, but she knew she had to support Jamie. Kim had, after all, flouted him. But she stood there looking very pretty and grown-up, giving reasoned arguments which Pat knew would not placate her father. In fact, they would only serve to infuriate as she got the better of him.

'I don't remember seeing that before,' Pat said, noticing a flash of gold as the necklace caught the light.

Kim's hand went up to her throat. 'Serena gave it to me.'

'I might have known,' Jamie said. 'I suppose it was her suggestion you go out with Ian.'

'I told her I like him.'

'In that case Tom knew about it too. I'm going to see him and get this sorted out. He wants to keep that interfering wife of his under control.' He held out his hand. 'Here, give it to me.'

'What?'

'The necklace – give it to me, I shall give it back to Serena. I don't want her trying to buy you off.'

'But she gave it to me!' Kim exclaimed. 'You've no right to take it away, it's not yours to give back.'

They glared at each other and Jamie took a step forward. Pat thought he was going to wrench the offending article from her neck.

'Look, it's late, let's all sleep on it,' she said, placing herself between them and edging Kim towards the hall. 'We'll talk about it in the morning when we've calmed down.'

'When he's calmed down you mean.'

Kim went to her bedroom and slammed the door.

*

Jamie threw open the farmhouse door and a blast of chilly air came in with him.

'I want a word with you,' he bellowed. 'Will you tell that wife of yours to stop interfering in my family's affairs.'

'And hello to you too Jamie. What's got you all hot under the collar this time – and could you keep your voice down, Serena's gone for a rest. She's due any minute now you know.'

'I don't care. Kim went out with your Ian after I'd told her not to. It seems Serena's been encouraging her, planting ideas in her head.'

'Now, wait a minute.'

'And you knew about it all along, didn't you? You knew Kim had taken a shine to that lad.'

'Will you calm down. Sit over there and we can talk about what's worrying you.'

'You know what's worrying me – and it ought to be worrying you. Kim's too young to be going out with somebody so much older than her.'

There was a creak on the stairs and the door from the hall opened.

'It's your fault,' Jamie said, pointing a finger at Serena. 'Why don't you mind your own bloody business.'

'Don't speak to Serena like that, she doesn't even know what you're on about. Can't you see she's....'

'All I can see is the bad influence she's having on Kim.'

'Now hold on,' Serena said. 'Are you saying I encouraged Ian and Kim to go out, because if you are, you couldn't be further from the truth. I don't think he's a suitable person – type of person for Kim either.'

'What's she confiding in you for anyway? It's her mother she should be talking to.'

'I can hardly stop her speaking to me; I don't know what she's going to say. I just happened to ask why she looked so miserable as it wasn't like her.'

Jamie turned to Tom. 'And why didn't you tell me and Pat?'

'Because I knew you'd get yourself in a state.'

'Too right.'

'Anyway,' Serena continued, 'I was quite unaware they had got together. Kim just told me she like him. Originally I thought she was keen on a boy at her school.'

'And another thing,' Jamie said not wanting to hear excuses, 'I don't want you giving Kim expensive presents, filling her head with ideas.' He reached into his pocket and threw the necklace on to the table where it lay like a thin elaborate snake.

Tom stared at it and then at Serena and for a moment he thought she was going to fly at Jamie. instead tears welled up in her eyes.

'Look what you've done,' he shouted furiously. 'All my life I've got you out of scrapes mostly of your own making, but this time you're on your own. I was under the impression we were your family, but if that's the way you feel about us, that's OK by me.'

Tom's steely-blue eyes were cold with anger. 'I must say I'm surprised that even you have so little consideration for Serena that you choose this, of all times, to vent your ill-temper. Now go home before you upset her any more.'

'It's all right, Tom, Jamie should be upset about Kim,' Serena said, dabbing her eyes.

'No, it's not all right.' He stood beside Serena his arm tightly round her shoulders. 'I presume you've finished all you wish to say, so you can push off.'

Jamie's cheeks were burning red, his lips pursed, his anger joined by a look of bewilderment. He opened his mouth to speak, but clamped it shut and left. They heard his car rev noisily and shoot up the track. It was a few moments after the sound had died before they spoke.

'You shouldn't have said that Tom, he was very upset. I expect we'll hear the full story from Pat. You must have known how he'd react.'

'He had no call to insult you like that no matter how upset he was – especially at this time. I'm fed up with his irrational outbursts.'

'I'll ring Pat and explain exactly what I said to Kim.'

'We have explained – but he doesn't want to listen.'

Serena gave a cry and doubled over in pain.

What's the matter?'

'A contraction. I had slight pains when I was upstairs.'

'What shall I do?'

'Nothing yet, don't panic. My case is all….' Another pain seized her.

'I'm going to ring the hospital,' Tom said.

*

'A boy, Mrs Cresswell, a handsome boy.'

The doctors drifted away and a nurse held the baby for her to see then it was wrapped up and taken away. Serena, almost too exhausted to speak, looked at Tom and smiled weakly. He nodded, his throat tight. He took one hand from hers and quickly wiped his eyes and found he was pouring with sweat.

'There you are,' the nurse said, putting the little bundle in her arms. Tom stood to get a better view. 'In a minute we're going to take him down to the Special Care Baby Unit just to be on the safe side.' Serena looked alarmed. 'Don't worry – it's just a precaution. He's a healthy nine pounds and very long. He'll be tall like you both. We just want to keep an eye on him overnight because he's had a stressful time.'

'He's not the only one,' she exclaimed.

'Nurse Carter will get you tidied up and then you can have a sleep. I expect your husband could do with a rest.'

Tom realised just how shattered he was. They had been at the hospital since Sunday afternoon and Serena had been in labour much of that time till Mr Gilberton recommended a caesarean.

'He looks very red,' Tom said. 'Has he got all his fingers and toes?'

'Yes, all there.'

Tom kissed her forehead and the baby's. 'Do you want me to stay?'

'No, you go. What day is it?'

Tom looked at his watch. 'Tuesday – half past midnight. You've had a rough time my darling.'

'You have a good rest and don't come back till you have. There's plenty for you to eat….'

'Yes, yes, I have looked after myself before.' He gave her another kiss. 'My clever mother hen.'

'Tom?' she said, as he reached the door. 'How about Alexander Jonathan?'

'Anything you say,' he said, relieved it was all over.

Part III

The Garage

Chapter 30

'Hi, here's your post.'

'More bills,' Jamie said gloomily, rolling up the shutter of the garage.

Colin glanced at the pile and handed it to him. 'Looks like it. You playing in the darts match this Saturday?'

Jamie slipped off the elastic band and flipped through the envelopes. 'Yeah.' he said to the disappearing postman.

Pat came down the path. 'Serena has had a boy, Alexander Jonathan. Nine pounds – big, wasn't it?'

'Here's a letter from your sister and a couple of catalogues.' He thrust them at her without looking up.

'She had to have a caesarean.'

He ran his thumb along an envelope. 'What else did Tom have to say?'

'He didn't – it was Lydia who rang. What exactly did you say on Sunday that Tom can not bring himself to tell us about the most momentous event in his life? I warned you, but you flew off in your usual hare-brained way. I reminded you the baby was due any minute. From what Lydia said they went to hospital soon after you left and she's been in labour from late Sunday till late last night.'

Jamie went to the back of the garage and Pat followed him.

'Come on, what was said? Tom doesn't take offence easily – certainly not where you're concerned, he knows you too well.'

'He told me to push off.'

'That's not like Tom.' Her eyes narrowed. 'Why?'

'I said I didn't want Serena meddling in our family's affairs.'

'And…?'

'He said he thought they were part of the family.'

'I despair of you sometimes. I don't…'

'Shut up! Shut up! I don't want to hear any more about them or their blasted baby. Just tell the kids they're not to go to the farm any more – and neither are you.'

'Now look here, if you don't want the children to go to the farm you do your own dirty work and explain why, but I think you're making a big mistake. In fact, I think you've made more than one big mistake. Going out with Ian Walker would have been a flash in the pan if you hadn't made such a fuss. Now you've made it a battleground. Kim's not a wayward girl. You were a tearaway from what I've heard. I bet your Mum and Dad let you have your head.'

'That's different, I was a boy, she needs protecting. Bloody hell, she's only fifteen.'

'All you've done is put her back up.'

'She's got to learn to do as she's told.'

Pat took a deep breath and let it out slowly. She shot at him as she turned to go. 'What you tell the children to do I will support, as I supported you over Kim, though I didn't agree with you. But do not tell me where I can and cannot go.'

Kim was in the kitchen in her dressing gown when Pat returned.

'Shall I get you some breakfast, love.'

'I can get it.'

'It's no trouble, I'll get some for both of you. I could do with another coffee. You start it while I get Tony out of bed, it's time he was up.'

When they were seated round the small table in the kitchen Pat said, 'Serena had a boy last night. He's to be called Alexander.'

Kim's eyes were bright with excitement. 'I didn't even know she'd gone to hospital. Did she go suddenly?'

'Late Sunday afternoon I gather.'

'Sunday? Why didn't Uncle Tom tell us sooner?' She studied her mother's face. 'What do you mean 'I gather'. What did Uncle Tom say when he rang?'

'Lydia Casleigh told me; he asked her to.'

Kim looked puzzled. 'Couldn't he have told you himself. He could have telephoned from the hospital, Serena must have been there – a day and a half before the baby was born.'

'She had a caesarean in the end because she was a long time in labour, so I expect Uncle Tom was with her all the time.'

'But why didn't he tell us when it was born, he knows we'd want to know straightaway.'

'I think Alexander is a sissy name,' Tony volunteered. 'There's a boy in my class…'

'Oh shut up, I think it's lovely. Alexander Cresswell. They go well together, don't you think Mum?'

'Yes.'

'What did he weigh?'

'Nine pounds, but I don't know any more than that,' Pat said sadly, wanting to know as much as Kim did and join in the rejoicing.

'When can we go and visit? Can I go and see Uncle Tom, I bet he's excited.'

'I think perhaps we'd better wait until…'

'What's up? Are you keeping something from me? Is the baby ill?'

'No, it's nothing like that, the baby's all right to the best of my knowledge. No, it's your Dad.'

Kim's face hardened. 'I get it, that row he had on Sunday – Dad won't speak to him.'

'Uncle Tom won't speak to Dad it seems.'

'He started it I bet, stupid man.'

'Kim.'

'Don't you like Dad any more?' Tony said unhappily.

'Of course she does.'

'No I don't. He mucks up everybody's life, mine, Uncle Tom's, Serena's. He'll probably start on you next.'

'That's enough, Kim.'

'I've got to get some things for school next week so I'll go into Maidstone on the eleven o'clock bus. Do you think they'll let me see Serena?'

Pat collected the plates from the table. She tipped washing-up liquid in the bowl and splashed in the hot water.

'Mum? What's the matter?'

'Could you ask Dad about…'

'If I can go into Maidstone. He'll be telling me next I can't go to school.'

'No, of course you can go to Maidstone. It's – it's Dad, he doesn't want you to go to the farm or to see Serena anymore.'

'Not go to see them – ever again! You must be joking.'

'Couldn't you just go and have a talk with him.'

'You don't talk to Dad nowadays, you just stand and listen. I'm going anyway and if I can see Serena I will. You can tell Dad what you like. I'll be sixteen in six months and then I can please myself what I do.'

'You'll still be living here.'

'I'll get myself a flat, or…' Her eyes brightened. 'I can live with Uncle Tom. I can look after the baby while Serena gets back to work.'

If Pat had not been so upset she would have laughed. 'Don't you think you're being a trifle naïve?'

'Well I hate it here,' she cried as she left the room.

*

'Where are you going?' Jamie demanded as he saw Kim stride across the forecourt.

'Into Maidstone, any objection?'

'Look 'ere, I don't want you going to the farm anymore.'

'Why?'

'We've had a row, Uncle Tom and me, and he said he didn't want to be part of the family.'

'I don't believe you, he wouldn't say anything like that. Anyway, it's you that had the row – not me. I shall go and see them if I want to.'

Jamie's face tightened. 'Can't you do anything I say?'

'Not if it's unreasonable.' She paused. 'Don't you want to see your new nephew?'

Her father turned away and disappeared into the rear of the garage. Kim shrugged and went down the hill to the bus stop.

At St Catherine's they told her visiting times were from three-thirty to five-thirty and seven-thirty to eight-thirty.

As she left the foyer of the hospital she saw her uncle.

'Uncle Tom,' she managed, before bursting into tears. 'They won't let me see Serena and the baby – and Dad says I'm not to see you anymore and he's stopped me seeing Ian. He's ruining my life. Can't you do something?'

She clung to him her arms round his neck, her head against his chest. Passers-by stared at them sympathetically as they stood on the steps.

'There, Kim, don't cry,' he said, raising an arm to pat her head. 'Let's go and get a drink.'

They found the canteen and he wove his way through the tables carrying the instant coffee.

'Here you are – feeling better?'

Kim sniffed. 'Not really.' She took the beaker from him. 'Please help me.'

Tom signed. 'I'm sorry, but your Dad said we weren't to

interfere. If he doesn't want you to see us you must do as he says.'

'But I want to see you – and the baby.' She burst into fresh tears and coffee spilled into her lap as her hand shook.

He took the paper cup and put it on the table. 'Look, Kim, I know this is difficult for you to understand but sometimes even adults can't make things work.' He took her hand. 'Your Dad was worried about you going out with Ian because he is a lot older than you are, and he thought we were encouraging you. We tried to explain but he wouldn't listen. I lost my temper because he was so rude to Serena and he took no account of the state she was in.

'Your Dad has always had a quick temper, as you know, and ever since he was a kid I've been the one to smooth things over. But now I've a family of my own and I'm not prepared to be the one to climb down. I know I could, but the fact is I don't want to. Do you understand?'

'No,' she said, raising her eyes to his. 'I don't.'

'You will just have to let things take their course and perhaps, in time, it'll get resolved.' He drank the last of his coffee. 'I'm anxious to see Serena and the baby. You sit for a few minutes and finish your drink. You're bound to see them about the village. I'm sorry it's like this, but there you are.' He gave her a kiss. 'I still love you.'

*

Lydia pricked up her ears – was that a car? She put down her book and strained to listen. Yes, that must be him. She waited for Edward to come upstairs.

'I thought you were going to stay in town.'

Edward strode across the room, loosening his tie and undoing the top button of his shirt. He gave her a peck on the cheek.

'That's not good enough. You've been away nearly a week and that's all you can manage.'

He smiled his slow smile. 'I wasn't intending to stop at that.' He went to the bathroom undressing as he went. Lydia thought how cleverly she was managing him but it was hard work constantly reassuring him he was loved.

'The plane wasn't delayed as long as we were led to believe,' he shouted from the bathroom, 'So I thought I'd come home.'

'Do you want the good news or the bad news first.'

Edward came to the door, his tall frame filling the doorway.

'There's nothing wrong with the children, is there?'

'No. Philippa keeps asking, "Where's Daddy gone" and we look at a map, but it doesn't mean anything to her.'

Edward's face softened at the mention of his daughter. 'So what's this good and bad news,' he asked, disappearing from view.

'Serena's had a boy, to be called Alexander.'

'Oh, that's wonderful. How is she?'

'She had a very long and painful labour, Tom said, and eventually had a caesarean.'

'When was this?' he spluttered as he cleaned his teeth.

'Late last night, about eleven or half past I think. Tom rang me this morning.'

'What's the bad news?

'It's that Tom asked me to tell Pat and Jamie about the baby.'

Edward switched off the light and came into the bedroom. 'You mean he didn't tell them himself – go round there?'

'Nope, just said would I do him a favour and tell them.'

'Perhaps he was in a hurry.'

'In too much of a hurry to ring his own brother about something so important – to ring us first. Those two might be as different as any two people can be, but they're devoted to each other in their own way.'

Lydia's eyes followed him as he moved about the room lost in thought. He hung his suit in the wardrobe and put his other clothes in the linen basket. He laid his towelling robe carefully over the chair and got into bed.

'I think they've had a row,' she said.

'Jamie's rowed with almost everyone in the village if you include those when he was a child. Do you know he once hit me on the head with a cricket bat? I've still got the scar. It's about the only time I saw Cressy lose her temper and she smacked him hard, which was very unusual. What makes you say that?'

'Pat sounded uncomfortable. She was pleased about the baby, but she seemed on the point of telling me something and then decided not to. She's very loyal, don't you think?'

'I don't know her very well.'

'You jolly well ought to,' Lydia admonished. 'She's as good as a sister-in-law to you, even if she isn't your type of person.'

'I never said that,' he said indignantly.

'Not in your class then.'

'I never said that either.'

Lydia slid down the bed deciding she had chided him enough. She flung an arm across him and twirled her fingers through the golden hairs on his chest.

'Now, tell me what you did while you were away.'

'Right now, I've got better things to do.'

*

'Mrs Cresswell, this is Gina Stone, Tony's Group Tutor.'

'Yes, Miss Stone, what can I do for you?'

'It's about Tony, is he ill?'

'Ill? Isn't he well enough to come home on the bus? Do you want me to fetch him?'

'No, he isn't here. He hasn't been here all week.'

'Not been there, but he's gone off every morning and come back on the bus.'

'This morning I caught up with Kim and asked about him but she said she wasn't responsible for her brother. It seemed so unlike her, but she obviously knew he wasn't in school.'

Pat did not know what to say.

'Mrs Cresswell, are you still there?'

'I'll try to get to the bottom of this when he comes in. I'm sorry you've had ring. I had no idea Tony had been truanting.'

'There's nothing wrong at home, is there?'

'Like what?' Pat said defensively

'Illness, bereavement or a sick pet. Children often can't express their feelings, they tend to bottle things up.'

'No, nothing like that. Thank you for letting me know. Goodbye.'

As she put the phone down she heard the back door open and close.

'Kim? Tony?'

'No, it's me. I've come to get a bill I left here somewhere.' Jamie rummaged around behind the can opener 'It's a bit early for them, isn't it?'

'The school's just been on the phone.'

'Um.'

'Tony's not been in school all week.'

Jamie looked up. 'Playing truant! Just wait till he gets in, I'll give him what for.'

'That's your solution to everything, isn't it? It's never occurred to you it might be your fault.'

'My fault that he's not in school.'

'Yes, yours. Haven't you noticed how unhappy he's been lately 'cause of you and Kim?'

'So that's all the thanks I get. Is trying to care for my daughter such a bad thing?' He swallowed. 'Shutting herself in her bedroom every evening, slipping out without saying where she's going. She's always told me before. All she does now is – is…'

'I can tell you one place she isn't and that's at the farm. She's desperate to see that baby. At least she is obeying you there.'

'You just look 'ere. If you want someone to blame it's Tom's wife, poking her nose in where it's not wanted.'

'Don't be so stupid Jamie.'

'I'm not stupid,' he shouted. 'What's the matter with you? Can't I count on you anymore.'

'You've always been able to count on me, but there comes a time…'

'So now you're deserting me.'

'I'm not, but you won't listen to reason. It's the same old story – somebody else's fault.'

'That's right, make me in the wrong like you always do.'

'That's not fair, I've always supported you where the children are concerned, even when I've not agreed, but this time things have got out of hand. This house used to be a nice place to be.' Pat began to cry. 'Now everyone wants out and that includes me.'

'Why don't you clear off then.'

Neither heard the back door open.

'Getting at you now, is he? I told you he would.'

'Kim.' Pat quickly wiped her eyes.

Jamie glared at his daughter. 'Did you know Tony wasn't at school?'

'Not until Wednesday.'

'Why didn't you tell me or your Mum?'

'I'm not his keeper.'

'Don't get clever with me.'

'I'm going to get changed,' Kim said, attempting to push past her father.

'I haven't finished yet,' he said, blocking her way.

She stood insolently staring straight ahead.

'Why didn't you tell us?'

'Why should I? As I said, I'm not responsible for what he does. I'm sure you'll be able to deal with it in your usual good-humoured manner.'

The slap resounded round the kitchen. The three of them stood stiffly, disbelievingly. Kim's hand went to her burning cheek and her eyes filled. Pat gave a horrified gasp and a vein in Jamie's forehead throbbed visibly. He gave a strangled cry and hurled himself through the back door nearly knocking over Tony who was just outside.

'You – come with me.' He grabbed Tony and hauled him round the bungalow and down the path to the garage.

'What are you going to do?' Pat cried, running after them.

'You keep out of this. I'm going to give him a bloody good hiding like he deserves.'

'Don't, please. You don't know your own strength.' She tried to get hold of him but he shrugged her off. 'Think of some other punishment, please Jamie, you'll hurt him.'

'That's the idea.'

In the garage he pushed Tony ahead of him towards the office. Tony backed up the side of a car and peered over his father's shoulder at his mother. '

Mum, what's wrong?'

'Miss Stone rang me.'

'You've been playing truant, haven't you? Haven't you? Jamie pushed him into the tiny office.

'Please come back to the house so we can talk about this properly,' Pat entreated.

'I'm dealing with this. It's obvious you're too soft with him.' He turned Tony. 'Bend over that desk.'

'Jamie don't.'

Tony threw a fearful look at his father as he grasped his shoulder and held him down. He swung his large hand and brought it across Tony's buttock. Tony gave a muffled yelp of pain and shock. Jamie struck him again and again.

Pat sensed Jamie had not only lost his temper but was out of control. She forced herself between them, grabbed Tony and pushed him out of the office. Jamie's next blow hit her. Jamie's eyes were unseeing as he stood, right arm partly raised. He let it fall to his side.

Pat was trembling as she let herself into the kitchen. He had never gone this far before. She went to Kim's bedroom where she found the two of them sitting on the bed.

'What does he think he's doing?' Kim started. 'He's a maniac.'

'Calm down,' Pat said, trying to bring some normality to an abnormal situation. She turned to Tony. 'Are you all right?'

He tried to look brave but only succeeded in looking more

vulnerable. 'He hurt me,' he whimpered.

'Show me.'

Tony pulled up his shirt and undid the top button of his trousers. He pushed them down to expose a weal across the lower half of his body where the desk had cut into him. The skin was broken in two places.

'Oh Tony love.' She felt like crying.

'He ought to be had up for assault,' Kim said.

'Don't make matters worse, please, it's all a misunderstanding. Dad just lost his temper. He's worried about you both.'

'You're always sticking up for him. Why don't you stand on your own feet and tell him to piss off.'

'Don't speak like that. He's a good father to you.'

'Was – he isn't any more.'

Shocked at what Kim was saying and the way she said it, Pat sat bewildered by the serious turn events were taking.

Eventually she said, 'You two stay in here. I'll get something to put on those cuts.'

'Humph, there's no danger of me getting in his way. I can assure you I never want to see or speak to him again. In fact, I was going to ring Uncle Tom and ask if he would take me away from this place.'

'Do you think he would take me too?' Tony asked tentatively.

'Please don't do anything hasty. I know you've been hard done by and I'm on your side. But you know what you Dad's like. He'll get over it soon and then he'll be his usual cheery self.'

'But he's never hit us like that before,' Kim said, putting her hand on her cheek.

Removing his hand from under Kim's and giving it a squeeze, Tony said, 'Let's do what Mum says.'

'Oh, very well. But I'm doing it for you – not him.' Her curly head jerked in the direction of the garage.

Pat sighed and left the two of them united as they had never been before.

Jamie did not come in for his dinner and Pat was not going to call him. He knew when meals were ready. The three of them ate their evening meal in reflective mood, conscious of the unoccupied place. When the meal was finished Kim disappeared and Tony sat in an armchair gazing into space. Pat came and sat opposite.

'Why didn't you go to school?'

'Dunno, s'pose I couldn't face it. It's not the same any more. Everyone's so miserable. Kim don't like Dad, and Dad don't like – he doesn't like anyone. An' we don't see Uncle Tom an' we haven't seen his baby, an' – an' I don't like Kim not liking Dad.' His eyes filled with tears. 'Why did Daddy hit me like that?'

The word 'Daddy', which he had not used for a couple of years, made Pat's throat constrict and she had trouble holding back her own tears.

'Why's he quarrelled with Uncle Tom? It all seems so silly.'

And there, thought Pat, you have summed it up precisely.

'I don't know what to say, Tony. Dad thought he was doing his best and Kim did go against him. Try to forget what he did; he wasn't himself. Perhaps he wasn't feeling very well.'

Tony considered this and, pleased with an explanation he could understand, said, 'I 'spect that's what it is. Perhaps he ought to see a doctor.'

'I'll suggest it to him, shall I?'

'Brill,' he said, brightening. 'Then Dr Gifford can give him some pills and we'll be all right again.'

If only Dr Gifford had the power Tony bestowed on him.

As Pat prepared for bed, there was still no sign of Jamie. She thought he had gone to the pub to drown his sorrows and have a sulk. There was a darts match coming up so he could be practising for that.

Feeling drained, she fell asleep almost immediately but woke to hear the church clock chiming. She put her foot over Jamie's side of the bed – it was cold. A glance at the clock showed it was eleven thirty. He should have been back ages ago.

She went down to the forecourt and to her surprise found the garage unlocked. She checked out the pub but all was quiet and dark, except for a light from a curtained upper window. Pat shut the garage door with difficulty, the noise sounding extraordinarily loud in the still night.

It was then she noticed Jamie's van was missing.

Chapter 31

Jamie parked the car at a meter. He had no idea why he had driven to Maidstone, all he knew was he could not face Pat and the children.

He pushed the door of the first pub he came to and a familiar, warm smoky atmosphere enveloped him. He ordered a pint, which he carried to a small table, took a sip and sat down. The office workers had departed and the evening drinkers were just arriving. The pub was not full, but nearly every table had someone sitting t it. He stared moodily into his beer.

'Mind if I sit here,' a voice said. Hardly raising his head Jamie nodded. 'Live locally?

'No, I live in Grassenden.'

'Where's that then?'

'About seven miles away.'

'I come from London, but I've come down to see the in-laws. Thought I'd come out for a breather.'

Jamie nodded again. He wished the man would go away, he was in no mood for chitchat. The voice droned on, but the mention of in-laws sent Jamie to thinking of his own.

Jamie had met Pat's father before he met her. Mr Hudson had brought his car into the garage where he was working at the time. It was nearly closing time and Mr Hudson said he was on his way home to Hemlow but did not like the strange noise the car was making but thought he might do more damage if he drove it. Jamie said it was too late now to do anything about it, but he could leave the car and he would take him home because he lived in Abbotts Lidiard.

Mr Hudson asked if he would care to come in and meet his wife. 'She's in a wheelchair, you see, and likes to meet new faces as she doesn't get out much.'

While he was drinking his tea, Pat came in from work. He was attracted to her, but did not do anything about it at the time. This was unusual for him, as waiting for appropriate moment was not one of his traits, and he already had a steady girlfriend. A few weeks later he met Pat in Maidstone and asked her out.

Pat was unlike any girl he had ever been out with. She was quiet and shy, not at all like the lively, bouncy girls he usually went for. He found out later though, she was not one to be pushed around. She was just over five feet, pretty with fine dark hair she had difficulty managing. His Mum liked her and told Jamie to snap her up before someone else did. Tom said he was not good enough for such a nice girl, and if he were going to ask Pat to marry him he would make sure she knew what she was letting herself in for. In spite of these dire warnings she did accept his proposal and they were married at St John's in Hemlow a year later.

'So they moved down here.'

Jamie raised his eyes to the speaker and slowly focused.

'Pardon?'

'I said the wife's parents moved here when the old lady died.'

'Oh, right, yes, that was a sensible thing to do.' Jamie had no idea what the man was talking about.

'Well, better get going before they send out a search party. Nice to have talked to you.'

'Yes, you too. Goodbye.'

Jamie bought himself another pint and returned to his seat. The pub burst into life as groups of boisterous lads rolled in, smoking, boasting, and laughing, much as he had at their age.

Hand-clasping young couples squeezed into corners and proceeded to kiss and caress in a manner even he had not contemplated as a teenager – not in public anyway. He was right to protect Kim if this was the way kids behaved nowadays. Why some of them seemed younger than her.

He glanced round the pub and noticed two women across the way from him. One was talking animatedly, but her companion was not listening and kept staring his way. Even in the dim lights of the pub he thought her face familiar. Every time he looked up he found the woman's eyes on him. Perhaps she had brought a car in sometime. She was about his age, maybe older. Blond, shoulder-length hair touched her wide-collared white blouse, which just about buttoned over her large bosom. She had on dangling earrings. She flashed a smile as if she knew him. He gave a weak one in return, drained his beer and went for another. When he returned the pub's large dog pushed his nose into his hand.

'Hello, old chap.' He stroked the animal behind the ears.

'You always liked dogs, didn't you? Hello, Jamie, you don't remember me, do you?'

He stared at her till recognition pierced his mind.

'Betsy.' Jamie jumped up, his face animated with pleasure. 'Fancy seeing you. I didn't realise – it's a bit dim in here. It must be – how long since we last saw each other? Twenty years?'

'Something like that.'

'Sit down here.'

'Mind if my friend…' She turned where her companion was in deep conversation with a man. 'Oh, she seems to have company.' Betsy took a chair and placed it close to Jamie's.

'What you doing here? Bit far from home. You still in Abbotts Lidiard?'

'No, I have a garage in Grassenden.'

'Married?'

'Yes.'

'Children?'

'Girl and a boy. And you?'

'I've got three boys. Jim's out at work, Kevin, he's the clever one, is soon starting college and the youngest, Steve is still at school.'

'And your husband?'

'He buggered off 'bout six years ago.'

'I'm sorry.'

'Don't be, he was a no good layabout. Couldn't keep a job and when he did have one he squandered the money on drink or expensive presents that were useless. In the end he just upped and left and I 'aven't seen him since.'

'Bet it's been a job bringing up three boys on your own.'

'Yeah, but they ain't bad boys considering. Steve needs a firm hand though. He was the one most affected by his Dad going but Jim's good with him.'

As the evening wore on Jamie lost all sense of time or how much he was drinking.

'You'd better come back to my place,' Betsy said, as she saw him grasp the table as they went to leave. 'I'll get you some coffee and try to sober you up. I live quite close.'

Jamie protested but realised he was not in a fit state to walk, let alone drive.

'Has your friend gone?'

'She waved to me as she went out.'

They reached a road of late Victorian terraced houses. Jamie leaned against the porch wall while Betsy fumbled in her copious bag for a key. Once inside they went along a tiled passage and she opened a door on to a staircase. With difficulty Jamie climbed the steep, narrow stairs covered with cheap carpet.

'Sit down there,' she said, 'while I get the coffee.'

Gratefully he sank into it. He screwed up his eyes and peered at the clock. He thought the time it said could not be right.

'Where're your boys?' he called to her.

Betsy came in with two mugs. 'Jim's taken Kevin on a week's holiday 'fore he starts college, and Steve is on a sleepover with a friend.'

'Wotchew looking at?' Jamie's voice was slurred with drink and tiredness.

She smiled. 'We had some good times, didn't we?'

'Yes,' he said, before his eyes closed and his head dropped to one side.

He half roused as she struggled with him to the bedroom. He fell on the bed and she covered him with a blanked, standing for several moments studying his face.

*

Jamie opened his eyes and raised his head, which felt like a cross between a pumpkin and a canon ball. He fell back on the pillow and tried to think what he had been doing. He had driven to Maidstone – there was a man talking about his wife's parents – Betsy!

This must be Betsy's place. Gingerly he pushed back the cover with his legs and lowered them over the side of the bed. He forced himself to sit up and sat with his head in his hands.

'You're awake at last,' Betsy said, peering round the door.

'What's the time?'

'Ten to nine.'

'I must get home. It's Saturday, isn't it? I've someone coming to collect a car and there's bound to be people wanting to book in.' He stood up but had to steady himself on a chest of drawers.

'I think you'd better have some breakfast first and clear your head a bit. You're not in a much better state now than you were last night. If you look in the bathroom I expect you'll find a razor and shaving cream. If not, you'll just have to make do with a wash.'

'Thanks Betsy.'

'Nice to hear you call me Betsy. No one 'cept you has ever called me that.'

The sight of the monster breakfast Betsy provided made him feel sick.

'I don't think I can eat this.'

'Go on, try, you'll feel better.'

'But you've only got a piece of toast and tea.' Jamie would much rather have had that.

She smiled at him fondly as he cut off a piece of sausage and slowly put it in his mouth. She bit into her toast and sipped her tea.

'Remember that time we stayed out all night when we'd missed the bus, in that shed at the edge of Mote Park. Full of equipment it was – not very comfortable.' She grinned. 'You were a bit of a lad.'

'Yeah, my Dad and Mum were none too pleased when I rolled up Sunday morning.'

'My old man gave me a hiding.'

Jamie thought about Kim. 'What did he say?'

'What didn't he say! Said I was a slut, a disgrace to them and he was a good mind to turn me out of the house. I don't think he would have done, but it frightened me at the time.'

'Did you mind what he said?'

'Of course, I was seventeen and old enough to know what I was doing – or so I thought. It wasn't that so much, it was the assumptions he made. And he wouldn't listen to what I wanted to say. If he had shown his disapproval it would have been enough. Young people know when they've done something wrong.'

'I shouted at my daughter and then I hit her. Now she won't speak to me.'

Betsy tut-tutted. 'How old is she?'

'Fifteen.'

'Difficult age – same as Steve. Is that why you were drowning your sorrows?'

He nodded 'Sort of. I don't really want to go into it.'

Betsy sat companionably munching her toast. Jamie managed one sausage and half the egg.

'I loved you, you know,' she said at last. 'I thought we had something going for us. I know I was young, but given time I thought we could have made a go of it. I was devastated when you gave me up.'

'I – I don't know what to say – I didn't know you felt that strong 'bout me.'

'No?' She reached for the unfinished meal. 'I was under no illusions, I knew you sometimes went out with other girls, but I thought perhaps I was a bit special.'

'You were,' he said truthfully.

'But not special enough.'

He looked down at his plate. 'I met Pat.'

'And she was special.'

'Yes, I suppose she was.'

Betsy took the plates into the kitchen. 'How's that brother of yours? Still farming? I always rather fancied him – sort of dark and mysterious. Not a bit like you. I could never understand why he weren't surrounded by girls. You never had any trouble.'

'He got married two years ago. They've just had a baby.'

'Really, left it a bit late, didn't he? What woman managed to capture him after all this time?'

'A very rich one.'

'Really,' she said again. She scrutinised his face. 'You don't like her.'

'Things aren't the same since she came on the scene. It was her fault that Kim and me fell out.'

'Is Kim your daughter.'

'Yes.'

'What does your wife think?'

'I don't want to talk about it. I must go now 'cause I've got to find out where I left the van. It wasn't far from the pub.'

'I think I know roughly where it could be. Give me a moment and we'll go and have a look.'

*

As Jamie drove into Grassenden he saw Edward's car parked outside the garage. That was all he needed. He went into the bungalow and through to the living room.

'There,' Pat said, giving a wan smile, 'I said you wouldn't be long. I told Edward you had to go into Maidstone to get some parts.'

'Yes, some parts – yes.'

'My car needs its big service and I wanted to book it in.'

'Right, let's go to the office.'

'I'll fetch Philippa,' Edward said.

Kim came into the hall holding the little girl by the hand. 'We've been looking at my toy animals, haven't we?'

'Come, look Dadda.'

'I've got to go to…' he began, but she grasped her father's hand and dragged him into Kim's bedroom. Pat prayed it was tidy, Edward gave her such an inferiority complex.

'Doesn't Philippa look like you, Mr Casleigh?'

'So I'm often told.'

'Who does Nicholas look like?'

'Oh, he resembles my wife.'

'What does Uncle Tom's baby look like?' Kim asked, avoiding her father's eye.

'Haven't you…?' He stopped. 'It's much like all new born babies.' He gave an embarrassed laugh. 'He's very long, has fair hair, but not much of it.' Edward appeared to be searching for something else to report. 'And he weighed nine pounds, but I expect you knew that.'

'No, we don't know anything,' Kim said. Pat gave her a nudge.

Philippa told her father to 'Come 'long.'

'Thank you for the coffee. Goodbye Pat, Kim.'

Jamie rolled up the shutter. He was just about to go in when a man appeared on the forecourt.

'There you are at last. I came earlier but you weren't open.' His voice was full of censure.

'I'm sorry, Mr Henderson. I was delayed in Maidstone longer than I thought. Your car is ready.'

'I wanted it at nine. I did tell you when I left it. I'm going up north and wanted to make an early start.'

'Go into the office,' he said to Edward. 'I'll just drive Mr Henderson's car into the road and get his bill.'

When he had gone he joined Edward in the office. He reached for his book and flipped through the pages. 'Wednesday OK?'

'If you don't mind my saying, Saturday morning seems a silly time to go and buy spares. You must get more people wanting to see you on Saturdays than any other time. You should remember you have to rely on people you know rather than passing trade, as you are such a small outfit. You can't afford to upset customers like Mr Henderson.'

'Look, Edward, you might own this garage, but I rent and run it. How I do it is up to me.'

Edward ran his hand through his hair. 'Talking about rent, I was going through my bank statements last night and I see the last two months have not been paid and another's due soon.'

'I'll look into it, OK?'

'I wanna go, Dadda,' Philippa whined.

'We're just going, my lovely. Wednesday then, Jamie.'

'Yep, Wednesday. It'll be ready when you come home.'

'You're not in any…'

'Come 'long, Dadda.'

'I'll leave the car on the forecourt as usual,' Edward called as he was dragged away. 'Lydia will drive me to the station.'

*

Pat was washing lettuce when Jamie came in at the end of the morning.

'Where are the children?'

'Kim's in Maidstone with Trudi and she's staying with her for the weekend. Tony will be in in a moment. He's cleaning out the rabbit.'

'How – how is he?'

'If you're really interested he's shocked as much as hurt.'

'Did I hurt him?'

'Of course you hurt him! He has a bruise right across his body where the edge of the desk caught him and it's broken the skin. You just don't realise how strong you are and he's only a child. You completely lost it, and yet again I've smoothed things over – trying to make excuses where there are none.'

He watched her as she moved around the kitchen putting ham on plates and making a salad. She strained the potatoes and put them in a bowl with a knob of butter.

'Here, take these', she said, thrusting two plates at him. She followed with the potatoes and salad bowl. 'Go and get the other plate, will you?'

Tony came in from the garden as Jamie picked up the last plate. Warily they eyed each other.

'I'm sorry – 'bout yesterday,' his father said.

Tony bounded across the kitchen and flung his arms round him and cried, then said, 'Mum says you're not well. Why don't you see Dr Gifford?'

Jamie was about to deny any illness but realised he had been given an escape route and assured his son he would do just that.

At the table Jamie glanced at Pat but she avoided his eye.

345

Chapter 32

'Did Dad tell you where he went Friday night,' Kim said when she came in from school.

'Yes, he drove to Maidstone and got drunk.' Her daughter gave a snort of disgust. 'And said he slept in the car all night.'

'How typical.'

'Did you have a good time at Trudi's?'

'That's right, change the subject. That might have worked once, but I'm grown up now.'

'I haven't any more to tell you.'

'In that case I'll go and change.'

Pat called after her, 'I'm popping over to the Stores. Shan't be long.'

She crossed the road and as she approached the Store she met Tom coming out. She rushed up and kissed him.

'It's so good to see you. How are you, and Serena and the baby?'

'I'm fine, so's the baby – but not Serena.'

'Is she ill?'

'Well, sort of. Anna says it's postnatal blues, but I think it's more than that. She comes in nearly every day, twice sometimes.'

'How kind of her.'

'I know, but we can't keep imposing on her. She has her own family to see to.'

'What does Dr Ferguson say?'

'When he first came she was all right. I suggested I call him again but Serena said he'd think she should be grateful she has a baby at all at her age.'

'But that's silly.'

'Try telling her that, you just can't reason with her.'

Pat looked at his worried face. 'Why didn't you call me?'

'I nearly did, but the situation – you know.' He rubbed his fingers by his temple in a gesture so familiar to her. 'I don't want there to be any more trouble.'

'Yes, I was told about it – his version anyway. I've not been to see you – not because I didn't want to, but I'm trying to keep the peace here. Jamie knows what I think about seeing you, but he's forbidden Kim or Tony to go to the farm. He and Kim aren't speaking after the Ian affair and Tony has been very upset by the whole thing. It's not been easy in the Cresswell household recently, I can tell you.'

'That makes two Cresswell households.'

'I'll come in the morning. Serena won't mind, will she?'

'She'll be pleased to see you, but don't take any notice if – if she says – she's inclined to be irrational.'

Pat put her hand on arm. 'Don't worry, I'll be down tomorrow. Give her my love and tell her I'm dying to see the baby.'

She watched him climb into the Landrover and waved before going into the store.

Pat took her basket to the counter.

'Hello, Pat. Did you see Tom?' Shirley Reece asked.

'Yes.'

'I thought he looked a bit harassed. I asked after his wife and baby, but he wasn't, you know, chatty. He just said they're all right. Who do you thing the baby's like?'

'Oh, er, like Serena – well fair hair like hers.'

'There's nothing wrong between them two, is there?' She jerked her head towards the garage.

'No, no. Jamie's been very busy lately.'

'Only I spoke to him last Tuesday, and he nearly bit me head off. Didn't seem at all excited about his nephew.'

'Well, you know what men are like, babies aren't their thing.'

Shirley took the items out of the basket and rung them up. 'That'll be £3.45.' Pat searched in her purse and gave her a note. 'Kim all right, is she?'

'Yes, what makes you ask?' Pat begun to think every question had a hidden motive, which, in Shirley's case, was probably true.

'Nothing. She just seemed a bit miserable when I saw her.'

'I can assure you we're all blooming with health.'

Shirley Reece looked unconvinced.

∗

'Was that Tom I saw you talking to?' Jamie demanded.

'Yes, Serena's not well and tomorrow I'm going to see what I can do.'

'I don't want you to go, you know how I feel about them.'

'But she's ill. Do you expect me to stay here knowing she needs help. She is our sister-in-law and part of the family.'

'Not mine. She messed up everything when she got her hands on Tom.'

'I don't see it like that.'

'So you're on their side now,' he spat out.

'No Jamie, there aren't any sides. We all need you – Tom and Serena included.'

Without warning her eyes filled with tears and she began to shake. She put her hand to her head.

'I've tried, heaven knows I've tried to keep things on an even keel, but I can't do it any more. You're on your own now.'

'OK,' he said savagely. 'OK, go and see them. Call on Edward and Lydia on the way back. What do you want with a common mechanic for a husband.'

Pat could only stare at him, shaking her head from side to side as the tears slid down her cheeks.

'And don't expect me in for dinner.'

*

'What's the matter?' Kim said. 'What is it? It's not Dad again, what's he done now?'

'I c-can't carry on trying to keep the peace, I just c-can't. Your Dad can be impossible at times, but I can usually win him round, and he is easy-going most of the time, isn't he?' She looked to Kim for verification, which was not forthcoming. 'Serena's not well and I said I'd go and see if I can help. Dad flew at me and accused me of siding with the enemy.' She began to cry again. 'And said I wasn't content with a c-common working man. I've never said or even thought such a thing.'

Pat put a small, damp handkerchief to her eyes.

'Here, have this.' Kim held out one of hers.

'Can I come too? I could help.'

'But you'll be at school.'

'I mean when I come home and at weekends.'

'I'd rather you didn't.'

'But Mum.'

'Don't add to my problems, please. Just do as your Dad wants and keep away from the farm.'

'Why do I have to do what he wants?'

'If you had not gone out without Dad's permission I would probably have talked him round, so you didn't do yourself any favours. Dad is not the only villain'.

*

When Pat arrived next morning she found Serena in the kitchen cuddling Alexander close and crying softly. Pat knelt down by her chair.

'I can't cope, Pat,' she sobbed. 'I don't know what to do? I'm so tired. I thought it would be easy, that I'd automatically know what to do, but I don't. He'll grow up knowing I've been a dreadful mother. He'll think I should have been his grandmother. Her increasing sobs upset Alexander and his lips trembled and he started to cry.

'Here, let me take him.'

Pat rocked the baby in her arms and cooed and talked to him. After a few moments he stopped crying.

'There, you see, you stopped him crying immediately.'

'It was only because he sensed you were upset.'

'He knows I'm no good as a mother. He cries all night and Tom sleeps so heavily he doesn't hear him. He says I'm to wake him but I don't want to because he's got to work next day.'

Pat thought the crying all night was a bit of an exaggeration but had been prepared by Tom. 'But you don't have to cope all on your own. That's not what being a mother is all about. If I'd known sooner, I'd have come down.'

'Anna comes in every day. She takes it all in her stride and she's got three children.'

'Don't forget she's younger than you.' Pat could have bitten off her tongue.

'So you think I'm too old to care for a baby?'

'No, of course I don't, that's not what I meant.'

Alexander had fallen asleep so Pat put him in his basket and covered him.

'Why don't you go and have a rest. I can clear up and prepare something for lunch. Will Tom be in for a drink?'

'He always comes in. He's so good and I'm horrible to him.' Fresh tears appeared. 'I never knew farmers worked so hard. I don't mean to be horrible.'

Pat put her arms round her. 'He understands. Now go upstairs and I'll bring you a drink. What would you like?'

Tom hung up his coat and gave a peek at the baby. 'How is she?'

'Very tearful. I've persuaded her to have a sleep. She's in a bad way and I think you must call Dr Ferguson whether she likes it or not.'

'I haven't been off the farm since they came home apart from yesterday. I don't like to leave her on her own.'

She handed him his mug. 'Now, what have you been doing for food.'

'Mostly I've had to get it myself. Some days she feels better than others and she'll have started preparing something, even if she hasn't finished it. At least there's plenty in the freezer, but even that's getting low.'

'Right, I'll have a good look round and see what's needed. Will Serena go out? Couldn't you all go out and shop together?'

'I don't think she will. She knows she doesn't look her best, and she holds herself in such low esteem she thinks everyone will be staring at her and thinking what a dreadful person she is.'

'Yes, I can see that. Still, let's cross each bridge as we get to it. I'll get something for lunch and prepare a casserole or something that you can dish up tonight.' She took their mugs to the sink. 'Is she feeding the baby herself?'

'Trying to, but I don't think she has enough milk – another failure in her eyes.'

'It's a vicious circle, the more she worries, the less likely she is to produce the milk. What about the health visitor?'

'She's public enemy number one. I think she's almost afraid to come here. Serena sees her as a constant reminder of her own inadequacy.'

'She must realise all is not well.'

'She's newly qualified, I believe. Serena intimidates her – you know how she is even when she is well'. Tom gave a crooked smile. 'What did Jamie say about you coming here?'

'Not pleased.'

Tom gave a sigh. 'Perhaps I should go and make my peace with him.'

'No!' Pat said, more sharply than she intended. 'You've enough to deal with at the moment. He's too used to others sorting out his life and making him think he's always right. Like the time you paid his fine.'

'That was Serena.'

'Don't ever tell him that.'

'I did, but he wouldn't believe me.'

'That's another thing, Jamie believes what he wants to believe.'

'Right,' Tom said, as he stood with his arm in one sleeve and mug in the other. 'I must get going.'

'Call the doctor in, don't bother going to the surgery,' Pat urged.

'OK, you did say you'll come tomorrow, didn't you?'

'Yes.'

'I do appreciate it. I hope it doesn't get you into too much trouble.'

Wishful thinking, she said to herself as she picked up the wide-awake, gurgling Alexander after his short nap.

Anna came soon after Tom left. 'Hello. Tom finally sent for you.'

'No, I met him in the High Street. I wish he had called.'

'I gather there has been some upset between Tom and Jamie.' Anna said. 'Serena thinks it was all her fault.'

'The frame of mind she's in, Serena would think it her fault if the crops failed and all the sheep died.'

'Isn't he beautiful?' Anna said as she looked at the baby. 'Mind if I pick him up?'

'Of course not. I'm leaving Serena to sleep as long as possible. I thought of getting in touch with Lydia and perhaps, between the three of us if you agree, we could keep things going. Faith could probably give a hand too.'

'It seems to be a bit more than the maternity blues.' Anna said as she waltzed round the kitchen table with the baby.

'Yes, it does,' Pat agreed. 'Dr Ferguson might be able to give her something.'

'I do hope so.'

*

Pat did not get home till three and parked in her usual place.

'Don't put it there,' Jamie shouted as she stepped out of the car.

'Why not? I always put it there.'

'Well I don't want you to now. OK?'

Pat let her breath out audibly. 'Where do you want it then?' she said, getting back into the driving seat.

'Park it in the road, but leave me room to drive the cars out.'

'Give me some credit,' she muttered under her breath.

'Do you want to know how Serena is?' Pat shouted to an invisible Jamie.

'No.'

'Can you tell me your eating arrangements. Can I expect you

in tonight?'

'Yes, I'll be in to eat.'

'Does that mean you'll be going out again.'

'If I feel like it.'

'You're being very childish.'

Pat heard him shout something, but could not be bothered to find out what it was.

'So Alexander's fair, long and chubby,' Kim said at dinner.

'I can see why she had a bad time, he is a big baby.'

'Who does he look like?'

'Difficult to say. I fancy he'll look like Serena, but babies change a lot.'

'I wish I could see him,' she said, looking wistfully at he mother. 'What's wrong with her?'

'We think it's postnatal depression. I told Tom to call in the doctor. She has been so efficient in the past she thinks she should be able to do everything perfectly. She's going to need a lot of support for a while. Anna Bartley, that's her friend and Lydia and me are going to get a rota going so she's not left on her own too long.'

Jamie came into the room, his hair still damp from the bath. Tony had already finished eating and Kim was putting her knife and fork together as Pat ate her last forkful.

'This is cold,' Jamie said, resting his fists on the table, knife and fork sentinel-like in the air.

'I told you I was about to serve up when you came in.'

'You could have put it in the oven.'

'You could have showered after dinner.'

'So,' Kim said, ignoring her father, 'the three of you are going to keep an eye on her.'

'Yes, and Lydia is…'

'Just as I said, isn't it? I knew you'd call on the Casleighs.'

'I didn't, Anna rang her.'

'Same thing.' Jamie pushed his plate away. 'I can't eat this. I'm going over the pub. I'll get something there.'

'Please yourself.' Pat took his plate and put it on the others.

'Thank God he's gone,' Kim said. 'It's like eating in a mortuary.'

'Dad isn't very well,' Tony said.

'Believe that, you'll believe anything.' Kim replied.

'Mum said, didn't you?'

Kim picked up the plates and took them into the kitchen.

'Bring in the pudding while you're out there.'

'Dad is going to see the doctor – he told me he would.' He looked confused and dejected and Pat's heart went out to him.

'I expect he will, he forgets because he's busy.'

'He hasn't got much work he told me.'

'When did Dad tell you that?'

'Sunday.'

'Shouldn't wonder if he hasn't driven all his customers away,' Kim declared as she put the dish on the table.

A worried frown appeared on Pat's face and the rest of the meal was eaten in uneasy silence.

Chapter 33

Nothing had gone right that morning and by midday Jamie had had enough. Pat had left for the farm telling him his sandwiches were in the fridge. She did not go so often now, he presumed because the woman was getting better – that is, if she was ever ill.

A pint might revive him. He washed his hands in the old-fashioned earthenware sink in the garage. He had not been to the pub for sometime. When he had first stopped eating his evening meal at home he had gone there for a snack, but that woman's illness was now common knowledge. He was asked how she was, what the baby looked like and was he pleased, till in the end he shouted at them not to mention Tom or his family ever again.

At night he and Pat lay in bed each clinging to their edge. Should they touch they quickly retreated to their designated half as if they had had an electric shock. He ached to make love to her, coupled with the desire to hurt her for what she was doing. He needed her, but she was not there – nobody was there. Why could they not see what that woman had done?

'Hello stranger, your usual,' Fred Braster asked.

'Yeah.'

Beer in hand he strolled across the empty bar to the darts board and glanced at the curling notice pinned there.

'*Dog & Bear*, Hemlow,' he read. 'Tough match that.' His eyes ran down the team selection. 'Not a hope of winning with that lot. Why, Paul Carver hardly knows which way round to hold a dart.'

'They miss you, you know. You'd be welcomed with open arms if you came back. We've lost the last five matches, two of them to pubs we've never lost to before.'

Before Jamie could reply the door opened with a crash. Jamie heard a familiar voice say, 'That gust pulled the door right out of my hand.'

'Right, Ian, what do you want?' Tom asked.

'Half of lager, please.'

'Mike?'

'Bitter, just a half.'

'Right Fred, two halves of bitter and half of lager.'

The landlord placed the dripping glasses on the towelling mats and glanced across the room. Tom saw his brows knit and followed his gaze.

Jamie wove his way through the tables, put his half-empty glass on the bar between them and walked out. Embarrassed, Fred and Mike stared at each other, Ian looked guilty and Tom felt wretched and angry.

Pat drove on to the forecourt just as Jamie crossed the road.

'It'll please you to know,' she said as she locked the car, 'that I shan't be going to the farm much now.' Without answering he went past her into the garage and lowered himself into the pit.

'Can't you see Tom and get this pointless situation settled. We can't keep on like this forever.'

'I've just seen him.'

'Oh, good, were you at the pub? Serena said he was going. What did you say – is it all cleared up?'

'I walked out as soon as he and his staff came in.'

'You stupid, stupid, brainless man! Here was a heaven-sent opportunity for you to heal this rift, but you couldn't even try.' Pat came further into the garage. 'All these years I've put up with your outbursts of temper and pigheadedness over matters that were not worth the fuss you were making. Tom bailed you out when you were a kid then I took over.

'Not any more, Jamie – not any more. Everything's spiralled out of all proportion by you and no one else but you. And when you go off to Maidstone – or wherever it is you go to avoid your family – you needn't come crawling back to my bed 'cause I don't want you there. You've made it clear you can do without any of us.'

Pat stormed out of the garage.

＊

Kim stood in the bay window of the bungalow watching a man pointing to the ground near his car, then pointing his finger at her father.

'What's that man shouting about, I wonder?'

Pat came and stood beside her. 'Where?'

'He arrived just as I came home from school. He doesn't half look fierce. What's Dad done now?'

'Perhaps he expected his car earlier like that Mr Henderson a few weeks back.'

'No, it's something to do with the car. Oh dear, more trouble.' Kim raised her shoulders and resignedly let them drop. 'Still, we won't hear the full story.' She turned to her mother. 'Can't you do anything about this quarrel, Mum? It's making you very unhappy.'

'No I can't, and yes it is, are the short answers. Do you know that at lunchtime Tom came in the pub and your Dad was there. Now, tell me, how many times has Tom been to the pub in recent weeks? None. How often does your Dad go midday? Rarely. Wouldn't you think fate had set up an ideal time for reconciliation? Does your father think so – no – he just walks out! I tell you Kim, I've really had enough.'

Kim thought she ought to be pleased at this outburst, but it made her as miserable as her mother and Tony. It was all right for her to be at war with her father, but the ripples in the pond were getting wider and wider. It was her fault, like her Mum said. She should not have gone out with Ian, even though Dad was making a fuss over nothing. Now there were mock exams to be done, she had not seen her baby cousin and she was still without a boyfriend. Dad was out every night and Mum was fed up – it was too much.

'You've a lot on your plate at the moment, haven't you, darling,' Pat said, giving her daughter a hug. 'And we're not helping. It's not as it was when you were little – when we could kiss things better and make everything right. I'm afraid it's all part of growing up when you realise your parents make mistakes and are silly and badly behaved.'

'That's what Uncle Tom said.'

Pat gave her another squeeze. 'Go and change then you can give Serena a ring and see if you can see them.'

'Can I really?'

'I think you've been punished enough. There is no reason why you should be part of someone else's quarrel.'

*

Jamie went to the *Kentish Hop* that evening as usual, but he did not know what was worse, being in *The Mitre* amongst friends, or sitting in a Maidstone pub in the hope he might meet Betsy again. He had walked round the streets nearby where he thought she lived, but all the roads looked the same, as did most of the houses.

He brushed his hand across his eyes and took a bite from a tuna sandwich. He was sick of sandwiches or something and chips and was never one for what he called fancy food. He gazed round the saloon bar. This one had fruit machines which beeped and jerked, periodically coughing money to its gleeful operator, only to suck it all back later in the evening.

'Hello Jamie, you 'ere again.'

His head shot up and he saw Betsy smiling down at him. He jumped up. 'I'm so glad you've come, I've been hoping you would. I couldn't find where you lived, you see. I tried to look for your house but couldn't remember the number or anything. Sit down, can I get you something?'

'I'm meeting Jim for a quick drink.' She glanced at her watch. 'He should be here any minute.'

'Well, I'll get you something now and I can buy one for him when he comes.'

Jamie brought her drink to the table.

'Do I gather life's still treating you badly?'

'Yeah, too true.'

'This'll be quite like old times then.'

'What d'you mean?'

'Oh, nothing.'

A voice beside him said, 'Hi Mum, been here long?'

'Hello, dear. No, 'bout five minutes.' She waved a hand towards Jamie. 'This is an old friend of mine, Jamie Cresswell. He lives in Grassenden. We used to know each other a long time ago – when we were young and silly.' Her eyes flicked from one to the other.

Jamie held out his hand, which was clasped in a grip as strong as his own. 'Let me get you a drink. What's your poison?'

From the bar he studied them both. Jim was a bit like Betsy, apart from his hair, which was curly and dark. He was an inch or two taller than himself, well built and had pale blue eyes that twinkled when he laughed.

'Where do you work?' he asked, handing Jim his drink.

'At Westlake's, the window people, on the industrial estate. What about you?'

'I run a garage in Grassenden.'

'I'd like to do that.'

'Jim got a bedsit a few months ago,' Betsy explained. 'It was too cramped for them to be sharing a bedroom. But it takes a lot of your money, don't it dear?' She patted his arm.

They chatted about Jim's job and he asked about the garage and seemed genuinely interested. When he had finished his drink he said he had better go as his friend was expecting him at Mcdonald's. Betsy said she should go too, as she did not want to leave Steve too long.

'I said I'd help with his homework,' she told Jamie. 'Can you imagine it? Me helping him when I was so dim at school.'

'You weren't dim. Anyway, who cares, you're a lovely girl.'

'You were always good for me,' she said smiling.

'Betsy, can I see you again? I'd like to talk something over with you.' She seemed reluctant. 'Please,' he entreated.

'What about?'

'Things.'

'Here?'

'No, no, too noisy.'

'How about the equipment hut in Mote Park?'

But Jamie was in no mood for jokes. 'A hotel lounge maybe?' What about *The County?* he suggested.

'But that's been closed for years.'

'Well you suggest somewhere, you know Maidstone better than I do.' He thought she was deliberately being awkward.

'But I don't move in hotel circles.'

'You don't have to go to hotels to know where they are.' he said shortly.

'You never did like criticism, did you?' Jamie looked sulkily into his drink. 'There's *The Falcon,*' she suggested.

'Where's that then?'

'On the Sittingbourne Road.'

'OK, tomorrow all right?'

'No, not tomorrow.'

'Friday then.'

'OK, I'll see if Jim'll take Steve out somewhere.'

He watched as she left. She could do with losing weight, he thought, though she had always been cuddly.

*

Jamie dressed with more care than usual and left the bungalow via the front door. Unfortunately for him, Tony was coming up the path as he endeavoured to slip out unobserved.

'Are you going out again? Why don't you stay here any more? You never used go out every night. And why don't you sleep with Mum?'

'I don't want to disturb your mother when I come in,' he lied. 'I've got to go out on business son. Something's cropped up recently. Don't worry about it, I'll be back.'

*

Jamie arrived at the hotel first and went through the foyer to the bar. It was quiet, just as he had hoped. A man and a woman were at a table beside a fire and two men in suits perched at the bar. He sat so he could see the entrance. When Betsy came in, she stood looking round self-consciously. She caught sight of him as he raised his hand. Her long earrings swung like crazy pendulums as she hurried over. He gave her a kiss on the cheek, which took her by surprise.

'Would you like a gin? That's what I'm having.'

'You look smart,' she said, eyeing him as he came back.

'As this was a hotel I thought I'd better spruce myself up a bit.' He threw a couple of packets of crisps on the table. 'This jacket and trousers only come out when we go on holiday as a rule.'

'I haven't any nice clothes. When you've a family to bring up on your own, there's not a lot of money left over. In fact, quite the opposite.'

'You look all right, Betsy,' he said kindly.

'You never took much interest in clothes, did you?'

'That's what Pat says.' Jamie had not intended to mention her.

'So why've you got me here?'

'I'm having trouble at the garage.'

'What sort of trouble?'

'Financial.'

'You've hit lucky with me than. I'm an expert on financial trouble. What you ain't got is an expert on how to get out of it. Why are you talking to me? What's your wife got to say?'

'I haven't spoken to her about it.'

'Why not?'

'We've – we're not talking.'

'I see.'

'She's gone over to the enemy.'

'Oh dear.'

Jamie shot her a frosty look. 'You don't seem to think it serious.'

Betsy composed her face. 'Go on.'

'She's been going down to the farm to sort out that woman. There's probably nothing wrong with her – just putting it on to get attention. I told Pat I didn't want her to go, but she's off just the same. Kim's going down there too now. Pat obviously said she could.' He paused. 'And that's deliberately against my wishes.'

'This woman is Tom's wife, I presume? Has she got a name?'

'Serena – silly stuck-up name. She's anything but serene. Got a temper like – like...'

'Yours.'

'I thought you'd be sympathetic.'

Several faces glanced their way at his raised voice and Betsy stared into her drink. They sat embarrassed till at last she said, 'What is this trouble you're in.'

'I can't make ends meet any more. There was a rent rise last year, the price of spares has rocketed and business has slackened. I had to get a new van and I can't even afford to have my name put on it. We shouldn't have gone on holiday this summer, but we booked it early in the year and I didn't like to disappoint the kids. When you're a one man band there's not a lot you can do.'

'Couldn't you tell your landlord how things are and that you'll make up any arrears when things pick up.'

'I'm already three months behind with the rent. The landlord's Edward Casleigh and I wouldn't want to go cap in hand to him.'

'Casleigh – that name sounds familiar.'

'He's that rich kid that my mother practically brought up.'

'Was that the one who got all uppity for no apparent reason?'

'Yeah, that one.'

'How did you get caught up with him?'

'He bought the garage and when he knew I was getting married he asked if I was interested. I had refused once, but it had a bungalow that went with it so....'

'Yes, I do see – that would be an attraction.'

'Well, what do you reckon?'

She laughed. 'What d'you think I can do about it? I can't even sort out my own money problems.'

'I need someone to help me think it through. I thought you might have some suggestions.'

'It's your wife you should be talking to. You're lucky you've got someone.'

'She wouldn't understand.'

'Really, I find that hard to believe.'

'So you won't help me?'

'It's not won't, it's can't. I've made two suggestions that have not met with your approval. What else can I say? What do you *want* me to say?'

'I haven't told you everything. I got careless once and didn't tighten something properly. When the man came to collect this car for a meeting that day, oil had leaked from the sump overnight and he had to wait till I fixed it. He said he had lost a lot of money and he was going to sue me. This man owns a firm and I could have had all his company cars to service. And,' Jamie added gloomily. 'To crown it all, Edward had recommended me, so that's two people I've upset.'

'Are you covered by insurance?'

'Of course, but I've still lost potential business which would have helped me out of this mess. Then there's Edward – he'll look down his nose. Betsy, what am I going to do?'

She took a sip from her glass. 'I'm sorry, I've no idea.' She shook her head sadly.

Jamie examined the hotel lounge. Thick patterned carpet, flocked wallpaper and mock candle lights with small red shades. On the wall were hunting prints and a framed aerial photograph of the hotel. He thought it would be a nice place to stay.

'You wouldn't spend the night with me, would you?'

Chapter 34

'It's me Mum,' Pat called as she let herself into her parents' house. She shut the front door and went into the living room where her mother sat in her wheelchair. Pat gave her a kiss. 'Dad in the garden?'

'Where else?'

'Fancy a breath of air?'

'That'd be nice, dear. Go and tell your father.'

'Has your cold gone?' Pat asked, when they had been walking for a while.

'Nearly.'

Pat brought her mother's chair close to the seat by the green and sat down. They watched the outfield being mown and she recalled the times when Hemlow played Grassenden and she informed Jamie she had to support Hemlow, no matter who he was playing for. That, he said, would all have to change when they were married. Not a chance she said, which led to Jamie chasing her and ended with lots of kisses.

'You look a bit peaky, Pat. You sure you're not doing too much? Are you still going to Tom's?'

'Not often. I just ring and see if Serena wants any help. She is much better.'

'Couldn't she have employed a nurse? After all, she's not short of a bob or two.'

'That wasn't the point, it was support and sympathy she needed; though I agree somebody else could have done the housework. I enjoyed helping.' Pat could have added it took her mind off other things. 'You know, Serena's not anything like I thought she was. I've got to know her quite well these past few weeks and I can see how Tom fell for her, he adores her. You should see the change she's made on that farmhouse. The kitchen looks like something out of a magazine.'

'Shows you what money can do,' her mother said practically.

'It's more than that. She has a real talent for making the best of what looks, well, you know what the farmhouse was like before they married.'

'It was a bit of a tip,' her mother admitted.

'I mean, it doesn't take money to have a hop bine trained over the range and dried flowers hanging from an old clothes airer. Apart from the things for her business and a couple of chairs, all other furniture is much the same. She's even thinking of having the range restored. I don't think Tom was very keen on that idea. I'll take you round one day if you like.'

'You sure she won't mind?'

'Course not, she likes to think she's part of a family.'

Pat wished she had not said that, it brought back all the anguish at home.

'There's something on your mind, Pat.'

Caught unawares by her mother's question, she felt hot tears begin to prick at the back of her eyes. Mrs Hudson turned her chair and put her hand on her daughter's knee.

'I think Jamie's found another woman,' Pat confessed.

Mrs Hudson looked shocked. 'No, surely not. What makes you say that?'

'It's a long story.'

'Time is what I've plenty of, darling.'

'You remember the row with Tom?'

'That not settled yet?'

'Not likely to from the way Jamie's behaving. He doesn't eat with us any more.'

'Where does he go then?'

'He started going to the pub, then I gather he lost his temper there because they kept asking about Tom's baby, so now he goes into Maidstone. At least I think that's where he goes.'

'Doesn't he come home at night?' her mother said, still registering surprise.

'Yes, he comes back, late. Eleven, half past, that sort of time.'

'What makes you think he's found someone else?'

Pat was quiet for a few moments. 'The first time he went off in a huff he was out all night. He said he had got drunk and slept in the car but when he returned he was washed and shaved. I didn't think about it at the time because Edward Casleigh was paying a rare visit and I was trying to find excuses why Jamie wasn't there on a Saturday morning.'

'He could have gone to a public convenience to wash.'

'But he wouldn't have any shaving tackle and he didn't bring any back.' Her fingers wound round one another. 'No, I'm sure he was at someone's house and I think he's still seeing this person.' Pat did not mention the smell of cheap perfume.

'Don't you think you might be jumping to conclusions? He could have met a man he knows.'

'Yes, he might.'

Mrs Hudson liked Jamie – they both did. He was fun to be with, even teased her about being in a wheelchair, but with such amiability that she never took offence. He called it her chariot and asked if she had ever had a part in Ben Hur. This was the first Pat had ever intimated he might be straying.

'Look, dear, don't do anything you'll regret. Talk with him, and get to the bottom of it.'

'We don't speak to each other. He sleeps in the living room on the settee.'

'Oh, I am sorry, but I still advise you not to think the worst.'

'That's all very well, but we can't go on like this. The quarrel with Tom is all Jamie's fault – there is no one else to blame. Kim's upset and this is an important time for her and poor Tony can't understand any of it.'

'What about Tom?'

'I've told him not to do anything.' Mrs Hudson raised her eyebrows. 'Both Tom and I are fed up with him. It's time he realised and faced the consequences of his stupid actions, instead of expecting others to straighten him out. He's not a child.'

Like her daughter, Mrs Hudson always sought solutions rather than confrontations. If Pat said she had done what she could, then she was sure she had. 'What are you going to do next.'

'I don't want to make things worse for the children's sake. If I challenge him – right or wrong – he'll fly into a rage and we'll be no further forward.'

'Couldn't you get someone else to talk to him.'

'Umph,' Pat snorted, sounding so like Kim. 'Is there anyone left?'

*

'You are looking so much better,' Lydia said as she took their coats and hung them in the cloakroom.

'A hundred percent,' Tom agreed.

'Hm, there's a nice smell coming from you kitchen. I haven't done any cooking to speak of since Alexander was born.'

Edward came along the passage. 'How are you? I've been kept informed of your progress. I haven't been to see you because I thought I might get in the way of all your attendants.' He smiled.

'You would not have been in the way, but I would have hated you to have seen me like I was.'

'Right, you two go along with Edward,' Lydia said, 'and he'll get you a drink.'

Edward led the way along to the drawing room where flames from a huge log fire burning in the inglenook made flickering patterns on the wood panels.

When Lydia joined them Tom and Edward were leaning against the wall by the fire talking about the farm and Serena was sitting in the leather settee holding a gin and tonic. Edward moved to the cabinet and brought over a sherry for her without interrupting his conversation with Tom.

Lydia sat beside Serena. 'How's Alexander?'

'Fine now, putting on weight and sleeps from tenish to about four or five.'

'Who's babysitting?'

'Kim. She rushes down as soon as she can so he won't be asleep before she gets there.'

Lydia studied Serena's face. She was as beautiful as ever but with a mature look, as if she had lived, instead of existed in some rarefied atmosphere like an orchid in a conservatory. Serena raised her eyes and caught Lydia's scrutiny.

'You don't know how grateful I've been to you all for helping me like you have.'

'We were glad....'

'No, don't stop me. These past weeks when I've felt so depressed and inadequate, I've come to realise what true friendship is. Before I only had acquaintances I thought were friends. But you have shown me such kindness.' She took a deep breath. 'What I'm trying to say, and what I should have plucked up courage to have asked long before now, is for your forgiveness.'

'But Serena, all that was forgotten long ago. Anyway you had your reasons.'

'That's no excuse for the way I treated you.'

'Don't give it another thought. Things are different now – for both of us.'

Lydia glanced at Edward who seemed to be more at ease with

himself as each week passed. He sensed her look and fondly smiled at her.

At the dining table Tom said, 'I don't think Pat has been looking well lately.'

'Doing too much looking after me,' Serena said.

'No, it's not that, it's Jamie.'

'He's just lost a good contract through sheer carelessness from what I can make out,' Edward said. 'I was shouting his praises to a friend of mine who wanted someone to service his firm's fleet of cars. He said he would take his car to the garage and I assured him he would not be disappointed. Then I get this angry call about oil leaking from the sump. He was furious and I was embarrassed. And he's lost the chance of further business. I don't know what's wrong with him. He's also behind…'

'It's all my fault,' Serena began.

'No it is not!' Tom interrupted forcefully.

'Well, what is it all about? Lydia told me something was up, but I thought it was Jamie being – well Jamie.'

Tom explained about the row and that they no longer spoke to each other.

'Jamie's everlasting having rows. They always blow over.'

'That's because Pat or I have smoothed things over. I was going to a few weeks ago, but Pat said it was time Jamie took responsibility for himself. She was quite adamant.'

'Did she?' Lydia said. 'That doesn't sound like Pat.'

'I think she's had enough, like I had at the time because I was not going to have him speaking to Serena the way he did. What he says to me is a different matter.'

Edward changed the subject and got up to refill their glasses.

*

Tom held the door of the Volvo open and turned to wave at Lydia and Edward.

'Are you sure you don't want to have a drive. The roads will be quiet this time of night.'

'No, I'll drive into the village tomorrow.'

Tom shut her door and went to his side. As he stopped at the end of the drive he said. 'It was a good evening, wasn't it, sweetheart? Did you enjoy it?'

'Yes, but I feel tired. I'm not used to this high life.' They glanced at each other and laughed. 'Who would have thought I'd ever say that.'

The security light shone on them like performers on a stage as they crossed to the farmhouse. An owl hooted close by.

'I never cease to be impressed every time I come into this room. Remember when you first came and cooked me that meal? I can't think why you didn't keep well away after that.'

'My fingers itched to get to work on this kitchen.'

'So that's the only reason you married me.'

'And you've only just realised?' Her green eyes twinkled and she smiled at Tom. 'Do you want a drink?'

'No, I've had enough. Anyway you're tired, and Alexander might wake early.'

'I think it's about time you did the early morning feed now he's on a bottle.'

'Why don't I keep my big mouth shut?'

Tom bolted the doors, switched off the lights and returned to give Serena a kiss.

'That's for starters.' He swept her up in his arms and tried to kiss her, unsuccessfully, as he carried her up the stairs.

'Shush,' she said, giggling, 'you'll wake Kim and the baby.'

*

Serena dropped Kim off at the Vicarage car park next morning and went for a coffee with Faith. She was told how well she looked and Alexander was cuddled and told he was the most beautiful baby that ever lived.

'He knows that, Faith, I've told him enough times.' She reached for a biscuit. 'I've had a letter from Jeremy.'

'Did you? What did he say?'

'It was very brief; said he had heard from Stephen Maltby that I'd had a son and wished us both well. It seemed rather sad somehow.'

'What do you mean?'

'He needn't have written at all, so presumably he was glad for me. I don't know, just a feeling I had as I read it.' Serena did not explain about Jeremy's inability to father children. Only Tom knew that – and Kim.

'What are you planning to do when you've left here?'

'I'm going to do some shopping, butcher's, baker's. I'll probably go to the Stores.'

'You'd better do that or Shirley Reece will never forgive you. She's already upset she hasn't had any information to impart to the villagers. What's Tom doing this morning?'

'He's going to walk into the village and meet me then we'll go for a short drive somewhere, maybe have lunch out. It rather depends on Alexander.'

'It's so good to see you,' Faith said at the door. 'Mind how you go.'

Serena left the Vicarage by the path that ran behind the village school. As she passed the gates of Ridge House she glanced up the drive at the two cars parked there. It seemed light years since she had lived there, since she had led the kind of life she was used to then. Was it only two years ago? She and Tom would soon be celebrating their anniversary. She wondered what sort of changes the new owners had made to the house on which she had once lavished so much time and money. She shrugged thinking to herself she did not much care.

'Mrs Detrale, how lovely to see you,' Mr Anders said. 'Have you brought the baby? Margery, come out here. It's Mrs Detrale with the new baby.'

Mrs Anders came from the back of the shop admonishing her husband for not calling her Mrs Cresswell. Alexander was produced, admired and smiled dutifully. This performance was repeated at the bakers so that by the time she had dealt with an ecstatic Shirley Reece, she felt quite tired. Alexander was no light weight when she was standing holding him.

It was with some misgiving that she crossed the road to go back up the hill. When she reached the bungalow she put Alexander's pushchair in the front garden and wove her way through the cars on the forecourt of the garage.

'Hello,' she called, her voice resounding in the interior.

'Just a minute madam and I'll be with you.' Jamie climbed from the pit wiping his hands on a cloth. He glanced up and his eyes narrowed.

'What the bloody hell are you doing here?'

'I just wanted to….' Her voice faltered as she saw the expression on his face, but she went on, 'I wanted to apologise for whatever you think I've done to upset you, and I thought you might like to see….'

'Get out, get away from here,' he spat out. 'You're not welcome.'

'Look Jamie, Tom is really upset by this.'

'If you hadn't wormed your way into our family, it would never have happened.'

368

Serena persisted. 'If you don't like me, I'll live with that, but don't keep up this quarrel with Tom. I don't want there to be a rift between you. Please, please make up with him.'

'Everything was all right between us till you came on the scene bringing your grand ideas.'

'But....'

'Not content with that you take Kim and Pat away.'

Jamie's face grew more florid and he took a step towards her. Serena was appalled by the look of hatred on his face and drew back alarmed as she saw his fists clench tightly by his sides. In spite of her resolve to keep calm, she felt anger build inside her at the injustice of his accusations and his stubborn intractability.

'It's no good talking to you, your mind's shut,' she shouted. 'I wish I'd never come.'

'So do I. It was silly of your husband to send you round to do his dirty work.'

Neither had seen Tom arrive till a large hand descended on Jamie's shoulder and turned him round.

Chapter 35

'If I'd known what Serena was intending to do,' Tom said, his voice slow and deliberate with scarce controlled anger, 'I'd have stopped her. Neither of us has any need to grovel to you.'

Jamie tried to shrug Tom's hand from his shoulder but it remained there, the fingers pressing into his overalls.

'Take your hands off me.'

The raised voices had attracted the attention of villagers, particularly those in the shop opposite.

'I'll go as soon as you apologise. Serena had no part in the accusations you made, and you know it. I won't have you speaking to her like that – I told you before.'

Pat and Kim rushed down the path and went to Serena who was standing in some agitation.

'Me apologise. To her!' Jamie was apoplectic and, as Pat and Kim feared and Tom anticipated, he swung his fist at him. But years of seeing his brother wound up for a fight made him alert and he parried the blow. Incensed, Jamie went for Tom forcing him to defend himself. When Jamie caught him with a glancing blow to the face, Tom let fly catching Jamie full in the face. He staggered, partly from the force and partly from surprise. Jamie rushed at his brother, but was met with another blow, which brought blood from his nose and lip and knocked him against the wall of the garage.

Jamie held his hand to his face and blood trickled through his fingers and across the back of his hand and dripped to the ground. Pat went over to him.

'Get out of the way, Pat,' he said, flinging his arm across her body.

'Stop it, you're doing no good. Come indoors and let me see to your face.'

'I'm not letting him get away with that.' He advanced on Tom. Serena shrieked at them to stop, but they were unheeding of any entreaties.

The crowd outside the shop had crossed the road and grown larger as word spread of the fight at the garage.

Tom held up his arms for protection from his brother's onslaught. Jamie's aggression built on pure rage was no match for Tom's cold, calculating judgement and when his guard was down, Tom caught him with a punch full in the face. Jamie's knees buckled and he sank to the ground shaking his head to clear it.

After staring expressionless at his brother, Tom turned away clutching the knuckles of his right hand. He walked over to Serena, said something and she pointed towards the Vicarage then to the front garden where Alexander was sleeping peacefully, oblivious of the trouble that had been festering since his short life began.

The crowd broke up. A few, who knew the brothers well, huddled together commenting in disbelief at the turn of events. Then they too dispersed.

✳

Jamie lay on the bed in the bungalow. In silence he let Pat clean his face. They avoided each other's eyes as she washed the cut nose and lip and smeared on ointment which made him wince. He had intended to go back into the garage, but when he stood up he felt dizzy and she made him rest.

Pat had made no comment on the fight and her lack of censure left him empty, as if there were now nothing left for him to fight against, to strive for – no point in existing. Kim's look of shame and embarrassment as he passed her on his way up the path had pierced him like an arrow.

Jamie buried his head in the pillow. He could hardly bear to think about Tom. He tried not to, but pictures of them at home as kids seeped into his mind. How he had admired and looked up to him. So easy going, always taking care of him at school, breaking up fights, stopping other children taunting him. Tom was clever, too, helping him with his homework.

He remembered his brother urging him to get qualifications and not to leave school and go out to work. Tom knew how much he longed to escape the boredom of study and because he thought so much of Tom he had taken notice. Money was tight after his father died, but Tom was always there giving him a little money while he was at college. When Tom started work, he made sure he had enough to go out occasionally for, as he told him, 'keeping you indoors every evening is tantamount to caging a lion.'

Jamie reached over to the other side of the bed and ran his hand over Pat's pillow, which smelled of her hair. He rolled on to his back and stared at the ceiling.

He heard Tony come in and ask where he was and caught the buzz of a reply then Tony saying loudly 'But what's wrong with him?' and Kim or Pat saying 'Shush' before the kitchen door shut and he was alone with the silence.

*

The church clock struck eleven. Pat wiped the tears from her cheeks with the edge of the sheet. During the afternoon she had gone to see how Jamie was, only to find he had returned to the garage. She had been sure he would want to eat with them after the fight with Tom, to feel his family round him, even if they were not totally sympathetic.

She thought it might be a good time, if there were such a time, to get together and discuss what could be done. At six o'clock she sent Tony to get his father only to be told the garage was shut and the van gone.

For the children's sake she kept her feelings under control as she served the evening meal, but now she was in bed, the tears could no longer be stemmed. How could Jamie be so callous, so unfeeling towards her and the children? He was off seeking solace in his woman's bed that he could not, or would not seek in hers.

She heard Jamie letting himself into the bungalow and the door of the drawing room close softly. Should she go and talk to him? What would she say? What has your lover got that I haven't? Don't you love me any more?

The sheet mopped up more tears. It was no good; she would have to find out for herself.

*

Pat peered through the evening gloom, desperately trying to keep Jamie's van in sight without being seen. When she reached Maidstone, the Sunday evening traffic merging from the left held her up and Jamie disappeared from view. Luckily, by the time she reached the bridge she could just see him on the Chatham road that skirted the river. He turned right and drove into a car park. She could not stop as she was on double yellow lines so she had to follow him in and drive speedily past as he got out. Pat saw a space and quickly drove into it. She tried to see in which direction he was heading and when she thought he was a safe distance away, she hurried after him as he turned towards the library.

To her surprise he went into a pub. Pat had convinced herself that he was going to her house and the intention had been to note the address and see what she could find out. Now she was in a fix. How was she to get in the door without being seen, let alone spy on him when in there? Maybe this had not been such a good idea after all. She bit her bottom lip. She was not going back now, not without seeing what he did of an evening.

Timidly she pushed open the Public Bar door, hoping she could see into the one that Jamie was in. She examined the interior to see where she could place herself to best advantage. It was dreadfully smoky and she wanted to cough but felt sure Jamie would hear her. Pat was embarrassed to discover she was the only woman. She sidled up to the bar.

'Yes, love,' the barman bellowed. 'What can I get you?'

Please don't speak so loudly she wanted to say. 'I'll have a – a white wine.'

'White wine,' he repeated, as if she had asked for a glass of poison.

Pat's face reddened. 'Yes, haven't you got any?'

The barman leaned forward. 'Look miss,' he said, conspiratorially, 'wouldn't you be better off in the Saloon Bar?' He tipped his head in that direction.

'I, er, I said I'd meet someone here, um, in this bar.'

'Well, in that case.'

He disappeared out of sight and was back in a flash. 'There you are Miss, that'll be £1.80.'

Glass in hand she turned from the bar to discover there was no table free. There was a space on a bench seat, but it meant sitting next to an unsavoury looking man with a cigarette dangling from his mouth. He was laughing with his equally unsavoury pals. Pat perched awkwardly on the seat.

The best that could be said about her situation was that it gave her a view, restricted somewhat by her height, through to the other bar. To say she felt ill-at-ease was an understatement. She raised a hand to her thumping head, which the thick atmosphere did nothing to alleviate.

'You got enough room there, duck?' the man said, moving slightly.

'Oh, yes, thank you. I'm waiting for a friend. He said he'd meet me here.'

Why on earth would he want to know that? She sat bolt upright but could only see tops of heads. Then Jamie came to the bar. Pat bowed her head, she was right in his eyeline. She slowly moved her head and peeped through lowered lashes as if this would make her less conspicuous. He was smiling as he paid for the drinks and took two glasses away.

So – he did have someone with him. This must be the rendezvous, the place where he got in the mood for his adulterous liaison. Pat stood up abruptly and the man beside her slopped his beer as it was halfway to his mouth. She marched up to the bar and glared over it.

'Another wine?'

'Yes,' she said sharply. There he was sitting with a woman who must be forty, if not more. Pat took some comfort from the fact she was not some young bimbo. But then it did not much matter how old she was, Jamie should not be with anyone.

'Your wine.'

'Thank you.'

Pat took a sip and resumed her examination. The barman cleared his throat.

'That'll be £1.80.'

Pat rummaged in her purse. She handed him the money but remained at the bar, not caring whether she was seen or not.

They appeared to have a familiar relationship, not formal as if they had met recently. Surely Jamie had not had a long-running affair going on for months. No, impossible. She always knew where he was – he was not good at lying anyway.

His choice surprised her. This woman was as different from herself as it was possible to get – big, buxom, blond and cheap, though she did have a cheery look.

A raised hand reached up to touch Jamie's face. Pat could tell from his gestures that he was explaining his account of the fight. Don't believe a word he says she almost called out.

The woman shook her head in sympathy and her long earrings glinted in the light.

Pat did not want to stay any longer, they could be there till closing time. Then again, they might retire to their love nest or some sordid hotel room – she did not want to know. Pat tipped down the rest of her wine, banged the glass on the counter and left.

*

'Who've you been fighting with this time?' Betsy asked as she touched his face with her pink-tipped finger.

'My brother.'

'With Tom?' she exclaimed. 'But he wouldn't hurt a fly.'

'Well, he's changed since he got married.'

He explained the previous day's events. She listened attentively.

'Where were you yesterday? I wanted to see you.' Jamie said.

'I took Steve out for the day. I don't often get a Saturday off from the supermarket so he never gets taken out like other kids, plus the fact I don't often have the money either. What did you want me for particularly.'

'I wanted to tell you about the fight and everything.'

'Now you have, what difference does a day make. Look, Jamie, I don't mind meeting you occasionally, but I've got responsibilities, too – like you have.'

'What are you trying to say?'

'I was so pleased to see you again, more than you probably realise. It's nice to have male company, but really you just wanted a shoulder to cry on, didn't you?'

'Why did you keep coming then?'

'Because – because you've brought back all the feeling I once had for you twenty years ago.'

'But you wouldn't sleep with me when I asked.'

'Not because I didn't want to, believe me. My life's pretty dreary in that department, but you asked for the wrong reasons.'

Betsy looked him straight in the eye, but he could not hold her gaze.

'The trouble with you is you don't know when you're well off. A lovely wife…' Jamie went to protest. 'I know I haven't met her but I can read between the lines. You've said enough for me to know that she's good for you. You have children you are proud of and a brother who should be your closest friend, not your enemy.'

'They're all against me.'

'That aint true, if you really thought hard enough without your pride and hot temper getting in the way, you'd cotton on. Go back, and thank your lucky stars that you have such a family.'

'There's still that woman of Tom's – I hate her.'

'Why?'

'Why!' he exclaimed, 'Haven't you been listening to what I've told you over the last few weeks.'

'I've done nothing else. Apart from when we first met, you have not once asked me how I manage, what I've done since we parted or my expectations for the future. It's been you, you, you and what I can do to put it right. The suggestions I've made haven't suited you. So now I'm telling you, go home and tell Pat about your money worries. Apologise to Kim for losing your head and ring Tom and ask if you can meet somewhere and find some common ground that you can agree on. If you can't bring yourself to like Tom's wife, avoid her, that shouldn't be difficult. She probably doesn't like you either, she's the odd one out in all this, not you. Have you thought about that?' Betsy stood up.

'You're not going, are you?'

'I think it's best. It's been wonderful seeing you again, Jamie and if circumstances had been different, well, who knows.' She slipped her arms in her coat. 'Don't try to get in touch because it's just preventing you from doing what should have been done weeks ago.' She kissed his forehead and her earring brushed his cheek. 'Bye Jamie – love you.'

Her eyes filled with tears as she left.

*

Pat got back home about eight-thirty. Kim came into the kitchen from the drawing room.

'You left in a hurry. Where've you been?'

'I went into Maidstone. A friend rang and asked if I'd meet her for a drink. She's – she's having some trouble with her son and wanted some advice.'

'What friend?'

'Oh, you wouldn't know. I used to go to school with her.'

'What's her name? Perhaps he goes to my school. I might be able to give you some information to pass on.'

'Oh, er, Carol Trescott.'

'Trescott, Trescott, no, can't say I know anyone of that name – not in my year anyway. Why does she want to talk to you if she hasn't seen you for a long time?'

'Oh, I don't know, Kim' Pat said impatiently. 'she just did.' Kim threw her a puzzled look. 'Where's Tony?'

'Watching television. It's a good film, Mum, hasn't long started so you've not missed much. Come and watch it with us.'

They went into the living room, Kim explaining what had happened so far. Tony told them to shush, as he could not hear what was going on.

Throughout the film Pat stared at the screen but had little idea what it was about. She knew it was a detective story with spectacular car chases, but it needed more concentration than she could give it.

Pat was back at the pub bar checking out her husband's fancy woman. An appropriate phrase, she thought, a tart with a heart. She recalled the dress she had been wearing, white background, big, bold, garish pattern, falling in crumpled folds covered by a shapeless cardigan that flowed over her ample bosom. Her coat, lying over the back of the chair, revealed a torn lining at the armhole.

The more she reflected on the rapport between them, the more she was convinced they had known each other for longer than a couple of months. Perhaps he had been having an affair for years. You heard of women who were completely unaware that their husbands had mistresses but she had considered they must have been pretty stupid, or just didn't want to know.

Tony leapt from his chair making her jump. The list of credits was disappearing rapidly from the top of the screen.

'I'll get us a drink,' Pat said.

'No, I'll do it, you stay there, Tony can help me. What do you want?'

Pat wondered if Kim had swallowed her story about the mythical Carol Trescott. She was sure she had not, she was far too smart – which was more than could be said for Jamie.

She went to bed early meaning to read till Jamie came in but she kept reading the same lines. She turned off the light and lay staring at the ceiling, waiting. The clock struck – he would be in soon.

Pat felt someone shaking her shoulder.

'Mum, Mum, wake up. It's the phone, there's someone on the phone. I don't know who it is. She wants to speak to you.'

Pat thought she had just dropped off, but a glance at the clock showed it was nearly five.

'Where's your Dad?'

'I don't know, he's not in the living room.'

Pat was fully awake now, a riot of thoughts racing through her head. She grabbed her dressing gown from the door and hurried into the living room.

'This is Pat Cresswell.'

'It's about your husband, he's had an accident.'

Chapter 36

'What sort of accident?'

'His van was found in a ditch on the....'

'Where is he? What's wrong?' Pat's legs felt weak and she fell into the armchair. 'Is he badly hurt?'

'He's here, in St Catherine's. He's got lots of injuries and he's – he's unconscious.'

Pat thought she had been talking to a nurse, but the unprofessional description of his injuries and the sound of a woman crying told her who was on the other end.

'I'll come now,' she said coldly.

'What's wrong?' Kim asked as she hovered anxiously beside her mother.

'It's Dad, he's in hospital, unconscious. He's had an accident.' Kim began to cry.

'Stop crying,' Pat said, more sharply than she intended. 'Ring Uncle Tom and tell him what's happened. I'm going to the hospital.'

'Can't I come? What about Tony?'

'Uncle Tom will bring you.'

'Supposing he won't come?'

'He'll come – tell him I need him.'

She was putting on her coat as Tony, sleepy-eyed, came from his bedroom.

'What's up? What's all the noise about?'

'Dad's had an accident. Kim'll explain when she's phoned Uncle Tom.'

Pat flew out of the door and leapt into her car, revving violently as she backed off the forecourt.

Pat headed for A & E and immediately saw who had phoned. She was sitting on a chair leaning forward her elbows resting on her knees, clutching a screwed-up handkerchief. The dark roots of her hair showed up under the harsh fluorescent lights.

'Was it you who rang me,' Pat said, standing over her.

The woman stood up so quickly she almost knocked Pat off her feet.

'Yes, I – I….'

'Where do you come into all this.'

'The hospital rang me.'

'Why didn't they ring me?'

'I don't know – I think they found my telephone number. I s'pose the police couldn't find anything else.'

'Where is he now?'

'He's in a cubicle over there. He looks – he looks dreadful.' She began to weep.

'What's your name?'

'Betty Gwynne.'

Pat crossed over to a desk. 'My husband is here. He's had an accident. I'm Pat Cresswell.'

Years of watching hospital dramas on television were no preparation for seeing Jamie lying unconscious. He had a drip in his arm, and a green tube came from his mouth. His face was grazed and the cuts had thin strips of white sticky tape across them. A lump came to her throat and tears pricked her eyes.

'Can I touch him?' she asked a blue coated nurse standing by the bed.

The nurse nodded and Pat gently held the tips of his bruised fingers. A doctor came through the curtains.

'What's wrong exactly?' she asked him.

'He has extensive bruising from his seat belt and there are various superficial wounds not of a serious nature, but there may be internal injuries. He was unconscious when found and it is this that is causing most concern. We're going to do a CT scan of his head.

'What could be wrong?' she probed.

'It might be severe concussion, it's difficult to tell, but we need to make sure nothing else is going on.'

Pat's heart sank. 'Such as?'

'There could be some bleeding in the brain, for instance.'

'Caused by the accident I suppose,' Pat said.

'Could be, but it could have caused the accident.'

She was about to question him some more when he said, 'Why don't you get a drink. I'll come and talk to you again when we've got the results.'

Pat took a deep breath and stared at Jamie for some moments before returning to the waiting area.

Betty was still there – she had forgotten all about her. She looked up enquiringly. Pat was tempted not to tell her anything, but she was so distressed, she had not the heart.

'Jamie's going for a brain scan.'

'He's not come to yet then?'

'That's what's worrying them.'

Dry-eyed, Pat watched the woman twisting her handkerchief round her fingers. 'Want a coffee?' she asked.

Pat waited at the machine behind a man on crutches and brought back the plastic beakers. They drank in silence. Pat had a hundred things she wanted to ask Betty Gwynne, but did not know where to start. She formed a couple of questions and was about to speak when the children came in with Tom. She turned her attention to them and reported in a matter-of-fact voice all she knew.

'They said the police are coming to speak to me. I don't know what I can tell them.'

'What did they say when they rang you?' Tom asked.

'They didn't, it was this woman.' Pat turned to Betty, but she had disappeared.

'That blond woman sitting near you?'

'Yes.'

'She went out as we came in.'

'What's she got to do with it?' Tom asked.

'She was evidently Jamie's bit on the side.'

'What d'you mean? He was seeing this woman!'

'I doubt it stopped at seeing her as you so delicately put it.'

Tony asked Kim what Mum was talking about and why she was so annoyed. A policeman and woman came over to them.

'Mrs Cresswell?'

'Yes.'

'We'd like to ask you some questions. This is WPC Kenley and I'm PC Deacon. We can talk in a room over there.' The policeman looked at Tom and the children. 'Do you want them with you.'

'This is my husband's brother.' She turned to Tom. 'Go and explain who you are and you might be able to see Jamie when he comes back.'

'OK, come on kids.'

Pat explained Jamie's movements up to leaving the bungalow,

omitting her visit to Maidstone. She, in turn, learned that Mrs Gwynne had left Jamie in the *Kentish Hop* at about eight fifteen. Surprise must have shown on her face because they asked if this meant anything to her. She had to reply that he was not usually home till eleven or thereabouts. She caught the meaningful look they exchanged and felt her cheeks burn. They said it was not known yet what time Jamie left the pub, but there had been no excess of alcohol in his blood so he could have left soon after his friend.

Pat asked where the accident had taken place and learned it was about three miles out of Maidstone and the van was on the wrong side of the road in a ditch – which was probably why it had not been seen earlier. There were no witnesses to the accident, no skid marks, nor was it known how long the van had been where it was found. It was notified to the police about two that morning, and even then the informant rang after he had got home to say he only thought he had seen a van.

When the police found it there was no identification on Jamie apart from a wallet, and that only contained money and a piece of paper with a telephone number. The rest she knew.

Pat thanked the police for their help and went back to the waiting area to be told by Tom that they had not seen Jamie as he was still at the scanner. They hung around talking in hushed voices about nothing in particular till a doctor came to the room. He sat down beside Pat and gently explained that the scan had shown the presence of a haemorrhage and her husband needed an urgent operation to remove the blood clot and stop the bleeding. They would shortly be transferring him to the Neurosurgical Unit at the General.

'He will go into the Intensive Care Unit there and they will put him on a ventilator to try to reduce the pressure in his skull.'

A nurse popped her head round the door. 'The ambulance has arrived.' She looked at Pat. 'There's room for you if you'd like to go with him.'

'Yes, yes I would.' Tom was frowning anxiously as Pat said to him, 'You will follow us, won't you?'

'Of course.'

Pat smiled weakly at Kim and Tony.

When they arrived at the General, Jamie was taken away. Pat sat anxiously, clammy hands clasped in her lap, awaiting the others. She paced the floor. They should be here by now; she did not want to sit alone having to think about what could happen to Jamie.

Tony rushed in. 'Where've they taken him?'

'He's being prepared for an operation.'

'What are they going to do?'

'Relieve the pressure and clip off the blood vessel.' Pat said crisply.

'How long's that going to take? When can we see him?' Kim asked.

'Two hours, the doctor said about two hours.'

'Is it serious – Daddy won't die, will he? Tony's face was a cross between that of a little old man and a small child.

'Of course not,' Pat almost shouted at him.

'Hospitals do wonderful things nowadays,' Tom said reassuringly. 'Look, why don't we all get something to eat. I don't know about you lot, but I'm starving.'

'I don't want to go, I want to stay here – now,' Tony said defiantly as if his uncle had suggested taking him to the Outer Hebrides for breakfast.

'Uncle Tom's right, none of us has eaten since last night, and I've just realised how hungry I am. There's nothing we can do till the operation's over.'

'But I'm coming straight back.' He glared at his mother.

The café was crowded with people breakfasting, and they had to sit at different tables.

'Are you all right, Pat?' Tom put his tray on the table and unloaded it. 'You seem different – hard – well, not hard exactly, not your usual self.'

'Oh?'

'Was Jamie really seeing another woman?'

'Yes, I followed him last night and saw her. He has been going out every night since your row and he never eats with us in the evening. He ceased sleeping with me weeks ago.'

'No, I didn't know that. I knew he didn't go to the pub, but I didn't know he went out every night. Didn't he come home?'

'Oh, yes, he was home around eleven. He was out long enough to – to do whatever he wanted to do.'

'It's just – you don't seem very upset about his condition.'

Pat put down her knife. 'Look, Tom, in the space of twelve hours, I've discovered and seen his mistress and learned that his injuries are such that he could die. You don't live with someone for nearly nineteen years without having deep feelings about him or her.' His lips trembled and tears spilled down her face. 'Of c-course I'm worried ab-bout h-him.'

Tom put out his hand to cover hers. 'I'm to blame for this. I should not have let it get to this state.'

Pat wiped her eyes. 'I didn't think he'd go as far as this when he considered we had failed him. It doesn't say much for us – the kids and me, does it? Or you?'

'He thinks the world of you, Pat. Perhaps there was something else worrying him, something he hasn't told you about.'

'Like what?'

'Money? Edward was telling us that he'd recommended a friend to the garage but Jamie made such a hash of it, he'd lost the chance of servicing a fleet of cars for the man's company.'

Pat frowned, calling to mind the man Kim had pointed out and the way he snapped at her when she asked when he was going to have his name painted on the van. And there was Tony saying Dad did not have much work.

'You could have something there. He hasn't let me near the books recently. I thought he was just being bloody-minded.'

They stayed at the hospital all day. Pat was washed out and the children looked tired. Tony asked so often when they would have some news that Pat almost screamed at him to shut up. At last someone approached.

'I'm Elena, I'm the nurse looking after your husband while he's in intensive care.'

'How is he? Was the operation successful?'

'He's doing as well as can be expected. You can see him now.'

The children rushed forward to follow her.

'Let your mother see him first.'

Their faces dropped and Pat said, 'Just a few minutes then I'll come and get you.'

Jamie looked like a stranger, with his shaved head and a stockinette cap keeping a dressing in place. A tube, taped round to the back of his neck, came from his mouth and a drip of clear fluid fed into his hand.

'He'll come round, won't he?'

The nurse smiled reassuringly showing even white teeth. 'Just talk to him, hold his hand; sing if you like. Anything to stimulate the senses.'

Pat sat close so she could slip her hand under his fingers. She spoke of their courtship. Carefree, easy-going, indulgent Jamie, giving her little gifts on silly pretexts such as six weeks since they had first met or two months since he had proposed. When they were engaged, she made him put a stop to these extravagances and reminded him they had to save. One or two tiffs resulted from this ultimatum, but he loved her and she was the steadying influence he needed.

'What went wrong Jamie?' she said, in a soft voice. 'Have you fallen out of love with me? Did you want to move on? Was nearing forty a milestone you couldn't cope with? Why didn't you talk to me?' She lifted the limp hand above the bed cover. 'Perhaps we never get to know the person we live closest to. There's always some secret part hidden from those we love. Come on, Jamie my darling, come back to me. We all care about you, Tom included and, if you'd let her, Serena as well. We could be so close like we used to be.' She rested her head on the hand that held Jamie's and felt the hot tears trickle across her hand. 'If Kim can get over meningitis, then you can get over this.'

The nurse came back. 'Shall I fetch your children?'

Kim could no longer hold back her tears when she saw her father. 'He looks so awful,' she sobbed. 'How long is he going to be like this?'

Pat looked questioningly at the nurse. 'Twenty-four hours perhaps, could be less, could be more. We can't say exactly.'

'What's that for?' Tony asked, trying to control his wavering voice.

'That monitor? It's to show how your Dad is reacting. We make various checks, blood pressure, heart rate, that sort of thing.'

Tony carefully inspected all the equipment anxious to know how it was going to affect his father and, Pat thought, it was to stop him crying.

Eventually Pat said they ought to be going home. 'I've the garage to sort out. People will have left cars and I'll have to be there to sort it out.'

'I'm not going. I want to stay here with Dad.' His voice accusing as if Pat had no right to leave his father.

'How will you get home?'

'What's wrong with a bus?'

'Nothing, but don't be late.'

'That's not likely, the last bus is 9.30,' Kim said.

'I'm quite capable of looking after myself,' Tony said aggressively. 'I could get a taxi.'

'I'll stay too, Mum, don't worry. We'll come home together and I'll make sure we get something to eat if you'll give me some money.'

*

'Thanks for coming back here,' Pat said, as Tom came in the kitchen door. 'I hope Serena's not annoyed with you spending so much time with us.'

'Don't be silly, of course she isn't. It's more likely to be Mike and Ian who are put out. Thank goodness they're competent. They asked after Jamie by the way.'

'That's good of them. Right, let's see what we can find out.'

Pat took a set of keys from a hook and marched purposefully to the garage. Tom rolled up the door. Inside the office she searched for the order book. After poring over files, bank statements and receipts, hampered by customers enquiring about their cars, they turned one another.

'So, it wasn't just about Ian Walker and Serena – he is in trouble. Why didn't he tell me? He's never kept anything from me before.'

'Perhaps he was too embarrassed.'

'Or things go so bad between us he couldn't.' She sighed. 'As if I haven't got enough to worry about.'

'You'll sort things out, you're not on your own. Kim will be a great help and you know you can count on us.'

When Pat went to the hospital on Tuesday Jamie was still unconscious. She talked to him about the children and the naughty or funny things they had done when they were little. She wondered whether to talk about Betty Gwynne, but felt silly thinking of what to say to someone who was not hearing.

'How is he?'

'Tony, you startled me.'

'Has he said anything yet?'

'No, the nurse told me to talk to him, so I have. Where's Kim?'

'I didn't see her when the bell went so I came on.'

'Sit here Tony. I'll go round the other side.'

She stared at his sullen face. He loved his Dad and Jamie had no failings as far as he was concerned and if he had, Tony did not want to know, or found reasons to excuse him.

Kim arrived, followed shortly by Tom, and the four of them talked about almost everything but Jamie's accident, till they were told there were too many people at the bedside.

'Have you been here all day,' Tom asked the children when they reached the waiting room.

'We've come from school,' Kim said.

'School!' he exclaimed. 'You've been to school!'

'Mum said we had missed one day and it would be better if we were doing something,' Kim said.

'I think she was mean making me go,' Tony said, 'I haven't got exams.'

Pat glared at Tom daring him to make any further comment.

Chapter 37

'How was he?' Serena asked when Tom came home.

'Not surfaced yet, I'm afraid. Tony said he had seen him move his hand and open and shut his eyes, but I think it was wishful thinking.'

'How's he taking it?'

'He's in a very strange mood, I've never seen Tony like that before. He's always so harum scarum.'

'It must be a shock to see his father like that.'

'He's also very anti-Mum. Poor Pat can't do or say anything right.'

Tom sat on the settee and leaned back covering his face with two hands and rubbing his eyes with his fingertips. 'Edward knows about Jamie, doesn't he?'

'Yes, I told Lydia.'

'Pat and I want to speak to him about the garage this evening.'

'Is Jamie in bad trouble?'

'It doesn't look good and there are so many factors we don't know. What insurance cover he's got while not working, is one thing. Then there are outstanding repairs and debts and, in the long term, getting back lost trade when he recovers.'

Serena sat beside him and took his hand.

Tom said, 'I shouldn't have let things go this far. I've let him down.'

'Don't try to do any soul-searching now. I've been through all that – what did I do wrong? Should I have done this or that and would it have made any difference? But you can't take all the responsibility for his actions even if he is your brother. I should not have interfered I know, I just wanted you to be friends again. You're certainly not responsible for his accident. Try to get things in proportion, darling. I'm sure it will work out in the end.'

*

It was not that he was unconcerned about Jamie, but Edward

did not see what could be gained by this meeting with Pat and Tom. It was Lydia who urged him to go.

Tom handed Edward a beer. 'We've asked you here because we hope you might want to help Jamie – and you are involved.'

'Involved?'

'It's not only the accident. The business has not been doing well and he's in debt.'

'Ah, I mentioned a while back about the rent, but I haven't heard anything since. He's also lost some good business.'

'I know,' Pat said.

'If you all knew about this, why weren't you helping Dad before.'

All heads jerked up at the angry voice. Tony was sitting at the dining room table. Edward was not even aware he was there. He stared at him now and was surprised how much he had grown. The glowering face reminded him of a young Jamie. What age was he? Eleven, twelve?'

Edward had never sent Jamie's children a card or present. He had hardly acknowledged their existence. What must Cressy have thought about him, that he could not be bothered to acknowledge her grandchildren? They would have been as dear to her as his children were to him.

'We didn't know till recently,' his mother said to Tony. 'In fact, you were the one who told me Dad hadn't as much work as usual. He hadn't mentioned it to me.'

'You hardly ever spoke to him,' he shouted.

'He was hardly ever here,' Pat said.

'That was your fault, you drove him away. You should've known 'bout the garage – you used to. I've heard you talking all about it – and doing the books.'

'He hasn't let me near the accounts for weeks,' Pat tried to explain, feeling more and more embarrassed.

'You don't care about him – none of you. Kim didn't do as she was told, Uncle Tom fights with him and you weren't the least upset about his accident. You don't care because if he dies you won't have to worry any more.' His voice broke and he rushed from the room.

A shocked, embarrassed silence descended on them. They all knew that what Tony said held some truth and guilt showed in the way each avoided the others eyes. Even Edward, who had least to do with the present situation, experienced a twinge of conscience.

Tom said, 'Shall I go and talk to him?'

Wearily Pat stroked her forehead, disturbing her fringe. 'Not just yet, he won't want you to see him crying.'

This remark reminded Edward how much he had hated his mother to see him cry. He would hold back his tears until his throat hurt. So adept had he become at hiding his feelings for fear of some harsh reaction that he could barely feel, or express any emotion of happiness or sorrow. He threw Pat an understanding smile.

'First of all, we wondered if you would wait for the rent?'

'I've waited three months already so another month or two won't make much difference.'

Proving just how unfeeling he had become, Edward immediately wished he could take it back.

'Thank you,' Pat said hurriedly as she saw Tom open his mouth to remonstrate. 'We'll try not to keep you waiting longer than is necessary.'

Edward caught Kim's eye and was left in no doubt her opinion of him.

'Is there anything else I can do?' he said placatingly.

'We haven't gone into it deeply enough to know what help we might need, but we'll bear your offer in mind.'

'I rang Jamie's friend at Thompson's this morning and he put me in touch with Sam Williams who has just retired. Sam said he would come over and see what he could do. He offered to work on Sunday to keep current business going. I'll know more when I see him. As the police don't yet know how the accident was caused or if there was another vehicle involved, the insurance company weren't very forthcoming about money.'

'Has he private health cover?' Edward queried.

'Of course, he's not that irresponsible,' Tom snapped.

'Can I visit him?' Edward said, wishing he were anywhere but here.

'I don't know – it was family only. I can ask when I go back tonight. I can say you're a very close friend.'

It crossed Edward's mind she was being sarcastic, but her face betrayed no such thought.

'Ok, let me know what they say. I'd better be going now.'

'I'll see you out,' Tom said.

At the door Edward said, 'I wanted a word with you. I'm thinking of buying a pony for Philippa and would like to keep it on the farm. I thought perhaps on Lower Field.'

'Lower Field can get marshy. I think it should be nearer the farmhouse – Dally's Field perhaps. What rent had you in mind?'

'Rent?'

'I'm not a benevolent institution, you know.'

'No, no, of course not. You don't mind then?'

'I'm quite happy as long as someone else is looking after it. Perhaps when Alexander is old enough, you'll let him ride. Do you realise our children have roughly the same age gap as we three had. Perhaps they'll be as friendly as we were – once. At least there will be a girl to keep them in order'

'Philippa will certainly do that, she's a real handful.'

'So I've heard.'

*

Jamie had been unconscious for well over forty-eight hours. As Pat reached the unit the nurse greeted her with the news that he had opened his eyes momentarily.

'He's been struggling with the tube in his mouth so we took it out to see how he manages. Keep talking to him as you have been doing,'

'Hello, darling.' She kissed his forehead. 'I hear you're coming back to us, we've all been so worried about you. I've sorted out the garage for the time being so there's nothing for you to worry about except getting better.'

Jamie's eyelids flickered. Pat moved her head closer, as it seemed as if his mouth were forming a kiss. She could feel his breath on her face.

'What is it Jamie? Are you wanting a drink?'

He looked at her with glazed eyes. 'Ber, ber,' was all she could make out. She called the nurse.

'He sounds as if he's trying to say my name,' she said excitedly.

'That's a good sign.' The nurse said in a loud, clear voice. 'Mr Cresswell. Wake up, your wife is here.' Jamie turned his head a fraction. 'I'll get the doctor.'

Pat bent over her husband and smoothed his forehead. 'Bessy,' he said, his voice faint and slurred. 'Bessy.' Pat stiffened and her fingers stayed poised above his face. She sat down jerkily.

The nurse returned with the doctor and they stood opposite. He saw her tears.

'It's an upsetting time I know, but the signs are good.' He shone a light into his eyes. 'Go on talking to him, move your fingers across his skin. He needs as much stimulation as you can give him.'

Pat scarcely noticed as they moved away from the bed. Betty, that was what he was trying to say. Betty. Such a lot had taken place and she had had so much to think about, it seemed like weeks rather than days since she had seen them together. All that worry and the first name he utters is hers.

Jamie seemed to retreat into a sleep and she rushed over to the nurse who told her it was not unusual.

At lunchtime Tony came in and Pat told him he was coming round. He bent over his father. 'Dad, it's me, Tony. Look at me, Dad.'

Jamie turned his head. 'Tony,' he whispered.

'He said my name, did you hear? Really he did.'

'Yes, I heard him. That's the first word he has said. Isn't that wonderful? He should recover quickly now.'

Jamie slowly focused on her. 'Pat,' he said.

'Hello.' She gave him a kiss.

In his slurred voice he said, 'Is this 'ospital?'

'Yes.'

'How long?'

'Since Monday,' Tony said eager to impart his knowledge. 'Uncle Tom brought Kim and me – it was almost the middle of the night.'

'Monday? When's that?'

'Day before yesterday,' said the newly arrived Kim, elbowing her brother to get closer. 'You were found in the van in a coma and you've had an operation.'

'Oh, Dad, I thought you were going to die.'

'Don't say that Tony!' Kim exclaimed.

Jamie closed his eyes. 'Not ready go yet.'

*

'How is he?' Tom asked as he came into the kitchen.

'Quiet and subdued – not very Jamie-like,' said Pat.

'He must take it easy now he's home.'

'Yes, I know,' Pat said listlessly, 'Go on in, he'll be pleased to see you.'

'Are you sure?' Tom had only visited Jamie in hospital once since he had come out of his coma. Little was said as Pat's parents were there.

'Yes, I'm sure.'

Jamie was sitting in his armchair, which had been moved into the bay. He was pale and drawn. Tony was sitting beside him flipping the pages of a motoring magazine.

'Keeping your Dad amused?' Tom said.

'I've been reading to him,' he said primly.

Jamie gave Tom a wry smile. 'Sit down. Tony, go and see if Mum can make us a cup of tea.'

'How are you feeling?'

'So-so, I didn't sleep very well last night. I was overtired. Dave Reece came, and a couple of the darts team – and David to rescue my soul. Pat's got someone to keep the garage going, did you know?'

Tom glanced at the magazine. 'Tony looking after you?'

'He reads about cars 'cause he thinks that's what I'm interested in. To tell you the truth, I don't want to think about cars – or anything.'

'You're not expected to, Pat has everything under control.'

'I know, she's been wonderful.'

Tom gazed across the road to Mr Anders' shop, neatly empty with rows of plastic leaves and in the middle the grinning pig dressed in striped apron and straw hat. He and Jamie used to stand outside and laugh at it every time they walked into Grassenden with their mother.

They both started to speak.

'Sorry, you go first Tom.'

'I was only going to remind you of the pig in Mr Anders' window.' He nodded toward the shop.

Jamie stared unseeing into the distance. 'Seems a long time since we were kids.'

Pat came in with tea and Tony put the cups on the saucers.

'Why don't you go to Peter's' Pat said. 'We'll keep Dad company till you get back.'

He gave his mother a withering look. 'I'd rather stay here.'

Pat poured the tea, but tears were not far beneath the surface.

'We were talking about the pig in Mr Anders' window. Your Dad and I used to love it when we came shopping with Granny as kids.'

'It used to amuse you and Kim too, didn't it?' Pat said.

Tony ignored her and took a cup from the tray and gave it to his Dad.

'Where's Kim?' Tom asked.

'She's at Trudi's.'

'She's always off somewhere,' Tony said, little realising how funny it sounded coming from someone who could hardly be contained indoors.

'She was here yesterday when Dad came home.'

'She knew you were taking care of me today,' Jamie said.

Tom thought how strange it was to hear his brother making the sort of diplomatic remark that usually came from Pat. Perhaps this would be a good moment.

'We were wondering – Serena asked – if you minded if she called in when she came shopping.' Tom realised by Jamie's face that he had misjudged the situation.

'No, I don't want to see her.'

'Now you've upset him. Why don't you leave him alone – we don't need you.'

'There's no call for you to speak like that. Uncle Tom's been very kind.'

'He could hardly be anything else considering what he's done.'

The cup in Jamie's hand rattled in the saucer as his hand shook. Tom reached over and took it from him. He put his hand on Jamie's shoulder and murmured, 'I'm sorry, I shouldn't have mentioned it. You look very tired. I'll come tomorrow, if that's all right.'

Jamie nodded and rested his head back on the armchair.

'I'll let myself out,' Tom said as he saw her rise to her feet.

Pat sank back gratefully. 'We'll see you tomorrow then.'

She and Jamie had slept together last night, but she didn't know what was expected of her. That Betty woman was always between them violating any natural feelings of sympathy and love that she had towards Jamie. Pat wanted to put her arms round him and give him a hug and say how wonderful it was to have him home, but she could not. They kissed each other, but it was perfunctory – the way it was with visitors.

'Dad's asleep, so I'm going to feed the rabbit, then I'll go and see Peter – for a little while.'

'Fine.' His mother's smile was not returned.

Tony was another complication she could do without. Pat wondered how much he had understood about Betty Gwynne when she had spoken so unguardedly at the hospital. Trouble was he was getting past the age when he could be fobbed off with an explanation that a tank could be driven through. Her rather immature son had grown up very fast in the last few weeks.

All Jamie said he could remember was driving along one minute and waking up in hospital the next. He assumed the police had sent for Pat and she had not disillusioned him.

Pat rested her head and through half closed eyes regarded her husband's sleeping face. The laughter lines round his eyes made him look haggard. His hair was stubbly where it was beginning to grow. The cuts on his face were hard scabs as if drawn with a crayon. He did not look like Jamie and the man she loved no longer loved her. He was a stranger physically and spiritually.

Even the children and taken up positions making her life almost unbearable in its complexity. 'This time, Jamie, you've dug yourself a hole that no one can get you out of, and you've dragged us all in with you.'

She closed her eyes and slept.

Chapter 38

Kim told Stewart to help himself to a biscuit and she went to the fridge for a drink. She heard her Dad call from the drawing room and sighed, wondering if he would make a scene about bringing home a boy who did not meet with this approval.

In the two weeks since leaving hospital Jamie had been depressed and quiet, apart from one brief flare up with Tony about fussing too much. They all skirted round each other like boxers waiting for an opening, but Kim could not decide who was waiting for what. She was disappointed in her father, but, on the other hand, she could not just stop loving someone who was the pivot of her life – especially as he was now so vulnerable.

'Come and meet my father,' she said.

Jamie was sitting in the bay, telephone table beside him, television turned his way and everything else he might need to hand.

'This is Stewart Lindell. He's come to get some notes from me and we're going to do a bit of revising together.'

'Lindell, Lindell,' Jamie repeated. 'Green Rover about two years old.'

'That's right, fancy you knowing that.'

Kim laughed. 'I'm afraid everyone in the village is known by their car. Rather like Jones the Milk or Evans the Post. Only here it's Harry the Honda.'

'That's rather clever,' Stewart said admiringly. He turned to Jamie. 'I heard about your accident, how are you?'

'Bored, but I haven't the will or energy to get up and do anything.'

'Dr Gifford came yesterday and said he should start going for a short walk every day and build up his strength gradually.' She looked at her father. 'Have you been today?'

He shook his head and smiled ruefully.

'I'll go with you tomorrow when I come home from school.'

'I noticed your garage is still open,' Stewart said.

'Yes, I've been lucky enough, or rather my wife has, to find someone to help out.'

They talked about the garage and cars and Kim hovered anxiously wanting to get Stewart on his own.

'We don't want to tire you out, Dad.' she said eventually, moving towards the door.

'No, all right, see you some other time Stewart.'

Kim glanced at her father before closing the door and saw him flop his head back and shut his eyes.

*

'So,' Sam said, as he watched Pat putting the garage books neatly in the filing cabinet, 'Jamie's ready to start work?'

'He's been home six weeks. Dr Gifford gave him the OK yesterday, but suggested he didn't do a full day to begin with. That's what I want to see you about. I see the book is pretty full. Will you be able to help out for another week or so? You've done a great job and I can't tell you how grateful we are.'

'You've done your bit too, ringing round, sending out invoices, balancing books, not to mention dashing off to buy parts I've needed.'

'It's surprising what I've learned doing that,' Pat said. 'Another week then?'

'Yeah, sure.' He slid into the pit. 'Jamie has wandered down here a few times, but he hasn't seemed that eager to start. Young Tony seems more enthusiastic.'

When she had told Tony it was dangerous in the garage, Pat was told that someone had to keep and eye on things if she was not interested. It was pointless trying to tell him she hardly had a moment to herself so hard was she 'keeping an eye on things.'

'I must apologise for him. I know he's been a pest, but he thinks he's safeguarding his Dad's interests. I heard him say he was definitely going to be a mechanic, that's probably why Jamie hasn't seemed keen to start back.' Pat chuckled as she went out on to the forecourt.

*

Tom felt conspicuous as he pushed Alexander into the Stores. Serena had wanted a few things and asked him to take the baby for a breath of fresh air. On the one hand he felt proud and on the other embarrassed. He seemed so large and the baby buggy so tiny.

He elbowed the tinkling door of the shop and clumsily manoeuvred the wheels over the threshold. There was hardly room for a pushchair between the shelves and he wondered if he should have left the Alexander outside.

Shirley Reece was beside herself at seeing the baby again.

'Hello stranger, I haven't seen you in ages. Bring the little darling over here so I can have a good look at him.'

He did as he was told, and the two women waiting to be served were indulgent and forbearing as she chucked Alexander under the chin and told him how he had grown and didn't he look like his mummy. A discreet cough reminded Shirley of her duty and Tom watched amused as she polished off her waiting customers with alacrity practically unknown in the store.

While Alexander was taken into the back to be shown off to Dave, Tom gathered everything on Serena's list.

'How's that brother of yours?' she asked on her return.

'What do you think, Shirley? You probably know better than I do.'

'Yes, um, he's sort of not lively like he used to be.'

'No,' He reached in his trouser pocket for his money. 'It's disconcerting when someone's character seems to change.'

'Have you made it up?' She sounded sincere.

'Yes, we're speaking to each other.' But not, he might have added, a return to brotherly love yet.

As he crossed the road to go up to the bungalow, Jamie appeared from the Hemlow Road. He was in jeans and white trainers, and his blue anorak was zipped up to his chin. His pinched face and the slight limp had aged him and he no longer seemed like his younger brother.

Walking head down and deep in thought, Jamie had not seen him and started when Tom said, 'Hello, taking your constitutional like the doctor ordered?'

'I've walked to Pat's Mum for a coffee. It's somewhere to go where I can rest halfway.'

Jamie glanced at the buggy. Alexander's woolly clad arms moved the blanket, which Shirley had pulled up high against the cold wind, revealing his face. His blue eyes seemed to focus on his uncle. They had reached the garage and Jamie asked if he were coming in.

'Yes, I was going to call.'

'I'll just have a quick word with Sam, then I'll be in. I'm

starting back on Monday.'

'That's great news, don't do too much too soon.'

'Hi, Uncle Tom, want a drink,' Kim said as he came in the kitchen.

'No thanks, I had one before I came out. That for your Mum.'

'No, it's for Stewart – we're revising.'

'Got yourself a boyfriend?'

Kim blushed. 'It's just schoolwork.' She looked pleadingly at her uncle. 'You won't tease me will you – not in front of him.'

'Well I don't know, you were pretty horrible to me a couple of years ago and I haven't forgiven you. Let's just say I'll think about it in case I want to blackmail you sometime.'

Kim stuck out her tongue, gave Alexander a kiss and asked after Serena before disappearing with the two mugs.

'Jamie's gone to my Mum's, he'll be back soon,' Pat said coming in from the garden.

'I've seen him – he's talking to Sam. Do you think he's fit enough to start work on Monday? He doesn't look all that well.'

'Physically he's fit or Dr Gifford wouldn't have given the go-ahead. Mentally I'm not so sure.'

'Things still bad between you?'

'Come into the living room. Here, give me the baby.'

Pat regarded Tom seriously. 'I've got to do something about this woman. I've waited hoping he'd tell me, but he hasn't.'

'Do you think you should be telling me this?'

'Maybe not, but I need someone to talk to.'

'So, what had you thought about doing?'

They heard the kitchen door slam which frightened Alexander and his lip curled and he began to cry.

'There's a strong wind out today,' Jamie said as he came into the room.

'There, there, darling,' Pat's soothing voice cooed at the baby. 'Did your naughty uncle frighten you?'

Jamie's head lifted on hearing the word uncle and he glanced at Tom.

'Not a very good introduction to my nephew upsetting him like that. Here, let me hold him.'

Jamie limped to his chair and held out his arms.

*

'Take care and good luck. Don't do too much and pack up if you get too tired, we can always get Sam to help out.'

'Yes, ma'am,' he replied.

'I can help you Dad, if it gets too much,' Tony offered.

'And I can learn how to do the bookkeeping, if you need me,' Kim said, not wanting to be left out.

'With all this help I might as well stay here and let you all get on with it.' Jamie gave one of his cheeky grins making them all feel life was getting back to normal.

When he had been sent off with lots of hugs and kisses, Pat took a crumpled slip of paper from her pocket and dialled the number written on it.

'Hello,' a voice answered.

'Betty Gwynne?'

'Yes.'

'It's Pat Cresswell.'

'How is he, has he fully recovered? I've been so worried 'bout him. The hospital told me he had been discharged.'

'I want to talk to you, when can we meet?'

'I'm just off to work. I can meet in my dinner break, that all right?'

'Where?'

'What about Seagars, in the cafeteria? It's near where I work. I can be there round one.'

*

Pat had given Jamie his coffee, examined him keenly and was assured he was feeling all right.

'I'm off to Maidstone to look for a winter coat and do a bit of shopping. Do you want anything?' Assured he did not, she gave him a Judas-kiss and drove off.

She had only been partly lying about the new coat, but as she walked through Ladies' Fashions and cast her eye along the rails, she blanched at the prices. One she particularly liked was eighty-nine pounds – quite out of the question.

The escalator took her to the top floor. She walked between displays of cosy bedrooms each with matching bedlinen and curtains. On the shelves were brightly coloured towels in orderly pyramids. Pat sighed. That was something else that could do with being replaced.

She hovered by the cafeteria where the smell of fried fish and casserole mingled inappropriately in the air. She saw Betty approaching wearing the same black coat and wondered if she had sewn the lining.

Betty gave a weak, embarrassed smile as she approached. Pat turned her back and joined the queue, which had built up in the few minutes since she had arrived. Pat led the way to a small table by the wall and they unloaded their trays.

'How is he?' Betty asked anxiously as she put the tray down beside her chair. She slipped off her coat to reveal her pink and green overall with a badge 'Betty Gwynne May I help you?' pinned to a pink square

'He started work today by himself. A friend has been keeping the garage going. Jamie did short days last week.'

'What about his injuries?'

Pat listed them dispassionately, glowering at Betty's effrontery.

'So, what stories had he been telling you? That his wife didn't understand him I suppose.' She took an angry bite from her sandwich and waited for the protest that it wasn't like that.

'Sort of.'

The nerve of the woman 'What d'you mean *sort of*.'

She took a sip of her tea and replaced her cup. 'It was my fault he had that accident, you know. I upset him.'

'I don't think so. A blood vessel burst in his head, which made him lose consciousness. It could have happened any time. He just lost control: there was no other car involved.'

Pat saw the look of relief on her face and regarded her gravely. How had they met? What did he say to introduce himself? What was the appeal of this woman who seemed not to have a great deal going for her? Her hair was fine like her own, but dyed and permed and in need of a trim. Her skin was fair with a soft bloom. A patch of powder clung to the soft hairs on her cheek and her lipstick showed hasty application. Her eyes, in the careworn face, were her redeeming feature, large and a clear mid blue.

Betty cut a sliver from her pizza. 'Jamie doesn't know you've come to see me, does he?'

'No, I was waiting for him to tell me when he felt better.'

'He wouldn't do that,' Betty said, the fork still in the air.

'And why not?' Pat almost shouted, annoyed she should be so certain what Jamie would or would not do.'

'Because he's like a child who won't admit he's done something wrong.'

'And what has he done wrong?'

'Not spoken to you like he should – like I told him to right at the beginning.'

'You have the audacity to sit there and say you told him to tell me you were having an affair?'

Betty's fork stopped halfway to her mouth and each stared at the other with incredulity.

'But – but – you didn't – you didn't think we were sleeping together? You didn't think that, did you? Oh dear.'

'But I saw you the night of the accident – I followed him. He's been meeting you every night for weeks.'

'No, no.' Betty shook her head vigorously. 'I haven't seen him regular, probably only about once a week. I first saw him in the pub one night 'bout middle of October. I was out with a friend and Jamie was drinking by himself and I spoke to him.'

'Why did you speak to him?'

'Why? Because I used to know him.'

Pat reached for her cup then paused. From the depths of her mind came a faint recollection. 'You must be Betsy.'

'I have been mentioned then.'

'Jamie didn't tell me he had a girlfriend when he first took me out, but your name cropped up occasionally later.'

Betty stared through the windows at the rooftops, thinking of their days together.

*

'Jamie.' Betsy gave him a kiss before getting into the old banger he had just bought.

'Hello, Betsy.'

'It's still moving then,' she said laughing.

'I'm a car mechanic, I can make anything move,' he imparted with a seriousness practically unknown to this twenty-year-old.

'If you say so.' She patted his knee as he got in beside her and started the engine.

For the first half-hour of the film he fidgeted and squirmed in his seat till she had to whisper, 'For heaven's sake, sit still.' She grabbed his arm, threaded it behind her head and waited for his hand to tighten about her.

At the end of the cops and robbers film, that she had not much enjoyed, Jamie removed his arm and left his seat.

'Let's have a bite to eat before we go home,' he said unexpectedly.

They were in the foyer and Betsy was fumbling to find the arm of her coat, annoyed that Jamie just stood looking at her.

'If you like,' she said surprised. They never did anything after a film because they knew she would get into trouble if she were in too late. It did not matter to her father that she was nearly eighteen. Betsy sensed something was amiss. They usually held hands at the very least and sneaked a kiss or two, but the arm she had sought in the cinema had rested unromantically on her shoulder throughout the film.

Now they were sitting at a plastic table, two cups of tea and a sad looking sandwich between them. Jamie was facing her but his eyes would not, or could not meet hers.

'Out with it Jamie. Who or what has upset you?'

As he did when caught out, he gave her a shamefaced look. 'Er, nothing's upset me.'

'Well, what is it?'

Betsy thought it must be something to do with work, or maybe he could not make the day they had carefully planned to celebrate his birthday, and was afraid to tell her. But the way he had behaved and the strange, furtive looks he had given her since they had come into the café filled her with foreboding.

'I, um.' he fumbled. 'I, er, I – I want to call it off.'

'Oh Jamie, after all the trouble arranging your birthday. What's wrong?'

'No, listen.' He reached over and put his hand on top of hers. The sinking feeling returned. 'I want to finish – not go out with you anymore.'

Never had she thought this was what he wanted to tell her. They were so close, so loving. Nothing in his behaviour till this evening had led her to believe he no longer cared for her. Not cared for – loved her. He did love her, hadn't he shown it? Hadn't she? The lump in her throat and the tears filling her eyes prevented her asking the obvious question.

'Don't cry.'

Betsy wanted to ask what she was supposed to do, fling her arms round him and say how lovely it was: just what she was hoping for. No words would come, not even of anger or reproach.

'I'm sorry, I know I've upset you. I didn't want to, really I didn't, but I've met....'

She couldn't bear to hear any more or even to know the reason. All she wanted was to get home so she could die in the privacy of her bedroom. She stood up and without looking at him she left.

'Betsy,' he called, then followed her out

'Come along,' he said taking her arm. 'I'll take you home.'

She pulled it away. 'I'll get a bus.'

'You'll be home even later and you know what you father's like.'

'You won't have to worry about that any more then.'

Two days later she had slipped out of her home in the middle of the night taking all her possessions and her Post Office book containing her wealth of fifty-six pounds, twenty-four pence.

*

'I thought Jamie was going to ask me to marry him,' Betty told Pat. 'That's how close we were – I thought we were. I knew there had been dating other girls on the odd occasion after he had first gone out with me, but I gradually became his only girl. We had made great plans for his birthday, that was when I thought he would propose.' Her voice wavered. 'I n-never knew 'bout you.'

Betty reached for a handkerchief from her overall pocket and wiped her eyes. 'I'm sorry. I've been so worried and I felt guilty because I was sure he had gone off in a temper because I had a go at him. I thought he had driven too fast – or something.'

Pat felt angry on Betty's behalf. 'You still love him, don't you?'

Betty nodded and dabbed her eyes again. 'But I wouldn't have done nothing to upset your marriage, really I wouldn't. I told him more than once to talk to you about the money worries he had. That's why, in the end, I said I wouldn't see him again, so when I was phoned…'

'You thought he was trying to end it all because you had failed him?'

'Yes.'

'I don't think he would have gone that far. These last two weeks he's seemed on the point of confiding in me. He knows I've found out about his finances – though neither of us has mentioned it – so it only remained for him to tell me about you.'

'How are things with the garage?'

'Not good. I've found someone to take care of the repairs and various people have rallied round in one way or another.'

'Tom as well? Jamie told me he'd had a fight with him. I couldn't believe it – not Tom, he was so easy-going.'

'Of course, you know him. That's why you disappeared so quickly that night.' Pat finished her tea. 'They've made it up more or less. Jamie's even acknowledged the baby's existence.'

'What's he like, the baby?'

'Bit like Tom, but he's going to take after his mother in looks I fancy.'

'Ah, the frightful Serena.'

'You heard about her?'

'Heard about her – he hardly talked of anything else. I think that's been the problem. Jamie loves his brother, looks up to him, and always has done. Perhaps he took the place of his father. They never quarrelled in all the time I knew them. Not like my brothers who seemed to do nothing else. Then Serena comes along and he thinks she's taking him away.'

'You seem very wise.'

'I sound like an agony aunt.' She grinned. 'But I know Jamie – and he hasn't changed.'

'Better than I do it seems.'

'You didn't know all the circumstances at the time and I am on the outside. You can see more clearly from there.' Betty took a sip of her tea. 'I presume he doesn't know the police told me about his accident first.'

'No.'

'Are you going to tell him about meeting me?'

'Eventually, when the moment's right. There's been too much deception. I've kidded myself that Jamie had to stand on his own feet, but he can't – though he will have to come to terms with not having Tom at his beck and call. I know he needs me and I shouldn't have deserted him. If only he'd realise what a lot of trouble he has caused.'

'Don't go on at him.' Betty gave a pleading smile.

'I'll play it cool.'

'I must hurry, I can lose my job if I'm back late. I'm glad we've cleared up one or two things. I would have hated for you to think that we … well, anyway I'm pleased to have met you.'

'So am I. Perhaps we could meet again sometime and I can tell you how he is.'

'No, I don't think so, it'll rake up too many memories. Let's leave it.' Betty put on her coat. 'Good bye.'

'Bye.' They touched hands and Pat watched her weave her way through Household Linens till she was lost from sight.

*

'What is it? What's the matter?' Pat sat up with a jerk and rested on her elbow. She could just make out his silhouette sitting bolt upright. She clicked on the bedside light and turned to him. Beads of sweat ran down Jamie's forehead and upper lip. He was staring straight ahead. Pat felt panicky.

'Aren't you feeling well, shall I send for a doctor?'

'No, I'm all right. I was having a bad dream that's all.'

She handed him a tissue and he dabbed his face.

'It was awful, Pat. I was working in the garage and when I came into the house the place was empty, no furniture, nothing, and there was a note which said you had all gone to America with Tom and Serena and you weren't coming back.'

'I'd never do anything like that.' She looked at the clock. 'It's only four-thirty, try and get back to sleep. Pat gave him a gentle push and, when he had settled, she pulled the covers up over his shoulders and put her arm round him.

'Are you still awake?' he said after five minutes.

'Yes.'

'There's something I want to tell you.'

'Can't it wait till morning.'

'No, I must tell you now or I won't do it at all, and I shan't have to see the look in your eyes.'

Just the soft tick of the clock disturbed the stillness of the early morning. Pat said nothing; she wanted to prove Betty wrong.

'I used to meet someone in Maidstone. It was Betsy, do you remember Betsy? I used to go out with her – before I met you. It was quite by accident,' he said quickly. 'She came over to me but I didn't recognise her.'

'Was it her you stayed with when you came home that Saturday Edward was here.'

'Yes, I was too drunk to drive.'

Pat tut-tutted.

'Next time I went I couldn't remember where she lived so I kept going to the same pub hoping she would turn up – and one evening she did.'

'So – every night you met this woman. Then what did you do – go back to her place?'

'I didn't meet her every night. She's got a boy at home so she couldn't get out often.'

'So what did you do when you met?'

'We sat and talked.'

'And you expect me to believe that's all you did, that you didn't slip off to some cheap hotel room?'

'Please believe me Pat, we didn't do anything wrong.'

'Going off and leaving me and the kids was wrong.'

'I know, I know, and I'm sorry. I needed to talk and she was there.'

'I was here, but you didn't talk to me. I had to find out about the trouble you were in after your accident.'

'You're not making this easy for me, are you?'

Pat smiled in the dim light of emerging dawn but resumed her serious, sceptical tone. 'So you sat and talked. Has she got a husband?'

'He left her.'

'How convenient.'

'With three children. The eldest is out at work now, Kevin's just started college and Steve is at school. He's about Kim's age. Perhaps she knows him.'

'We'll have to ask her.' Pat said coolly. 'And what tale did you tell this Betsy?'

Jamie rolled on to his back. 'How miserable I was and that I didn't know what to do about Kim and Tom.'

'It must have been like a thousand and one nights, you keeping her entertained week after week. What advice did she give you?'

'She said that you were the one I should be talking to.'

'Very wise, then why didn't you?'

'I couldn't, I didn't know where or how to start. It all seemed such a mess. But I was going to. Betsy said she wasn't going to see me anymore so after she went I finished my drink and drove around in the van trying to think what I'd say to you – then I had the accident.'

'I'd like to meet this Betsy, she sounds too good to be true.'

'I think you'd like her.'

'You really are telling me the truth about not sleeping with her?'

'Yes, but….'

'But what?'

'Nothing.'

'Is that all you've got to tell me.'

'Yes.'

'I'm glad you found the courage to tell me. Betty told me you wouldn't.'

'Betty! You've seen her! Do you mean to tell me you made me go through all that – when you knew all the time?'

'I don't think you're in any position to talk about anguish, Jamie, and I only found out the truth today when I met her.'

Pat revealed how she had followed him and her meeting with Betty at the hospital.

'When you came home I hoped you'd tell me about her. I thought you were on the point of doing so more than once.'

'I was, but I felt so weak I couldn't face it.'

'And I couldn't leave it hanging over me any longer, so I contacted her this morning and between us we sorted things out. But I don't think you did her any favours. She loved you and still does and you raked up the past.'

'I don't deserve you – and I didn't deserve Betsy either.'

They both lay quietly, not moving, not speaking.

'Pat?'

'Yes.'

'I want to make love to you.'

Pat snuggled up close and gave him a kiss. 'I've missed you, darling, no one to warm my feet on.'

'I was hoping to be a bit more than a hot water bottle.'

Chapter 39

The children crowded at the stop waiting for the school bus to turn the corner from the Hemlow Road. By the time it had been to Grimley Heath and Hemlow, the Grassenden children had little choice where to sit. In the folds of her skirt Stewart found Kim's fingers as they stood close. Each hoped there would be a seat together and Stewart was going to make sure the younger kids did not push on first.

Kim was in a state of euphoria. Schoolwork had become an altogether more pleasant experience as the two of them worked together at each other's houses. Never had a holiday passed so quickly or revision been such a pleasure, especially when a kiss was exchanged. All was right with her world again.

A few days after her Dad had returned to work they had sat in the living room and Mum and Dad explained what had happened and the misunderstanding that had occurred between them. Kim thought her father particularly brave to expose his weakness to them.

Tony, not so worldly wise, asked, 'But what did you do together that upset Mum?'

'We didn't do anything, just talked in a pub.'

'Why was Mum upset then?'

'Because she thought we were?'

'You were what?'

'Having an affair.'

'What does that mean exactly?' Tony said moodily. 'Nobody ever explains these things. All I know is it's something wrong, like it was with Uncle Tom and Serena, and I didn't understand that either.'

By this time Kim would have gladly sunk through the floor, but Tony had a lesson in matrimonial discord which no biology textbook could have given him. It kept him subdued for all of two days.

'If any of this gets out around the village,' Kim said later, pointing an intimidating finger at him, 'I shall know it's you and I'll make your life a misery such as you wouldn't believe possible.' By the look of alarm on his face the threat was taken to heart.

Kim checked him out now as he stood shouting at Peter who was not more than an arm's length away, gesticulating about something he had done in the holiday.

There was still coolness between her Dad and Uncle Tom. Luckily he and Serena had been to America over Christmas so there had been no embarrassment over Christmas entertaining.

'Did your Uncle have a good time in America?' Steward asked when they were seated.

'Yes. He also had his birthday over there and they made quite a fuss of him. Serena's brother lives in a place called Kent? Uncle Tom says nearly all the towns in New England are named after places in this country.'

'I suppose the first settlers did that so they wouldn't feel so homesick.'

'Are you coming round tonight?' Kim asked, but before she got an answer someone at the back of the bus called to no one in particular.

'Hey, How long have Stewart Lindell and Kim Cresswell been an item. Nice Christmas present for him'

The whole of the downstairs laughed and gawped at the red-faced pair. Stewart squeezed her hand.

*

'I think I'm ready to start my business again,' Serena said as she cleared the table. 'It'll be like starting from scratch as I hardly got going last year.'

'Are you sure? What are you going to do about Alexander?'

'Whenever I can I shall take him with me and Lydia says she will have him if I can't.'

Serena saw him frown. 'What's the matter?'

'I don't like the idea of farming him out, especially at the Manor.'

'You still feel under obligation to Edward, don't you?'

'I never feel under obligation to him,' Tom lied, his face flushing. 'It's just I don't want Alexander handed around. I want him brought up her with us, like Jamie and I were, not pushed from pillar to post like Edward was.'

'Am I likely to do that? Don't you think you're being a bit old fashioned? Your mother used to take both of you to the Manor – you told me so. I shall endeavour not to take on large events, to begin with anyway.'

Tom was partly mollified. 'I don't want you to do too much,' he muttered.

She came up to him and kissed his ear. 'I feel fine, really, never better. That holiday did me the world of good – and you too.'

There was a tap on the door and Kim put her head round. 'Can we come in?'

'Of course. Hello Stewart,' Tom said.

'Where's Alexander?' Kim asked eagerly.

'He's asleep, he'll be awake in a minute.'

'We've just seen that man who used to work here, the one you didn't like – Jack something.'

'Jack? Oh you mean Joe Lotter.'

'Yes, that's him.'

'What was wrong with him?' Serena asked.

'He was the one who took Chris' place but he was sullen and bad tempered. After he had been particularly rude to Mike one day, I told the agency I didn't want him again. None of the farmers round here have had him working for them.'

Stewart said, 'He looked scruffy.'

'And surly,' Kim added. 'I don't know if he recognised me, but he turned his head away as we came near.'

'Was this on the footpath?'

'In the lane actually, opposite the Manor, but he looked as if he'd just come from the footpath.'

'Does he come from round here?' Serena asked.

'He did live on the other side of Maidstone – used to come in on a moped.'

'That sounds like Alexander. Come up, Kim, I'm sure your uncle can find something to talk about with Stewart.'

'Oh yes,' Tom grinned. 'I've got plenty to talk about. I can tell Stewart all about…'

'Uncle Tom,' Kim warned, 'you never know when you might need a babysitter urgently. You just stick to showing Stewart round the farm.'

'How's your Dad?' Serena asked as she changed the baby.

'All right, he manages to work all day, but I never used to see him sleep in the evening.'

'He still has a limp Tom says.'

'Yes, it's better than it was. It's worse towards the end of the day, and he speaks more slowly when he's tired.'

'Stewart seems a nice boy. Your Dad approves of him I hope.'

Kim picked up the baby. 'Yes, I wish you and Dad could be friendly again.'

'So do I, but look what happened when I tried to do something.'

'But other things were going on then, trouble at the garage and…' Kim did not finish. She was not sure what Uncle Tom had told Serena.

They went down to the kitchen and Alexander was strapped in his chair and a rattle put into his hand.

'At least Tom and your father are speaking, that's what concerned me most. You see I've never really had a family, close like yours is. Because my father was abroad so often or moving around the country, my brother and I were sent to boarding school when we were old enough so we never had a settled home life. My brother went to America when he was in his early twenties.'

'What about your mother, weren't you close to her?'

'We got on all right when we were together, but she was always following my father wherever he was posted. It made for a very unsettled life for her. We were rarely all together to form close relationships.'

'It must be wonderful for you to have Tom and Alexander then.'

'I never thought I could be so happy.'

'He's lovely, my Uncle Tom. I was going to marry him myself when I grew up.'

'What good taste you have?'

'I hope I marry someone like him.'

Fervently Serena replied. 'So do I, you could do a lot worse, believe me.'

*

Serena tapped the pencil on her teeth as she sat at the kitchen table. The baby was fed but she had not bothered with something for herself. Tom would not be in till the evening as he had gone to a farm auction to see if he could pick up a secondhand tractor.

Lovingly her eyes rested on her six-month old son as he gazed with his pale blue eyes at the dried flowers above him.

'Your Dad's an old fusspot sometimes, saying he didn't want

you farmed out around the village. As if I would my precious. I can hardly bear to be parted from you myself.'

She had just written Birthday Present, Advertising on her paper when the kitchen door was flung open.

'Who the hell are you?' she demanded, as a shifty-eyed individual stepped into the room.

He gazed round the kitchen. 'Cor, what a change. I wouldn't have believed a room could alter so much.'

'Who are you? How dare you walk into my house.'

'Now, now, don't get your knickers in a twist.'

'Get out of her. If you're wanting Tom he's gone – Tom's down Toilers Field.'

'I don't think so, love. I saw 'im in the High Street with his brother not much more than half an hour ago.'

'He'll be back soon.' She glanced anxiously at the clock. 'He said he'd come straight back when he'd spoken to Jamie.'

Unconcerned the man's small eyes flicked around the room alighting on Alexander.

'That yours? Heard Tom got himself hitched, but hadn't heard he'd had a brat. Dark horse that man.'

Beneath the table Serena's hands were kneading themselves together. She felt panic rise like floodwater and with it pent-up anger waiting to uncoil. She must keep control – the man looked unpredictable.

'Are you going to wait for him?'

He walked over to Alexander and stood over him and it was all Serena could do not to push him away. The baby smiled and idiotically she wanted to tell him he was not the sort of man he should smile at.

The phone rang in the office making her start. She leaped from the chair and ran to answer it before he could say anything.

'Abbey Farm.' She turned to find the man leaning against the door frame picking his teeth.

The voice at the other end said, 'Tell Tom when he gets back that I've heard of a Hayter orchard mower for sale. I think he might be interested.'

'Mr Green, how lovely to hear from you.'

'What? It's Jamie – not Mr Green.'

'Tom's not here at the moment…'

'I know, I spoke to him a little while ago…'

'… he'll be in fairly soon. Can you come now?'

'What are you playing at?'

'He'll be pleased to see you, Mr Green. So will I?'

'Don't play silly games, Serena, just give him the message.' He rang off.

The man pushed himself off the frame with his shoulder as she replaced the phone and sauntered back into the kitchen. Serena followed, apprehension labouring every step.

'Where was I? Oh yes, the baby, what's his name?'

'Alexander,' she forced out.

'Nice.'

To Serena's relief he moved away and sat down at the table.

'My name's Joe – Joe Lotter. I used to work 'ere couple of years back. Did he tell you?'

'Er, no.'

'No, 'e wouldn't. I wouldn't be worth mentioning. He gave me the push and the agency took me off their books. It was all his fault. I was a good worker, even Tom said I was good. I couldn't get no work after that.' His face darkened.

'I've got to make a telephone call,' she said, walking over to her phone.

Joe leaped up with startling speed. 'No you don't,' he said, 'I don't want you fetching no one. Si' down.'

It was as much as she could do to keep her temper as she eased herself on to the edge of the kitchen chair. Please Mike, Ian, someone – please come.

'What do you want here anyway?' she asked.

'Well now, a cup of tea wouldn't be a bad idea.'

Fighting the desire to tell him to get it himself, she moved slowly to the dresser and fetched a cup and saucer, which she put on a tray. With similar lack of haste she poured milk into a jug and only then did she put on the kettle. Though she could not bear to look at his face, she knew his eyes were watching every move.

'This aint the sort of place I'd expect a tasty little piece like you to end up. How did Tom manage it?'

The boiling water splashed into the pot. 'I've known him a long time. I lived in the village.' She pushed the tray towards him.

'Not 'aving one yourself, Mrs Cresswell?'

'No.'

'Not good enough for you, I suppose. You're just like Tom and all the others.' He poured out his tea.

Serena pricked up her ears. Was that a crunch on the gravel? Joe did not appear to have heard. Alexander started grizzling and they both turned to look at him. When she looked back she saw a face at the window and gave a gasp.

'What's up, what's the matter?' Joe jumped up as Jamie came in.

'Watch out Jamie,' Serena shouted as she saw Joe grab his cup and throw the contents at him. Jamie cried out in pain as the hot liquid caught his face.

Joe rushed over to Alexander and stood over him the teapot in his hand, the spout suspended over the baby's head.

'No,' she shrieked, and with superhuman effort hurled herself at Joe. The pot fell and tea spilled over her arm. She screamed.

Jamie staggered over to them his hand clutched to his face.

'Take the baby, take the baby,' she yelled at him.

'No you don't,' Joe said. He grabbed the handle of the baby seat.

Serena, in agony, tried to wrestle it away while Jamie struggled with the man.

Alexander, who first thought this was some new game to amuse him, let out a yell at the noise and the rough treatment he was getting. With two people to cope with Joe had to let go and Serena snatched the seat away.

Jamie, fists flying, went for him. The younger man was getting the better of the injured Jamie till Serena brought a huge meat dish down on the back of Joe's head. He staggered and fell, catching himself on the corner of the range.

They stood panting as they stared at the man's crumpled form. 'I'll call the police.'

When she came off the phone Joe was shaking his head as he started to come round. She gave Jamie a carving knife saying, 'You'd better guard him just in case,' and went to pacify an aggrieved Alexander who had been unceremoniously thrust into the hall.

Jamie bent over the man, one hand to his face and the other clutching the knife. Serena was holding out her burning arm like a demented scarecrow. It did not escape either of them how ludicrous they must look and they started to laugh.

'We'd better get these burns attended to.' She went to the fridge and put ice cubes into a bowl. She soaked a cloth in the water and handed it to Jamie. She put her arm under the cold running water where she found instant relief from the excruciating pain.

The farm kitchen was crowded. The whole Cresswell clan had gathered in relays to hear the fantastic story. Serena told her side then Jamie went on.

'I rang Serena to give Tom a message and she kept making strange references to a Mr Green. I thought she was mucking about so I put the phone down, but as I thought about the funny remarks, I knew there was something not quite right. I knew Tom wasn't there and Mike and Ian were sure to be in the fields, so I thought I'd better investigate.'

'Why didn't you tell me where you were going, I could've come with you,' Pat said.

'I thought I'd look silly if I went there and nothing was up.'

'She would have made you a cup of tea,' Tom said.

'Don't talk to me about tea,' Serena said.

'Me neither, I never knew burns could be so painful.'

'What did the police do, Dad?' Tony asked, 'I wish I'd been here.'

'They came quickly, didn't they Jamie?' Serena said.

'Yeah, and wasn't I glad because I had visions of having to keep Joe under control and I wasn't feeling in the mood for more fighting. I don't think the police would have taken kindly to me stabbing him. They asked a few questions then took him away. He was concussed and I'm not surprised the force Serena brought down that dish on his head.'

'You don't know how pleased I was to see you peering through that window. I'd been trying to think what else I could do to get help.'

'Did he actually threaten to do something to you?' Tom asked.

'No, but he was very menacing, obviously had a grudge against you. I don't know if he was going to do anything if Jamie hadn't arrived. I was most afraid for Alexander.'

'What happened to him all this time?' Kim asked.

'He thought it was a huge game till he was piggy in the middle. When he was finally pulled away, I practically threw him in the hall and shut the door. You should have heard him howling.'

'Will you have to be questioned by the police again, Dad?'

'Yes, both of us will.'

'Cool. I hope I'm there.'

'I rang the surgery because neither of us was in a fit state to drive there and they contacted Dr Ferguson who was on his rounds. He gave us the once over.'

Serena insisted they all stay for a meal. With three arms between them she and Pat set about preparing it. Alexander was put in Kim's charge and all thoughts of baby-routine were forgotten.

While they were eating Serena cast her eye round the table as they talked animatedly to each other.

They all listened as Tony made Jamie repeat the story with many interjections of 'And what did you do then, Dad?'

At the end of the meal Pat and Tom said the hero and heroine of the hour deserved a rest and sent them into the best room. Tony was persuaded to stay in the kitchen with them and Kim put her baby cousin to bed.

'I hope you don't hurt as much as I do?' Jamie said as they settled themselves in the armchairs.

'I feel I want to chop off my arm and put it in the fridge. It must be worse for you after all you've been through.'

'I could have done without it, that's for sure. Still I'm glad I came down. There's no knowing what that man might have done.'

'When you rang I didn't know what to say without arousing his suspicions. When you rang off I nearly cried. I wished I hadn't seen you at the window then I wouldn't have given you away so soon.'

'It turned out all right, thank goodness.'

There was a period of pregnant silence and Serena spoke.

'As they have diplomatically left us alone, can we call a truce? I honestly had no thoughts of upsetting you. I like you – all of you, and I want to be part of the family.'

'I'm sorry too, I lose my temper easily.'

'You and me both, but I am getting it under control. Tom is a calming influence.'

'Always has been.' There was a long pause. 'I was jealous you know.'

'I thought perhaps you were, but there was no need. I don't want to take him away from you. There's enough of Tom for both of us.'

Jamie held out his hand. 'Friends then?'

'Brother- and sister-in-law,' she said, getting up and giving him a kiss and hugging him as they all came into the best room.

Epilogue

Betsy sat on the floor, back against a cupboard. Scattered around her were boxes, old knitting patterns, pamphlets and long out-of-date brochures. A small tin box was by her knee and she was gazing at a snapshot, a gentle smile playing round her lips.

The living room door opened pushing the pile of discarded items along the floor.

'What are you doing, Mum?'

'Hello, love. I was looking for something when I came across these old snaps and got carried away.'

'Let's have a look?'

Steve sat beside her and she handed them to him one by one.

'Here's one of your uncles.' She pointed. 'That's Cliff, that's Bob and Les. They must have been feeling particularly pally that day. You couldn't usually get them anywhere near each other.'

'Uncle Bob's got a beard,' Steve exclaimed.

'Yeah, didn't last long, your Auntie Karen didn't like it. That was taken just before he got married I think. Here's one of Gramps and Grandma.' Betsy handed him another. 'That's your cousin Natalie when she was about a year old.'

When they had all been seen, Steve leaned forward and took the one lying in Betsy's lap.

'When was this taken? Who's that with Jim? He peered more closely. 'Oh, it's you. How old were you there?'

'About seventeen.'

'It can't be Jim then. Who is it?'

'Someone I used to know before I met your Dad.'

Steve studied the man's face. 'He doesn't half look like our Jim.'

Betsy took the photograph from him and stared at it.

'Yes, he does rather, doesn't he?